A FATAL PACT

A DI CROW NOVEL

HJ REED

INKUBATOR
BOOKS

Published by Inkubator Books
www.inkubatorbooks.com

Copyright © 2024 by HJ Reed

HJ Reed has asserted her right to be identified as the author of this work.

ISBN (eBook): 978-1-83756-310-4
ISBN (Paperback): 978-1-83756-311-1
ISBN (Hardback): 978-1-83756-312-8

A FATAL PACT is a work of fiction. People, places, events, and situations are the product of the author's imagination. Any resemblance to actual persons, living or dead is entirely coincidental.

No part of this book may be reproduced, stored in any retrieval system, or transmitted by any means without the prior written permission of the publisher.

1

I'm dragged into consciousness, choking for breath, as though a steel girder is pressing down on me, and there's a hot, wet sensation in my left ear. I get a fleeting recollection of the day I was shot in the head and struggle, unsuccessfully, to push myself upright. *I'm going to die*, I conclude, and as if to emphasise the point, a cacophony of ringing bells accompanies the feeling of impending doom. *Fuck it!* I decide, thinking that maybe just letting it happen is the best idea. It takes a minute to become fully aware that I'm in my bed, and ninety pounds of Doberman pinscher is lying across my chest, insistently poking its tongue in my ear. It's another thirty seconds before I realise that the noise is actually my mobile.

'For God's sake, Blue, get off!'

Bluebell, my eighteen-month-old canine companion, bodyguard and alarm clock, responds with a typically adolescent disdainful 'woof'. I manage to shift her bulk just enough to reach the phone, and as I snatch it up, I notice the time – six thirty on a Sunday morning.

'Jesus bloody Christ!' I mutter, bracing myself to give whoever is on the other end a pretty good idea of my current state of mind. I press the 'talk' button. 'What the hell do you mean by—'

'Sorry to ruin your beauty sleep, Al.'

It's Grace Helston, my DSI. I take a deep breath and restrict myself to, 'I should sodding well hope so. Do you know what time it is? And unless you've forgotten, it's my day off.'

'Correction,' Grace says calmly. 'It *was* your day off. I need you to get over to West Hill. Somebody's dug up two bodies in their garden.'

'In their garden?' I take a moment to think it through. 'What the hell is anyone doing gardening at six o'clock in the morning? And can't Polly handle it? I thought she was on shift over the weekend.'

'Apparently the owners were up early, taking down an old shed. They found bones and rang us half an hour ago. Polly's on her way, but I want you there as well, Al. From the information we've got so far, it doesn't look to be your average gangland killing. I've got a horrible feeling this one's going to hit the media, and I don't want to be accused of not putting a senior officer onto it when it does. So make yourself a strong coffee, kick the dog off your bed and get down there.'

'How do you know the dog's on my bed?' I retort, but do as I'm told, and boot a grumbling Bluebell onto the floor, the phone wedged to my ear as Grace gives me the address. 'Jesus Christ almighty,' I comment once the line's gone dead and I'm heading for the kettle.

. . .

HALF AN HOUR later I climb out of my brand-new VW hatchback – one with a dog barrier in the back. My trusty old rust bucket just couldn't cope with a full-sized Doberman lolling in the back seat, chewing the already tattered leather upholstery. Bluebell, by now well used to my complete lack of routine, pricks up her ears, grunts the canine equivalent of 'bloody hell, here we go again', and flops down on her blanket, preparing for a long wait.

The house, a Victorian semi-detached on Oakfield Road, one of the less down-market enclaves of West Hill, is already cordoned off with blue police tape, behind which a little swarm of white-suited SOCOs are going about their business in the back garden. Polly Sillitoe, my DI, ducks under the tape and heads towards me, peeling her paper coverall down to her waist and trying to walk and take off the plastic overshoes at the same time. She manages to snag the heel of the left one – the one encasing her artificial foot – with her right toe, but has to wait until she reaches me to rip the other one off with her fingers. These days, eighteen months after having her leg amputated just below the knee following a vicious and deliberate dog attack, the injury is barely noticeable to most observers, just surfacing now and again when fine motor movements are needed.

'Good morning, boss.'

'Nice to see you've still got a sense of humour,' is all I can say to that, trying to stretch out the kinks in my back. 'I don't suppose there's a tea wagon anywhere round here?'

She grins and turns back to the little group of police officers at the front gate. 'Hey, Connie!' She beckons, and a young PC trots across to us. 'Do us a favour and nip round to the garage. One latte and one black, three sugars.'

'You'll have to give me the money,' the PC retorts, looking none too pleased. 'I left my wallet at home.'

I dig into my pocket and bring out a couple of crumpled twenty-pound notes. 'My shout,' I tell her. 'Coffee all round, and biscuits if there's enough change.'

She manages a reluctant smile. 'Yes, sir. Thank you, sir,' and stalks off, muttering something along the lines of, 'Who was your servant last week?'

'So what's the story?' I ask Polly when she's gone.

'We're still waiting for the pathologist to give us a verdict,' she says, 'but it looks like the bodies have been there quite a while – an adult and a child of around three or four, if the size of the skeleton is anything to go by.'

'Oh, Jesus!' I suddenly understand why I've been dragged away from my long-awaited day off.

'Are you okay, boss?' Sillitoe is looking concerned, and I realise my hand has developed a slight twitch, an occasional reminder of the furrow that bullet left in my frontal lobe.

'I'm fine, Polly. Go on.'

She nods. 'The property was purchased by a couple …' She consults her notes. 'Paul and Andrew Maitland, just under two months ago on 24 July. They've been working on the garden for a couple of weeks and had decided to replace the shed. They were digging a hole for a concrete foundation for the new one and found the bodies around a foot down. The shed had been there a long time by the look of what's left of it, so it's unlikely either of the new owners were in any way involved. As soon as they dug up the first bones, they recognised them as human and called the police.'

'Okay, so we're looking at previous owners. Any information on them?'

'I've sent Daz Jackson to haul the estate agents out of bed. I bet that will make their Sunday morning.'

'Good. If I have to bloody suffer, so can they. What else?'

Her gaze shifts to her feet, and she looks distinctly uncomfortable.

'What?'

She shuffles and clears her throat. 'I thought it would be a good idea to get further checks under way, and you know what the IT lot are like. No chance of getting hold of them on a weekend, and when you do, they say they're backed up for weeks. So …' She takes a deep breath. 'I gave John Larson a call and said you were on the case and could he help out. Hope you don't mind, boss.'

'Fucking hell, Polly,' is my first reaction. 'Does the DSI know about this?'

'I thought—' she begins, but we're interrupted by the PC, clutching a cardboard tray full of paper coffee cups, a bag of chocolate chip cookies balanced on the top.

'Your change, sir,' she says, handing me a fifty-pence piece and pointing at two of the cups. 'Latte and black with sugar. There was enough left for a cookie each.'

'Thank you, Constable,' I say, thinking I could probably have fed myself for a week with half what I've just spent on crap coffee and a biscuit. I'm cheered up, however, by the thought that Polly's idea does have a bright side. If I can be yanked out of bed at some ungodly hour, so can my son-in-law.

'Boss?' Sillitoe asks, still looking concerned, and I realise I'm grinning.

'Don't worry, Polly,' I tell her. 'It's a good idea. I'll square it with Grace later. Given what we might be dealing with, I don't think she'll object to a bit of queue jumping. After all, it's what Larson is paid for these days.'

I take a sip of my coffee, which actually isn't all that bad, and nearly spill it as Sillitoe nudges my arm and jerks her head towards the end of the street.

'Shit!' she hisses, whacking the lid back on her cup. 'Didn't take them long, did it?'

I glance over her shoulder and see a white van coming up on us fast, emblazoned with a BBC logo. Inevitably, it's the first of many, and I know that within the next hour or so, the street will be rammed solid with a mix of media and nosy neighbours. 'Bloody hell,' I agree. 'Come on, let's go and see if the pathologist's got anything for us.'

She nods. I check on Bluebell dozing contentedly in the back of the hatch, and we both head up the side path to the back garden, leaving instructions with the uniforms to keep a sharp eye on the cordon.

The pathologist, Maggie Ainsworth, has maintained a reputation for brutal efficiency coupled with a worrying enthusiasm for corpses for as long as I can remember. As we round the corner of the house, she looks up and gives us a wave, then turns back to her two assistants, who are busy preparing to move the bodies, not into the usual black body bags but onto large metal trays – a clear indication that whoever the individuals were, there isn't much left of them. Maggie finishes giving instructions to her team and strides over to join us, ripping off her mask to reveal a wide grin that, given the circumstances, is a bit disconcerting, even to those who, like me, are well used to it.

'Morning, Al,' she says, the grin getting even wider. 'Not often we see you up and about at this time of day.'

'Morning, Maggie. Believe me, it wasn't my idea. I just hope you're going to make it worth the effort.'

'It's an interesting one, that's for sure,' she replies, and turns to Sillitoe. 'It's good to see you, Inspector. How's the leg coming along? You know, it's such a shame the hospital incinerated the redundant bit – it would have made an excellent teaching aid for my trainees.'

Sillitoe colours at that, highlighting the white scar running across her left cheek, another disfiguring legacy of the attack. Nevertheless, she manages a smile.

'You should have let me know, professor,' she says sweetly. 'I would have asked them to frame it for you.'

Maggie laughs. 'Ah, well, too late now. Anyway, we can't stand here chatting all day. I must say, this is one of the more intriguing cases I've had lately. Usually there are at least a few body parts to look at. I haven't had to examine pure skeletal remains for a year or two.'

'They've been there quite a while, then?' I ask. 'Any idea how long?'

She shakes her head. 'Not precisely, no. I'm going to have to do a fair few tests, and I'll probably only be able to approximate to, say, within five years or so. My instinct is telling me they've been there maybe twenty or thirty years, but I can't be certain at this stage.'

'Anything you can be certain of?' I ask, thinking that Grace might have played down the urgency just a little bit and given me an extra hour in bed. I decide to take it up with her later.

Maggie frowns and then nods. 'I can tell you that there are two bodies, both intact, and it doesn't look like they've been moved – all the bones are in the right places. The first is an adult female, I'd say definitely under thirty, possibly early twenties, from looking at the bone development. The second is an infant male, I'd guess between three and five, but I can't be more definite.'

I open my mouth to ask the next obvious question, but Maggie holds up a hand. 'I've only had a quick glance, but it looks like both individuals sustained a number of injuries, although I can't tell you yet whether they were all inflicted at the time of death. However, what did kill them both was a hefty whack on the head. Both skulls have clear and very similar damage, possibly caused by the same heavy, blunt instrument – hammer, mallet, brick – something like that. I should be able to tell you more later. I think you are, without doubt, looking at two unnatural deaths.'

'Bloody hell,' I mutter, even though murder was more or less a foregone conclusion. People don't just keel over and get buried under garden sheds by accident. 'Any chance of identifying them?'

'I should be able to secure DNA,' she replies, 'and get it run through all our databases. There is one odd thing, though.' She frowns again. 'I had a quick look at the teeth of the adult. Obviously, I haven't had time to do a detailed examination, but if I'm right about the age of the remains, the condition of the teeth is very poor indeed – in fact, more what you might find in someone of low to moderate income living in early Victorian times. There is no evidence of dental treatment of any kind, and some of the teeth are quite decayed.'

'Probably no chance of identification through dental records,' I add. 'Bugger.'

'Quite so. It might make any identification much more difficult, if not impossible.' She glances over her shoulder at the assistants, who have finished loading the bones onto the trays and are preparing to move them across to a waiting van for transportation to the pathology lab. 'Right. I'll get off. Nothing on today, so I'll go and sort Cyril out and get onto it this afternoon. I'm unlikely to have anything for you until tomorrow, so don't bother asking. I'll be in touch.'

She gives us both a cheery wave and stomps back over to her assistants.

'Cyril?' Sillitoe asks, scowling after her. 'I thought the old bat lived alone.'

'Not quite,' I say, grinning. 'Cyril is an overfed geriatric shih tzu. Bloody thing spends all its time eating, shitting and farting, with an emphasis on the farting. Believe me, Polly, if you ever get invited round to Maggie's, remember to take a biohazard suit.'

She nods slowly. 'That explains a lot. What now, boss?'

I shrug. 'Not a lot to do until we've got something to go on. Just make sure we've got full statements from the Maitlands and the estate agents, and get uniforms to keep the site secure. Then go home and take some time. It's not as if we're starting an urgent manhunt for a murderer who's still got fresh blood dripping down their shirt. It's looking like a cold case, so all we can do is wait for the pathology report. How's Robbie, by the way? All good at home?'

'So-so. I think she's still coming to terms with things, you know? But we're managing.'

I give her shoulder a squeeze. 'Tell me about it. It'll be fine. Just give her time.'

Both of us know that's probably a lie. Police work and relationships are mutually exclusive for all but the lucky few. Having a romantic involvement with another police officer, and especially one on the same team, is an even bigger recipe for disaster. Still, it's their business. I have enough to contend with when it comes to treading on eggshells where family matters are concerned. Talking of which, as we turn to follow the forensic team, my phone shrills into life. It's Larson. My daughter, Rosie, is cooking a Sunday lunch, and my grandson, Ben, wants to see Bluebell. Would I like to come over?

'In other words,' I say, 'you want to talk to me about Polly Sillitoe's call, yes?'

I almost feel him blushing at the other end of the line. 'Ah. You know about that?'

'Of course I know. What do you expect? I'm her boss.' I let him stew for a minute before adding, 'I think she's right. Tell Rosie thanks, and I'll see you around one.'

I hang up and shoulder my way through what has now become a scrum of reporters and rubberneckers to my car, leaving Sillitoe to organise the crowd control. I've got a few hours before I'm expected for lunch, so I head off to the calm haven of Ashton Court country park on the other side of town, where I can give Bluebell a run and focus my mind on events that might have led to a woman and child ending up underneath a garden shed.

2

It takes a fair effort to haul myself out of my armchair and follow my son-in-law out into the kitchen, where we set about clearing up the remains of an excellent and very traditional lunch of roast beef followed by an apple crumble, provided by Joyce, my ex-mother-in-law. She and my ex-wife, Chrissie, have taken our twenty-month-old granddaughter, Alex, to the play park, and young Ben is out in the back garden, playing ball with Bluebell. I watch them through the kitchen window as I rinse pans and hand them to Larson, busy packing the dishwasher – fetch, sit, treat, throw, repeat – and wonder how long it's been since I was able to enjoy such simple pleasures. Probably, I conclude, not since the day I first stepped out on the beat in West Hill.

I realise it's gone quiet and that Larson is watching too. 'He's a natural,' he comments. 'The other day he told me he was going to be a vet. I wouldn't be surprised. Most kids go through phases and lose interest, but since we gave in to having guinea pigs and a rabbit last year, he hasn't missed a day feeding them, cleaning them out, the whole thing. Blue's on a whole different level, though. He lives for his visits with that dog.'

He pauses, shuffling and looking at his feet. We have the sort of relationship that definitely doesn't include heart-to-heart revelations over pints and packets of crisps, owing mainly to my unreasonable attitude to sharing my daughter's affection with a high-flying, high-salaried, highly sensitive partner – everything I'm not. I really have to deal with it – sometime. For now, I manage, 'You got something to say, son?'

He treats me to a long-suffering smile. 'I was only thinking,' he says after another long hesitation, 'I was surprised you accepted the offer of a Doberman after what happened with that Greek bastard, and what his dog did to Polly. I know you did it for Ben, and it was a great thing to do, but …' He shrugs. 'You know?'

I know exactly what he's asking, but as always, my brain struggles to find an adequate answer. My second and final brush with Darius Kyriaku, premier assassin for Greece's largest organised crime group and psychopath obsessed with raising killer Dobermans, isn't something I want to be forced to recall just after a very good Sunday lunch. For me, and probably everyone else involved, the memory is still raw, particularly as one of his dogs was responsible for tearing off a good chunk of my DI's left leg. A few years before that, of course, Kyriaku fired the bullet that finished up embedded in my brain and almost ended my career – permanently. I realise I've been unconsciously massaging the scar on my right temple, and Larson has turned away, fiddling with the control panel on the dishwasher.

He glances back at me and mutters, 'Sorry.'

It occurs to me that my son-in-law deserves some sort of explanation. After all, he was a part of the same operation and came within a whisker of being a victim himself. We've never really talked about it, aside from expressing our mutual relief when Kyriaku, as we half expected, was found dead in his remand cell three days before the start of his trial. An artistic sketch of the Greek goddess Medusa, insignia of his criminal organisation, had been carved into his chest with a razor blade, which had then been used to cut his throat. As far as I know, the prison authorities are still trying to identify the killer. I move my attention back to the garden, where Ben is happily running around with Bluebell. Rosie has joined them for a three-way game of 'catch', Blue scampering after any stray balls that roll into the bushes.

'I suppose it was partly for Ben,' I say finally, 'but not entirely. He desperately wanted a dog, you and Rosie couldn't cope with one, and when I took those stolen pups back to the breeder after Kyriaku's arrest, she sort of convinced me a dog might be a better treatment for PTSD than avoiding sessions with a psychiatrist. Believe me, son, it was my intention to persuade you and Rosie to take her once you'd got used to the idea, but ...'

Larson leans back against the counter and gives me an incredulous stare, then bursts out laughing. 'But you fell for her,' he finishes for me. 'Somehow, that dog found your soft spot – I knew there had to be one somewhere!'

'She's a working dog,' I protest, throwing down the tea towel and giving him a glare of my own. 'Deterrent, guard dog, station mascot, whatever you want to call it – she earns her keep. Still,' I admit, 'one thing's true – she's a damn sight more effective than a psychiatrist. Polly couldn't go near so much as a Chihuahua when she came out of hospital, but once she got used to Blue, she started to recover much faster than she would have sitting in a room with some overpaid, under-skilled shrink.'

'Don't let Rosie hear you say that,' he says, still grinning. 'She's constantly moaning about how little trainee forensic psychologists get paid. It's true, though, what you say about Polly – she's done amazingly well to get back to anything like normal, considering what she's been through.'

I nod my agreement, although I can't help thinking that for Polly and me, and perhaps for my son-in-law as well, the real legacy of our fight against Medusa is that none of us will ever feel normal again.

Rosie, glowing from her exertions, joins us in the kitchen and makes a beeline for the kettle. 'Those two are going to be out there till it gets dark,' she comments, grabbing mugs and tea bags and dumping them on the kitchen table. 'I swear, I just can't keep up with Ben anymore – I don't know where he gets his energy from.'

'I blame the parents,' I tell her. 'You were exactly the same when you were his age.'

She grunts, sloshes boiling water into the mugs, and roots a carton of milk out of the fridge.

'Well, now that it's just the three of us, you can both sit down and tell me what's going on with those bodies you've found over in West Hill.'

Larson and I exchange a look. Boundless energy isn't the only thing my daughter has inherited – she's also developed her mother's uncanny ability to get her men exactly where she wants them. We both know that any attempt to escape will be met with utter failure. We obediently leave off our kitchen duties and join her at the table.

'I take it there have been news reports already?' I ask.

She nods. 'BBC and ITV at lunchtime, and on the local radio. Not much detail, though, just two bodies, a female and a child, found early this morning under a shed and could have been there some time. Is that true?'

One thing about my daughter – she doesn't shrink away from the gruesome details. 'As far as it goes, yes,' I reply. 'The pathologist estimates between twenty and thirty years or so, but we won't know much more until she's done all the tests. It's difficult when there's nothing left but bones. She was able to say that they weren't moved from somewhere else though, so presumably they were put there pretty soon after death.'

Rosie echoes my first thoughts on the matter. 'Who the hell starts digging up shed foundations at six o'clock in the morning? They must be dead popular with the neighbours!'

'Apparently the Maitlands do,' I say. 'Or, at least, that's what they say they were doing. Sillitoe is still there getting detailed statements from them and the rest of the street. I haven't seen them yet, but it's unlikely they had anything to do with it – they've only been living there a couple of months.'

'I've been asked to look into previous owners,' Larson puts in. 'I've been working on it since I got the call this morning.'

'Anything?' I ask.

'Not a lot, yet. There's nothing on the electoral roll, so whoever lived there previously didn't register to vote. According to the 2011 census information, the property was owned by a Joseph Drake, aged forty-six, living with –

presumably – his partner, Pauline Drake. He was still living in the house in 2021, with a daughter, Millie Drake, aged six, but minus Pauline.' He looks at me and shrugs apologetically. 'The next step is to check the information for 2001, then go through the land registry, but I haven't had the chance yet. Chrissie hauled me out to peel potatoes.'

Right on cue, the front door bursts open, sending a crack like a pistol shot down the hall and setting off a brief but violent tremor in my right hand, one of the few remaining outward effects of the bullet damage to my frontal lobe. I grip the table until it subsides, listening to the commotion as Chrissie and Joyce disentangle Alex from her pushchair and deal with coats, shoes and the general paraphernalia involved in taking a toddler to the park.

A few seconds later, Alex charges into the kitchen, pink faced and minus one sock, yelling, 'Gandi!' at the top of her lungs – she hasn't quite managed to get her tongue around 'Grandad' yet. She makes a wild leap for my lap, and I just manage to catch her before she bangs her head on the edge of the kitchen table.

'You realise you're going to be stuck with that?' Rosie points out, doing her best not to giggle.

'Bloody hell,' I mutter, trying, without success, to think of a more inappropriate comparison than with the world's most famous advocate of non-violence.

Chrissie, following close behind, hands me the missing sock and leans back against the worktop. 'I suppose you three have been talking shop all this time,' she comments, aiming her disapproving stare at me.

I take my cue, restore the sock to my granddaughter's foot, hand her over to Rosie and get to my feet, feeling a sudden need for the peaceful haven of my own sofa and a chance to think. 'Whatever gave you that idea, Chris?' I say, moving over to the window to call Bluebell in, and giving her a quick hug on the way.

She melts a little and pecks my cheek. 'I just wish ...' She doesn't finish the sentence, simply nods, resigned. 'Take care, Al – please?'

'I always do,' I lie, and head for the door.

It's well past eleven by the time I settle myself with my daily ration of whisky to watch the late-evening local news roundup. As expected, it's dominated by a sensationalist, but mostly fact-free report of the gruesome find at number 24 Oakfield Road. Thankfully, uniform have done a good job keeping press and public well back behind the cordons, far enough to make things difficult, although not impossible for the cameras, even those with state-of-the-art zoom lenses. There's a brief statement from a suitably blank-faced Sillitoe to the assembled press – yes, we can confirm that human remains have been found, and no, we have no further information at this stage. The report finishes with the usual, 'we will bring you more on this story in our next bulletin,' and the scene switches to the sports results.

I must have dozed off on the sofa, because I come to with a start, replaying the conversation I had with Rosie and Larson earlier – *Who the hell starts digging up shed foundations at six o'clock in the morning?* But there were no foundations, so the question should have been, 'Who the hell builds a shed without putting down a concrete base first?' The answer is, either an idiot or someone who needs to cover up two dead bodies in a hurry. So whoever put up the shed is likely to have been responsible for the deaths, or at least complicit. If we can find out when it was built, it will probably give us a more accurate timeline than Maggie's examination of the remains. I pick up my phone to call Sillitoe, and realise just in time that it's gone 2 a.m. I send a brief text message telling her to meet me in my office first thing in the morning, and head upstairs to catch up on some much-needed sleep.

3

Getting promoted has both advantages and disadvantages. On the one hand, it means I spend more time in a slightly better-quality office chair behind a slightly larger desk, one with room underneath for Blue to hide out when things aren't too hectic. My canine companion has become one of West Hill's worst-kept secrets, and her presence guarantees I catch up with more or less every officer in the station on a daily basis, from trainee constables to DSI Helston, who has taken to keeping a bag of gravy bones in her filing cabinet alongside the whisky bottle and breakfast croissants. If head office has got wind of it, so far there's been no reaction. I suspect Chief Constable Gosford is simply biding his time, waiting for my first major fuck-up to make his move. Meanwhile, my chief problem with dog ownership is preventing everyone who enters the office from slipping her black pudding and slices of bacon from the canteen. The main culprit, naturally, is our desk sergeant, George Saint, who has decided that dog, like man, can survive on a diet of pasties and sausage rolls.

On the downside, it didn't take me long to discover that the reason the DCI's desk is bigger is because it's a metaphor for the now mostly electronic, but still vastly increased piles of paperwork being chucked onto it, everything from witness statements to requests for reimbursement of the cost of a double espresso bought for an informant.

When I complained to Grace, her response was simply, 'Think yourself lucky. At least you don't have to put up with the chief constable's excuses for not inviting me to play golf.'

'You hate golf,' I reminded her.

'That's not the bloody point!' She slammed her mug onto my desk hard enough to dent the MDF. 'Men play golf. Senior female officers don't even get the chance to tell them to stick it up their arses. I swear, Al, one of these days I'll take it up just to spite them, and then I'll challenge them to a match. It'll be worth it just to see Gosford paying for the cocktails at the nineteenth hole!'

THIS MORNING, I think as I'm bundling Blue into the car, is going to be one of the better days, not least because acting as SIO on a murder case gives me a free hand when it comes to handing the usual West Hill gang wars and petty drug deals over to the latest bunch of trainee constables, currently overseen by Dave Fosbury, Polly Sillitoe's counterpart in uniform. It also, naturally, means I can hand over the relevant paperwork as well. I head over to Clifton, drop off Blue with Joyce, and make it to West Hill station at just gone half seven. George Saint, installed as usual at the front desk, jumps in surprise and almost chokes on his bacon sandwich.

'Bloody hell,' he splutters, 'did somebody put a firework down your trousers?'

'Better,' I reply, resting an elbow on the counter next to the assault-proof screen. 'Pulled a couple of skeletons out of the closet.'

He gives me a rumbling chuckle. 'So I heard. Nothing like a good murder to get the upper ranks off their arses. Mind you, Polly's beaten you to it – she was in half an hour ago.' The grin dissolves. 'I hear one of the bodies is a little kiddie – mother and child, do you think?'

'No way of knowing until we get the DNA back,' I reply, 'but it looks likely. Keep a close eye on the switchboard today, George. Anything that comes through, put it straight through to me or Polly, okay?'

'Will do, Al. By the way,' he adds as I make my way over to the lift, 'don't forget to find something interesting for young Daz Jackson today.'

I give him a puzzled look, but then remember – it's Daz's first day as the squad's newly promoted sergeant. By tradition, the first job given to any officer jumping up a rank from constable has to be either the muckiest or most tedious on offer that particular day. My own first day as detective sergeant was spent sitting in a freezing cold transport café car park following a tip-off that a couple of local lads were aiming to nick a container load of French lamb carcasses destined for a local supermarket. Neither the thieves nor the container showed up.

'Sodding hell,' I mutter to myself, and then, 'Is he in yet?'

George nods. 'Last I heard, he'd locked himself in the second-floor gents' – he's probably planning to stay there until you and Polly have gone back out.'

'That's all I bloody well need,' is my final comment as I step into the lift and head up to the squad room.

When I get there, everybody is already at their desks,

heads down, clicking away at keyboards, the atmosphere thick with a combination of perspiration and coffee fumes. There's a subdued ripple of greetings as I make my way through to my office at the end of the room, one of two partitioned spaces, the other occupied by DI Sillitoe. I had the chance to take over Grace's office on the next floor following my promotion, but knew I wouldn't feel comfortable so far away from the general hubbub of everyday policing. It was a decision that Grace wholly approved of, since it meant she didn't have to move either.

Sillitoe is already hovering by my door. 'Morning, boss.' There's a definite caffeine-fuelled glint in her eye, reminding me I've only had one coffee so far, and that part of my mind is drifting back to George's bacon sandwich.

'Go on in, Polly,' I tell her. 'I'll just be a minute. Colin?'

Colin Draper, our youngest and newest DC, bobs his head up from behind his computer screen and gives me a resentful look.

'Nip down to the canteen and get me my usual, will you? Tell them I'll settle up at the end of the week.'

'Sir.' He reluctantly gets to his feet to a chorus of 'and while you're there …' requests.

'The rest of you can sodding well get your own,' I add, then join Sillitoe in my office, shutting the door on the squad's rumbles of protest. 'Okay, Polly,' I say, sitting down and gesturing to a chair on the other side of the desk. 'What have we got so far?'

'Not a lot that's useful,' she replies, 'at least, not yet. I've spoken to Maggie Ainsworth, and she says she's managed to get some decent samples from both victims. She's promised to fast-track the analysis and hopes she'll have something for us later today. I've spoken to the estate agent who handled the sale in July. He says it was on the market with vacant possession, and he's not sure how long it was empty before it was put up for sale. He reckons it can't have been long, though, as there was no build-up of dust or damp. The place looked as if it had been well cared for and recently redecorated throughout.'

'Redecorated?' Something pricks at the back of my neck. 'Who the hell spends money on redecorating a whole house if they intend to move straight after?'

She shrugs. 'According to the agent, a lot of people these days. It's been a buyer's market the last couple of years, so sellers are desperate to give their properties an edge.'

There's a knock on the door, and DC Draper comes in clutching coffee and a carton containing, I hope, a bacon sandwich. 'Thanks, Colin,' I say. 'We'll have a quick briefing in around ten minutes. Is Sergeant Jackson here yet?'

'Not seen him, sir,' he replies, struggling to hold in a grin.

'Try the second-floor toilet,' I tell him. 'And if he's not here in five, I'll have him searching through the rubbish bins over at Vista House for the rest of the week.'

'Yes, sir.' He manages to make it to the other side of the door before the grin hits his face.

'Okay,' I say, setting the carton aside for the moment and taking a good shot of coffee. 'First, we've got two bodies that we think were tipped into a shallow grave sometime between the late 1990s and early 2000s, then covered up with a very hastily constructed garden shed – so hasty that whoever built it didn't bother laying a proper foundation.' I silently send thanks to Rosie for pointing that out.

'Maybe they just weren't very good at DIY?' Sillitoe suggests.

'Maybe. In fact, definitely. So, as I can't imagine a

murderer hauling his or her victims over a random fence in the middle of the night, burying them and building a shed over the top, we're looking at whoever was living in the house at the time being either the killer, or at the very least an accessory, who needed to cover their tracks in a hurry.'

'Agreed,' she says. 'Second?'

'Second, Larson's working on it, and so far, he has Joseph Drake living in the house in 2011. He's checking further back now. The trouble is, if he finds Drake there in 2001, and Maggie is right, that's bang in the middle of our window for time of death. He's a suspect, but maybe not the only one. We have to go further back to see who was living there in the 1990s.'

'Bugger,' she comments. 'Not a slam dunk, then.'

'It never bloody well is. Maybe we'll get lucky, but I doubt it.' I take another shot of coffee. 'Third, in 2011, Drake was living there with a partner, probably wife, but in 2021 the wife was off the census, and he was living with a six-year-old daughter. Maybe he got divorced, or the wife died. Whichever, we need to know what happened to her, and if she's alive, she needs to be questioned. I'm sure Larson is already on it, but we need to get all the information we can from neighbours, work colleagues, whatever. She's not our corpse – the timings don't fit, especially given the age of the daughter, so she must be on record somewhere. Plus, right now, we have no idea where Drake and his daughter are. I think that's plenty to be getting on with while we're waiting for forensic reports to come through, unless you can think of anything I haven't mentioned.'

'Not right now.' She shrugs. 'Do you want me to get the troops mustered?'

'Give me a couple of minutes – I've an urgent matter to attend to first.'

Her eyes drift to my rapidly cooling bacon sandwich. 'Good.' She grins. 'That'll give me time to set up the coffee machine. I should have done it first thing, but we're out of filters. Robbie said she'd pick some up on her way in to save us trailing down to the canteen every five minutes.'

I'VE JUST STARTED the morning briefing when Daz Jackson, flanked by DC Draper, finally makes his appearance to a chorus of cheers and whistles.

'Sorry we're late, sir,' Draper announces. 'Daz got pulled over in the corridor on suspicion of being drunk in charge of a lavatory brush, and had to do a breathalyser.'

There's another round of cheers and sniggers as Daz makes his way to his desk, red-faced and scowling. Sillitoe and I exchange a look. If Jackson is going to gain the respect of the squad, he needs to start now, and an intervention from either of us will make it harder in the long run. I see his mouth tighten into a thin line, and he shoots to his feet, scraping his chair across the vinyl with a painful screech. There's instant silence.

'For fuck's sake, you lot!' He glares round the room. 'We've got the killer of a woman and child out there somewhere, and you're sat in here behaving like a bunch of pricks on a stag night. So do us all a favour, shut the fuck up, and let's get on with the job, okay?'

There's a short pause, followed by a subdued response, in unison. 'Sorry, Sarge.'

I give Jackson a slight nod – he's going to be fine.

'Right,' I say. 'The Maitlands have been moved to a hotel

apartment in Redcliffe for the duration, and I need a family liaison officer with them.' I turn to DC Karen Wyatt. 'Karen, you're our qualified FLO. Get over there, stay with them and find out everything you can about what they've done in the house since they moved in – painting or decorating, whether any furniture was still there when they moved in, anything unusual they've noticed, even whether they've put a shelf up or put in extra electrics. If anything was left behind by Drake, let forensics know, and they can put it on their list for analysis.'

Wyatt nods. 'I'm on it, boss.'

I carry on assigning tasks – two DCs observing and reporting back from the crime scene, and one, Ollie White, a young IT graduate who, like my son-in-law, has developed an unhealthy interest in policing, to liaise with Larson and assist if needed. Finally, I get to Daz, and there's an expectant hush. I decide I don't have the luxury to bugger about.

'Sorry to disappoint you all,' I say, 'but the party games will have to wait. Daz, I want you down at Oakfield Road. Take Robbie and Colin with you. Go door to door, find out where the older residents are, especially those who have been there twenty years or more, and get everything you can out of them, who the previous occupants were and so on. See if anyone remembers that shed going up, and if so, who built it. Find out how well they knew Drake and his wife. The younger families might have information about the daughter, too – if they have kids the same age who played with her, we could get something useful there. Go easy, though, if children need to be spoken to. Put them on a list, get parental consent, and we'll go through the proper channels for interviewing minors.'

Jackson gives me a grateful smile. 'Will do, boss.'

'Okay, that's it. Anything you find, pass it on to Polly, even if it seems trivial.'

Within a minute, the room is empty except for me, Sillitoe and Ollie White, who is busy on the phone, communing with Larson.

'Maybe I should get over there and give them a hand,' Sillitoe suggests, but I shake my head.

'I know it's frustrating, Polly, but somebody's got to mind the shop. If we're both here, we can respond more quickly if anything kicks off.'

'You think it will? What's the back of your neck telling you?'

'Something, but I haven't translated it yet,' I admit. 'Whatever it's saying, I don't think it's good.'

'Bloody hell,' she replies. 'I suppose I'd better go upstairs and get Grace up to speed.'

She's halfway across the squad room when the phone rings in my office. I gesture for her to wait, and answer it.

'I thought you should know,' George says. 'A call has come in from Ashton Road primary school. The headteacher saw the news and wanted to register her concern. Millie Drake is on her roll and hasn't been seen since the beginning of July.'

'July? Damn it, George, that's two and a half months ago!'

'Yes, well …' There's a pause, during which I can hear a wrapper being removed from something edible.

'For God's sake, George, get on with it,' I snap, knowing full well he'll take his time no matter what I say.

'She reported the absence to the council on the eleventh of July,' he says through a mouthful of something, 'and they put Millie on the non-attendance list, but couldn't get hold of the parent or guardian. Then they did what all overworked and understaffed councils do, put it on a very long list to deal with after the summer holiday. It's two weeks into the autumn term, and they haven't got round to investigating yet.'

I stifle a groan. 'Sounds like one of us needs to get over there.'

'No need,' he says. 'I've asked her to come in straight away. She's left the deputy head in charge, and she's on her way, should be here in the next half hour.'

'Thanks, George.' I put the phone down and fill Sillitoe in. She takes the words right out of my mouth.

'Jesus fucking Christ!'

4

Grace sits back and massages her temples, finally coming up with the obvious. 'Jesus, Al. This doesn't sound good.'

'No, ma'am,' Sillitoe and I agree in unison.

Sillitoe gives me an encouraging nod, and I take a deep breath. 'The thing is, ma'am, I think we need to consider—'

'I'm well aware of what we need to consider, Chief Inspector,' Grace snaps back, 'and I'm bloody well considering, okay?' She takes a couple of deep breaths, then looks from one to the other of us. We wait in silence until she makes up her mind and nods. 'Right. This is what we're going to do and not do. We are *not* going to rip a whole house apart unless we have a solid reason for it. We *are* going to see if we can find a solid reason. Polly, perhaps you could go and see the Maitlands and explain that we might be looking at a bit more than a simple search of the premises. It will be a lot easier if they are onside. I'll give the go-ahead to get a dog handler into the house, and Al, I'll back you up if forensics start moaning about manpower and budgets. If there's anything to justify messing with the structure, we'll find it.'

'In the meantime,' I say, 'we need to get Joseph and Millie Drake flagged nationwide as missing – they could be anywhere – well, somewhere else, at any rate.'

Grace gives me a weak smile. 'I suppose it's worth being optimistic until we know otherwise. I'll give a short statement to the press at lunchtime, enough to keep them quiet without giving them too much information. If I do it, it might keep the focus off you two for the time being.'

Her phone rings. She picks up, listens, says, 'Thanks, George,' and turns to me. 'There's a Cicely Henstridge downstairs asking for you.'

'Good. That'll be the headteacher. Maybe she can shed some light.' I get up, Sillitoe right behind me.

'Good luck,' Grace calls after us as we make our way to the lift.

'I'll go over to Oakfield Road when I've seen the Maitlands,' Polly says as we reach reception, 'keep an eye on the forensic team.' There's a slight air of triumph in her voice at the overrule of my decision to chain her to the office. I smile inwardly. I would have felt exactly the same.

'Good idea,' I reply. 'I'll let you know if I get anything useful from the headteacher; then I'll chase up Maggie.'

'What about Larson?' she asks.

What about him? I think, unfairly. 'I'll catch up with him tonight,' I say, 'and if he finds anything before then, I'm sure he'll let us know.'

CICELY HENSTRIDGE IS the perfect image of a formidable controller of small children. I guess she's in her early sixties, a stocky figure ploughing towards me like a galleon in full sail. I'm briefly reminded of my own primary school days and am tempted to put my hand up rather than hold it out for her to shake. Thankfully I do the latter.

'Ms Henstridge – I'm Chief Inspector Crow. Thank you for coming. Can I arrange some tea or coffee?'

'It's "Mrs", Chief Inspector, and thank you for seeing me. Coffee would be very nice.'

I raise an eyebrow at George as she breezes through the door I'm holding open for her, and he heads for the back office to find a constable for kettle duties.

'You're Rosie Crow's dad, aren't you?' she asks as we settle in one of the interview rooms. I nod, and she continues, 'I remember teaching her years ago – a real handful and sharp as a tack. We've got Ben now, of course – he was in the same class as Millie Drake.'

That statement brings me up short, and I silently curse myself for not getting my facts together before now. Millie Drake is Ben's age and attends – or did attend – the same school, so naturally they'll know each other. I also realise I've met Cicely Henstridge before, some twenty-odd years ago at a couple of parents' evenings when Rosie was a pupil. Clearly, she recognised me at once despite the passage of decades. I'm saved more awkwardness by the arrival of a pot of coffee and biscuits. I pour us both a cup, and as I pass one to the headmistress, I see she's smiling.

'Don't worry – I'm sure I've put on a few pounds, not to say wrinkles, since we last met. That's the thing about teachers – we never forget a face. Names, though …' She shrugs. 'But we're not here to reminisce. I've been concerned about Millie for some time, and when I saw the news this morning, an alarm bell really started ringing. If something's happened to her ...' She shakes her head and reaches for a biscuit.

'I'd like you to take me through those concerns, Mrs Henstridge,' I say, 'perhaps from the point she first went missing, back in July? I understand that was when she stopped attending school?'

She nods. 'Millie's last day in school was Friday, eighth of July. She didn't turn up on Monday the eleventh, and nobody has seen her since. We usually leave it a few days, to give the parents a chance to get in touch. I'm afraid there's always a bit of a rash of absences just before the summer holiday. Parents try to get a holiday in before the prices shoot up when term ends. I was chasing eight unauthorised absences that week – I looked them up before I called you. It's usually a case of waiting for the families to get back from the Costa del Sol, or wherever they've gone, then issuing a fine, which is a poor deterrent – it's much less than the extra cost of the same holiday after the schools break up. That would have been on the twenty-second of July.'

'You said you'd had concerns about Millie for some time?' I prompt.

She takes a sip of coffee. 'Yes. She was a quiet, uncommunicative child – the sort who keeps to herself, doesn't make friends easily. She was always very well turned out; clean, neatly dressed and diligent. Academically, she was ahead of her years, and sometimes that can lead to a child being either disruptive or mentally "absent" in class. They get bored and frustrated, and schools don't have the funding to deal adequately with children at the extreme ends of the spectrum. Millie, though, was never a moment's trouble.'

'Millie sounds like a model pupil,' I point out, refilling her coffee cup and trying to swallow my growing impatience.

'So, aside from an unauthorised holiday, what were you concerned about?'

Henstridge blinks and takes another biscuit. 'I'm sorry – I'm sure you're not interested in her academic record. Last year, just after the Easter break, things started to change. She became even more uncommunicative, her grades dropped dramatically, and she began to turn up for school looking a bit, well, untidy – clothes unwashed, odd socks, hair not so well combed, that sort of thing. I contacted the father, and he told me his wife had left him without warning, leaving him to look after Millie by himself. Of course, we were very sympathetic and offered to help in any way we could, but he refused, said he'd sort something out. I called Millie into my office to make sure she was coping, but didn't get much out of her. With hindsight, perhaps she had been told not to talk to us, although at the time there was nothing I could put my finger on, so I just put it down to grief at her mother's disappearance. There was certainly nothing to make me consider calling social services in. After my conversation with Mr Drake, things did improve a bit in terms of her clothing, hygiene and so on, but her grades continued to fall, and I noted she was losing weight, although not dramatically.'

'And how often did you meet the parents? I mean, aside from phone calls, did either of them ever visit the school?'

'The father just twice. Once when Millie started at the school, and once when she was unwell, and we had to call a parent in to take her home.'

'And the mother?'

She frowns, thinking, and finally says, 'Never. Her mother never visited the school, and I never spoke to her on the phone either. It was always the father.'

The prickling at the back of my neck turns into a full-blown knot in my stomach. 'Okay. A child is missing, the mother has never been seen, father and child vanish into thin air. So, when did you think to alert the authorities?'

She bristles. 'Contrary to popular belief, Chief Inspector Crow, a teacher's work does not end when the children go on holiday. When Millie hadn't returned by the end of term, I made every effort to contact her father, without success. A week into the summer holiday I reported her absence to the relevant council department, who promised to investigate further, but everyone knows that nothing gets done in late July and August. Finally, I heard from another member of staff that they may have moved out of the area. The thing is, there is no record of Millie being added to the roll in another school. If she had, we would have been contacted and asked to remove her from ours. I've been chasing it up for the last couple of weeks, and then I saw the news, about the bodies being found, and I thought … I mean …'

She comes to a halt, looks away and wipes a hand across her brow.

'Mrs Henstridge,' I say, as gently as I can despite an urge to throttle the woman for not raising the alarm earlier, even though, if I'm being rational, the fault lies squarely with the educational bureaucracy. 'We haven't been able to identify the remains yet, but whoever they are, I can assure you, neither of them is Millie Drake.'

She whips out a handkerchief, dabs her eyes and gives me a dubious look. 'You're sure? You're absolutely sure?'

'We're sure. I'm afraid I can't tell you any more than that, but as far as we're concerned at this stage, Millie and her father are simply missing. You've given us some valuable information. Thank you for coming in – we'll let you know if we need to speak to you again.'

I conduct her back to the front desk, where George is waiting, waving and pointing at the switchboard. I show Henstridge out and go across to him. 'What is it, George?'

'Maggie Ainsworth. She says can you go across to the lab as soon as you're free.'

'Did she say anything else?'

'Nope – but she did sound as if she'd found a winning lottery ticket in someone's stomach contents.'

'Right.' I try to put a brake on my imagination. 'Ring her back, will you, and tell her I'm on my way?'

George nods, and I dash upstairs to grab my coat.

5

Twenty minutes later I press the entrance buzzer to the pathology lab, feeling slightly less queasy than usual. At least on this occasion I won't have to sit through a minute examination of some poor sod's internal organs. Maggie lets me in, and we head up to her office.

'I'm about to have lunch,' she says, pouring us both coffee. 'You want some?' She rips the lid off a plastic container and has a rummage. 'Egg and cress or liver pâté today. Which do you fancy?'

Somehow, sitting right next to a room full of dissected bodies doesn't do much for my appetite. 'Thanks for the offer, Maggie, but I'll stick with coffee if it's all the same to you.'

She grins and pulls an egg and cress sandwich out of its wrapper. 'And people say policemen have strong stomachs,' she comments, tucking in with almost ghoulish enthusiasm. 'But don't worry – there wasn't that much to get squeamish about this time. All bones and no guts.'

'George Saint said you had some news,' I say, bringing the conversation back to safer ground.

She nods. 'I have indeed, and I think you're going to find it interesting. I managed to get some decent hair samples from both sets of remains, and even better, some flakes of skin still adhering to one or two of the bones. I started running them through the analysis yesterday and got the results around an hour ago.' She pauses and, when I don't say anything, gives me a mock frown. 'You can thank me later.'

'Sorry, Maggie – I'm very grateful. What have you found?'

She takes another bite of sandwich and washes it down with coffee. 'Okay. The adult first – female, late teens to early twenties, although I'd be more inclined to put her at the younger end of that range. It's difficult to say because there is possible evidence of a degree of malnutrition, perhaps an eating disorder or lack of access to food. It's very hard to be definite from an examination of bones and teeth, but if you pushed me, I'd say it's likely.'

'Why? A hunch or something more definite?'

'Hunch?' She sighs in irritation. 'Pathologists, DCI Crow, do not work on hunches.' She clicks at her keyboard, then turns her computer screen so we can both see. The display shows several images of human bones – legs, arms and ribcage. She clicks on a leg to enlarge it. 'Look here,' she says, pointing out a faint horizontal line. 'This is the left leg. There's a fracture in the tibia, healed, so the injury was sustained well before death, possibly much earlier.' She points again. 'Here are two more. There are a couple of similar fractures to the right leg, and one to the tibia. We also have a broken wrist and scarring to the ribs. There is evidence of skeletal damage consistent with an eating disorder, although similar problems could be the result of coeliac disease, bowel disease or cystic fibrosis. I can't rule out any particular cause.'

'What about abuse?' I ask.

'Depends whether you want to include the bloody great hole in the back of her skull,' she replies with a shrug. 'But in terms of the historic injuries, again, it's hard to say. Neglect, quite possibly, but the fractures might be accidental. As for identification, as I suspected, there's not much chance of hooking out a dental record, and there are no DNA matches on any of our databases. However, she might perhaps have been hospitalised at some point, so worth a try? It's a long shot, but you never know.'

'Bloody hell!' I try to imagine how long it might take to narrow it down to the thousands – probably tens of thousands – of medical records stretching back before the millennium. Unless we get a very lucky break, it's likely an impossible task.

She smiles. 'I know – not quite what you want to hear. But ...' She holds up a finger. 'I might have something to cheer you up. We've had a lot more luck with the child. You might want to get yourself another coffee.'

'For fuck's sake, Maggie!' I push my chair back and grab the coffee jug, then realise I'm smiling too. When Maggie says she's had some luck, you can guarantee there's big news on the way. She also does very good coffee. I refill both our cups. 'I'm listening.'

She nods. 'The infant remains are male. And I'd pin the age to approximately three years old. Again, it's hard to say exactly, and there is evidence of a number of greenstick fractures, one of which resulted in a slight deformation of the left radius.'

'You're saying the child had broken bones that were left untreated? Jesus Christ!'

'It looks like it,' Maggie replies, 'which lends some weight to an argument that both mother and child were victims of neglect at the very least. And yes, DNA confirms that we have a mother and son here. What's interesting, though ...' There's an infuriating pause while she unwraps another packet of sandwiches. 'You're sure you don't want one? It's very good pâté – Cyril loves it.'

I catch the glint in her eye and take the bait. 'Just get on with it, Maggie!'

She chews, swallows and grins. 'Well, we've drawn a blank as far as identifying the mother goes, but we do know who the child's father is – or to be more accurate, who the father *was*.'

Again, there's a pause for dramatic effect. This time I simply fold my arms, keep my mouth shut and let her have her moment.

'Do you remember Jimmy Harris?' she says finally.

That makes me sit up. 'You've got to be bloody joking,' is all I can think to say as I absorb that bit of information. 'You mean *the* Jimmy Harris – ran with Shark Johnson's lot until Craig Tyler beat him to death in the car park under Vista House?'

'That's the one,' Maggie says. 'Back in 2003, I did the post-mortem, and you were the one who got Tyler put away, if I remember correctly.'

I nod. 'I was still a lowly PC then, and Craig Tyler was my biggest arrest. The bastard broke my arm, too!' It takes another minute for things to sink in. 'You're saying that this child is Jimmy Harris's? Are you sure you haven't mixed up a couple of samples!'

'There's no doubt,' Maggie says, ignoring the suggestion. 'It's an exact match. Plus, I pulled out the record of Jimmy's post-mortem, and guess what? The actual cause of death was a blow to the back of the head with a heavy blunt instrument – exactly the same as the bodies we have here. I'd even hazard a guess it was the same object that caused all the deaths, from the size and shape of the holes in all three skulls. Don't quote me on that, though.'

My mind is starting to race as I process the implications of Maggie's findings. 'If that's true,' I think aloud, 'we've got three murders that probably occurred at around the same time, with the same killer.'

'There's no concrete evidence for that,' Maggie reminds me, 'but what there is would suggest something of the sort. It fits with my estimate of the age of the remains. A murder weapon would help, if you've got one stuffed in an evidence bag somewhere.'

'We never found it,' I tell her. 'Tyler admitted giving Jimmy a beating, but denied murder. He was convicted anyway – the jury didn't think twice once they'd seen the photos of the body, and if that wasn't enough, Tyler completely lost it in court and tried to punch his defence counsel. The verdict took less than half an hour.'

'Looks like you may have grounds to charge him with a couple more,' Maggie suggests. 'If you like, I can do some more work on the three head wounds, see if we can get a definite match.'

'Yes, please, Maggie – that would be useful. Meanwhile I'll track Tyler down. He's still in prison, and last I heard, was turned down for parole a couple of years or so ago. He's never admitted to the murder, so the chances are he'll be in for another five years at least.'

I'M BACK in my car, taking a few minutes to mull over the idea that Craig Tyler might be not only a first-class thug, but also a child killer, when my mobile shakes me out of my thoughts.

'Boss?'

'How's it going, Polly?'

'I think you should come over to Oakfield Road. The DSI sent a dog handler down, and he thinks he's found something.'

'Found what? And where?'

'He's not sure. It's behind one of the walls. It could be dead rats or a pigeon or ...' She leaves the sentence unfinished.

'Shit!' I say, then realise that's not very helpful. 'Okay, Polly, I'm on my way. I'll let Grace know. In the meantime, keep the area clear, and—'

'I know what to do,' she snaps irritably. 'Tell Grace we might need to take the wall down.' She hangs up.

I feel rather than hear Grace's groan at the other end of the line. 'You'd better be bloody sure, Al, if we're going to start ripping the house to bits.' There's a pause and then, 'Okay – I suppose there's only one way to find out. I'll get a team down there, but please try to cause as little damage as possible. The chief constable's moaning about budgets enough as it is.'

'I'll do my best,' I tell her, hang up and key the ignition.

6

I arrive at Oakfield Road to find Sillitoe hovering by the front gate, looking distinctly unhappy. I battle my way through the barrage of reporters and spectators, then duck under the cordon. Before I have time to say anything, she grabs my arm and propels me through the front door, slamming it behind us.

'Fucking hell!' She leans back against the wall and rubs a hand across her forehead. 'If this carries on, we'll have to call in riot control. It's like the siege of Leningrad out there, and it's got worse since the demolition team moved in.' She sucks in a breath between clenched teeth. '*And* I've got a bloody headache!'

I give her a pat on the shoulder. 'If you want to take a couple of hours, I can take over here,' I suggest. 'Give yourself a break and get some food – and a packet of painkillers?'

She straightens. 'No, boss, I'll be fine. It was my call to take the wall down, and I want to be here. We were just waiting for you to get started.'

'Fair enough,' I say. 'But at least we can get that cordon

moved back.' I go through to the back door, where a couple of PCs are keeping an eye on a large blue plastic tent where the shed used to be. I give one of them instructions to move the cordons to block each end of the street. It won't stop some of the reporters wheedling their way into nearby residents' front bedrooms, but it will help clear the road. 'Okay,' I say when he's trotted off to see to it, 'where's the wall, and where's the dog?'

Sillitoe leads me upstairs to the large, bay-windowed front bedroom, where a line of police tape forms a makeshift barrier running from the doorway to the window. It gives us a narrow corridor to stand and watch the proceedings. On the other side of the tape, three officers in paper boiler suits are in a huddle next to a section of the bedroom wall, having an animated discussion involving a lot of pointing and grunting. On our side, a uniformed officer in a high-vis vest is looking on, a paper coffee cup in one hand, a dog lead in the other, at the end of which a spaniel is fidgeting, panting and thumping its tail on the floorboards, its attention firmly fixed on the gaggle by the wall.

'This is PC Dent, boss,' Sillitoe says.

Dent straightens up. 'Mike Dent, sir,' he says, then points to the spaniel, who is still fixated on the wall. 'And this is Flossie.'

I give him a nod. 'So what makes you think it's worth knocking a hole in somebody's house, Constable?'

Dent grins. 'It's not me who calls the shots, sir. Flossie thinks so, and that's good enough for me.'

I rephrase, making sure my irritation isn't open to interpretation. 'All right – what makes Flossie think it's worth it?'

Dent isn't fazed. 'Our Flossie's as bright as a pin, sir. Of course, we can't say precisely what's in there, but something is. She's trained to pick up a range of smells, in particular, the scent of human residue. That could be human remains, old artefacts that people have handled – anything connected to a historic human presence. She's used at archaeological digs and so on, or old grave sites, and she can distinguish between recent traces and older ones. The stronger the scent, the bigger the reaction – and this time she barked her head off, so I'd put my pension on there being something behind that wall, sir.'

'I'll make a note of that,' I comment. 'Okay, let's see what we've got.'

Sillitoe calls over one of the group of SOCOs, a woman with a pile of blond hair stuffed into a disposable plastic cap, giving the top of her head a precarious wobble and reminding me of one of Ben's favourite cartoon characters. 'What do you think?' Sillitoe asks.

The woman shrugs. 'It should be easy enough. The recesses on each side of the chimney breast have been bricked in, but there's a space around a foot wide behind each partition. I must admit it's an odd way to do it. Most people have built in wardrobes on either side in these old Victorian houses, or occasionally a stud wall to even things up and provide insulation. I've never come across a layer of bricks before.'

'Go carefully,' I tell her. 'We want to cause as little damage as possible. The DI and I will be downstairs. Give us a shout as soon as you're through.'

The woman nods and turns back to her team. Sillitoe and I head down to the kitchen and through into the back garden, quiet now except for the rustle of the plastic tent in the wind. I fill her in on Maggie's findings, and she lets her breath out in a soft whistle.

'That's a lot to get our heads round. You think Craig Tyler killed Jimmy, then went after the woman and child?'

'It's possible. The thing is, I know it's a long time ago, but I can't remember any talk of Jimmy Harris having a family – he was barely out of his teens when he got himself murdered. There was never a suggestion that it was anything more than a straightforward territorial scrap between rival gangs. The idea of going after a woman and child doesn't quite fit, even if Maggie does say the same weapon might have been used. There's always been an unwritten rule on the street when it comes to reprisals involving bystanders, innocent or not. Still, Tyler was, and I'm sure still is, a very nasty bastard, so there might have been more to it.'

Sillitoe leans back against the wall and closes her eyes, thinking it through. 'So,' she says slowly, 'if Tyler killed the two bodies we've just dug up, then who built the shed? Drake, or whoever was living in the house at the time, must have been involved. Otherwise, it's too much of a coincidence.' She draws herself up and looks at me. 'What's the plan, then, boss?'

'I'm buggered if I know,' I reply. 'It's all getting too damned complicated.' I take a leaf out of my DI's book and give myself a minute to think. 'Right,' I say finally. 'I need to talk to Tyler and to Shark Johnson as well if I can set up a meeting. Shark and Jimmy were practically joined at the hip back in the day, and he's been gunning for Tyler ever since. If anyone knows what went on, he will. What about Daz? Has he turned anything up from the neighbours yet?'

'He's still at it,' she replies. 'Last I heard, he was on his seventh lot of tea and cake. It's difficult to stop some of the older residents once they get going. Robbie and Colin are trawling the streets either side. The thing is, there are a lot of families who have been here generations, especially in the houses that used to be council owned.'

'Okay. I suppose that means we might strike lucky. Tell everyone to get back to the office by 6 p.m. for a catch-up.'

I'm about to leave when the back door bursts open, and a PC sticks his head round. 'They've knocked through upstairs, sir,' he says. 'They say can you go up?'

Sillitoe and I exchange a look and trail back inside and up to the bedroom. PC Dent is standing in the corner, looking very uncomfortable, unlike Flossie the spaniel, who is sniffing enthusiastically and straining at the leash. The SOCO team leader comes across to us, carrying a plastic bag in the tips of two gloved fingers, holding it at arm's length. There's another sealed package tucked under her other arm.

She greets me with a curt nod. 'Chief Inspector, if you were hoping for another body, I'm afraid I have to disappoint you – unless you are interested in a dead cat.' She holds up the bag, wrinkling her nose in distaste. 'It's fairly desiccated, I'm afraid, but not so much that it can possibly be confused with human remains.' She sends a withering glare in PC Dent's direction.

Sillitoe has turned a little pale. 'Oh, for fuck's sake,' she mutters while taking a sudden and intense interest in her shoelaces.

'And what else have you got there?' I ask, pointing at the other package.

'A shoebox,' the woman answers. 'It's not in very good condition, I'm afraid. The damp has got to it and fused the lid. I haven't tried to open it, but from the weight, I'd guess it contains documents of some sort – photographs, certificates, that sort of thing.'

I mull this information for a moment. 'Okay,' I say. 'Two

questions. First, what's in that box that is so important someone went to all the trouble of building a brick wall to hide it? Second, how the hell did the cat manage to get stuck in there?' I don't wait for an answer, but pull out my mobile and dial.

'DCI Crow – don't tell me – you changed your mind about the liver pâté. Luckily for you, I've got a couple left.'

'Thanks, Maggie, but I'd hate to deprive you. I'm sending some samples over. Can you get started on them right away?'

'Depends how good the bribe is.'

'A bottle of Jura?'

'Send them over. You can drop the Scotch in later.'

I turn back to the SOCO. 'Can you get both of those over to Maggie at the lab? I need to know how long that cat's been in there, the age and contents of the box, and while you're at it, take her a sample of the brick and mortar used in the wall, to see if we can get anything from that.'

She shrugs. 'If you say so. I'll send someone straight over. Anything else?'

'Take a look at the other rooms, see if there are any more hidey-holes. You never know.'

Sillitoe follows me out to my car, looking like she's caught a whiff of rotting cat. 'Sorry, boss,' she says. 'Grace is going to have a bloody field day with this.'

'I wouldn't worry,' I reply. 'I would have made the same call. Besides, it's pretty clear something isn't right. There's no obvious way that cat could have got into the cavity and got itself stuck, and it's my bet that whatever is in that box, someone wanted to conceal it. Plus, we didn't find another human body, and as far as I'm concerned, that's good news.'

'I suppose so,' she says, sounding unconvinced. 'So what now?'

I check my watch. It's nearly 2.30 p.m. 'Stay here and make sure the team goes over every inch of that house. You might as well make use of the dog, too, while it's here. It might look daft as hell, but it was excited about something, so you never know. Oh, and call Larson; tell him I want him at the six o'clock briefing. I'm going to set up an interview with Tyler – he got moved back to Bristol a couple of years ago, so it shouldn't be a problem – and then chase down Shark, see what he's got to say.'

I get off the phone to Grace as I pull into the staff car park of what used to be the secondary school, now known as Ashton Road Learning Academy, just up the road from the primary school attended by my grandson and, until recently, Millie Drake. Grace has taken on the task of arranging an urgent interview with Tyler. Getting Shark Johnson to agree to a cosy chat without having to arrest him first is slightly more complicated. I make my way to the school's main reception desk, hoping that an agreement I made with him eighteen or so months ago is still holding up. I announce myself to the school secretary and get shown straight up to the principal's office.

Mr Carver is a burly, no-nonsense type, around my age, his round face half obscured by a thick salt-and-pepper beard, and decked out in lime green corduroys, Hush Puppies and a bright orange felt waistcoat. He wouldn't, I think, look out of place in the upstairs room of a trendy pub, finger jammed in one ear, giving a nasal rendition of 'Streets of London'. He gets up and comes round the desk to shake my hand.

'Chief Inspector Crow – do come in. Can I get you anything? Tea? Coffee?'

The handshake is firm, and there's a humorous glint in

his eye that fits well with his flamboyant dress sense. I can't help but warm to him as he invites me to take one of two leather armchairs by a large window with a view over the playing field.

'Thanks,' I say. 'I'm fine. I'd like to have a word with one of your pupils, if he's in school today – Clive Gingell?'

'Clive?' His eyes narrow. 'Why? He's not in any trouble, I hope.'

'Not at all,' I reply, trying to put on my best reassuring smile. 'It's just that I have some news about a mutual friend of ours, and I'd like to pass on a message.'

'Hmm.' Carver goes back to his desk and fiddles with his computer. 'You're in luck, Chief Inspector. He's actually in today – in an English class if the register is correct. I can ask him to come up here if you like. I'm afraid I will have to be present, though, if that's all right?'

'Of course.'

Carver makes a phone call down to the school secretary, then comes back to his armchair. 'It shouldn't take more than a few minutes. Clive's an odd little chap – very bright, but his own worst enemy. He'd make a great footballer, too, but he does have a habit of thumping the opposition when they get in his way. He was suspended for aggressive behaviour a few months ago, but his mother must have had strong words with him, because he's been much better since he came back.'

I smile inwardly. Whoever had 'words' with him, it sure as hell wasn't his mother. A minute or so later, there's a knock at the door, and Clive appears, hands jammed resolutely in the pockets of a pair of black jeans, bottle green school sweatshirt tied round his waist. He's grown a bit since I last saw him – he must be over fourteen now, and the arms, on display below the sleeves of his T-shirt, are starting to put on a bit of muscle. He's also suffering from a decent eruption of acne, and stinks of knock-off aftershave, despite the lack of bum fluff on his chin.

He gives Carver a brief glance, then directs his attention to me, lifts his chin and sniffs. 'What the fuck do you want?'

'Clive!' Carver takes in a sharp breath, but I hold up a hand.

'It's quite all right. Good to see you doing so well, Clive. Jermaine keeping an eye on you, is he?'

He scowls. 'Yeah, right. Like I said, Bird Man, what do you want?'

'A small favour, if you can,' I answer. 'I'd like to have a chat with Jermaine, and I thought you might be able to give him a message for me.'

'What makes you think he'll want to talk to you?' he counters, doing his best to hold up his image of a refugee from *Fight Club*.

'He will when you give him the message,' I say. 'Tell him I want to talk to him about Jimmy Harris.'

Clive frowns. 'Who? I've never heard of him.'

'Way before your time, son. Shark will know, though, and I guarantee he'll want to see me. I also guarantee he won't be best pleased if you don't pass on the message. I'll be waiting for his answer – you know where to find me.'

Clive's response is an awkward shrug as he heads for the door, but Carver stops him.

'Clive?'

The boy turns, one hand on the door handle. 'Yes, Mr Carver?'

'Next time I see you,' the principal says, 'I want you properly dressed – no jeans, and if you must take your sweatshirt off, I want to see a shirt and tie, understood?'

Clive flushes and clenches his fists, but after a moment's thought simply says, 'Yes, Mr Carver,' then disappears down the corridor.

'I must admit I've got a bit of a soft spot for that lad,' Carver tells me. 'He could really make something of himself with a bit – well, a lot – more application.'

'I'll mention it when I next see his … his mother,' I say. I hold out a hand. 'Thank you for letting me speak to him. You've been very helpful.'

'Anything we can do to help the police, Chief Inspector. Feel free to get in touch any time.'

Back in my car, I realise I haven't eaten since breakfast. There's still well over an hour until the squad's daily debriefing, so I head off to collect Blue from my ex-mother-in-law, hoping I'll be able to take advantage of her latest batch cooking session while I'm there.

7

I arrive back at the station just in time to catch Daz, Robbie and Colin piling out of Daz's battered Ford Fiesta. I walk over to join them as Robbie flips the hatch open and pulls out two packed supermarket carrier bags.

'I thought you three were interviewing,' I comment, 'not doing your weekly shop.'

Daz looks affronted. 'We've been at it all day, boss,' he protests. 'Can't help it if everyone in the street thinks they're auditioning for *The Great British Bake Off*. We tried to refuse, but they wouldn't take no for an answer.' He turns to the other two, who both nod vigorously.

'We were just being polite,' Robbie puts in, giving me her 'butter wouldn't melt' face. 'We're supposed to be friendly, put witnesses at their ease in order to gain their confidence and extract detailed information.'

'Don't you quote the bloody interview handbook at me,' I snap, but then can't help grinning myself. 'So what have you got?'

'Carrot cake, Victoria sponge, chocolate brownies ...' She sticks her nose into one of the bags. 'One chap insisted we have a whole cheese and onion pie, and there's a big bag of homemade sausage rolls—'

'That's enough!' I hold up a hand. 'Just don't forget to slip George Saint a sausage roll on your way up. If he hears he's missed out, he'll sulk for the rest of the week.'

'Will do, boss,' she says, grinning, and they head off inside.

'And I hope cake isn't all you've bloody well got!' I call after them, and I take a deep breath. At least there's still one section of the West Hill community that isn't trying to blow our heads off or pelt us with empty beer cans, dog shit and the odd Molotov cocktail.

I reach the squad room, Bluebell in tow, just in time to grab the last chocolate brownie.

'Everyone's here, boss,' Sillitoe says through a mouthful of fruit scone. 'I've brought them up to speed on the finds at the house.'

I do a quick sweep and catch sight of Larson, who gives me a non-committal nod.

'Okay,' I say, bringing them to order. 'Before we start, I don't want to catch anyone trying to sneak Blue a sausage roll, understood?' There's a murmur of agreement through the general sound of chewing. 'Right. Karen, you first. Anything from the Maitlands?'

'Not much,' she says. 'They said there was no furniture left in the house when they moved in, and nothing in the loft. The carpets were in a pretty bad state, so the first thing they did was rip them all out and lay new throughout. The flooring company took the old stuff away – it's probably in the landfill by now. The kitchen units are still there, but apparently they were pretty filthy, so they went over the whole lot with bleach and God knows what else. Same with the walls. New oven, dishwasher and washing machine. It could be worth trying to get traces from the kitchen, but it doesn't sound hopeful. Sorry, boss.'

'Thanks, Karen. Daz, what about you – aside from acting as guest judge at the Church Fete bake off?'

Daz clears his throat and grins. 'It took a while, but between us we got some reliable info. We didn't have much luck with the newer residents, though. Quite a few are renters and tend to keep to their own circles. None of them had much to say about Joseph Drake except to say they might recognise him in the street, and none of them had ever seen his partner or even knew he had one. The older folk generally didn't like him much, and one or two said they felt sorry for the little girl, as they never saw her out playing, and her father always took her to school and picked her up. Again, they couldn't say anything for sure about the mother. One woman said she'd knocked on the door once, back in the late 2000s, with a fruit cake for Mrs Drake – being nosy about the invisible neighbour I'd guess. She told me Drake thanked her for the cake, then said his wife suffered with her nerves and had a thing about meeting people.'

'I suppose you would have trouble chatting to people if you were buried in the back garden,' Robbie puts in.

'A good point,' I say, 'but don't forget we haven't any evidence that the body is Pauline Drake – at least not yet. So, Daz, what is this "reliable info" you say you've got?'

'Well, between us we managed to get four accounts that were very similar concerning the previous owner. He was an old guy by the name of Fred Mackintosh, lived alone – his wife died in the Bristol Blitz, and he never remarried. He died in 1998, aged ninety-something. The house passed to his younger brother, Arthur, who never lived in it, but according to these neighbours rented it out for a year or two. Then he died, and the place was empty for a while before Drake moved in – that would have been in the early 2000s. We couldn't get anyone to be more precise. I've passed the information on to Mr Larson. As far as the shed goes, several people remember it going up, but it could have been any time between the late 1990s and early 2000s. I'm afraid that's it, boss.'

'Damn,' I mutter, thinking that the dates cut right across the period we're interested in, and don't bring us any closer to identifying a prime suspect for the murders. I realise that Daz, Robbie and Colin are exchanging crestfallen looks, give myself a mental kick up the arse and dredge up a smile. 'Thanks, you three. Good work.' I turn to Larson and, not quite able to overcome my unreasonable aversion to using his first name, raise an eyebrow instead.

'That partly bears out what I've been able to dig up so far,' he says. 'The younger brother, Arthur, inherited the house, but died six months later in January 1999. It was never actually rented out at that point. It passed to his daughter, June Fletcher, née Mackintosh, and was sold to Drake in June 1999 as a cash purchase. The thing is, Drake can't have moved in straight away. The house is shown as unoccupied in the 2001 census, and I haven't been able to verify for how long, or when precisely Drake and his family moved in. I'm currently trying to trace June Fletcher and get copies of utility bills for that period – they should confirm whether or not the property was empty for any length of time.'

'That's bloody marvellous,' is all I can think of to say. 'We don't know when Drake moved in, and we don't know who was living there before him. Nobody ever saw his wife, so for all we know, she could have been a figment of his imagination. We can't identify the adult victim except to say that she seems to have had an affair with a local drug dealer and gave birth to his child – and we can't ask the dealer because he got himself murdered twenty years ago.' I take a minute to remind myself that everyone is doing their best; it's not their fault things are complicated. Plus, it's not as if we don't have any leads to follow. 'Okay, everyone,' I conclude, which triggers glimmers of relief among the team. 'We'll call it a day and make a fresh start in the morning.'

Everyone troops out until there's just me, Sillitoe and Larson.

'What now?' Larson asks, but I don't get a chance to reply, as the door bursts open and Grace strides in, looking very tired and slightly irritated.

'I don't suppose any of you lot thought to save me a piece of cake?' she says, heading across to the depleted bags on Robbie's desk. Word travels fast.

'Help yourself,' I reply, and she roots about, coming up with a chunk of cheese and onion pie.

'I hear,' she says after a couple of bites, 'that we've just spent God knows how much uncovering a dead cat. It's a pity you couldn't have thrown in a couple of pigeons and a rat, just to make it worth the expense. And to make matters worse, you've asked Maggie Ainsworth to do a bloody postmortem on it!'

Sillitoe's face reddens, and she shuffles her good foot. 'I thought it was worth—' she starts, but I interrupt her.

'The fact is, ma'am, the search uncovered a deliberately created cavity containing not only the cat, but a box of documents that may well prove to be relevant to the murders. They're in pretty poor shape, but I've asked Maggie to do what she can with those, too. Plus, I'm pretty sure the cat didn't end up there accidentally. I want to know if somebody killed it and then threw it behind the wall.'

Grace thinks about this for a minute and then nods. 'Okay, Al, fair enough.' She turns to Sillitoe. 'And you think there may be more of these cavities in the house?'

'It's possible, ma'am,' she says, looking relieved. 'I'd like to keep the dog handler on and go through the rest of the house, just to make sure.'

'Don't forget,' I add, 'we've got a missing man and an eight-year-old child, and according to the information we gathered today, no one has ever set eyes on Millie Drake's mother or even spoken to her on the phone as far as we know. There could be an innocent explanation, of course, and the bodies we've found may be unconnected.'

Grace snorts. 'You mean, you've got Craig Tyler in the frame, and Joseph Drake might have spontaneously decided to build his shed precisely where the victims were buried. That makes perfect sense.'

'Or,' I say, 'Drake might not have been there, somebody else built the shed, and the false wall in the house might have been put there while the property was empty, before he moved in. Right now, there's no way of knowing.'

'Except we do know,' Grace counters, 'that Drake and his daughter have vanished into thin air, not to mention the invisible wife. Jesus bloody Christ!'

She pops the final piece of pie into her mouth and sighs.

'Okay. Polly, go ahead and make sure we haven't got any more surprises in that house. I'll argue the toss with the chief constable over the budget. We'll also need to talk to the children who were in Millie Drake's class, and her teachers, see if we can build a picture of her home life and get any clues as to where she and her father may have gone.'

'I can get DC Robbins onto that,' I say, although it was already on my 'to do' list.

Grace finally cracks a small smile. 'I've managed to get an interview with Tyler, Al. They are expecting you at one p.m. tomorrow. Don't hold your breath – he's been protesting his innocence since the day he was sentenced, so I'm not sure how much you'll get out of him. Still, he might find it harder to fend off three murders than one.' She rubs the crumbs off her hands and makes for the door. 'Keep me posted,' she says, gives Larson a cursory nod, then disappears down the corridor.

Sillitoe lets out a long breath. 'Thanks, boss.'

'Don't thank me yet, Polly,' I say. 'You'll be the one filling all the forms out for the expenses. For now, though, get yourself home and let Robbie know I want her down at Ashton Road school tomorrow. Mrs Henstridge is the head; she can get the contact details from George to arrange it.'

Sillitoe rolls her eyes. 'Robbie's going to love that – she hates kids.'

Finally, Larson and I are left alone, and I suddenly feel awkward, not quite knowing how to phrase my next request. My son-in-law, though, is ahead of me.

'I've already spoken to Rosie,' he says, risking a smile, which widens when I blink at him in surprise. 'You're going to say you need to interview Ben,' he goes on. 'It's fine. She said to tell you to come over when we've finished here, and we can both sit in if needed. I doubt if he'll be able to tell you much. Millie was in his class, but from what he's said, he didn't know her very well, and they weren't in the same circle of friends. You might be able to get more out of him – it's what you do, after all.'

'Yes, it is,' I reply, then, under my breath, 'Bloody hell!'

8

I'm sitting on one side of Rosie's kitchen table, and my grandson on the other, swinging his legs and fidgeting with excitement. He's brought his PlayStation down from his bedroom and has placed it strategically at the end of the table to make it look like an old-style recording machine. Larson and Rosie have been positioned on either side of the door, trying to keep straight faces.

'You're supposed to read me my rights,' Ben says. 'You can't ask me anything unless I'm under caution!'

'I only caution people if they're being arrested,' I explain, 'and you haven't been arrested.'

'Oh.' His face falls. 'Why not? Inspector Morse is always arresting people whether they've done a crime or not. If they haven't, he has to let them go, but he always arrests them first.'

'Maybe I should arrest your father instead,' I suggest, 'for letting you stay up late and watch unsuitable TV.'

'In my defence,' Larson puts in, 'all the old cop shows are on daytime TV these days, so I plead not guilty.'

'Anyway, Ben,' I go on, 'I can ask you questions because you are doing something much more important. You are "helping us with our enquiries".'

'Yay!' Ben bounces in his chair. 'Cool! That means I get to help you catch the perp!'

Rosie stifles a giggle. 'He watches the reruns of *Cagney & Lacey* as well,' she explains.

I catch myself just before I swear. 'Listen, Ben,' I say, putting on the most serious face I can manage. 'There's a girl around your age missing, and we're trying very hard to find out where she is in case anything has happened to her. It's really important you tell us everything you can about her.'

He nods, straightens in his chair. 'You mean Millie Drake, from my class,' he says, wrinkling his nose.

'That's right. Can you tell me anything about her?'

He shakes his head. 'Not really. She wasn't friends with anybody. I tried talking to her when she came into our class last year, but she told me to fuck off.' He blushes and glances at his mother, who frowns, but doesn't comment.

'Go on, Ben,' she says, nodding encouragement. 'Just say the truth – anything might help.'

'Well …' He keeps his eyes on the table. 'Nobody liked her. Her clothes were dirty, and she smelled. Some of the others in our class bullied her and called her names.' His eyes shoot up. 'I didn't though, honest. Mr Chase said we should be kind to her because her mum wasn't there anymore, so I did, but Millie just told me to bugger off.' He shrugs. 'I did try, Grandad, but she was rude back, so I stopped.'

'I'm sure you did, Ben,' I say. 'Don't worry, you're being really helpful.' He grins at that and sits up straighter. 'Is there anything else you can tell me?' I ask. 'Even the smallest thing could be important.'

He sits for a while in silence, brow furrowed, then says, 'I heard Mr Chase and Mrs Henstridge talking on Friday, at break. But you mustn't tell them – I left my apple on my table and went in to fetch it. We're not supposed to go back inside unless a teacher's there. Will I get in trouble?'

'I won't tell if you don't.' I shake my head. 'They were talking about Millie?'

He nods. 'Mr Chase said he thought it was funny that all Millie's stuff was still in her locker, and that if she'd moved somewhere else, they ought to take it out and keep it somewhere out of the way until they could send it to her. Mrs Henstridge said that was a good idea and she'd see about it. Then they came out of the cloakroom. I got my apple and ran back outside before they saw me.'

I stare at Ben for a minute. 'You said I wouldn't get in trouble,' he reminds me with a worried look, and I realise my expression is probably scaring him.

'You're not in any trouble,' I reassure him. 'In fact, you've just given me some really important information. Well done, Ben!'

He beams at me. 'Does that mean I've helped you with your enquiries?'

'It definitely does,' I confirm, and he twists his head to look at his parents.

'Can I have an extra half an hour on the PlayStation, then?' he asks. 'That's how long I've been helping.' He holds up his wrist and taps his watch, for emphasis.

'I suppose so,' Larson replies, 'but not a minute more, okay?'

'Cool!' Ben grabs the machine off the table and disappears upstairs.

'You want a coffee before you go?' Rosie asks.

I shake my head. 'Thanks, but I should be getting home. Give me a minute, though – I need to make a call.'

Sillitoe answers on the third ring. 'Anything the matter, boss?'

'Nothing apart from the usual,' I say. 'Is Robbie there?'

She hesitates, then, 'Hang on a minute.'

There's a long pause, and then DC Robbins comes on the line. 'Is there something you need, sir?'

'Has Polly told you I want you over at the school in the morning?'

'Yes, sir.' She doesn't sound too enthusiastic about it.

'Good. Before you talk to the children, I want to you ask Henstridge if she's moved Millie Drake's things out of her locker yet. If she has, she will have stored them somewhere. Take a pile of evidence bags with you, get everything you can that belongs to her and bring it back to West Hill when you've finished at the school.'

'Okay, sir, will do. Anything else?'

'No, that's all. I'll see you both tomorrow.' I hang up and head home for what I hope will be some much-needed uninterrupted sleep.

I finally make it to my lounge, having taken Blue round the block, fed her and poured myself a reasonable slug of whisky for 'medicinal purposes', only to find a plastic bag knotted round the outside handle of my patio door. I know at once who's left it. I don't have a back gate, and there's only one person who makes an occasional habit of scaling my fence to leave messages. I open the door, grab it and bring it inside. The curt note is to the point.

Tomorrow. 4 p.m. Usual place.

It's good timing, although it might have been better to get Shark Johnson's side of the story before interviewing Craig Tyler. I decide, though, that it doesn't make that much difference, as when it comes to giving unbiased, objective accounts of events, both of them are evasive at best, at worst pathological liars, especially when it comes to the police. The truth is likely to be somewhere in the middle, if there is any truth to be got out of either. I decide enough is enough, turn on the TV for the late news, down the Scotch and close my eyes.

I'VE JUST TURNED into the near stationary traffic jam that is Bristol's seemingly endless rush hour when my mobile rings. Predictably, I haven't gotten round to connecting it to the car's Bluetooth – or, to be more accurate, haven't bullied my son-in-law into doing it for me, so I let it ring until it goes to voicemail. Two minutes and two hundred yards later, it rings again and carries on ringing on and off for the next twenty minutes until I finally pull into the police station car park. It starts up again as I walk through to the front desk, where George immediately flags me down.

'I wouldn't bother going up,' he calls out. 'Polly's on her way down. She's been trying to get hold of you.'

'Why?' I ask. I finally dig out my phone – seven missed calls, all from Sillitoe. Damn.

George gives me a superior grin. 'Looks like the shit's hit the fan, Al. I've got some spare boxers in my locker if you need to borrow some.'

That thought is just a step past reasonable at eight

o'clock in the morning. 'Thanks, George, but I think I'll manage.'

The security door slams open, and Sillitoe strides into the front office. 'For fuck's sake, boss, don't you ever answer your phone?'

'Sorry, Polly, caught in traffic – what's up?'

'We need to get over to Oakfield Road. They've found another one.'

Dear God. I close my eyes and count to five. 'Okay. You drive. You can fill me in on the way.'

She guns down the Bristol Road in her two-seater BMW automatic – necessary, is her excuse, as her artificial leg can't cope with a clutch pedal – as if we're rehearsing for an episode of *The Sweeney*. 'I don't know much,' she says, between bouts of swearing at drivers who don't get out of her way quickly enough. 'Only that Flossie the dog kept on barking her head off, and eventually they realised there was another cavity directly above in the loft space. They took it down an hour ago and found another body. *Not* a cat. Maggie's been called, and she should be there any time now.'

'Bloody hell. What are the rest of the team doing?'

'Robbie's gone to the school, Karen is with the Maitlands, and Ollie is trying to trace Drake and his daughter. Maggie called through and asked if John Larson could go over to the lab to help with the contents of that shoe box we pulled out of the wall yesterday. Daz and Colin are mopping up the door to door; then they're going to meet us at the house.'

Thankfully, when we reach the cordon at the end of Oakfield Road, the crowd of onlookers has more or less dispersed, leaving just a gaggle of reporters and a single TV newscast van. A duty officer lets us through, and we climb the stairs to find a member of the forensic team at the foot of a fragile-looking loft ladder, busy bagging and tagging an assortment of items that presumably have been handed down from above. Maggie's head appears in the hatchway.

'Morning, both,' she says cheerfully. 'Only room for one of you up here, I'm afraid. You'll find a spare suit in the back bedroom.'

I look at Sillitoe, who shrugs and points to her left foot. 'Sodding hell,' I mutter, and take off my jacket.

Suited and booted, I make my way up the rickety ladder and over to where Maggie and two of her assistants are crouched in the eaves in the far corner, being careful not to put my foot through a bedroom ceiling. She beckons me closer.

'Take a look. We haven't moved her yet – I think we might need to take a bit more of the wall down first, but it'll be tricky without disturbing the corpse while we're at it.'

I nod, stick my head into the cavity, then pull it back sharply, banging my ear on a wooden strut. 'Damn it!' I take a deep breath and try again. A bright light has been hung from a beam, illuminating the body of what appears, from the remains of the clothing, to be a young woman hunched in the corner of the tiny space, arms clasped around knees that are drawn up to the chin, the face, no more than two feet away from mine, staring straight at me – or it would be if it had any eyes. I withdraw my head, more carefully this time, and take a deep breath. 'Jesus!'

'Yes, she's a bit disconcerting, isn't she?' Maggie says, giving me a pat on the shoulder. 'It'll be a lot better when we get her out, but that might take an hour or two.'

'Anything you can tell me now?' I ask.

'Not much.' She shakes her head. 'Female, from the

skeletal structure and the fragments of clothing – floral print by the look of it. Quite young, I'd guess, maybe late teens or early twenties, from the bone development. I haven't been able to look at her properly yet, so I can't tell you if there are any signs of violence, but from the position and attitude of the body, it's possible she was alive when she was put here. She was sitting, you see – hunched, as if she'd tried to get out and given up – a difficult position to emulate if she was already dead. Put that together with the damage to the fingernails, and it's a pretty good bet.'

'Good God,' is all I can say for a moment. 'Do you think there's any link between this body and the ones in the garden?' I ask after a pause.

'You mean apart from all three being in the same property?' Maggie shakes her head. 'It's impossible to say at this point, but I can tell you that this one is a lot more recent – two or three years old, maybe? I'll know more once I've got her in the lab. One thing's for sure.' She curls her lip in a grimace. 'Whoever was living here would have had a plague of flies to deal with. Good for us, though – if nothing else, it will confirm she died here and was not moved later. It's all about larvae and the remains of the cases, plus the dead flies – they are all over the place.'

I leave Maggie to it and make my way back down the ladder to where Sillitoe is waiting. She raises an eyebrow. 'You really don't want to go up there,' I tell her, ripping off the paper suit with a sigh of relief.

She gives me a suspicious look. 'You're saying I'm not up to a dead body?'

'Believe me,' I reply, 'nobody's up to that one except Maggie. Best leave it to her.'

'Right. So what happens now?'

I pull out my phone. 'I'd like you to stay here until Daz turns up, then get back to the station and coordinate. I'm going to talk to Grace and get an upgraded alert out for Drake and his daughter – it's pretty clear now that he's top of the suspect list, and Millie could be in danger. Tell Daz to keep the search going and tear this house apart if necessary. If you need me, I'll be at the pathology lab with Larson, then at the prison.'

There's a long pause after I finish explaining the situation to Grace, during which I can hear her breathing; it doesn't take much effort to imagine her clenched teeth. 'For God's sake, Al!' she says finally. 'It's been nearly three months. They could be anywhere by now. Can you get hold of any photos – from the school, or perhaps passport or driving licence records?'

'I'm going to see Larson now,' I tell her. 'I'll put him onto it, and DC White as well. Nothing's turned up in the house – apart from the body. If anyone digs up a photo, I'll let you know.'

I hang up as Jackson and Draper come through the front gate. I go out to meet them. 'I want you to go round again,' I tell them, 'and see if anyone ever took a snap of Drake or Millie. You never know, they might have been caught on camera at some point in the last few years.'

Daz looks heavenward. 'Come on, boss – you must be joking! It's taken us more than a day to get statements.'

'And it would have been a lot quicker if you'd eaten less cake,' I point out. 'So no cups of tea, no chats, just have they got photos of the neighbours or not.'

'Okay, boss.' They slope off back down the path, shoulders hunched, muttering.

'That's Daz's initiation sorted,' Sillitoe says, coming up behind me. 'Poor sod!'

I turn to her with a smile. 'With rank comes responsibility, Polly. Talking of which, when things are finished here, I want you to go back with Maggie and observe the post-mortem. If I know her, she'll want to put everything else on the back burner and get on with it.'

'Bloody marvellous,' she comments. 'You certainly know how to make someone's day. Aren't you going to be there?'

'For some of it, maybe. It depends how long it takes them to get the body to the morgue, and what Larson's come up with.'

She looks distinctly unhappy at the prospect. 'Right, boss. Looks like I'll be skipping lunch, then.'

'I'm sorry, Polly,' I say. 'Somebody needs to be there, and it's important I interview Craig Tyler myself. I doubt he'll talk to anyone else – probably won't talk to me either, but I have to give it a shot.'

I go off to find a PC to give me a lift to the pathology lab, leaving Polly staring mournfully at the ground.

9

I find Larson hunched in front of a huge, curved computer monitor in a small office next to Maggie's. The desk is surrounded by an assortment of machines taking up almost all the floor space. The only thing I recognise apart from the computer is a filter coffee machine bubbling away to itself on a bookshelf in the far corner, next to a stack of plastic cups and a bowl of sugar. I make a beeline for it and pour myself some.

Larson sighs, sits back in his chair and stretches. 'Good morning to you, too.' He points at the coffee machine. 'I don't suppose there's a chance you could pour me one while you're there?'

It would be churlish not to, so I oblige – milk, I remember, and no sugar. 'I don't suppose you've heard the latest,' I comment, handing him the cup as I explain what I've just witnessed at Oakfield Road.

'Jesus,' is the best he can do. 'Sorry. I've been working on these all morning.' He points at a set of blurred images on his giant screen.

'And what are "these" exactly?' I ask.

'Come and look,' he says, gesturing to the empty chair beside him. I perch myself on it. 'These are documents from the box you found yesterday,' he explains. 'They are all in bad shape – a lot of damp and mould and so on. The forensic team have managed to separate a lot of them, and I've scanned them. I'm hoping I'll be able to reconstruct the content, or at least get some sort of approximation, using AI and other digital techniques.'

'What kind of documents?' I squint at the fuzzy contents of the screen – there must be at least twenty images, and next to each a pale square, some heavily blotched with brown or grey stains, most showing a line or two of smudged, virtually unreadable ink. I realise I'm holding my breath. 'Photographs,' I murmur as I take in a long gulp of air, hardly daring to hope. 'Christ, son! We might have photographs of the victims here.'

He nods. 'If we have, there are a hell of a lot of them – either a lot of victims, or pictures of individuals taken at different times and ages. I'm trying to establish that now. Some of these are in such bad condition it's impossible to tell whether the subjects are male or female, never mind the same person.'

He picks up a pen and taps two of the photos. At once, they spring out as much larger images, side by side. Both are cracked and soiled, as if someone has screwed them up and thrown them into a bin full of damp tea bags. From what can be seen of the clothing, it's clear both snaps are of girls, one young, the other older, both taken from a distance, and both look like badly focused casual snaps. The older girl's face is half missing where the photo has been torn, and that of the younger is so faded it's barely visible. The other difference is that one photo is in black and white, the other in washed-out colour.

He clicks on the monochrome picture of the younger one, and it fills the whole screen. 'I've been working on these two, as they aren't quite as badly damaged as some of the others.' There's more fiddling, and with each click of the mouse, the figure becomes slightly clearer. Eventually, I see a girl of around thirteen or so, long hair, possibly blond, dressed in a flimsy skirt, or maybe dress, beneath a thick, oversized sweater. She's standing against a wooden panel fence in what is most likely a garden. She isn't smiling. It's as if she's been forced to pose. The only other thing of note is that she isn't wearing shoes or socks. More clicks, and the other picture fills the screen. Larson goes through the same process, and the older figure becomes more defined. At once I can see that it's the same garden, the same fence, and exactly the same pose. Half the face is missing, but the hair, definitely blond, is the same, and so is the expression.

'You think that's the same girl?' I ask.

'Wait,' Larson replies, and carries on with the mouse. A grid appears in the area where the rest of the face should be, and very slowly, one point at a time, the gap fills in with a rough reconstruction of the missing portion.

'My God!' I can't help saying.

'If the technology is accurate,' he says, 'and I'm pretty sure it is, then we're looking at two photos of the same person, in the same place, taken maybe five or six years apart. If you ask me, it's a bit creepy.'

'You've got that right,' I agree, feeling a shiver run up my spine. 'Do you have any idea when these were taken?'

He shakes his head. 'Not yet. The forensic people are trying to date the paper, but it could take a while. The fact that the first is in black and white doesn't mean much. It could simply be an old camera and film. The clothing doesn't give much away either. We could be looking at the 1950s or the 2020s.'

I think for a minute, then pull out my phone and dial Sillitoe. 'Are you at the house?' I ask.

'Yes – they're still dismantling the wall in the loft.'

'Good. I want you to take a few pictures of the garden. Get every angle you can, but especially the back and side fencing. Taken from a distance of ...'

I glance at Larson, who thinks and says, 'Anything from four to six metres.'

I pass it on, then add, 'Do it now, and send them to Larson.'

'I'm on it, boss.'

We wait a few minutes; then Larson's phone pings with incoming messages. He transfers them to the computer and brings up the new photos on one side of the screen, the two old ones on the other. We stare at them in silence for a couple of minutes; then Larson sits back, voicing my own thought. 'Bugger it!'

Wherever the two girls were photographed, it wasn't in the back garden of Oakfield Road. But they were taken in somebody's garden. 'So where the hell is it?' I say aloud.

Larson looks at me. 'Not just where – when, and who's the photographer? And who hid them behind a false wall, and why?'

I think for a moment. 'Is that all there was in the box – just photos?'

'No. There was an assortment of stuff. I didn't really see, but there was a pile of things in evidence bags – jewellery maybe, all small items. I was assigned the documents, nothing else.'

'Okay.' I get up. 'Come on, let's go and find out what else there is.'

He follows me down the corridor to where a couple of white-coated forensic technicians are working in a jungle of microscopes, centrifuges and other lab equipment. A notice above the door, illuminated in red, reads *Restricted Area. Do Not Enter*. I press the buzzer next to the door, and one of the techs comes across and presses the intercom button.

'Can I help you?' she says, in a tone that makes it clear she's not happy about being disturbed.

I introduce myself and hold up my warrant card for emphasis. 'I'm interested in the box brought in from Oakfield Road,' I explain. 'I need a full inventory of the contents, plus anything else you've managed to analyse so far.'

She almost laughs. 'Chief Inspector, I'm sure you realise how long it takes to run the kind of tests you've asked for. While I understand your impatience, I'm sure you wouldn't want us to cut any corners.' She pauses before adding meaningfully, 'Or waste any time.'

I take a deep breath. 'And I'm sure,' I say, 'that given we already have two dead young women and a dead child, and given that any information you can give us may well help us catch the bastard who did it before your workload goes up by at least one more body, you won't object to sharing that information with us. Preferably now.'

She glares, sighs, finally nods. 'Wait there.'

She disappears to the far end of the lab and through a door. A few minutes later there are footsteps behind us, and she reappears from yet another door, minus mask and gloves.

'This way, please,' she says, and we follow her to an office twice the size of the cubbyhole Larson is squeezed into. 'Take a seat, Chief Inspector, Mr Larson.' She gestures to the chairs on the visitor side of the desk and sits opposite us, her expression softening a little. She looks exhausted.

'You will have to forgive me,' she offers. 'I'm afraid we're all playing catch-up – it's always like this in September, with everyone wanting to take time off in August. I've just spoken to Professor Ainsworth, and she asked me to give you whatever assistance you need.' She taps away at her computer keyboard for a few seconds, and a printer starts whirring. She waits until it goes back into hibernation, grabs a stack of sheets from the tray, divides it into three and hands us each a copy.

'As you can see,' she says, 'there was quite an assortment stuffed in there. The non-paper articles are listed first – they run to almost two pages. The other two sheets are documents, mostly photographs. We are dealing with each item separately, testing for DNA, bodily fluids, fingerprints and so on. We have a specialist dealing with the documents, and he's feeding them on to Mr Larson as they become available.'

I scan the first sheet. She's right. It really is a jumble of items, all small, and all relating to women or girls – watches, bracelets, rings, hair slides, lipsticks, earrings … I sit up, taking in a breath. Not pairs of earrings – single earrings. I flip the sheet and run a finger down the next page. More slides, a small, beaded coin purse, more jewellery, and more single earrings. I look up at the technician. 'These items – would you say they were valuable? Somebody's nest egg put in the wall to stop them being stolen?'

Her mouth quirks into a humourless smile, and she shakes her head. 'I'd say the opposite. Aside from a couple of things, most of it is pure tat.'

'The kind of thing a child would buy with pocket money?' I ask.

She thinks, then says, 'Very possibly, yes – a child or a young teen. Some of it is cheap plastic, the kind of stuff you used to get taped to the front of kids' comics. But there are a couple of earrings that are quite valuable – would be worth even more if they were a pair, and three or four rings, one with quite a sizeable diamond, probably worth a thousand or more.'

I look down the inventory again and count seven earrings – all single. 'So there were no pairs at all?'

She purses her lips. 'None – which is a bit weird, wouldn't you say? God knows what happened to the others.'

I get up, folding the sheets and shoving them in my jacket. 'Thank you. You've been very helpful.' I stop myself from adding *eventually*.

Larson follows suit, looking a bit confused, and holds out a hand to the technician, who gives him a bright smile as she shakes it and says, 'Not at all.' The smile dissolves into a flinty stare as she turns back to me. 'Glad to be of service, Chief Inspector.'

'By the way,' I say as I reach the door, 'Maggie did ask you to give us whatever assistance we need, yes?'

Her eyes narrow suspiciously. 'Yes,' she agrees, with some reluctance. 'Is there something else I can do for you?'

'Just one thing, for now,' I reply. 'You can fast-track the DNA testing on all the items on this list. It's vital we know as soon as possible whether they all belonged to one person or several.'

Her eyes widen, and she stares for a moment in disbelief, then sniffs. 'I'll see what I can do.' She grabs her copy of the printout and sweeps past us back down the corridor to the lab.

As we make our way back to Larson's cubbyhole, he gives me a look, brows furrowing. 'It doesn't make sense,' he ventures. 'Someone goes to all the trouble of hiding a box of old pictures and keepsakes, very few of which have any value.'

I stop walking, turn to face him. 'You might call them keepsakes,' I say. 'I call them trophies. I'm willing to bet a month's salary the results show that those trinkets all belong to different people, and that each one of them is a victim, one way or another. The best we can hope is that they aren't all dead.'

For a moment he just stares, the colour draining from his face, until he finally blinks and mutters, 'Trophies?'

If he's going to carry on in this job, he's got a lot to learn. I pat him on the shoulder. 'Congratulations, son. Welcome to my world.'

10

I follow a burly prison officer down an echoing corridor tastefully decorated in regulation vomit green, through a battered metal door into an interview room containing a desk and two chairs, all bolted to the floor.

'I'm afraid our Craig's not in the best of moods today,' the officer tells me. 'Mind you, he's hardly ever in the best of moods. He's particularly upset at having to talk to you. His type tends to hold grudges, especially against their arresting officers. We'll have to keep him in cuffs, just to be on the safe side, and he won't like that either.'

I nod my understanding, and he gets onto his radio to pass on the message that we're ready. A minute later, Tyler appears in the doorway, flanked by an even burlier officer. Even so, the man is dwarfed by his prisoner. Craig Tyler was nineteen when he was convicted and now looks as if he's spent the last twenty years amusing himself in the prison gym. Close-cropped hair, a grotesque assortment of tattoos, mostly homemade, covering arms, neck and probably the rest of him; he's all muscle, shoulders almost brushing the door frame on both sides as he swaggers in and lowers himself onto one of the chairs. One of the officers cuffs a wrist to a chair leg, but he doesn't seem to notice, just keeps his eyes on me, one lip curling in a silent snarl.

'Do you want one of us to stay?' the first officer asks.

'No, thanks,' I say. 'Craig and I are going to be fine.'

The two of them exchange a look. 'If you're sure, Chief Inspector,' he replies, and they both shuffle out, leaving the door slightly ajar.

'You're looking well, Craig,' I say, taking the seat on the other side of the table, uncomfortably close to the arm that isn't chained to the chair. 'Been keeping yourself fit, by the look of it.'

The chain on the cuff is just long enough for him to fold his arms across his massive chest, so he does, then leans back and gives me a glassy stare. Okay. Passing the time of day isn't an option – on to plan B. 'I'm sorry to take up your valuable time, Craig. I imagine you've got plenty of things to be getting on with. It's a courtesy call really, to let you know we'll be charging you with two more murders.' I practise my reassuring smile. 'Don't worry, you don't have to do anything or even talk to me if you don't want to. You'll be hearing from us in due course.'

While I've been talking, his eyes have widened, and now his mouth joins the club, revealing a set of yellowing teeth that have been filed to points. Then, without warning, he lunges forward, draws back a fist as solid as a brick, and lets fly. It takes all my self-restraint to stay in my chair and keep my eyes on his without flinching. The chain on his other wrist catches; he roars in frustration and slumps back into his seat.

'You fucking bastard!' he mutters, draws back his head to

aim a gob of phlegm, and thankfully thinks better of it. 'What the hell are you talking about?' he growls, rubbing his wrist where the cuff has bitten in. 'You're telling me you're fitting me up with another murder? And when am I supposed to have done it? I've been in here twenty fucking years, thanks to you! And I never did nothing in the first fucking place. You know that as well as me. I never killed Harris, and I never killed nobody else. You're just a lying arsehole, Crow – a pimply little shit back then, and nothing's changed.'

'Oh, come on, Craig. One or two things have changed,' I reply. 'I'm not so little anymore, and I never had pimples. I hear you're still hanging on to your story, though – an innocent man, framed by the police and convicted by a bent jury. If you'd owned up to it, you would have been out by now.'

'So you could fit me up again?' He curls his lip in a contemptuous snarl. 'Yeah, right. Who am I supposed to have murdered while I've been banged up in here? Maybe I robbed a bank while the screws weren't looking, or blew up a bus station while I was out prowling the streets on a night.' He jerks a finger at the security camera in the ceiling. 'Geoffrey will tell you – he gives me a key at lights out so I can run around wasting people – more fun than listening to the radio.' He laughs. 'You, Crow, are a real fucking tosser. The day I get out, you'll be top of my list.'

'*If* you get out,' I tell him, 'but thanks for the heads-up. I'll bear it in mind.'

He sits back with a sigh. 'Go on, then. Enlighten me. Who am I supposed to have murdered this time, and – just so I know – how did I do it? Stabbed them to death, maybe? Shot them? Slipped bad gear in their cocoa? Go on – surprise me. Oh, and while you're at it, you might as well tell me their loved one's address as well, so I can send a condolence card.'

'How about a blow to the head with a blunt instrument?' I suggest. 'Same way you did for Jimmy Harris. Thing is, Craig, we've just dug up the bodies, and they have the same fatal injuries, and they were killed at the same time, summer 2003, using what we think is the same weapon.'

His eyes narrow. 'So you've decided to put me in the frame to save time and give you a nice quick result?' He gives me a slow handclap. 'Well done, Chief Inspector Crow. Now we know how you got promoted.' He injects the *Chief Inspector* with a dose of sarcasm.

'You see, Craig,' I go on, 'this time it wasn't just another lowlife dealer you took off the street, it was a woman and a very young child. Jimmy's woman, and Jimmy's son. Now, that's against every rule in the book, so once Shark Johnson's lot find out – and you can guarantee they will – it won't matter if I make the charge stick or not, you're stuffed either way. Much safer to own up and get it over with. You'll probably live a lot longer.'

Hatred is one thing, and no more than I was expecting, but what I definitely don't expect is the wave of pure shock that passes across his face. For a moment, he scrabbles for words, eyes closed, shaking his head in disbelief. When he finally speaks, the words come out in a hiss through clenched teeth, his massive body trembling with fury.

'You fucking bastard, Crow! You must be bloody terrified I'll get out one day soon.' He barks out a laugh and shakes his head again. 'I didn't think even you would stoop that low. But let me tell you something – little Jimmy Harris, he never had no girlfriend, and he never had no kids. I know that for a fact. Jimmy wasn't wired that way, know what I mean? I knew it, Shark Johnson knew it, and so did everybody else on the street. Jimmy wasn't into women. He got his kicks elsewhere – ask anyone. He would have bloody loved it in here, been in his element, so to speak. He would have been the most popular kid on the block. You start dribbling a story like that, and see how far you get. As for pinning some random murder on me, forget it. Even Shark won't give you the time of day with that one.'

It's my turn to be taken aback. From his reaction, I almost believe him – almost. 'Is that why you killed Jimmy?' I ask. 'Because he was gay?'

'I didn't fucking kill him!' he spits. 'I beat him up because he ripped me off. I held my hands up to that. But I swore to the jury, and I still swear, he was alive when I left him. It was street business, no more, no less, and you never had any evidence it was anything else. You never found no weapon, no prints, no nothing. You're pissing in the wind, Crow, so why don't you fuck off and fit up somebody else?' He turns his attention to the TV camera in the ceiling. 'Geoffrey? I'm done here. Time for my afternoon tea.'

I take my cue and get up as 'Geoffrey' appears promptly in the doorway, the second officer following close behind. 'I think you'd better leave first, sir,' Geoffrey advises.

I don't disagree. At the door I turn back to Tyler, who has reverted to his blank, fish-eye stare. 'You're wrong about one thing,' I tell him. 'Jimmy Harris might have been gay, but it didn't stop him being a father. We have the DNA, Craig. You'll be hearing from me.'

His stream of threats and curses follows me all the way back down the corridor.

. . .

IT'S JUST GONE three when I get back to West Hill, leaving me enough time to grab a quick sandwich and catch up with Ollie White in the office before heading off to my rendezvous with Shark Johnson.

'There's nothing, sir,' he says. 'I've checked with Mr Larson, and we haven't got anything on Joseph Drake or Pauline Drake and hardly anything on the daughter either. It's almost like they don't exist. Mr Larson says it's almost like some of the traveller families – you know, people who live "off grid", work for cash and don't stay in one place long enough to register with doctors or other services. But this guy had a house, paid his electricity bills and so on.'

'So how did he pay?' I ask. 'He must have a bank account somewhere. Nobody can survive without one these days.'

'We're investigating that, sir. He paid for the main services at post offices, in cash according to the electricity and water companies, and possibly bought food that way as well. But you're right – it's virtually impossible to live without a bank account of some sort, and twenty-odd years ago he bought the house for cash, at a listed price of £68,000. That's a lot to hand over in a suitcase.'

'Okay, Ollie. Keep at it.' I let out a frustrated sigh. 'I'll catch up with Larson this evening.'

'One more thing, sir,' he says as I head for the door. 'Robbie came in around eleven with a bag of Millie's stuff from the school. She asked me to tell you she's dropped it off at the lab, and Professor Ainsworth is going to prioritise it. You might want to pop over to the lab later?'

'Thanks, Ollie. I'll do that.'

Out in the corridor, I stand still and take a couple of deep breaths. Quite aside from three dead bodies, not including the cat, and the missing Drakes, something is very wrong, and I have the feeling things are going to get a lot worse before they get better. I look down at my left hand. It's twitching, just slightly, as it still does now and then when a vague apprehension takes me over. I grit my teeth and set off for Vista House and my meeting with Shark.

Jermaine 'Shark' Johnson is waiting at our normal meeting place, a spot under the only working strip light in the car park underneath Vista House, the near derelict low-rise block that West Hill's dealers and addicts have called home for the last twenty-odd years. I make my way down the pitch-dark ramp, watched from above by one of Shark's minders, a shaven-headed specimen around the same size as Craig Tyler in his stockinged feet. I make my way across to Shark, trying to ignore the mingled scents of old piss, dried vomit and spray paint. He's leaning against a pillar, working on a roll-up, his Ray-Bans pushed up over his dreadlocks.

'Clive said you want to talk about Jimmy,' he says, without looking up. 'So talk, Bird Man.'

It's as much of a greeting as I'm going to get. 'You and Craig Tyler,' I start, trying to pick my words carefully, 'you never got along, even before his run-in with Jimmy.'

He looks up sharply, fishes out his gold Ronson, lights his roll-up and blows a stream of smoke in my face. 'Talk about Jimmy, you said. Tyler's a piece of shit, and if you hadn't poked your nose in back then, he'd be where he should be, same place as Jimmy, instead of getting room service in a government hotel.'

'And you would have been signing the same register, Shark. I did my job, followed my rules, just as you follow yours. The thing is, I reckon maybe Craig Tyler might have been making his rules up as he went along, and I think you might be able to tell me if I'm right.'

He pushes himself upright, flicks his dog-end across the concrete and starts rolling another. 'Okay, Bird Man – I'm listening.'

'Did Jimmy have a girlfriend, back in the day?'

The corner of his mouth twitches in a humourless grin. 'Not that I knew. Not to say he didn't take what he wanted now and again, sometimes girls, and sometimes ...' He shrugs. 'Most times one of the lads. That's how it was back then. That's how Jimmy was.'

I try to remind myself that in West Hill's underworld, violence of all sorts is as commonplace as a kettle in a kitchen. 'You mean rape? Sexual assault? What?'

Shark shrugs again. 'Whatever. He was one of those who liked it rough, know what I mean? All I'll say is he was a good mate – the best. What he did in his spare time wasn't my business. I never asked; he never told. But he had a reputation on the street.' He gives me a look, more suspicious than usual. 'So what worm you got in your beak now, Bird? Jimmy's long dead; this is old history. And what's it got to do with Tyler?'

I decide to get straight to it. 'You didn't know Jimmy had a kid?' Shark's look of pure shock answers that one. I nod. 'A little boy. He was around three when he died. We found him and his mother a couple of days ago over in Oakfield Road. I'll guess you know all about that already.'

I've seen Shark Johnson in a lot of different moods, but until now I never thought he was the type to be struck dumb. For a moment his mouth opens and closes, but nothing comes out. When it finally does, it's a murderous hiss. 'What the fuck ...?'

'I'm not lying, Shark,' I say quickly. 'We took DNA, and it's definitely Jimmy's boy – his and the dead woman's. They were killed around the same time and buried in the garden. That's all I can say, but I thought you'd want to know.'

I see him trembling with the effort of keeping his temper under control, lips clamped so tight they almost disappear, fists clenched, eyes on his feet. He draws in a huge breath, lets it out slowly.

'Like I said,' he growls. 'What's it to do with Tyler? You saying he did for Jimmy, then went after the kid?' He jerks his head up, eyes boring into mine. 'That what you're saying, Bird Man? If it is, I swear, he's a dead man, no matter where he is, you got me?'

He flicks the Ronson, lights his second roll-up, then slumps back against the pillar. Up until now, I've been pretty much drawing the same conclusion. Tyler killed Jimmy, then took his hammer, or whatever he used, for a walk down to Oakfield Road and did the same to his family. But Tyler wasn't lying to me earlier, at least, not about the kind of man Jimmy Harris was. Shark has just confirmed it.

I meet his eye. 'The God's honest truth is I don't know. Maybe he did, and maybe he didn't. All I know is somebody did it, and I'm not going to stop until I get whoever it was. In the meantime, Tyler is being watched, so my advice is don't do anything stupid, okay? Giving you a heads-up, nothing else.'

Shark nods, straightens again, then turns away. 'We're done here. When you know, send a message.'

'I'm sorry,' I say. 'About the boy and the woman. They didn't deserve it.'

He doesn't turn round, but lifts a hand and walks away.

Back out in the daylight, my phone rings. It's Maggie.

'I've got something for you,' she says, sounding far more enthusiastic than anyone should who's been awake since dawn poking about in dead bodies. 'Can you get over here? You won't regret it, Al, I promise.'

I look at my watch. It's just past five. 'I'll be half an hour,' I tell her as I head for my car.

11

It's nearer six by the time I get through the traffic and up to Maggie's office. Larson is there, looking a little queasy. Maggie glances up from her papers and gives me a bright smile.

'Come on in, Al,' she says. 'Your colleague here was good enough to join us for the post-mortem this morning. Pity you couldn't make it. It was very interesting.'

'Ah.' I look at Larson, who gives me a weak smile and turns even greener. 'I take it you've got some news, then?'

Maggie sits back in her chair, interlaces her fingers across her stomach and treats me to a self-satisfied grin. I can't help but let out an exasperated groan. I sometimes think that if she hadn't taken up pathology, she would have made a pretty good career for herself in the theatre.

'I thought you'd be pleased,' she comments, noting my expression. 'I've been analysing samples all afternoon, and so have two of my assistants. I suppose I'd better start at the beginning.'

'How about you just start, Maggie?' I growl. 'It's been a

long day for everyone, and we've both got dogs to get back to.'

'Right you are,' she replies, 'but if you want everything, I'm afraid your Bluebell will have to wait a bit longer. First things first – the body in the wall is female, late teens or early twenties – roughly the same age at time of death as the one in the garden. I've estimated that she died approximately two years ago.'

'That ties in with the disappearance of Pauline Drake,' Larson puts in.

Maggie nods. 'Precisely so. As I understand it, nobody met Pauline Drake before that, but given we have a corpse and the timescale fits, I don't think there is any doubt. There's more on that, but I'll go through the post-mortem stuff first. Unlike the first body, this one has no single wound, or group of wounds, that can be identified as the cause of death. However, there are some similarities, including an apparent lack of recent dental or medical care, but nothing that would lead to a fatality.'

I glance at Larson, suddenly understanding why he looks distinctly out of sorts. On top of having attended his first post-mortem, he would have heard this information during the procedure. 'You're saying she was definitely walled up while she was still alive, then left there to die?'

'It's highly likely,' Maggie replies. 'It is also possible she had a sudden heart attack, stroke, or was asphyxiated, and whoever found her panicked and didn't know what to do with the body. Without more information, it's hard to say. However, the damage to the fingernails would lead me to conclude she did try to get out. I've told the team to look for corresponding marks on the walls inside the cavity.'

I struggle, not quite successfully, to keep my imagination

under control. I manage to restrict myself to, 'Bloody hell!' There's a short silence; then I say, 'You said you had been doing some analyses?'

'More than some,' she answers. 'Three of us have been looking at DNA samples all day, from the box, the body and from items your DC Robbins brought in, which luckily for us included a hairbrush, various toiletries and PE kit. We're still getting results in, but there's some very interesting information already. First, the body in the wall has the same genetic makeup as the child in the garden. Given the ages of the two sets of remains at time of death, I would hazard a guess they were quite possibly fraternal twins. If not, they were born very close together.'

'Are you serious? You're saying the woman in the garden was the mother of them both? And Jimmy Harris was the father?'

She nods. 'Exactly. One died twenty-odd years ago from a blow to the head. The other lived until around two or three years ago, and she died inside the house in a completely different way.'

I give myself a minute to let this sink in. From the startled look on Larson's face, I realise this revelation is new to him, too.

'There's more,' Maggie goes on. 'I've got a DNA result from the hairs found on Millie Drake's hairbrush. Without doubt, the body in the loft was Millie's mother. Millie's father is unknown.'

'So it could be Joseph Drake?' I ask, although I know that can't be confirmed. But then another thought strikes me. 'Wait a minute – you say the body in the loft was between maybe eighteen and twenty-two years old when she died.

Millie, as far as we know, is eight years old. That means the mother would have been in her early teens when Millie was born – fourteen, fifteen maybe?'

'Very likely, yes.' Maggie sighs. 'And the same goes for the grandmother. The body under the shed would have given birth at a similar age.'

'Jesus!' I rub a hand across my forehead and almost give way to Grace's habit of massaging my temples between finger and thumb. 'What the hell is going on here?'

'There's something else,' a voice pipes up. I realise it's Larson, his tone almost apologetic.

'Go on, son,' I say, wondering how much more I can cope with without a stiff drink. 'Don't keep us in suspense.'

He colours a little and gives me a look bordering on irritation. 'Well,' he says, 'there were some remains of the clothing she was wearing – the woman from the loft, at the post-mortem.' He turns pale again and shifts in his seat. 'I thought they looked familiar, so I asked for photographs and compared them with the clothes the girl in the photos from the box was wearing, you know, the two I showed you. They were the same – almost identical, as far as I could tell, a white dress with a floral print, and a thick dark green sweater with a rib pattern, what Rosie would call a fisherman's knit.'

'So you think the body in the morgue is the girl in the photographs?' I ask.

He shakes his head. 'That's just it. The photos are of a girl with blond hair – very blond, almost white. But the hair of the dead woman is much darker – a sort of mousy brown.'

'Hair dye?' I suggest.

'Possibly, but I don't think so, not unless the eyebrows

were dyed as well. They are clearly visible in the reconstructed colour print we have from the box. But that's not the only thing. I said the clothing was almost identical, but not quite. I haven't managed to date the photographs precisely yet, but they are definitely more than ten years old, so the dead woman inside the house is too young to be the subject. They could possibly be of the first victim, from the garden, but not the second. The other factor is the age of the clothes. The sweater we don't know – we'll have to analyse the yarn and trace it to the manufacturer, but the dress is definitely relatively new, or at least well preserved, as there are little signs of wear; it's been handmade on a domestic machine by the look of it, possibly by someone local. The fabric is a Liberty print that's been available with only minor changes since the 1930s. Very popular apparently, and in demand for period dramas and theatre productions.'

'And how do you know all this?' I ask, feeling, I have to admit, impressed.

'I set up a Zoom call with Liberty's design department in London.' He shrugs. 'They were very helpful.'

I'm saved the effort of telling him he's done a good job by the trill of my mobile. It's Sillitoe.

'I thought you'd want to know,' she says, 'Daz scored a hit with one of the neighbours. They managed to dig out an old photo of Drake. He was caught on camera when they were taking a picture of their grandkids in the street. They reckon it was around six years ago. There are no official school photographs of Millie – she was unaccountably sick on days they were taken, but believe it or not, the neighbours also got a snap of Millie at a school sports day a few years later – the grandchildren are around the same age, so she would have been six or so at the time. Ollie's working on the images now, but he could do with a bit of help from Mr Larson.'

'That's great, Polly,' I reply. 'Give Daz a big pat on the back from me. Is everyone in the office again now?'

'Yes, just about. The DSI says she wants to sit in, and she'll be down in half an hour or so.'

'Good. I just need to finish up here, so I'll be back around the same time, and I'll bring Larson with me.' I hang up and turn to Maggie. 'Anything else I need to know?'

'One more thing,' she says. 'We're still working on the contents of the box. There are a lot of samples to get through, and some of them may be impossible to analyse in terms of fingerprints or DNA – jewellery, plastic bracelets, that sort of thing. But so far, we've managed to get results from three of the earrings and two hair slides. I know it might not be what you want to hear, but they did all have traces of DNA from different individuals. There was, however, one common thread. All the items so far were handled by one person, and that person has a different DNA profile to Millie Drake.'

Larson and I exchange a look, but neither of us can speak. He gives me a nod of acknowledgement.

Not keepsakes – trophies.

THE ATMOSPHERE in the squad room is one of tense expectation. The latest news has obviously gone around, and aside from the occasional low-voiced exchange, everyone is focused on computer screens or printouts. Sillitoe is in her office, and so is Grace, perched on the edge of the desk. Larson makes straight for Ollie White's workstation, grabbing a spare chair on the way, and I carry on through to see Grace.

'I've had a call from Maggie,' Grace says abruptly. 'Finding Drake and his daughter must take priority over everything else.'

My first reaction is to think that maybe my boss should apply for *Mastermind* – specialist subject, stating the bloody obvious. I raise an eyebrow. 'Yes, ma'am.'

She sighs, finger and thumb rubbing her temples. 'Sorry, Al. Been a long day, and I've a feeling it's going to get longer. At least we've got a picture of Drake now, and hopefully Larson and White can clean it up enough to use for an appeal.'

'An appeal? Bloody hell, Grace, you can't be serious!' I glance at Sillitoe, who raises her palms to indicate it wasn't her idea. 'If we broadcast his photo, it's only likely to send him underground and make our job harder.'

'Try telling that to the chief constable,' Grace hisses back, through gritted teeth. 'He seems to think publicity is the answer to everything. Not that he wants to stand in front of the camera himself this time – he wants me to be the patsy. I've been slotted into *Breakfast West* at some stupid time in the morning tomorrow.'

'That explains why Gosford doesn't want to do it,' Sillitoe puts in. 'Lazy bugger!'

Grace shakes her head, and I can tell from the way she's clamped her lips into a tight line that she's got something more to say, and whatever it is, it isn't good.

'There's something else, Al,' she says after a long pause, 'and you're not going to like it.'

'There's a surprise,' I comment. 'After the day I've had, I doubt anything you say could make it any worse.'

She gives me a grim smile. 'I wouldn't be too sure. Apparently, Craig Tyler has demanded a meeting with his brief, with a view to lodging an appeal. You'll be getting a summons to head office in the morning for a meeting with CC Gosford to, as he put it, "discuss the matter".'

'Oh, for fuck's sake!' I was wrong. Suddenly, I feel a damn sight worse. 'As if we haven't got anything better to bloody well do – that bastard is as guilty as hell, Grace – you know that as well as I do, and not just of murdering Jimmy Harris. He's trying to wriggle out of being charged with the other two.'

'That may well be true, Al,' Grace counters, 'but if he is guilty of killing the woman and child at Oakfield Road, you need watertight evidence, and you haven't got it. Right now, it looks like we have another suspect for those murders, and if Drake did do it, he could have killed Harris as well. If it turns out he did, we're looking at a wrongful conviction and the shitstorm that goes with it, with you, as the arresting officer, right in the middle. So' – she pushes herself upright and heads for the door – 'I want decent blow-ups of Drake and his daughter ready for circulation to every force in the country by first thing tomorrow morning, and I don't care if Larson and DC White have to stay up all night.'

With that, she stalks out, stopping for a brief word with Larson. I see him nod and turn back to the computer screen, he and Ollie deep in conversation and mouse clicks.

'You want me to finish up here, boss?' Sillitoe asks after a short, but meaningful silence. 'If you don't mind my saying so, you look all-in.'

I manage to summon up a weak grin. 'So do you, Polly.' I look at my watch. It's past half seven, and everyone's been at it more or less since dawn. 'Maybe we ought to call it a night and start fresh in the morning. Tell everyone we'll have a briefing tomorrow at seven – we might even get to watch the DSI on TV.'

Sillitoe rolls her eyes. 'Sure, boss. We're all looking forward to that one.'

Larson flags me down as I make my way out. 'DC White and I are going back to my place,' he tells me. 'My computers there have got better software than I can access here. With a bit of luck …'

'Spare me the details,' I say wearily. 'Is Rosie okay with that?'

He nods. 'I called her, and she's going to order a takeout for everyone.' After a pause he adds, 'You can come along if you like.'

'Thanks,' I reply, 'but I've got other plans.'

George Saint is pulling on his overcoat when I reach the front desk. 'Fancy a pint, George?' I ask as he trundles his way through to the front reception.

'Evening, Al,' he replies, eyebrows coming together in what passes for mild suspicion. 'If I remember right, last time you offered to buy me a pint, I ended up spending the whole night in the freezing cold, staking out the Rising Sun in the arse end of West Hill.'

'You got an arrest out of it, George,' I remind him, 'so don't complain. Besides, it was nearly twenty years ago – far too long to bear a grudge.'

His mouth twitches in what passes for a grin. 'One pint every twenty years? You need to watch yourself, Al. You don't want to get a reputation for being a soft touch.' His expression droops back into its default position – non-committal. 'So what hole have you dug yourself into this time? And is it worth throwing in pie and chips to go with the beer?'

I can't help but chuckle. 'You read my mind, George. Pie and chips it is – and downtown, not in West Hill. I need to swing by and pick up Bluebell on the way, if that's okay with you?'

'Just one thing,' he mutters as we head out to my car. 'You mention anything to do with surveillance, and the deal's off.'

12

The sun is well below the horizon when I finally pull up in a spot twenty metres or so from the Georgian townhouse in Clifton jointly owned by my ex-wife and ex-mother-in-law. I'm about to get out of the car when I see their front door open, and Chrissie emerges – not the Chrissie I'm used to seeing these days, but one who, for a fleeting moment, catapults me back to the days when we were newly married and childless, doing all the things doting couples did in those days, going for meals out, to the theatre or the pictures, even to the odd dance club when I got home from a late shift. I watch, frozen, as she pulls on an overcoat – her favourite one, a smart little number in black cashmere that cost me a month's salary and weeks of searching the rails of John Lewis and House of Fraser for a tenth-anniversary present. Beneath the coat is a dress I gave her for a birthday well over fifteen years ago, a long evening dress in a shade of royal blue, shimmering where it's illuminated by the security light, and beneath that a pair of glitzy heels. Add to that matching pearl earrings and choker – she looks absolutely beautiful. She turns to say something, presumably to Joyce, out of sight in the doorway, stoops to pat Bluebell, whose head pokes across the threshold, strides purposefully down onto the pavement and into a flashy sports car, which glides smoothly away, thankfully not in our direction.

'Someone's got money to burn,' George comments from the passenger seat. 'That's a top-of-the-range Tesla – not much change from a hundred grand.'

I realise my hands are welded to the steering wheel, which is the only thing stopping them from trembling uncontrollably, and my legs are locked so tight I can't move. I try to open my mouth, but my jaw isn't working either.

I feel George's hand on my arm. 'Easy, Al,' he says. 'It might be nothing.'

I close my eyes and take several deep breaths, and finally the tremor starts to subside. I risk taking my hands off the wheel. They are still shaking, but it's manageable. 'Stay there,' I tell him when I can trust myself to speak. 'I'm going to get Blue.' Without waiting for a reply, I head unsteadily up the road to the house.

Joyce greets me with a smile as Blue bounds out, barking with delight and struggling to keep all four paws on the ground, which is just as well, as even the gentlest nudge would knock me over. Somehow, I smile back and tickle Blue's ears while I fumble with her lead. 'Sorry I'm so late,' I say. 'Things are a bit hectic just now.'

'It's not a problem, Al,' Joyce replies, still smiling. 'We've been babysitting Ben and Alex too – they've all had a lovely time.'

'And Chrissie?' I manage to ask. Her smile falters a little.

'I'm sorry, Al, you've just missed her.' There's a slight hesitation, then, 'She had to go out.'

'Ah.' An awkward pause until I add, 'Never mind. I may need you to take Blue tomorrow. Is that okay?'

The smile returns to full beam. 'No problem. I can have her all day if you like; just bring her over when you're ready.'

'Thanks.' As I make my way back to the car with Bluebell, Joyce's last sentence starts to worm its insidious way into the compartment of my brain labelled 'Paranoia' – *I can have her all day.*

Not *we*.

'Like I said,' George says, spearing a chunky triple-cooked chip on the end of his fork and waving it in a gesture of dismissal. 'It could be anything. You don't even know if the driver was a bloke – believe it or not, Al, there are lots of women own expensive cars. My niece is a real petrol head – just got herself a classic Aston Martin *and* paid cash. My brother-in-law is spitting nails, says there are better things for her to spend her money on.'

'If she's a petrol head,' I reply, glaring morosely at my largely untouched steak pie, 'she wouldn't be driving around in a bloody Tesla, would she?'

George pops the chip in his mouth, deliberately avoiding my eye. 'Leave it, Al. You're divorced, remember? Chrissie can do whatever she likes, and it's nothing to do with you, right?'

'Right – like take up with a conman who steals her savings and nearly gets her killed,' I snap back, remembering Terry Markham, the bastard who pretended to be her boyfriend but in fact scammed her out of her – no, *our* – life savings and almost got her and Rosie killed. George is fidgeting on the other side of the table. 'What?' I demand; then it dawns on me. 'You got the number plate, didn't you? Bloody hell, George. Come on, hand it over.'

He finally puts down his fork. 'Al, you don't want—'

'I said hand the sodding thing over, or do I have to go through your pockets myself?'

'You know it's illegal to use the police computer for personal business?'

'For fuck's sake, George!'

He heaves a huge sigh, pulls out a pen, scribbles on a paper napkin and pushes it across to me. 'Just watch yourself, Al,' he warns, retrieving his cutlery and resuming his attack on the pie. 'Don't do anything stupid. Talking of which, you didn't buy me dinner to discuss your ex-wife. Maybe you should tell me what else is on your mind?'

He's got a point. I force my mind away from Chrissie and back to the plot. 'You remember Craig Tyler?'

He grunts. 'Wish I didn't. Why? What's he done now? I thought he was still banged up, at least for another five years.'

'He's about to lodge an appeal,' I say, 'and it looks like his request might be granted.'

I'm treated to the rare sight of George Saint with fork frozen between plate and mouth. 'You're joking!'

'I wish I were,' I reply. 'The chief constable wants to see me first thing in the morning. My bet is Tyler will go for whatever he can get away with – wrongful arrest, unsafe conviction, lack of evidence, you name it. And now an alternative suspect's popped up, so he might be in with a chance.'

George sits back and takes a long, slow draught of his beer. Eventually he sets down his glass, his expression putting me in mind of a ruminating cow. 'You know,' he says finally, 'I'm not sure I like the sound of that.'

'For God's sake, George!' My frustration level is getting close to the red zone. 'I've got Grace throwing the bloody obvious at me. I could do without you getting on the bandwagon. Tyler has already made open threats about getting his own back on his arresting officers, and if my memory doesn't fail me, that means you and me.'

'I suppose it does.' A fleeting smile brushes his lips. 'Those were the days – two keen constables out on the town. I could run a mile in under six minutes back then, and you could do it in less than five.' The smile vanishes. 'First big name on the scoreboard for both of us, and if you're asking if I had any doubts – no, not for a single minute. He was a nasty piece of work then, and nothing's changed. Mind you, so was Jimmy Harris, and it was gang warfare, blood in the streets for months before Tyler finally finished it. Harris got killed, Tyler got convicted, and decent folks could go out after dark again. That's how it was. If the chief constable asks, that's what I'll tell him – in court if necessary.'

'And the woman and child?' I ask. 'You reckon Tyler did for them as well?'

His brow furrows. 'You want the truth, Al? I'm not sure. Fights among the menfolk, that was expected. But to go after a toddler? I know it looks possible, from what I've heard, but somehow I can't see it.' He shrugs. 'You need a murder weapon, Al. If you haven't got the smoking gun, I can't see you have a case for charging him with the other two. Jimmy Harris, though – Tyler did that one, and he's where he should be. If he's let out, it will be a crime against justice. That's my opinion.' He looks straight at me. 'I hope it was worth the pie and chips.'

'Thanks, George.' It's the longest speech I've heard him make in a long time – probably since he gave evidence against Craig Tyler in court. 'When I went to see him, I was pretty certain he'd done all three, but now I'm not so sure. The problem is, every bit of evidence we gather points more and more to Drake, and if it turns out the bodies in the garden were down to him, there's a good chance Tyler's appeal will go through. Like you say, we need the murder weapon, and if we couldn't find it twenty years ago, there's bugger all chance of finding it now.' I sigh, utterly deflated. 'You want me to drop you home?'

'Nah. My Sheila's just down the road, and I said I might drop in with a bag of donuts they had on offer at Gregg's this afternoon. Did I tell you she's pregnant again? Got a craving for dough and jam.'

'Chip off the old block, then,' I comment, which draws a chortle from him. 'I'm off to see Rosie before I turn in. Larson's doing some late hours, and I want to make sure he isn't neglecting her.'

'See Rosie, my arse!' George remarks, pushing back his chair and hauling himself upright. 'You're going to get that poor son-in-law of yours to look up that number plate. For Christ's sake, Al – it's nearly ten o'clock! Give them a break and go home. He's a good lad, and he deserves more from you than he gets.'

'Thanks for the advice. Next time I need the family counselling service, I'll give you a call.'

George's smile returns. 'Go easy, Al – and watch your back.'

With that, he gives me a wave and disappears into the night.

. . .

I sit in the car outside Rosie's house for a good fifteen minutes, wrestling with my conscience and the burning desire to have my question answered. Desire finally wins, but instead of ringing the doorbell – it's 10.30 p.m. by this time, I punch in Larson's mobile number. He answers in two rings.

'This is a bit late, even for you,' he says. 'Has something happened?'

I want to say *Yes! My ex-wife is chasing around town dressed to kill with some flashy bastard in a Tesla, and I want to know what the hell is going on!*

'No,' I say. 'Sorry, it's a bit late. It's nothing that won't wait.'

I hear a sigh on the other end of the line. 'Ollie is still here, and I was just making coffee. You want to come over?'

'Sounds good. I'll be with you in five minutes,' I say, figuring that it's a suitable interval to avoid admitting I've been hanging about outside like a rookie on a stakeout.

Rosie answers the door, a finger to her lips. I take off my shoes and follow her on tiptoe into the kitchen. She looks ragged. 'Alex has got a back tooth coming,' she explains, sinking onto a chair and massaging one foot, then the other. 'I feel like I haven't slept for a week. Plus, work is crazy. At least Ben's old enough to occupy himself most of the time, and Mum and Gran are helping out.'

'I'm surprised your mother has the time,' I blurt out before I can stop myself, then add quickly, and with just as little thought, 'I don't suppose their father is helping much.'

She gives me a glare that would do Chrissie justice. 'For God's sake, Dad—'

'I know.' I hold up my hands. 'I've got him working all

hours, and that wasn't fair. I'm sorry, sweetheart. I'm a bit wound up with this case. It's making me act like an arse.'

She keeps up the disapproving stare for several more seconds before she melts, then relaxes back into her chair with a sigh. 'John's wound up too. I've never seen him this upset – or this determined. He hardly stopped to eat when he and Ollie – DC White, I mean – got in. They've been upstairs in the study ever since. I had to move Alex's cot into the lounge in case they disturbed her.'

As if on cue, there's a rustle on the stairs, the sound of the front door opening and closing quietly, and Larson creeps in to join us, looking utterly exhausted. He gives me a nod and heads for the coffee machine. 'Ollie's gone home. He was done in.' He moves across to peck Rosie's cheek. 'You want coffee?'

She shakes her head. 'I want sleep. I'll leave you two to it. I've set up the sofa bed in the lounge with Alex, so you don't have to worry about keeping me awake.' She hauls herself to her feet, kisses us both and disappears.

'We've managed to dig up a few things you might be interested in,' he says, handing me a black coffee and the sugar bowl. 'Come on up, and I'll show you.'

We make our way up the stairs like a couple of veteran housebreakers, careful to make as little noise as possible. Waking my granddaughter isn't an option. The only thing on my mind as we make our ascent is the crumpled serviette in my pocket containing the scribbled licence plate of the Tesla, and how I'm going to persuade my son-in-law to access the DVLA database. As he shuts the door to his study behind us, I lock up completely. It strikes me with the force of a jet of freezing water that what I'm intending to do is wrong on every level I can think of. What kind of bastard spies on his ex-wife, no matter what the excuse? In my case, I've almost convinced myself that it's fear for her safety – almost, but not quite. Even worse, I'm contemplating strong-arming Larson into breaking the law for the sake of what the small, half-decent voice inside me is telling me is plain jealousy. I realise my hand is in my pocket, gripping the napkin so tightly my fingers are starting to ache.

'Are you all right?' Larson asks, a concerned look on his face.

I release the treacherous bit of paper as if it's a hot coal. 'Fine,' I reply, and force a smile. 'Tired, that's all. Come on, show me what you've got.'

He slides into his office chair and brings up a head and shoulders image of a man, perhaps in his mid-fifties, not facing the camera head on, but looking as if he's just realised a photo is being taken and is in the process of turning away. He's a second too late, and his face is quite clear.

'That's Drake?' I ask.

Larson nods. 'That's him,' he replies, and then brings up another image, full face this time, and much younger, perhaps mid to late twenties.

I look from one to the other, mentally trying to make allowances for the age difference. 'That's Drake, too,' I conclude.

He smiles. 'It's the same man, without any doubt,' he says. 'But this man' – he points to the younger image – 'isn't Joseph Drake.'

13

I shift my gaze from one photo to the other. My son-in-law is right – it is the same man without any doubt. 'What do you mean it isn't Joseph Drake?' I ask. 'You're not making any sense.'

'This,' he says, pointing again to the younger image, 'according to the photo ID he had to have when he worked for a few weeks as a bricklayer for a building company in the early 1990s, is Kevin Porter, age twenty-eight.'

He clicks a few more times, and a third image appears, this time a head and shoulders school photograph of an unsmiling boy in a grey sweater and a tie with red, blue and black stripes. The link is harder to see, but it's there. 'So what is he calling himself here?' I ask, understanding.

'Kenneth Hughes. He was eleven when this was taken.'

'Where?' I ask. 'Do we know the school?'

He nods. 'This is Chepstow Comprehensive School, 1976. He was a pupil there for two years, then disappeared off the radar. I'm trying to fill in some of the blanks between his leaving at thirteen and turning up as Kevin Porter fifteen years later. However, I do have an address for 1976 to '78 as The Old Farm, St Arvons.'

He looks at me, and I know we're both having the same thought. 'We're chasing a bloody ghost,' I comment. 'He could have changed his identity God knows how many times in the last forty years.'

Larson nods. 'And the chances are, he will be doing it again soon if he hasn't already.'

'Bloody hell,' I mutter. 'This is going to be near impossible. Have you got any suggestions?'

'A couple,' he replies. 'First, the school photo was taken before he reached the age of sixteen, so it's possible Kenneth Hughes is his real name. It's also likely that he was living either at home with a family or in care in the Chepstow area. He may have parents, relatives or carers still alive. I can make a start on trying to trace them first thing in the morning.'

'And second?' I ask.

'Second, it looks like he doesn't just change his name, he adopts a whole new identity every time, which allows him to operate more or less normally, or less abnormally, under that name. For example, he buys property, pays bills and so on. I don't know if it's possible, but I can try to find out if there is some means of flagging up requests for a new photo ID using his photograph. It might be a hiding to nothing, but I can try.'

'Okay, son.' I give him a very uncharacteristic pat on the shoulder as I get up. Equally uncharacteristically, I say, 'You're doing a great job. Just make sure you're not up all night – the way this case is going, I don't think it's going to be over anytime soon.'

He gives me a weak smile, and as I carefully pull the door closed, I see his head turn back to the screen. Back at my car,

I put my hand in my pocket to fish out my keys, and my fingers brush against the paper napkin. 'Fucking hell,' I mumble as I make my way home.

UNLIKE MY LAST visit to Chief Constable Gosford's office a year or so ago, I'm not ushered to an armchair or offered coffee and biscuits. Instead, I'm left standing while Gosford paces up and down in front of his floor-to-ceiling picture window with views out over the Bristol Channel, hands behind his back, puffing and snorting like a beached walrus.

'What the devil were you thinking, Crow?' he splutters at last, spinning round to glare at me so fast it makes me feel dizzy. 'I mean, for God's sake! You should have known confronting him and accusing him of more murders so close to his parole hearing would result in something like this.' He strides across to his desk, collapses into his chair and slams a palm onto the polished mahogany. 'You don't have any evidence regarding the bodies at Oakfield Road, and it was circumstantial evidence that got him to court in the first place. The only thing you've succeeded in doing is casting doubt on the original conviction. It's a bloody mess, Chief Inspector, and I'll tell you this – if he's successful, somebody's head will roll, and you can be damned sure it won't be mine!'

I give it a minute to make sure the initial storm has blown over, then ask, 'Do we know who his brief is, sir?'

He slumps back and runs a hand across his brow. 'I'll give you three guesses,' he says, 'and sit down, for goodness' sake.'

Clearly, the rant has come to an end for now, so I warily take a chair opposite him. 'Don't tell me – Carol Dodds?'

He nods miserably. 'You know what her record is like. She would have got the Yorkshire Ripper off with a caution.' He meets my eye. 'You and I both know Tyler is as guilty as hell of murdering Harris. But you're not one hundred per cent sure he killed the other two, and without a murder weapon with his fingerprints on it, you'll never prove it. For what it's worth, I think he probably did, but what I think isn't worth a damn – and the same goes for you.'

I can't argue with that. 'What do you want me to do?' I ask. 'If you want me to step aside, I'm sure DI Sillitoe will do an excellent job.'

He barks out a laugh. 'That would be just perfect, wouldn't it? We might as well put a banner out the front of the station with "West Hill police are idiots" written on it. No, Chief Inspector Crow, I don't want you to step aside. What I want you to do is find the murder weapon, preferably with Craig Tyler's fingerprints on it. I also want you to find Joseph Drake and his daughter before yet another body turns up. From what we know so far, it seems likely Drake and Tyler were working together and, for my money, Drake was the senior partner. Maybe he paid Tyler to get rid of all three of them. It's a shame you didn't think to ask that question instead of hurling unsupported accusations, yes?'

I have to admit Gosford has a point, and I kick myself that the possibility didn't occur to me. 'Yes, sir,' I say. 'But what about the fourth victim, the one inside the house? Tyler couldn't have been responsible – he was in prison – so either Drake did it, or hired somebody else. My bet's on Drake, but if he was willing to murder Millie's mother, why take the risk of involving someone else?'

'That, Chief Inspector, is what you're going to find out – and sooner rather than later. We need this sorted before

Tyler gets a date for an appeal hearing, and ...' He gives me a fleeting smile. 'Believe it or not, I'm quite satisfied you're the man to do it.' He waves a hand in dismissal. 'Bloody well go and get on with it.'

BY THE TIME I get back to West Hill, the squad room is empty except for White and Larson, both glued to computer screens, and Sillitoe and Grace huddled in the DI's office. I grab a coffee from the machine and join them.

Grace looks up and smiles. 'You didn't get put in detention, then?'

'Gosford isn't that stupid,' I reply, pulling up a chair. 'Besides, he did have a point. I let myself get blindsided by the similarities in the method the killer used. I should have been more careful. Still, it's done. I just wish Carol bloody Dodds wasn't Tyler's brief. She's the last thing we need.'

Grace and Sillitoe exchange a look. 'Did he tell you where he's off to later this morning?' Grace asks.

'The golf course, if he's true to form,' I suggest bitterly.

'Yes, of course. But the important point is, who with. He just happens to be tackling nine holes before lunch with Martin Connor.'

'You mean *the* Martin Connor, Lord Justice of Appeal?'

'That's the one – an old school chum of Gosford's brother-in-law, apparently, down visiting family for a few days.'

I realise I'm grinning despite myself. 'The cunning old fox! He could have bloody told me. If he gets Connor onside, it'll make Dodds's life a lot more difficult.'

'I'd say it will clip her wings a bit,' Sillitoe comments, 'but she's not scared of going up against the big boys.'

'Still,' Grace puts in, 'for the moment it's not our problem. What's your next move?'

'Contact Chepstow police,' I answer, 'and see if I can see someone over there this morning. Maybe they can point me in the direction of The Old Farm, if such a place exists.'

'I'd better stay here,' Sillitoe says, clearly reluctant. 'Daz and Robbie are still at Oakfield Road, and I've asked Colin to come in and help Ollie on the phone lines. After that appeal this morning, we've been getting a shed load of calls – too many for two of us to handle, and most of them time wasters. With luck it will calm down a bit this afternoon.'

'I told the chief constable it would happen,' Grace grumbles, 'but he insisted we had to be "seen to be doing something". Stupid idea, it's a complete waste of our time.'

I shrug. 'You never know, something might come out of it – somebody who knew him by another of his aliases perhaps?'

'I hope you're right,' Grace says. 'You'd better get off to Wales.' As I make for the door, she adds, 'Take John Larson with you. He looks as if he needs a bit of fresh air, and it was him who ferreted out the address. It'll do him good to get out from behind that computer.'

'Grace …' She gives me a look I know well – the one that says the idea is non-negotiable. With a sigh I head back into the squad room and tell Larson to grab his coat.

14

I've lost count of the number of times I've made the crossing over the Bristol Channel, but the view from the famous Severn Bridge linking Bristol to Chepstow never fails to impress, even in dull weather. Today, the water is reflecting the glow of early autumn sunshine, reminding me of family outings back when Rosie was small, to Chepstow Castle or the Forest of Dean.

Larson must be having similar thoughts. 'We brought Alex over for the first time at the end of the summer holiday,' he says, smiling at the memory. 'She was just old enough to realise how high up above the water we were. She wasn't scared, just fascinated at how small the boats were.'

'Rosie was the same,' I reply. 'She kept wanting to get out and look over the railings.'

For once it's Larson who changes the subject, letting the brief moment of connection slide. 'I spent half of last night seeing what I could find out about The Old Farm. I hoped I'd have some luck tracing the occupants, maybe find other members of the Hughes family.'

'And did you? Find anything?'

'I'm not sure.'

I glance across at him, take note of his furrowed brow as he searches for the right words. I find his habit of hesitating before he speaks is beyond irritating, but resist the urge to tell him to bloody well spit it out, grit my teeth and wait. We're just coming to the end of the crossing, we're around ten minutes from Chepstow police station, so he might as well take some thinking time.

It's at least another minute before he finally comes up with an explanation. 'There is a place called The Old Farm,' he says, 'but it isn't a farm, it's a small house or cottage in the grounds of a much larger building. From the map it looks no bigger than maybe two-up two-down, and it's by itself, in a dip in the surrounding land. But what's interesting is the larger building. It looks like an old hospital or asylum, very Victorian gothic, and in the 1930s it was taken over for use as Wye Cross approved school. It was converted into Wye Cross community home in the 1970s, but from what little time I had to read up on it, the regime probably didn't change a great deal. Hopefully your contact will be able to tell us more.'

'He grew up in an approved school? Jesus!'

'That's what I can't be sure about. They were closed institutions, yet the photograph we have of him as a child was taken at the local comprehensive school. There may be a logical explanation, but right now it doesn't make sense.'

I can see the problem and also the reason for his hesitation. There is a lot of temptation to make assumptions. Perhaps Hughes was a criminal back then – but perhaps not. I pull into the police station car park and take a breath. 'Come on,' I say. 'Let's see what the locals can tell us.'

We're met at the front desk by a sharply dressed kid who looks as if he's only just discovered the business end of a razor and goes to the same gym as my son-in-law. The chief difference between them is that while Larson is decked out in his usual shabby-chic jeans, T-shirt and blazer, this guy looks as if his pale grey silk suit and eye-watering pink tie come from the reject pile of a Milan catwalk. He might as well have a sign glued to his forehead with 'fast track' written on it. He walks across and holds out a hand.

'Chief Inspector Crow? Very pleased to meet you, sir,' he says, in a Home Counties public school accent. 'I'm Inspector Jerry Forbes – I've been asked to look after you.'

He and Larson exchange introductions, and Forbes ushers us through to his office. 'I'm afraid the period you're looking at is a bit before my time, but I got in touch with one of our former sergeants, Dave Evans, who was here way back. He retired a decade or so ago and still lives in Chepstow. He said he was happy to come in – should be here any minute. In the meantime, I'll do my best. Can I get you some coffee?'

Despite my initial misgivings, I find myself warming to our host, and from the reaction of the young DC who appears almost instantly with coffee and biscuits, he seems to be well liked by the rank and file. 'Thanks, Phil,' Forbes says as the DC treats us to a bright smile, sets down the tray and disappears. 'Now,' he continues, gesturing for us to help ourselves, 'what exactly do you need to know? I assume it concerns the chap who was on the *Breakfast West* appeal this morning. You think he might have come across the border into our area?'

'It's a possibility. What information we have suggests he grew up here, at Wye Cross.'

'Good God!' Forbes recoils slightly. 'Like I said, it's way before my time, but if what I've been told is true, nobody who was in that place would want to go back there.'

Before he can say any more, there's a knock on the door, and a man bearing an uncanny resemblance to George Saint squeezes his way into the small office. From the look of his waistline, he survived the police force on the same diet of pastry and doughnuts.

'You've got a job for me, Inspector?' he asks Forbes in a soft, lilting Welsh accent, then nods to us as he wedges himself into a corner. 'Morning, gents.'

'Good of you to come in, Dave,' Forbes replies. 'This is Chief Inspector Crow, from Bristol, and Mr Larson – digital forensics, wasn't it?' Larson nods, and he goes on, 'They're after a murder suspect and think he might have landed on our patch – a place called The Old Farm. You know the area better than most, and I thought you might be able to help out.'

Evans frowns and scratches the back of his neck. 'The Old Farm? You mean the caretaker's cottage over at Wye Cross? That's been derelict for years – I can't see anyone holing up there.'

'Nevertheless,' I put in, 'I'd really appreciate it if you could take us for a look round, maybe give us some background on the way?'

Out of the corner of my eye, I see Forbes breathe a little sigh of relief. 'An excellent idea, Chief Inspector. If you do have any suspicions your man is nearby, I trust you will give me a heads-up? In the meantime, good luck. I'm afraid I need to go and brief my team. We've got a gang of organised car thieves under surveillance, and if we're lucky, we should get them rounded up by the end of the day.'

With that, he edges past us and out of the tiny office. Ex-sergeant Evans grabs a couple of biscuits off the desk and gives us a satisfied grin. 'Chocolate Hobnobs. Young Jerry must want to impress you. Well, gentlemen, shall we get going?'

We set off, Evans in the passenger seat giving directions, Larson in the back. 'So,' Evans says, 'has he got a name, this murder suspect of yours?'

'Several,' I reply, 'but the most likely one is Kenneth Hughes. We have a school photograph of him from 1976, and The Old Farm is the address given. He would have been eleven then.'

I realise Evans is staring at me. 'You have a picture?' he says. Larson obliges, digging out a copy and handing it to him. He peers at it, grunts and clicks his tongue before handing it back. 'Well, well – little Kenny Hughes. There's a face I haven't seen for a good while.'

'You know him?'

'Back in the day,' Evans replies. 'This is your murder suspect?' He shakes his head. 'We thought, back then, he might end up in a fair bit of trouble, one way or another, but murder? Who's he meant to have killed, then? I suppose you can't tell me that, seeing as I'm not serving anymore.'

'I'm afraid not,' I reply as he nudges my arm and points to a turning off the main road. 'At least, not yet. But you don't seem that surprised?'

'Not really – more sad, I suppose. I'm surprised you don't know the story, it made the headlines over here for weeks, but I expect you're used to all sorts over in the city – too busy to take notice of things happening out in the sticks.'

'That's true,' I agree. 'We tend to have our hands pretty full most of the time. What happened?'

The road I've been driving down has been getting gradually narrower and rougher, trees and other vegetation encroaching on the tarmac until we can't go any further without risking a burst tyre or worse. There's an old, rusting set of iron gates a hundred metres further along, secured with a massive padlock, although the masonry on either side has partially crumbled away, making it a fairly easy task to scramble through the gaps in the wall.

'This is as far as we go,' Evans says, completely unnecessarily. 'We'll have to go the rest of the way on foot. I'll fill you in on the history on the way.'

I spend the next few minutes concentrating on not tripping over brambles and fallen bricks, wishing I'd worn hiking boots instead of brogues. Evans seems oblivious to the terrain, clambering nimbly over the various obstacles despite his bulk. Larson, kitted out in designer trainers, seems to be enjoying the opportunity to show off the fruits of his labours in the gym. Finally, we make it through a gap in the wall to find ourselves on more level ground, in what, clearly, were once the well-tended grounds of a fairly large estate. The driveway is pitted, but still more or less intact, and leads up to an imposing, if decaying, Victorian building sitting at the top of a gentle rise around a quarter of a mile away. Even at this distance I can see that most of the windows have been boarded up, and those that haven't have very little glass left intact. The general effect is of the perfect film set for a gothic horror movie, something that Chrissie would describe as 'giving her the creeps'.

'That's Wye Cross House,' Evans explains. 'It closed in 1983, and the estate was bought by a developer who couldn't get the planning permissions he needed and eventually went bankrupt. There have been several attempts since, but the more time goes on, the more decay sets in and the more expensive it becomes, and nobody's got the money or the will to take it on. The building's listed, you see, so it can't be demolished, and conversion would be uneconomic for most developers. Mind you, I think most of us locals, including the police – and don't say I said this, mind – would be happy to see some vandal or other set fire to the bloody place and raze it to the ground.'

I can't help but smile. 'I know what you mean,' I reply, thinking of Vista House in West Hill. I'm also thinking that like George Saint, Dave Evans is pretty sharp; appearances, in both cases, are deceptive. 'So, what about Kenneth Hughes? He was an inmate here?'

Evans chuckles. 'It's far more complicated than that, Chief Inspector. His dad worked here, back in the 1960s and '70s. It was an approved school then, and Iain Hughes was caretaker and head groundsman. He took up the job in' – he pauses to think – '1963 if I recall. I can just about remember, but I was only a kid back then. Mostly, I only know because of the sensation later on. Hughes moved into the caretaker's cottage with his young wife, and less than a year later they had Kenny. The cottage used to be a farmhouse, before Victorian times, so the name stuck – The Old Farm. Not the sort of farmhouse we know today, of course – a ramshackle place, tiny, with hardly enough room for a family. It's just on the other side of the rise.'

We've been trudging up the driveway as he talks, and the closer we get to the gloomy edifice in front of us, the more oppressive it becomes. A shiver runs down my spine, and I look across at Larson, who has been very quiet since we left the police station. He's staring at the building with a look somewhere between amazement and horror on his face.

'There were children locked up in here?' he mutters, half to himself. 'It's unimaginable.'

'That's as may be,' Evans replies, 'but it's the way things happened, right up to the time you were born, I expect. Some were criminals – juvenile delinquents, we called them in those times – but not all, not by any means. A lot of kids ended up here simply because their parents couldn't cope, or they had a minor tussle with the school or with the police and no one knew what to do with them. Things have improved a bit since then, thank God, but the system's still far from perfect.'

'You were going to tell us about Kenny Hughes,' I prompt, steering Evans back on track.

'So I was,' he says. 'The cottage is on the other side. Follow me.' He leads us round the side of Wye Cross House, or what's left of it, and into the remains of what was once a large kitchen garden. There are the remains of wooden sheds and three or four collapsed greenhouses, and vegetable beds arranged in a grid pattern, each bordered by low brick walls. 'They used to grow most of their own food here,' he explains, 'and ship the surplus out to Chepstow, to the prison and the hospital mostly. But there's The Old Farm, down at the bottom of the slope, see? It's got the hillside in front and the woods behind. Back in the 1800s, they mainly farmed sheep here, and still did right up to the 1950s. Then the last farming tenant died, and the local authority decided to let the place out to a caretaker for the school.'

I squint down the long, sloping meadow beyond the kitchen garden to the woods and make out a small, derelict stone cottage jutting out of the trees. Evans leads us down the slope, the grass wet and slippery from recent showers, and by the time we reach the cottage, we're all soaked to the knees. It's a dark, miserable place, most of the light cut off by the encroaching woodland. There is no garden – the front door opens straight out onto the meadow, with just a narrow gravel path between the grass and the stone walls. I catch Larson's eye. He's having the same thoughts as me. This would have been a pretty difficult place to bring up a child – aside from the main house, the nearest habitation would be, at a guess, three or four miles away, and the general atmosphere of isolation and oppression might even have been worse when the buildings were occupied, surrounded by fences, barbed wire and all the other security paraphernalia associated with a juvenile detention centre back in the 1960s and 1970s.

Evans catches my expression and answers my unspoken question. 'There was a mains water supply here, piped down from the main house, but no mains electricity. A generator was put in just before Hughes took up the post, and there's a septic tank. It wasn't the kind of job that would have suited everybody, but Iain Hughes was a bit of a loner, by all accounts. He kept himself to himself, and the same went for his wife, Janet. Nobody saw much of her, or young Kenny when he was born, but rumour had it they were very close.'

'How old were they?' Larson suddenly pipes up. 'I mean, when Kenny was born, how old was Janet?'

Evans gives him a sidelong look. 'Funny you should ask that. She was very young – from what I heard, there was a bit of a scandal where she came from, down in the Valleys. From a very religious family, so the story goes, and ran off with Iain when she was just fourteen. Maybe that's why he took the job here, hoping they wouldn't be found. She wasn't much older when Kenny was born – it was illegal, and by rights he should have been arrested, but by the time it all came out, she was over sixteen, and a blind eye was turned. I think the council was just relieved someone had taken on the job. Iain was much older, around forty or so by then.'

I grudgingly admit to myself that Larson's question is one I wouldn't have thought to ask, yet it has shed a sudden light on Drake's – or Hughes's – possible motives and mental state. I need to sharpen up.

Evans is still talking. 'Janet wasn't Iain's first wife. He'd been married before – was still married, by some accounts – to an Englishwoman, somewhere up in Yorkshire. He'd left her to go off with Janet, but not before she had a child, another boy. He'd be, what – some five years older than Kenny, if the rumours are true. I can't tell you the name, or where they might be, or even if the other family exists, but it's what I heard at the time.'

My brain is jumping in several directions at once. I take a deep breath, trying to rein in my impatience. Diet isn't the only thing Evans has in common with George Saint. He also likes to take his time, tell the story his way, and no amount of prodding is going to make him alter course. 'So what happened?' I ask. 'You said the family made the headlines. How? And when?'

'Ah,' he says, giving me a satisfied grin, gearing up for the main event. 'That would have been in 1978. Kenny had been at the secondary school a couple of years, so that would make him thirteen at the time. Iain had put in for some holiday time; people assumed to take the family off somewhere for a couple of weeks. That was in August of '78. Nobody thought anything of it until he never turned up for work a fortnight later. At first, there wasn't too much of a fuss, the director of Wye Cross thought he'd probably just been held up and wasn't able to phone through to let them know. The phone lines were a bit unreliable anyway. But when he still hadn't appeared two days later, someone thought to come down to the cottage to see what was going on, and found Kenny all by himself. Apparently, he had no idea where his father was, hadn't seen him for the whole fortnight. He'd been left to fend for himself, with no money and no food. He'd been taking food from the kitchen garden, and he was old enough to work the generator and all that. He hadn't told anyone because he was scared of being taken into care. He said he thought his father was bound to come back eventually. But he never did. He disappeared off the face of the earth. All his clothes were gone, too. The police put out an alert, searched the whole area, but nothing. Iain didn't have a car – just a motorbike and sidecar, and there was no sign of that either. Everyone assumed he'd just driven off, and a runaway itinerant wasn't exactly high priority, so the incident was filed and forgotten. He was just another low-risk missing person.'

'You say "he",' I point out. 'What about the mother? Where was she while all this was going on?'

Evans grunts and raises an eyebrow. 'Ah,' he pronounces after a pause. 'That's the question. Nobody knows. Young Kenny refused to say a word when he was asked, and there were rumours going round after Iain disappeared that Janet had been long gone – some said she ran off when Kenny was still a baby and Iain kept it quiet. Others thought she'd walked out more recently. There was even talk that Iain had murdered her and then fled the scene. The truth is, nobody knows, the police at the time weren't interested in a couple of itinerant nobodies, and it's still a complete mystery.' He shrugs. 'Maybe we'll find out, now you city boys are on the case.'

'But what happened to Kenny?' Larson asks. 'They couldn't just leave him there. Was he taken into care?'

'I'm afraid he was.' Evans nods slowly. 'The thing is, he wasn't the easiest of kids to deal with. He made one hell of a fuss, and in the end the social services had to call in the police to get him out of the cottage. He barricaded himself in and threatened the social workers with knives at first, then his dad's shotgun. They did get him out eventually, but one officer was stabbed – not fatally, thank God – and it all ended up with the courts thinking the best place for him was Wye Cross House. So, in the space of a few weeks, he went from being the caretaker's son to being locked up in the main house. He stayed there until he was sixteen; then he was chucked out onto the street. A sad business for all concerned.'

'And his parents were never found?' Larson is shaking his head in disbelief.

'Not to this day,' Evans replies. 'There was no sense to it – none at all. I can't help thinking young Kenny could have really made something of himself. He was a very bright lad and seemed to enjoy studying at the secondary school, although he did have social problems, on account of being so isolated at home, I suppose. Being put into Wye Cross wouldn't have helped with either. But what was done was done.' He shrugs again. 'I'm sorry to hear he's got himself into trouble. Maybe if he'd had a lucky break or two later on …'

There's a silence when Evans finishes his tale of woe. After a moment, Larson ventures up to the front door of the cottage and pushes. It swings open, creaking on its hinges, to reveal a pitted slate flagstone floor, the sort that would cost an arm and a leg to have installed these days. These slates, however, are probably at least a couple of hundred years old, worn by generations of feet. Larson grabs my arm, points at the floor – and beyond to the ancient stone fireplace. It takes me a minute to realise what's got him so excited. The floor is clean, free of the years of dust one would expect to see in a derelict building. In the centre of the fireplace is a pile of ashes – not the old, blackened remains of a blaze, but fresh and pale grey, the kind of ash you would find where seasoned logs have been recently burned. I take a step forward and can even catch the scent of smoke. A vagrant might stay here a night and build a makeshift fire, but what tramp on his travels would sweep the floor, clean the mantel of the fireplace?

It's Evans who voices our thoughts. 'Kenny's been here – hasn't he?'

15

It's mid-afternoon by the time Jerry Forbes comes striding down the slope towards us, trouser legs stuffed into a pair of wellington boots, accompanied by the DC who served us tea earlier, plus half a dozen uniformed constables.

'Sorry about your car thieves,' I say as he reaches us.

He shrugs. 'Can't be helped, Chief Inspector. I've left a couple of officers on surveillance outside the garage they use, but to tell you the truth, I think it will be a no-show, at least today. Two of the gang have been spotted over in Newport. Besides, I'd say a murder suspect and missing girl take precedence, wouldn't you? That's what your chief constable's told mine, anyway.' He waves his DC across. 'I didn't introduce you earlier – this is Phil Jones, also known as Phil the Tea. We thought you might be getting a bit peckish by now.'

Phil the Tea unhooks a rucksack from his shoulder, rummages and pulls out four packs of ham sandwiches and a flask. 'There you go, sirs,' he says, with a grin. 'Best we could do at short notice – I think there's a cheese one in here somewhere if you'd prefer.'

'Ham's fine,' I say on behalf of us all, my stomach reminding me it's had nothing since breakfast. Nobody objects, and we all dig in, Forbes included, gathered in a huddle on the path outside the cottage.

'Looks like your boss and mine have been having a bit of a conference,' Forbes says. 'From our point of view, there are a couple of concerns. If Hughes has been back here, there must be a reason over and above simple nostalgia. He might be stashing trophies here or even, God forbid, bodies. The trouble is, he might have access to the main house as well, and it would take significant time and manpower to comb that from top to bottom. If we're going to do that, we need some pretty solid evidence we'll find something; otherwise we can't justify the resources.'

'Tell me about it.' I give him a wry grin. 'You said there were a couple of concerns?'

Forbes frowns, the same expression on his face that my son-in-law uses when he's trying to formulate the right words. Finally, with an apologetic glance at Evans, he says, 'Back in 1978, when Kenneth Hughes's parents disappeared, there was what I could only call – sorry, Dave – a cursory investigation. They were pretty isolated here and hadn't integrated well with the local community. I think it would also be fair to say that Iain Hughes had a reputation for itinerant behaviour.'

'That's true enough,' Evans put in, 'but not unusual in these parts. Workers came and went all the time – farm workers, travelling folk, manual labourers, tradesmen. People went where the work was, possibly more than they do now. It wasn't unusual for families to do a moonlight flit when the work dried up, usually owing rent, or credit run up at the local shops.'

'Except the Hughes family didn't pay rent,' Forbes says. 'The cottage came with the job, and they didn't have any other debts. They simply disappeared, leaving nothing except their son. Looking at the records, there was a search of the surrounding areas, and neighbouring forces were asked to keep an eye out. There was no sign of them, so they were classed as missing persons and consigned to a filing cabinet in the basement. But what if they didn't move on? What if they are still here? Given what we now know about Kenneth Hughes —'

Evans gets in before me. 'You're saying they might have been murdered? And Kenny Hughes might have done it?' He shakes his head. 'He was no more than a lad, a pretty scrawny one at that, if I remember right. Iain Hughes was a big man; he had a bit of a temper, too. I can't see it, and neither did my governor in the original investigation.'

'Inspector Forbes has a point, though,' Larson puts in. 'There are more ways to commit murder than brute strength. He could have poisoned them or something …' He trails off and looks at me.

'I don't think poison's his style,' I say. 'But we can't discount the possibility. If he can wall his wife up alive, who knows what he's been capable of in the past?'

To give him credit, Forbes simply raises an eyebrow. 'Did he, by God?' he mutters, then straightens and rubs his hands. 'Right. Let's do a sweep of the cottage and the immediate surroundings, see if anything looks like it's been disturbed.'

'Disturbed?' Evans looks confused. 'Why would he disturb anything? If he did do for his parents like you suggest, and buried them round here, any disturbance would have long disappeared by now – it was forty-odd years ago, and if they weren't found then, they'd be impossible to find now.'

'You weren't looking then,' I point out, 'and he came here for something. Maybe he wanted to check his handiwork was where he left it – and, in my experience, that's nearly always a mistake.' I turn to Forbes. 'Apart from Hughes – presuming it was him – and now us, it looks like nobody's been anywhere near here for years. The grass is knee high, and the wood's choked with brambles.'

'I'm ahead of you, Chief Inspector,' Forbes responds with a smile. 'If he has been wandering around, there will be a path, even if it's difficult to see. I'll tell everyone to go very carefully, and if there's so much as a bent blade of grass, we'll know about it. In the meantime, it won't hurt to have a look round the inside of the place – you coming?'

He ducks through the low doorway, and I follow, telling Larson and Evans to stay outside. The place is hardly big enough for two adults to move around without bumping into each other.

'Well,' he says once we're alone, 'do I pass muster?'

The question wrong-foots me completely. 'What on earth do you mean?' I ask.

He laughs. 'I saw the look on your face when you arrived. Fast-track boy from Dimwit University, doesn't know his arse from his elbow, right?'

I stare at him, unsure how to respond, and in the end decide honesty is the best bet. 'Something like that,' I admit, 'but first impressions aren't always accurate. Although you did join up as a graduate, yes?'

'That's right. I studied classics at Oxford, mostly just to

annoy my dad. I would have ended up in the police anyway, but didn't want him to think he'd got one over on me. Everyone has to rebel a bit, don't you think?'

I've already decided he's damned good at his job, fast track or not, but on top of that, he's piqued my interest. 'Your father wanted you to be a policeman? Christ – if I'd had a son, I'd have done my best to put him off!'

'It's the family business,' he explains. 'Five generations and counting. My great-great-grandfather was one of the first official constables in this area, and my great-grandfather one of the first detectives. Both my grandfather and my father ended up as chief inspectors, so you can see I've a lot of examples to follow. Mind you, it was a struggle proving myself to the troops. Believe me, it's not easy when your uncle is assistant chief constable. That's why I decided to come out here – a bit more under the radar.' He's grinning as he says this, and I can understand his problem. Anything that smacks of nepotism is likely to be taken badly by the rank and file. He gives me a sly wink. 'It's still pretty useful when you need to do a bit of arm twisting, though. If we can pick up anything worth pursuing, I should be able to badger Uncle Freddie for the manpower to follow it up.'

He reaches into his jacket pocket, pulls out a telescopic metal pointer of the sort teachers use to point at whiteboards, and uses it to poke through the fresh ash in the fireplace.

'Looks like he hasn't burned anything apart from wood,' he comments, 'and the place has been cleaned to within an inch of its life. Whatever else he is, he's careful.'

'Let's hope he's too bloody careful,' I say. 'Everyone makes at least one mistake, and maybe his problem is that it makes us look for that mistake a bit more closely.'

'Agreed.' He makes his way to the narrow staircase leading up to two tiny bedrooms on the first floor. The first is empty except for a camp bed neatly folded and stacked in a corner – no bedding. 'Looks like he's been having a field day with the mop and bucket up here, too,' Forbes says, shaking his head. 'I'll see if we can get any prints off the bed, but somehow I think he'll have thought of that.' He sighs. 'That's all we need – a psychopath with a bleach habit.'

The second room has no bed, but a large wardrobe dating back, at a guess, to the 1930s taking up half the space. I take a clean handkerchief out of my pocket and gingerly open the door. For a moment, both of us stand frozen, staring at the contents. Then I pull myself together and shout down to Larson.

Like us, he stops dead in the doorway, mouth open, staring. Forbes looks from one to the other of us. 'Someone want to tell me what this is all about?' he asks.

I gesture to Larson, who swallows and finds his voice. 'When we found the victim walled up in Drake's – or Hughes's, or whatever his name is – in his house, there were fragments of clothing on the body. By the look of it, these garments are identical in every respect. I mean, Jesus! How many has he got?'

The entire wardrobe is stacked with polythene bags neatly separated into piles. There are dresses, sweaters, ladies' underwear and shoes. There must be at least twenty of each, all exactly the same.

'What's the bet there are no prints on any of these either?' Forbes says.

'I'll save my money,' I reply. 'But what the hell is he doing? A straightforward serial killer is one thing, and it's likely that's what we've got, but this guy looks to be a complete nutcase! There's absolutely no sense in any of it, at least not so far.'

Larson clears his throat, and we both look at him. 'You've got an idea, son?' I ask.

'Maybe.' He gives me his long-suffering look, then shrugs. 'What if it's all about his mother?'

'His mother?' Forbes frowns. 'How?'

'Well ...' Larson gestures to the wardrobe. 'The clothes, for one thing. They are what a girl might have worn in the 1950s or early '60s. Sergeant Evans said that Iain Hughes was much older than his wife, that Janet had Kenneth when she was in her teens. That means she would only have been in her early twenties when she disappeared. The two female victims we've found were also in their late teens or early twenties, and one of them was dressed in exactly these clothes. Maybe the other one was as well. So perhaps he's recreating what his mother was wearing when he last saw her – sort of trying to bring his mother back, keep her alive in his mind ...' He sighs. 'Or something like that?'

I look again at the pile of clothes in the wardrobe. He might well have a point. Before I can answer, though, there's a shout from downstairs.

'Sir – I think we've got something.'

Forbes raises an eyebrow and heads back down the stairs. I follow, leaving Larson still staring at the contents of the wardrobe, a thoughtful expression on his face. We emerge into the September sunshine to find DC Phil 'the Tea' Jones shuffling impatiently from foot to foot, cheeks pink with excitement, like a schoolboy who's found a tenner in the washing basket.

'What is it, Phil?' Forbes asks.

'A path, sir, round the back, leading through the woods.

It's very faint, whoever went that way was careful, but it's recent. The undergrowth is so thick nobody could have gotten through without treading on the ground cover.'

He leads the way round the side of the cottage and points. At first, I can't see any sign of disturbance, but as we get closer, I catch sight of a couple of definite indentations in the brambles, and a little further in, a broken branch at around waist height. Someone, or something, has made the faint trail, but it could easily have been an animal of some sort, a deer, perhaps, or a fox.

'Well spotted, Constable,' Forbes says, with an eager grin, and I realise then that if we want to see where it goes, we're going to have to follow it, and probably get scratched to pieces by the vicious brambles that have run wild over every inch of the woodland. I glance at Forbes's sensible knee-length wellingtons, and then at my own ridiculously inadequate shoes.

'Oh, shit,' I mutter.

Forbes looks at me, and the grin gets wider. 'Don't worry, Chief Inspector,' he says. 'I'll go first and make a path for you – unless you'd rather stay here and wait.'

That isn't an option, so I give him a reluctant nod, and we set off, DC Jones in the lead, moving slowly so as not to miss any signs of the previous passage.

The going is slow and painful despite Forbes doing his best to hold the worst of the thorns aside with his wellington boot. By the time we manage to push our way into a clearing some hundred metres in, my ankles are covered in scratches, and my trousers are so torn I'm going to have to buy a new suit. Larson has caught up with us, and we all emerge into a small space where the brambles are much sparser and there's clear sky overhead. Forbes strides forward, and we hear the distinct clunk of metal under his feet.

'The septic tank,' he says, tapping the ground with his foot. 'It would have been much more accessible at one time, but we've got forty-odd years of unchecked growth here, and the trees have simply grown around it. It's definitely what he was heading for. The vegetation has been pushed aside to give access to the main hatch.'

I peer over his shoulder and see the metal inspection cover, just large enough for a man to squeeze through. Forbes crouches beside it, examining the seal. I feel the hairs on the back of my neck start to prickle. Forbes pushes himself upright and turns to me.

'Looks like it's been opened recently,' he says, and for the first time in our brief acquaintance, I see him grimace. 'I'm afraid we're going to have to get a team down here and open it up.'

16

After a wait of almost two hours, during which my feet, encased in sopping wet socks, have become entirely numb, Forbes comes across, stuffing his mobile back in his pocket and looking distinctly irritated.

'Sorry about the delay,' he says. 'Apparently nothing can be done today – there are only a few hours of light left, and if there is anything down there, I don't suppose it will be going anywhere. I've managed to get the powers that be to organise an expert for ten o'clock tomorrow morning. I'll post a couple of officers here overnight, and you're welcome to come back and observe.'

'Thanks,' I say, 'I'll do that.' We shake hands; then Larson and I set off on the long, uncomfortable tramp back to my car.

Surprisingly, there's a mobile signal, and as we walk, Sillitoe and I swap notes. The morning's TV appeal has so far resulted, as we suspected, in a waste of manpower fielding calls. Thankfully, there have been no further gruesome findings at Oakfield Road, but all that does, I remind her, is leave a question mark concerning the owners of the other items found in the box hidden in the wall. The analysis of those is still ongoing, so there is nothing we can do but wait until Maggie is ready with her full report. It's going to be way past six by the time we get back across the bridge, so I arrange a briefing for the morning and leave her to the crank calls.

I glance across at my son-in-law trudging along beside me in silence. He looks dazed. In the time I've known him, I've come to realise he's not without backbone, and he's never shied away from putting himself in harm's way when it really matters. He's proved that more than once. In the rare moments when I'm being honest with myself, I have to admit he's a pretty good detective, at least when he's sitting in front of a computer screen. The last couple of days have been a whole new experience for him, and the strain is starting to show. There's a big difference between solving a murder as an intellectual puzzle, and standing in a mortuary watching a victim being dissected, or being present at a crime scene knowing the next thing you'll see is a corpse. Even the most veteran police officers never really get used to that. Rookie PCs have been known to faint, throw up, or both, at their first sight of a dead and mutilated human being, or during their first post-mortem.

As if reading my thoughts, he turns to me. 'Since you were going to ask,' he says, 'I didn't pass out, and I wasn't sick. In fact, I asked to be present.' He sighs, looks down at his feet. 'I thought I should, somehow, seeing as I was poking about in the poor woman's life – seemed right I should see her death, too.' He pauses, then adds, 'But I wish I bloody well hadn't. I can't get it out of my head.'

'Actually,' I tell him, 'I wasn't going to ask.' It's my turn to hesitate before saying, more gently, 'It's not just you, son. We do it because we have to. If we don't look the real meaning of violence in the eye, who will? My first time, I spent nearly the whole event in the toilet.'

I realise I'm talking to him just as I would to any other rookie on their first stint at West Hill. He raises his eyebrows. 'Thanks. That makes me feel a hell of a lot better.'

We've reached the car, and as I'm fumbling for my keys, I surprise myself by saying, 'I don't know about you, but I need to be here in the morning when they take the lid off that tank. Perhaps you'd like to join me, get a bit more first-hand experience?'

He catches the note of challenge in my voice. 'That's very kind,' he says, lips curling into a smile. 'I'd love to.'

WE SPEND the journey back to Bristol in silence. Until now, my mind has been focused on Drake, or Hughes, or whatever his name turns out to be. As we get closer to Clifton, though, the only thing on my mind is whether Chrissie is going to be home and, if she is, what the hell am I going to say to her? I'm still trying to decide when I pull up outside the house.

Rosie answers the door. She gives Larson a hug and pecks my cheek. 'Come on in,' she says. 'Gran's cooked dinner for everyone.' She pulls me aside. 'Ben's in the garden with Blue. There's something bothering him, but he says he'll only talk to you. Do you mind?'

'Of course not,' I reply. 'I'll go and find him. Is your mother at home?'

Just like Joyce the night before, there's that slight hesitation before she says, 'No, not right now. She had to go out – a business meeting. She said she might be home quite late, and not to wait for her to eat.'

Business meeting? What the bloody hell is going on? Has Chrissie asked my daughter to lie for her? I take hold of myself. Like George says, what my ex-wife decides to do in her spare time is none of my business. My head knows it – the trouble is, the rest of me doesn't seem to be getting the message. What's really making me furious is that if Rosie and Joyce are covering for her, the chances are so is Larson, and they're all treating me like an idiot. Luckily, I've got enough sense left to keep my mouth firmly shut.

I make my way out into the back garden, where I find Ben sitting on the wooden bench behind Joyce's kitchen garden, Blue sprawled over his lap. She jumps up when she sees me and gives me her usual joyful bark, tail thrashing against my legs. *At least*, I think bitterly, *someone is pleased to see me.* Ben, on the other hand, hasn't moved or even looked up. I sit down beside him.

'Hey, Ben. How's it going?' He doesn't answer, but leans against me, wanting a hug. I put an arm around him while Blue sits quietly in front of us, the canine equivalent of curiosity on her face as her eyes flit between us. 'You want to tell me what's on your mind?' I ask when he doesn't say anything. I find myself hoping he hasn't inherited his father's hesitation habit.

Finally, his head comes up, and he looks me in the eye. 'Is Millie dead?' he asks simply, but determinedly, his expression challenging me to give an honest answer. This time it's Rosie I see in him, and I almost smile despite the seriousness of the question.

'I don't know, Ben,' I answer. 'It's my job to investigate what's happened to her, and that's what I'm doing right now.'

His gaze drops to his feet again. 'It's my fault, Grandad,' he says, close to tears, his voice trembling.

'How do you work that out?' I ask, then, trying to lighten the tone, 'If you'd murdered somebody, I would have found out by now. I'm a pretty good detective, you know.'

To my horror, he bursts into tears. I tighten my hug and make comforting noises while Blue does her best to sympathise, whining and licking his leg. 'Come on, Ben,' I say. 'How could it possibly be your fault? That doesn't make any sense.' I delve in my pocket and pull out my handkerchief. I wipe his eyes, and he blows his nose, recovering himself.

'I wasn't nice to her,' he admits. 'I told her she was a stink bomb and nobody liked her, and then she disappeared. If I hadn't said that, she wouldn't have run away, and she'd still be here.'

'That's just it,' I tell him. 'She didn't run away, so you can't be to blame. Her father took her somewhere, and we don't know where – not yet anyway. Maybe you weren't as nice to her as you could have been, but then, you did try, and she told you to bugger off, isn't that right?'

He nods miserably.

'So,' I go on, 'you did your best, and none of us likes everybody. I'll tell you something if you promise not to tell anyone.'

He looks up. 'Okay, Grandad, I promise.'

'Sometimes I'm pretty nasty to people too. I say things I shouldn't, but everybody does. But that doesn't mean I'm responsible for everything bad that happens to them. We all do it now and then, even when we're grown up. We try not to, but we get used to it, too, that's all.'

At last, he smiles. 'Yeah,' he says. 'I heard Mum and Dad talking once. Dad was really upset, and Mum said not to worry about it, because you could be a right arsehole, and it just meant you liked him. I mean, adults are weird. But it's kinda cool!'

I stare at his innocent face for a second, then can't help but laugh. 'Yes,' I agree. 'Adults are weird. And your dad isn't dead because I was acting like an arsehole, is he? So, I think we can safely say that as far as we know, neither is Millie?'

He reaches up and gives me a hug. 'Thanks, Grandad. I knew you'd understand.' He dashes inside to see if dinner is ready, leaving me with the uncomfortable thought that Rosie might be right, at least when it comes to my relationship with my son-in-law.

During dinner, nobody mentions Chrissie, and there seems to be a secret agreement to skirt round the subject of her increasingly frequent absences. Thankfully, I'm hungry enough to make myself focus on Joyce's cooking despite the growing shadow of paranoia that is spreading from the murky depths to the forefront of my mind. The 'rational explanation', which I've almost convinced myself does not involve a new relationship, is rapidly turning into a vain hope. Once or twice, Rosie gives me a concerned look, and I realise my expression is probably reflecting my misery. I manage a weak smile, crossing my fingers that my unsociable attitude is put down to my being in charge of a multiple murder case.

Finally, the plates are cleared away, and Rosie announces her intention to stay over with the children. 'Ben's got an Inset day tomorrow,' she explains. 'I know you're busy with your case, and he'd love to spend the day with Blue, so why don't you leave her here? I've taken a day off, so we can all go for a day in the country. Maybe you could drop John off on your way home? You both look like you could do with a good night's sleep.'

Larson and I exchange a look. 'Fine,' I reply, not trusting myself to say more. After five minutes of goodbyes, we extricate ourselves and set off for the Larson house, each buried in our own thoughts.

Larson comes to life as I pull into his driveway. 'I don't suppose you fancy some coffee?' he asks tentatively. 'I've had a few thoughts I'd like to run past you if you're not too tired.'

I weigh it up for a second, then nod. Any distraction is better than sitting in my own lounge imagining what my ex-wife might be up to. I follow him inside, and we settle at the kitchen table with a much-needed strong coffee each.

'So,' I say, forcing my thoughts to the matter in hand, 'what are you thinking, son?'

'Well ...' He sits back with a sigh. 'Stop me if you think this is all what you'd call bullshit, but firstly, I don't think Millie is dead.'

I raise an eyebrow. I've been thinking the same thing myself. 'Okay. Why not?'

'She hasn't reached the critical age,' he replies. 'The body under the shed was late teens or early twenties, and so was the victim in the wall. My bet is that his mother died at the same sort of age, and he waits until his victims are the right age for him to relive the events of his own childhood. It would make sense, in a warped kind of way.'

'Bloody hell, son,' I can't help saying. 'Have you been talking to Rosie?'

He colours a little. 'Actually, we did discuss it while you were in the garden with Ben. I hope that wasn't breaking any rules. She is a forensic psychologist now, after all.'

Much to his consternation, I burst out laughing. 'Jesus! What kind of family are we?' Hard on that thought, another follows. No wonder Chrissie's decided she wants to be well away from it all.

He gives me a rueful grin. 'Yeah, I know. But if that *is* what's happening, it must mean there are more victims. We've got the box full of what are probably reminders of the women he's "chosen" from age sixteen to the present day. So where did they come from? He must be selecting his victims to some sort of timetable. Suppose he abducts girls at a certain age, keeps them until they are at the age when his mother dies, or at least disappears, then he makes them disappear in the same way?'

He's got a point. 'Okay, but that doesn't explain Millie. What if he only originally abducted one girl, and he's been breeding his victims ever since? He waits until the daughter is old enough, gets her pregnant, then kills the mother as soon as she hits the critical age?' I realise as I say this, that if true, it's even more warped and much harder to verify.

'I don't think so.' He shakes his head. 'If that were the case, there wouldn't be so many trophies in the box – the timescale involved wouldn't fit. Plus, don't forget, Millie's mother wasn't his daughter – Jimmy Harris was the father. What if he can't have children, or has – you know – sexual difficulties. Maybe he got Harris to have sex with Millie's grandmother as some kind of last resort? And add to that, the DNA profile of the person who handled the contents of the box doesn't match the profile from Millie.'

He's right. My mind suddenly switches up a gear. 'Jimmy Harris was a known homosexual,' I say, half to myself. 'Both Tyler and Shark Johnson have said as much. But suppose he was paid to provide sperm, to a sperm bank perhaps, and

Kenny Hughes got hold of it? And suppose Hughes also used a donor for Millie's mother? For some reason – God only knows what – he wants children, and that's the driving force behind the abductions. But maybe he can't – he's possibly impotent, so he's been forced to use another method.'

'But until around twenty years ago, sperm banks were hard to come by unless referred by health services, and it might not have occurred to him to go down that route,' Larson puts in. 'So he takes women, tries to get them pregnant, and murders them when it fails. And because he only wanted a female child to fulfil the pattern, he got rid of the boy.' He takes a slug of his coffee and meets my eye. 'But if that's the case, why leave it so long? Why not kill the male child at birth?'

'A good point,' I say, 'and a question we can't answer – yet.' Another thought occurs to me. 'Wait a minute – he was detained in Wye Cross for a couple of years. That means he would have had contact with a fair few delinquents and gang members back then and may well have kept up with them after his release. It's reasonable to assume he'd have knowledge of who was who in local gang circles, get some of them to do the odd job for him now and then. That makes it more conceivable he might have had a private deal with Harris, which will make proving anything more difficult. It doesn't mean he didn't try official channels first, though, so it's worth a shot. Plus, we need to know where – and who – he's been before. That might not be easy.'

'Didn't Evans say Kenny Hughes's father had been married before?' Larson asks. 'If we could find the half-brother, it could at least give us a clue as to the area Iain Hughes was in before he moved to Chepstow. Perhaps Iain's former wife is still around. That's worth checking too.'

'You're damned right it is,' I reply, looking at my son-in-law with fresh eyes. 'I don't know about you, but I'm knackered. Let's get the troops going on it in the morning before we head back to Chepstow.'

He smiles. 'See you tomorrow, Chief Inspector.'

At the door I take a chance. 'John,' I say, and at once he takes a step back, eyebrows arching. I take a deep breath. There's no point messing about. 'Has Chrissie – you know – got someone else?'

He turns a little pale, but looks me in the eye. 'The truth? I don't know. She's been going out a lot recently, but I swear to you, I've no idea where or what for. I asked Rosie, and she put the barriers up – told me not to ask. Joyce did the same.' He shrugs. 'I don't know what to say except that I'm as much in the dark as you are. That's the honest truth. But whatever she's doing,' he adds, 'I'm sure she'll tell us when she's ready.'

I believe him. I step outside. 'See you in the morning.' There's nothing more to say.

17

After a quick meeting with Grace and Sillitoe, during which we agree to add finding Iain Hughes's former wife and son to the priority list, and put Ollie to work investigating sperm banks, Larson and I set off. We're in Chepstow by 9 a.m. to be told Forbes and his team are already out at Wye Cross. Dave Evans is waiting for us, and half an hour later we're all standing around The Old Farm's septic tank, watching two figures suiting themselves up in protective clothing while a 4x4 unloads a pile of cutting equipment onto the brambles. Thankfully, we don't have to repeat the previous day's long trek from the road, as a path has been cleared for police vehicles, and the gate opened to allow us through. Forbes trots across to join us, accompanied by Phil the Tea lugging a rucksack, from which he pulls two huge flasks and plastic cups.

'Coffee and milk,' he explains, pointing to the flasks. He does a bit more delving and comes up with a handful of sugar sachets.

Forbes grins. 'Good morning,' he says, unscrewing the

flask, filling five cups and handing them round. 'Might as well be comfortable while we're waiting. The drainage chap says he'll be ready any minute now, and there's a forensics officer to watch him in case there's anything down there we don't want disturbed. The records show the tank was flushed back in 1979, so with a bit of luck, it won't be too bad once we get it open.' He licks a finger and sticks it in the air, like an overgrown Boy Scout. 'Good,' he adds. 'We're upwind – and it looks like they're getting started.'

We sip our coffee and watch as the engineer gets to work on the tank's inspection hatch. It should be rusted solid after forty years of disuse, but our suspicions are confirmed when the thing lifts open smoothly with barely a squeak. The five of us exchange looks. The tank has been opened recently, and there's not much doubt as to who will have opened it.

'That's one question answered,' Larson mutters as the man grabs a torch from his belt, turns it on and sticks his head down the shaft.

A second later, he jerks to his feet and waves frantically to the second investigator, who hurries up to join him, takes a look down the hole and reacts the same way, almost dropping her torch. She takes a step backwards on unsteady legs, and for a minute I think she's going to faint. Thankfully, she recovers herself and starts to make her way over to us.

'Well,' Forbes remarks dryly, 'whatever's in there, I think we can safely assume it's more than a pile of shit.' He digs in his jacket and pulls out a small hip flask as the woman comes up to us, tearing off her mask and pushing back her hood. She's pale-faced, beads of sweat on her forehead. 'Here,' he says, unscrewing the flask and thrusting it into her hand. 'For medicinal purposes – I won't tell if you don't.'

She takes a swallow, and I catch the scent of brandy.

After a short pause she nods and hands the flask back. 'Thanks.' She shakes her head. 'Sorry about that. I'll be fine.'

'I'm sure you will – don't worry about it,' Forbes replies, stashing the flask back in his inside pocket. 'Just take your time.' He turns to us. 'This is Meera Kumar,' he says, giving her a pat on the shoulder. 'I'm afraid she drew the short straw this morning.' She holds out a hand, and Larson and I introduce ourselves. 'I take it there's something of interest down there, Meera?' he asks after she's had time to take a couple of deep breaths.

She nods, then screws her eyes shut as if trying to banish an unpleasant image. We all wait, giving her time. 'I'm sorry,' she says finally. 'It was just a bit of a shock, that's all. Not a very pleasant one, I'm afraid. If we want to investigate properly, we're going to have to take the entire top of the tank off and get a team down there.'

'To investigate what?' Forbes asks gently, managing by some miracle to keep the impatience we're all feeling out of his voice.

She swallows. 'Bodies, Inspector. I mean, not just bodies – there are bones – piles of bones.' She shakes her head. 'I've never seen anything like it. It's ...' she searches for a word, and ends with, 'unbelievable.'

There's a long silence until finally Forbes scratches his head and mutters, 'Oh, shit!' Then, 'Sorry. No pun intended.'

'How many?' I ask. 'Can you give us an estimate?'

'It's hard to say,' Meera replies. 'But, at a rough guess, maybe half a dozen, possibly more. They are all at different stages of decomposition by the look of it, and very carefully placed. It's as if someone has constructed their own sort of mausoleum, with different groupings – I only caught a glimpse, but even so, I could see a method of sorts. We won't know more until we can get decent access.'

Forbes glances at me. 'We ought to take a look,' he suggests, his tone less enthusiastic than usual. Then, to Meera, 'Do we have any spare suits?'

'A couple, I think,' she replies, and goes off to root through the back of the van.

Dave Evans, who has so far said nothing, lets out a groan and sinks back against the crumbling remains of a dry-stone wall. 'I don't understand it,' he mumbles. 'The place was searched – why didn't anyone think to look in there? God, what a mess!'

Forbes goes across to him at once and puts a hand on his arm. 'Maybe it was searched,' he says. 'We don't know yet how long those bodies have been there. But, even so, you can't blame yourself. You were a lowly PC in those days, not the senior investigating officer. If something was missed, it will be down to whoever was in charge. Besides, if what you've told us is true, there was no indication that any crime had taken place aside from leaving a child to fend for himself.' His brow furrows; then he says, 'In fact, it's my bet that whatever is in the tank now was put in later. Kenny Hughes was found alone in the house in 1978, right?'

Evans nods. 'That's right, and the search for the parents began straight away – it would have been towards the end of August.'

'And the records tell us the tank was flushed in 1979 – the following year. So even if it had been opened during the search, nothing would have been found. Kenny Hughes – if it was him, and if Iain and Janet Hughes are in there – must have come back and disposed of the bodies in the tank later, after it had been pumped out.'

'But your officer says there are more than two sets of remains,' Larson adds. He thinks for a minute and then goes on, 'Maybe he only realised he had the perfect dumping ground after the tank was emptied. He stashes the bodies until he has the opportunity to move them, then brings them here.'

It's a decent explanation. 'So what about the victims in Bristol?' I ask. 'Two were there for twenty years, and the third at least two, according to Maggie. Why didn't he move those sooner? Why wait all this time?'

There's a long silence while we try to come up with an answer. It's Forbes who finally snaps his fingers and announces, 'Got it!' We all look at him. 'Because the tank was full,' he says. 'If I read Kenny Hughes right, he's crazy in all sorts of ways, and one of them is a severe case of OCD. I mean, look at the cottage, the obsessive cleaning and tidying. If he'd thought about it for a minute, he would have realised it was a dead giveaway. He probably did, but couldn't help himself. These septic tanks are smaller than you'd think, I'd guess no more than six feet square. Meera said the remains were set out with care, as if it were a mausoleum. So to get his corpses into the exact position he wanted them, he'd have to wait until the state of decomposition allowed him to add another. He probably aimed to move your Bristol bodies eventually, but something spooked him, and he was forced to leave them where they were.'

He steps away, punching a number into his mobile, presumably to request more forensic backup. Meera makes her way back to us, carrying a bundle of protective clothing.

'Just two suits until the rest of the team gets here,' she says. 'Who wants them?'

I give Larson a questioning look, and he shakes his head. 'Be my guest.'

Forbes stows his phone and grabs one of the bundles. I take the other. A few minutes later we're crouching over the inspection hatch, shining torches down into what can only be described as a mass grave.

'Dear God!' Forbes hisses under his breath. 'Meera's right – there must be at least half a dozen here. And look at how they are laid out. I've never seen anything like it.'

'Neither have I,' I say.

The bodies are closely set into two neat rows, the heads of the first row pointing in the opposite direction to the second. The width of the tank can't be more than three or four feet, the length around six feet, and the effect is a little like a tightly packed can of sardines. I had expected to smell sewage, but the overriding stench is of dead, decaying flesh. Just once in my career I've attended an exhumation, and the unmistakeable smell of the rotting corpse as the coffin was opened is one I will never forget. I grit my teeth and force myself to examine the arrangement more closely.

'At the risk of stating the obvious, it looks like the most recent victims have been laid over the older ones,' Forbes says, jabbing his metal pointer over the hatch. 'The ones at the bottom are completely decomposed and could well have been there since the end of the 1970s or early '80s. The top ones are – well – shall we just say more recent?'

I nod. 'Less than twenty years, would you say?'

'I would,' he replies, pointing to one of the uppermost bodies. 'I'd guess this one is no more than ten years old, possibly much less. We won't know for sure until the forensic team's had a good root about.'

'Oh, Christ!' I pull out my phone and, after a couple of

tries, manage to stab the right number through my plastic gloves. Sillitoe answers. 'Have the SOCOs finished at Oakfield Road yet?' I ask.

'Almost,' she replies. 'Last I heard, they were going to start packing up this afternoon. No more bodies, thank goodness.'

'There's a reason for that,' I say grimly. 'There *were* bodies – one at least, but he moved it. I'm willing to bet I'm looking at it right now. Get onto the team, Polly, and ask them to go over everything again, and to assume there are more possible sites in the house and garden. If they find any space that might have been used to hide a victim for, say, a year or more, they need to go over it for traces even if it looks squeaky clean.'

'Boss – are you sure? They're not going to like it.'

'I don't give a damn if they like it or not, as long as they bloody well do it,' I tell her. 'I'll explain when I get back, although God knows when that will be. I need to stay here until we've got some sort of liaison set up, especially between the forensic teams here and at home. If anything else comes through, let me know straight away.'

'Will do, boss,' she says, and hangs up without any further questions.

Forbes has been waiting patiently, and now jabs his pointer again, shining his torch down its length. I follow the beam to the bottom of the tank, where a small fragment of rotted cloth is just about visible. I nod to indicate that I've seen it, and he moves the pointer up to another section of cloth, larger this time and slightly less decayed. The newest bodies, at the top, make it obvious.

'Now we know,' he says, 'why he wanted all those identical dresses.'

We exchange a look, the craziness and the horror hitting us both at the same time. 'Jesus,' I manage after a long pause. 'I've seen some things, but ...'

'Yes,' he says, wiping a hand across his brow. 'What kind of bloody madman are we dealing with?'

18

The operation to open up the septic tank completely takes well over two hours of painstaking cutting and drilling by engineers, watched over by an eagle-eyed forensic team. The pathologist, Douglas Fitzjohn, a lanky man in his forties with thick spectacles and a goatee beard, spends the time bobbing up and down impatiently on the balls of his feet, punctuating this little dance with frequent jerks of his arms and hissing intakes of breath at every puff of dust or debris from the sections as they are meticulously removed.

As the last chunks of earth and concrete are finally cleared, Forbes, Larson and I, suitably kitted out, are allowed to move forward to join Fitzjohn and a team of half a dozen SOCOs near the rim of the tank. I feel Larson, wedged in next to me, shudder as he catches his first sight of the contents, and I turn to him, raise a questioning eyebrow. He's gone as white as a sheet, but manages to give me a nod. The remains visible from the inspection hatch are now fully exposed, and even the forensic officers have stopped in their tracks, silent, staring at the horror of it all. For a full minute the only sound is of one poor devil who, unable to cope, is busy vomiting his breakfast into the brambles.

For me and Jerry Forbes, already knowing what to expect, it isn't the sight of the mass grave that makes us freeze. The tank has two compartments. The second is much smaller, what the engineer has described as a pump chamber to release clarified liquid from the tank into the surrounding soil. Inside this second space, a perfectly reconstructed skeleton has been propped against the rear wall in a sitting position, giving just enough room for the legs to be stretched out along the width of the tank. The arms have been carefully placed in the lap. If all this isn't bizarre enough, it's wearing clothes – what looks like an intact, unstained dress in the same fabric as all the others, and a green ribbed sweater. Poked through the fingers of the skeletal hands is the stem of a single, shrivelled rose.

Forbes doesn't speak, but points to something just above the skull. I squint along the line of his pointer and can just make out a mesh of fine, almost invisible wires snaking up the wall of the tank. We look more closely and pick out more running across the floor. I realise, with a small shock, that the wires are attached to specific parts of the skeleton – shoulders, head and the articulated joints – turning it into some kind of macabre puppet.

'What the bloody hell ...?' I mutter, half to myself.

Forbes rubs his chin, considering. 'Look at the bones,' he says in a low voice. 'They've been cleaned. The other victims, the ones in the main chamber, have simply been left to rot, but not this one. It looks like the whole skeleton has been deconstructed, each bone bleached and polished, possibly even coated with some kind of sealant, and then the whole thing put back together, just as you would if you were making one up for a lab in a medical school. If you look carefully, you can see where screws and wires have been inserted to keep the bones in place.'

My eyesight isn't as good as his, and I have to peer into the space for several seconds before I spot the glint of a brass screw embedded in one of the ankles. 'What about the other wires?' I ask, puzzled.

As we've been talking, Larson has crouched down to join us. 'The inspection hatch for this compartment was much smaller, according to the engineer,' he explains. 'It was too small for him to get down there to arrange the body, so he attached wires to all the joints so that he could manipulate it into the pose he wanted from the surface.' He shakes his head. 'It must have been really difficult to do, and taken him a long time – like putting a ship in a bottle.'

'At first, yes,' Forbes puts in. 'But he's been taking it out regularly to put new clothes on it, place a flower in its hand and put it back in precisely the same position. My guess is he's been doing it on a certain date every year – the anniversary of the death, do you think?'

'And if this is – or was – his mother,' I add, 'he's been coming back to tidy her up every year for at least forty years.'

Forbes smiles grimly. 'That's one hell of a lot of practice.'

Our musings are interrupted by Fitzjohn, who walks up to us, flapping his arms in a shooing motion. 'Move along, please, gentlemen,' he says in a high-pitched squeak, glaring at us through fogged spectacles. 'We've got a lot to get through if we want to get this lot sorted out before dark.'

We do as we're told, and leave the forensic team to get on with the unenviable process of cataloguing, measuring and finally removing all the remains from both the tank's chambers.

'What now?' Larson asks as we make our way back to where Dave Evans and DC Jones are waiting.

'Back to the station,' Forbes replies. 'You've got three victims so far, and I'd say we've got at least six here if not more, and they may not all be local. I suggest our first move is to set up an official cross-border investigation to make it easy for our two forces to work together. I've already been in touch with Uncle Freddie, and he's setting up an online meeting with your people as we speak. Once that's done, we can make sure we're not wasting time duplicating avenues of inquiry.'

I nod my agreement. 'After that, I'd say we've got a list of priorities longer than the bridge across the Bristol Channel,' I comment. 'It's my guess his victims were abducted as young girls, so they are likely to be listed as missing, but we don't know where from or precisely when. It's going to be like finding a bunch of needles in a proverbial haystack. We've got a half-brother with no name, and a former wife who's probably dead by now. And, of course, we're still looking for Hughes, who has likely changed his name again already, and Millie, whose most recent photo is at least two years old.'

'That's not all we've got,' Larson reminds me. 'The photos in the box are still being cleaned up. We've managed to get clear reconstructions of two of the victims' faces, and the lab has been working on the others. With luck, we might be able to get good approximations of more victims and then run them through the missing persons database to see if any matches turn up.'

Forbes turns to my son-in-law with a surprised, but appreciative look. 'You really think that's possible? From what the chief inspector's said, those photographs are pretty much beyond repair.'

'If it's possible,' I butt in, 'this is the man to do it. As soon as we find out what we've got, he'll be on it full time.'

'Good. I'd offer some resources from here, but ...' Forbes jerks a thumb towards the activity behind us. 'We're going to have our hands pretty full for the next few days. Meanwhile, let's get this meeting out of the way so we can all get on with it.'

With that, he heads off to the 4x4 parked on the slope by the cottage, and we follow, glad to put some distance between us and the tank's gruesome contents.

BACK AT THE POLICE STATION, a video call has been set up between ourselves, CC Gosford, Grace, Sillitoe and ACC Forbes, who has made the trip to Chepstow from Newport. The similarity between him and his nephew is striking. Both are tall and lanky, with the same blond hair and Roman nose, and when the ACC speaks, it's with the same clipped public school accent. P. G. Wodehouse, I think to myself, could easily have based the character of Bertie Wooster on a Forbes ancestor. The greeting between the two could not have been more formal, Jerry Forbes, deliberately at attention, addressing his superior officer as 'Sir,' while his uncle's response of 'Good to see you, Inspector,' is delivered deadpan, although not without a glint of humour in the eyes.

ACC Forbes turns to us. 'Chief Inspector Crow, I'm delighted to meet you. Your reputation precedes you over here, but in a good way, I assure you. And Mr Larson – quite a technology expert, I'm told.' He finally cracks a smile. 'Well, between the four of us, this is quite a family gathering.' The smile vanishes. 'But, sadly, not under the best of circumstances. Shall we get on with it?'

We all file through to a small office, where an officer I haven't met is busy connecting a laptop to a large screen on the wall. He looks up as we enter, and stands to attention. Forbes Jnr introduces him as Detective Sergeant Peters.

'Our equivalent of your Mr Larson here,' he says with a grin.

'I doubt that,' Peters replies, blushing slightly. 'Computers are just a hobby for me – can't compete with the professionals!'

My son-in-law simply smiles, colouring a little himself.

'Okay,' I suggest. 'If we've finished with the mutual appreciation society, are we ready to get down to business?'

'Quite right,' Jnr agrees as his uncle settles himself at the head of the table in front of the large screen, me on his right, his nephew to the left. Larson sits next to me, and Peters fires up the conference app, then hovers in a corner.

A moment later, the screen comes to life, and a similar arrangement appears, CC Gosford flanked by Grace and Sillitoe. The two senior officers exchange polite greetings, there's a round of introductions, and ACC Forbes defers at once to Gosford, the higher-ranking officer.

'I think we are all aware of the extreme gravity of the situation,' he begins, with his usual talent for stating the bloody obvious. 'From our point of view, it's likely that the burial site on your patch contains victims who were murdered on ours. I understand Chief Inspector Crow has requested an additional forensic search of the property in Oakfield Road, and I can confirm that we are currently seeking evidence of further crimes in the house and garden.

We have issued a nationwide alert to all forces concerning Hughes, aka Drake, and his daughter. In addition—'

Gosford's summary is interrupted by a scuffle in the background, and DC Ollie White appears briefly on the screen, flushed with excitement. He thrusts a note into Sillitoe's hand and hovers behind her, fidgeting impatiently until the chief constable gives him a warning glare, and he retreats out of view. There's a pause while Sillitoe reads the note and passes it to Gosford, who does likewise and hands it on to Grace. Eventually, Gosford clears his throat and turns back to the webcam, clearly surprised.

'Well,' he says, a note of excitement in his voice, 'it seems that whoever is in your septic tank, Iain Hughes isn't among them. DC White here has managed to trace him. He's still alive, in his nineties, resident in a nursing home just outside Cardiff.'

Forbes Jnr and I exchange a look, which doesn't go unnoticed by Uncle Freddie. 'Might I suggest Forbes and Chief Inspector Crow get down there as soon as this meeting is concluded?' he says. 'Assuming Hughes is compos mentis, he may have valuable information.'

Gosford nods. 'I'd like Mr Larson back here, though, as soon as possible. We need to get back to work on the analysis of the photographs from Oakfield Road, and DC White has his hands full trawling through the records trying to trace the previous wife and son. Hopefully, that may not be necessary once we've spoken to Iain Hughes.'

It's Grace's turn to pipe up. 'It might also be a good idea to share forensic resources,' she says, 'given the possible number of victims you have. Professor Ainsworth and Professor Fitzjohn will get through the job quicker if they work together.'

'Excellent.' ACC Forbes smiles. 'We'll get some of the bodies transported over to your lab, and the rest to Fitzjohn's in Newport. It's likely to take a while to get everything catalogued, so in the meantime I'll tell Fitzjohn to send one of his assistants over to liaise with Professor Ainsworth straight away – she can give Mr Larson a lift while she's at it.'

The meeting carries on for another few minutes, sorting out the fine details, and then the link terminates. ACC Forbes lets out a long breath.

'At least your lot are offering to help with the forensics,' he says, giving me the same crooked grin I've seen several times on his nephew's face. 'I hope they are quicker than ours. Still, Doug Fitzjohn hasn't had a case like this for years, maybe never, and when I saw him this morning, he was jumping around as if he'd been poked in the rear end with a bayonet.'

'Don't worry about Maggie Ainsworth,' I say. 'She's dropped everything for this one, and between them, we should have some results through pretty quickly.'

He holds out a hand. 'I look forward to working with you, Chief Inspector.'

'Likewise,' I reply, and he sweeps out of the room, leaving me, Jerry Forbes and Larson blinking at each other.

My mobile pings – a text from Sillitoe giving the address of the nursing home. I show it to Forbes, who groans. 'Jesus! That's probably the worst care home in Wales. It's been subject to five court proceedings in the last two years – a wonder it hasn't been closed down.' He sighs. 'Ah, well, I suppose I'd better tell them we're coming so they have time to spray some disinfectant round the place.' He turns to Larson. 'I'll let the front desk know where you are. Knowing Uncle Freddie, he'll have someone already on the way to pick you up. There'll be time for a coffee, though, if you want one. The canteen is down the corridor, third on the left.'

Larson nods. 'I guess I'll see you later,' he says to me. 'Do you want me to ask Joyce to hang onto Bluebell tonight?'

I suddenly feel like a bad parent neglecting a favourite child, and that sends my mind back to the days on the beat when I regularly arrived home in the early hours and only ever saw Rosie when she was asleep.

'No,' I tell him. 'I'll come back as soon as I've finished at the nursing home. I'll pick her up by nine at the latest.'

While we've been talking, Forbes has been on his mobile. 'Okay,' he says, jerking his head towards the door, 'let's go.' Under his breath, he mutters, 'And if anyone offers you a cup of tea, I'd advise you to politely decline.'

19

My first impression of Cedar Grove nursing home is that it fits DI Forbes's assessment perfectly. The building probably started out as someone's red-brick suburban mansion house, a mass of classic gable windows and a wide entrance porch enclosed by a pergola that might once have been smothered in climbing roses or honeysuckle. Now, not much of the pergola is left standing, and what remains is a tangle of rotted planks hanging from rusted nails around the scuffed and peeling entrance door. The view from the ground-floor windows is obscured by half a dozen or so industrial waste bins, some of which are overflowing with God knows what. I try to keep my eyes fixed on the path.

Forbes voices the thought in both our minds. 'May the Lord preserve us from ever ending up in a place like this,' he mutters as he reaches for the security intercom.

'Amen to that,' I answer, 'although I doubt any of the poor buggers in here have had any choice.' I can't help thinking that just a few years ago I was on the verge of spending my final years washed, dressed and wheeled around by strangers, listening to an endless stream of private gossip between nurses treating me as if I were already dead – in other words, a shining example of the perils of making a career in the police force.

Forbes presses the buzzer and, after a long wait, is rewarded by a shrill female voice demanding our credentials. He announces us, and the door lock clicks open. He puts on the kind of non-committal expression that I can never quite manage in situations like this, and we go inside, into a wide hall with a reception desk to the right of the door, a staircase to the left. The stench of disinfectant is almost overpowering, and a yellow hazard notice propped on the grey vinyl floor announces 'Wet Floor'. Forbes throws me an *I told you so* glance, then, following protocol, nods for me, as senior officer, to take the lead.

I step up to the desk, from behind which a middle-aged woman in a beige uniform is giving us a blank, unwelcoming stare. 'Chief Inspector Crow,' I say, although she must already know who we are, since she let us in, 'and Inspector Forbes. We telephoned you earlier.'

There's a short pause, during which she looks us up and down as if we're candidates for residency, then scrapes back her chair and gets to her feet, but remains firmly planted behind her desk.

'You asked to see Mr Hughes,' she says. 'May I ask the reason? He's a very old man, in delicate health, and we wouldn't like to think of him being upset. We take our duty of care towards him very seriously.'

At this, Forbes, standing behind me, manages to smother whatever retort he was going to make with a cough.

'I'm afraid I can't tell you the reason for our visit, Mrs …'

Forbes deliberately leans forward across the desk to scrutinise the name badge pinned to her collar. Not politically correct, but effective. She tries to take a step back, is blocked by her chair and flops down into it. 'Ah, forgive me – *Miss* Turner.' He straightens up. 'I assure you, Mr Hughes is not in any trouble as far as we know. He's simply helping with our enquiries. We won't take up much of his time, I promise you, and I'm sure you wouldn't want to obstruct the police in the course of their duties ...'

'All right, all right,' she says, holding up her hands in defeat. She shoots back to her feet and finally makes it out from behind the desk. 'He's in the day room at present, if you'd like to follow me.'

She struts down the corridor, pumps squeaking on the vinyl, to a large, shabby room containing, on one side, a selection of armchairs and sofas that look like they're fresh from the recycling centre, clustered round a TV pumping out a daytime soap, the volume so low I doubt any of the smattering of residents watching can hear it. The other half is taken up by a couple of Formica-topped tables dating, I guess, from the 1960s, one of which is piled with a selection of board games. In the far corner, in a gap between two of the rubbish carts we passed on our way in, a very elderly man in a wheelchair is staring out at the world outside.

Miss Turner jabs a finger in his direction. 'That's Mr Hughes,' she informs us. 'I'd be grateful if you didn't keep him too long. As I said, his health is poor, and his medication is due in half an hour. We've told him to expect you.'

'While we're with him,' I tell her, 'we'd be grateful if you could dig out the details of his next of kin.'

Her response is a derisive snort. 'He hasn't got a next of

kin. That type never do.' With that, she turns and squeaks her way back to the reception desk.

'Duty of care? Jesus bloody Christ!' I comment under my breath.

'Agreed,' Forbes replies. 'Well, I suppose we'd better get on with it. I was hoping the poor sod's still got his brain cells intact, but given where he is, I'm not so sure that would be a good thing.'

We advance on the wheelchair, not quite knowing what to expect, but only need to get halfway before he turns to us, and it's clear from the glint in his eye and the knowing grin that whatever else Iain Hughes might be suffering from, his mind is still razor sharp.

'I was wondering when you lot would turn up,' he says before either of us has a chance to speak.

'Really?' I ask, and hold out a hand. 'I'm Chief Inspector Crow, Bristol police, and this is Inspector Forbes, from Chepstow. Why would you have been wondering that, Mr Hughes?'

He ignores both my hand and the question, gripping the rims of his wheels. With a supreme effort, he manages to turn the chair round. 'Get me out of this bloody room, why don't you? They won't let us into the grounds on our own – health and safety, they say. Health and safety, my arse! Just damned lazy, the lot of them. They can't argue with a couple of policemen though, can they?' He makes another wheezing effort and inches dangerously close to my feet.

Forbes slips neatly behind him and takes the handles of the wheelchair. 'Lead on, Mr Hughes,' he says brightly. 'I'm sure with your help, we can all sneak out the back way.'

This draws a chuckle from Hughes, and he directs us down a maze of narrow corridors to a steel fire door at the back of the building. I push the bar, and we troop out onto a concrete yard cluttered with yet more bins, this time for kitchen waste, swapping the smell of disinfectant for the odour of overboiled cabbage. In the centre of the yard an ancient, solitary oak tree shelters a couple of wooden benches facing out towards a busy main road, an outlook infinitely preferable to that of the institution behind us. Hughes waves us to the benches, and we sit, hidden from view by the oak's thick trunk. He takes in a deep breath and lets it out slowly, savouring the air, fresh but for the diesel fumes from vehicles queueing at the traffic lights just along the road.

'You don't seem surprised to see us,' I say when we're all settled.

His response is an amused grunt. 'I was starting to place bets on who'd get to me first – you or the grim reaper. Looks like you just about beat him to it, no thanks to the bastards in here. I reckon that bitch Turner's taking backhanders from the council to get rid of us old folk and save them a packet running shit heaps like this.'

'That's a serious accusation, Mr Hughes,' Forbes points out. 'Can you provide any evidence?'

'I bet I could if I could get this bloody contraption,' he slaps his wheelchair, 'through her office door. She's put an extra inch of frame all the way round to stop us inmates getting in.'

'Really?' Forbes raises an eyebrow. 'I'll be sure to check on that on the way out. I'm sure it'll be in breach of some building regulation or other.'

'To get back to business,' I say, injecting a slight edge into my tone, 'perhaps you'd like to tell us why you were expecting a visit from the police?'

'Well, let's see ...' Hughes turns his gaze skyward, stroking his chin in mock thought. 'It could be sex with a minor – although you're getting on for sixty years too late with that one. Or poaching wild pigs in the Forest of Dean? I'm afraid I barbequed the last of them a good while ago, so you're a bit stuck for evidence there. So my guess is it's not me you're after. You've finally cottoned on to Kenny, and you think I might know where he is, right?'

'And do you?' I ask. 'Know where Kenny is?'

He snorts his contempt. 'Do I buggery! And believe me, if I did, I'd be the first to hand you a gun and tell you to go and shoot the little shit. The last time I laid eyes on him, he was thirteen years old, and he was a nasty little beggar even at that age. He's had plenty of time to get a lot worse since those days. What's he done, then? Finally killed somebody? I wouldn't be surprised. It was bound to happen sooner or later.'

I open my mouth, but Forbes jumps in. 'We'd like to know a little bit more about Kenny, if you're up to it,' he says, keeping his tone sympathetic, encouraging – the perfect 'good cop'. 'What was he like as a child? How did he get on with you and his mother? Whatever you can tell us will help.'

Hughes shakes his head, but in despair rather than refusal. I have to admit that he isn't what I expected. He may have been a rogue in his day, rough at the edges, but the description Dave Evans gave of his character doesn't quite ring true. I don't feel as if I'm looking at a real criminal or an abusive father. Rather, Iain Hughes is a man who may have bent the law now and then to keep his head above water, but who, ultimately, was judged by the attitudes of his time towards socially deprived itinerant workers and their families, betrayed by the authorities and family alike, and condemned to end his days in the modern equivalent of the poor house.

When he speaks, his tone has lost its abrasive edge, and he seems to shrink into the chair, his gaze drifting to his knees as he travels back into what is clearly a painful past.

'Worst mistake I ever made,' he says, rubbing a hand across his brow, 'leaving Carrie, going off with Janet. We were doing all right, me, Carrie and little Danny. We weren't rich, but we had enough to get by. I made a decent living doing carpentry, a bit of electrical, you know, odd jobs round and about, and a bit of farm work too, when it was needed. The thing is, when we had Danny, things changed. Carrie, she – well, she was tired all the time, taken up with the baby, and all that – you know what I mean.' He looks up, searching our faces for understanding. 'Are you married?' he asks, directing the question at me. 'Got children?'

'Divorced,' I tell him. 'And yes, I have a daughter.'

'Ah.' He shrugs. 'You know what I mean, then.'

I resist the urge to say something I might regret. My impression of Hughes swerves again. He's been hiding something for a very long time, and we're about to hear a confession he hoped he'd never have to make – even to himself. Forbes shoots me a worried glance, and with an effort I straighten the fingers that have unconsciously formed into a fist. 'So,' I say, keeping my voice even, 'you weren't getting what you wanted at home, and you decided to look elsewhere?'

He looks away again. 'I was stupid. But not at first. It never entered my head, not until I got a call from this minister over in one of the villages outside Pontypool, wanting some work done on his chapel. It was around two weeks' worth and too far for me to travel every day, so he offered me bed and board. Things weren't so good between me and Carrie, and we agreed it would be good to have a bit of a break, so I took the job. Danny would have been just coming up to four by then and getting to be a bit of a handful – not that I didn't love him, of course. It's just, well, he never gave us any peace – kids don't at that age.'

'And that's when you met Janet?' Forbes asks, shunting the story along.

Hughes nods. 'Little Janet, the minister's daughter – all sugar and spice on the outside, but on the inside – I don't blame her, mind. Fourteen years old and stuck in a half-abandoned mining village in the Valleys, couldn't so much as sneeze without it got back to her parents, and they were proper God botherers. Most of the young lads had left, gone to find work in Swansea or Cardiff. She was lonely, and so was I, although I'm ashamed to say it. One thing led to another, and she ended up pregnant with Kenny. She refused to get rid of it, said I was her only way out, and if I didn't stand by her, take her away and look after her, she'd accuse me of rape, and as she was only fourteen, you know what that would have meant.'

He paused, shaking his head as if to shake the memories away. 'You've got to understand,' he says, a pleading look in his eyes. 'I didn't know, not till afterwards, how young she was. She looked twenty-one when she changed out of the awful clothes her parents dressed her in. They introduced her as their daughter, and they were quite elderly, so I assumed the kid was well over the age of consent. I fell for her lies, and, looking back, I know I should have done it different. But that's how it was back then. We had free love, communes, Jimi Hendrix, dope, and fuck the future. In the

Valleys, though, there weren't any miniskirts or pop concerts or women's lib or the pill. There was church on Sunday, warped Christian values, and the young people got out the minute they could. For the lads, it wasn't so hard, but the girls were stuck between a rock and a hard place, judged for wearing a skirt more than half an inch above the knee, beaten by their parents for having a lipstick in their handbag. No, I don't blame her for taking her chance, and I was the mug who fell for it.'

He pauses for breath, and I can see from Forbes's expression that we're thinking the same thing. Whatever excuses Iain Hughes has made to himself over the years, and whatever the circumstances, he's just confessed to having sexual intercourse with a minor. There's not a decent police officer in the country who wouldn't have been happy to see him sent down for at least ten years. If it had been my Rosie, he wouldn't have gotten as far as the courtroom, and it would have been me doing time for murder. We could charge him, given what he's told us, but given his age and state of health, he hasn't got more than a few months left at most. Added to that, without evidence of a genetic relationship between Kenny and Iain, all we have is an old man's recollection of events – in other words, hearsay.

'So you left Carrie and ran away with Janet and took the caretaker's job at Wye Cross?' Forbes asks.

Hughes sighs. 'Carrie left me, took the boy and went back up north to her parents. She remarried after the divorce, but we stayed in touch for a while, on account of Danny. Me and Janet rubbed along well enough. We weren't in love, but she was a sweet thing at the start and for a while was just happy to be away from her parents, doing for me, and Kenny when he came along. She was playing house, like a kid with a new toy, you know? I was sure she'd grow up, get tired of it, and of me, once the hard work started as Kenny got older. But she didn't. She and Kenny, they had this sort of – well, connection is the only way I can describe it. Not the normal way a mother is with a baby. This was different, and the older Kenny got, the closer they were. It was like I didn't exist; they were in their own world. I tried to be a dad to him, but he wouldn't have it. If I took him anywhere without her, he'd just scream and scream until we got home. The older he got, the worse things were.'

He stops, eyes closed, the silence stretching so long I think he's fallen asleep.

'Mr Hughes,' Forbes says gently, 'please, go on.'

The old man blinks and shifts in his chair. 'He must have been around five,' he goes on, 'when I found him in the woods behind the cottage. He'd made himself a sort of den out there, and he'd nicked a metal cage from the school garden – one of the fine mesh ones we used to keep rats and birds off the soft fruit. He'd got hold of this cat and had it in the cage. He was putting live rats in, two or three at a time, watching them fight. Rats can be nasty buggers if they're cornered, and the cat was badly bitten. I got the cat out and chased Kenny back into the house. I was boiling mad, but he hid behind Janet, and she said if I ever laid a finger on him, she'd go to the police and tell them I'd taken her off against her will, and kept her and Kenny locked up in the house all this time.'

'So to save your own skin, you looked the other way,' I say, 'while your son turned into a psychopath.' Despite struggling to keep my tone professional, I can't help but let a touch of contempt trickle into my voice.

Hughes bristles. 'You're the marriage guidance expert

now, are you? Police force branching out into social work, is it? From what you've told me, things didn't work out so well for you, either.'

Now I really do seriously consider thumping him, but Forbes says quickly, 'I'm sure you did your best under the circumstances, Mr Hughes. Please, do go on.'

Hughes snarls at me, grunts, then nods. 'Around that time, Carrie got a job, and she got back in touch to say Danny was eager to see me, and it would help her out if I could have him in the school holidays, as they were both working, and he wasn't old enough to be home alone. Janet wasn't too happy, but I figured it might even things out a bit, and maybe Danny would have a good influence on Kenny, him being an older brother and all. Me and Danny, we got on straight away, but Kenny hated him. He played all sorts of nasty tricks on him, tried to get him in trouble whenever he could. Janet had a little pottery figure she really loved – the one thing she brought with her from home. Kenny broke it and blamed Danny. Janet took his side as usual. One time he put broken glass in Danny's bed, and on another, cleaning fluid in his juice. I told Danny he should tell Carrie to make another arrangement, and I'd come and visit him in York instead, but he said no. He liked being in the countryside with me and said he could handle Kenny. It carried on like that for a few years, and all the time Kenny was growing up and getting worse. Janet couldn't see it – or if she did, she ignored it.'

He pauses, working himself up to something. After another sigh, he pulls himself together and carries on.

'Danny was fifteen, down for the summer holidays, and Kenny was just coming up to eleven. Kenny was up to his tricks, and Danny decided he'd had enough. They had a huge fight, out in the field, and Danny broke Kenny's nose. After that, things went quiet. Janet wouldn't hear a word against her boy. Kenny acted the innocent, said he forgave Danny, it was an accident, and they should make up, let it go. It was all crap, of course. He was up to something. So I kept my eyes open, and sure enough, the day before Danny was due to leave, I caught Kenny creeping downstairs in the middle of the night, to where Danny was sleeping. At first, I couldn't believe what was happening. The little shit had a hammer, and I saw him raise his arm, take a swing at Danny's head. I threw myself at him, managed to knock him sideways – the hammer caught Danny's skull, but didn't break it, thank God. I got him to hospital, and he had a dozen stitches and a concussion, but that's all.'

He shakes his head, as if he still can't bring himself to believe what he witnessed.

'Kenny was going to kill him,' he says. 'He was actually going to kill him. If I hadn't been there, Danny would be dead. God knows what Kenny thought he was going to do afterwards if he'd succeeded. Not even his mother would have been able to cover up that one! I should have called the police, had the bastard taken away, but Danny persuaded me not to. He knew Janet had a hold over me, and didn't want to risk her carrying out her threat and me being sent to prison. He went back to York straight from the hospital. From that moment, though, it was over between me and Janet. All I wanted was to get out of that house. To be honest, the pair of them deserved each other.'

'I stuck it for another couple of years – Kenny was at big school by then, and he seemed to calm down. He was a bright boy, if something took his fancy. Maybe he'd scared himself, realised he could have been put away for what he did to Danny. Anyway, it didn't last. It all blew up again when he was thirteen. He got in trouble for bullying; then he got caught trying to touch up a first-year girl – an eleven-year-old. She reported him, and he was lucky he didn't end up in juvenile court. I decided the time had come. I booked a couple of weeks' leave, told Janet I was going to get away by myself for a while. She was happy enough – we were hardly speaking by then. I left, and I never went back. I've not heard a word from either of them since, and I hope I never will. That's it. I don't know anything else, and I don't know where they are now – in hell, if there's any justice in the world. Maybe I'll find out soon enough. I've not got long, and I'll be glad to be out of it. Do what you like – I've got nothing more to say.'

There's a long silence; then Forbes asks, 'You're sure you have no idea where Kenny might have gone – a favourite place, somewhere he went when he wanted to be alone, for example?'

He gives a contemptuous snort. 'Favourite place? His favourite place was behind his mother's skirts. Find her, and you'll find him. As for where she is, I don't know, and I don't care, as long as it's away from me.'

'Mr Hughes,' I say carefully, 'I'm afraid we have a pretty good idea of where she might be. We've found a body, near to your old cottage at Wye Cross.' I decide it's probably not a good idea to give the details of what we've found, or precisely where. 'We believe it may be Janet, and, if so, she's been dead for a very long time – probably since just after you left. We also think Kenny may be responsible for her death, so you can understand it's very important we find him. He has a young girl with him, and she may be in danger. You're absolutely sure you have no idea where he might have gone?'

His head jerks up, the look in his eyes one of complete bewilderment, like a boxer who's just been floored by a killer punch.

'Janet's dead? And you're saying Kenny did it? But he wouldn't – he couldn't – not Janet ...'

I realise he's crying and mumbling between ragged breaths, 'All this time – all this time I thought ...' He shakes his head. 'I should never have left her. I shouldn't have gone, left her on her own. It's all my fault ...'

'We're very sorry, Mr Hughes,' Forbes says quietly. 'What about Danny? Do you know what happened to him, where he is now?'

But it's no good. Hughes carries on mumbling, lost in whatever hell he's been carrying around with him all these decades. There's a noise behind us, and we turn to see Miss Turner stomping across the yard towards us.

'Mr Hughes!' she shouts as she spots us, shrill as a banshee. 'I've told you before about—'

Her tirade is cut short by Forbes, who grabs her arm and leads her away, back towards the house. 'If I were you, Miss Turner,' he says in a tone I haven't heard him use before – quiet, but containing more than a hint of menace, 'I'd leave Mr Hughes for a while. He's just had some very bad news. I'm sure his medications can wait a few minutes. In the meantime, I suggest you go back inside and get on with' – he waves a hand vaguely in the air – 'well, whatever you have to get on with. I'm sure you must be very busy, and you wouldn't want Chief Inspector Crow and I to witness what might be interpreted as threatening behaviour towards one of your patients. That certainly wouldn't go down well with social services. We've given Mr Hughes our contact details, should he have any *further information* for us – you understand?'

Her mouth flaps soundlessly for a few seconds; then she turns and marches stiffly back inside.

'What an unpleasant woman,' Forbes remarks. 'I don't think we can do any more here, Chief Inspector, do you?'

I glance back at Hughes still hunched in his chair, weeping. 'We're done here,' I agree, and we follow the road back round to where we've left the car at the front entrance. As we make our way back to Chepstow, there's one thing Hughes told us that I can't get out of my mind. *The little shit had a hammer, and I saw him take a swing at Danny's head.* If that's true – and we need to find Danny Hughes to verify it – where does that leave Craig Tyler's appeal against his conviction for the murder of Jimmy Harris, never mind the two bodies under the shed at Oakfield Road? I just about manage not to voice my response to that.

20

Grace leans back in her chair and grabs a bottle of Scotch and three glasses from the bottom drawer of her filing cabinet. She pours three generous slugs, one each for herself, me and Sillitoe. We sip in silence until Sillitoe voices what we're all thinking.

'Do we really need to act on this?' she asks. 'I mean, all we've got is a wild story by an old man who probably can't remember what he did yesterday, never mind forty-odd years ago. We've got enough on our plates as it is, chasing after Kenny Hughes and trying to identify God knows how many dead bodies. We all know Craig Tyler deserves to be where he is, for goodness' sake.'

'Great idea,' Grace comments. 'And what do you think will happen when Carol Dodds finds out about it? If we can find Iain Hughes, so can she, and once he tells her that we know about Danny and did nothing, where does that leave us when it comes to the appeal? We'll be on a hiding to nothing, and you know it.'

'You're both forgetting one thing,' I say. 'It might not be

important to either of you, but it bloody well is to me. If I put somebody away, I want it to be for something they've actually done. Otherwise, what's the point? Tyler might be a toe-rag, and he's probably done more than he's been convicted for. But if I fucked up his arrest, I'll hold my hands up. That's the end of it. If you two don't want to play along, I'll sodding well do it on my own – and if that's the end of my career, so be it.'

Grace gives me a grim smile. 'Nobody is above the law,' she pronounces, then, with a pointed look at Sillitoe, 'especially not us. If you want to get any further in this force, you'd better bloody well remember it.'

Sillitoe blushes and mumbles, 'Yes, ma'am.'

'That doesn't mean I don't agree with you,' Grace says after a suitable pause. 'Tyler is a menace to society, and he deserves to be locked up for the rest of his natural life – which means we need to find some real evidence before we get well and truly screwed over by Dodds and her crew. Meanwhile, we add Danny Hughes to the list and make sure we get to him before they do. I know that means more work for us, but—'

She's interrupted by a tap at the door, and Larson pokes his head round. 'Sorry,' he says, 'but we've turned up a few things we thought you'd want to know about straight away.'

'Come on in and pull up a chair,' Grace says, reaching for the bottle. 'We could do with some positive news in here. Scotch?'

He comes in, eyeing me suspiciously. 'Aren't you driving?' he asks. 'And no, thanks, I'd better stick to coffee.' He waggles the mug in his hand.

'In that case,' I tell him, 'I'll have another, and you can give me a lift home.'

He sighs, but doesn't object, and flops down.

'Go on, then,' Grace says. 'Make our day.'

'Ollie and I have been liaising with forensics.' He grins. 'And they've just come through with an initial report. There were six bodies in the main part of the septic tank, plus the older one in the pump section. That makes ten altogether, with the three found in Bristol. All are female except for the infant male at Oakfield Road.'

'At least that means Danny isn't down there,' I put in. 'Given the way he works, I think it's safe to assume Kenny disposes of all his victims in the same way.'

'Hang on,' Sillitoe puts in. 'Isn't that a bit of a leap? Clearly, the two under the shed are different. Aren't you making another assumption – that Tyler killed the mother and child?'

'Polly's got a point,' Grace points out. 'Right now, we have no idea which victim belongs to which killer, so best to keep an open mind, yes?'

I hold up my hands. They're right, and yes, I'm making an assumption, even if, deep in my gut, I believe I'm right.

'Maggie did a quick scan of the skulls,' Larson continues, 'and none of them were killed by a blow to the head except for the two we know about – well, three if we include Jimmy Harris. They follow the pattern of the body found in the wall. No injuries, and possibly died of thirst or starvation, or at least from an injury that doesn't show up in the skeleton – they won't know for sure until more tests have been done. She says it's only a preliminary finding, and if there's anything different, she'll let us know. Oh – she also says the cat went the same way, and that it precedes the death of the woman found in the wall at Oakfield Road. She says it might be worth considering whether the cat was a sort of practice run to make sure things would work.'

'Hang on,' I say, piecing things together. Everybody waits. I get my thoughts in order and give it a try. 'Firstly, I doubt the cat was a practice run. It's my bet that at least some of the victims in the tank predate Kenny Hughes's purchase of Oakfield Road. If that's the case, there are other houses, either bought or rented under other aliases. We need to find the aliases and the other properties – with luck they will give us more forensic evidence and help us trace all the victims.'

'I may be able to help with that,' Larson interrupts. We all look at him. 'We've found Joseph Drake – or, to be more accurate, Ollie has. Joseph Drake was born in Reigate on the twentieth of June 1965. He died on the second of September in the same year and was buried in an existing family grave in Reigate cemetery. The family had dispensation to conduct a burial on account of his grandfather being a former curate of St Mary Magdelene church and so having a family plot. Kenny Hughes was born on the first of July 1965, and he's probably taking the identities of infants born around the same time and who only lived a week or two. Ollie is delving in the records now for possible candidates, but it could take a while, if we manage it at all. Infant mortality in 1965 was very similar to today, though, so the figures are quite low. Our main problem is that Hughes might have built up several identities over a number of years, and he might be using one now that he set up twenty or more years ago.'

'Good work,' Grace says. 'Tell DC White to keep it up. Any more on the photographs?'

'I was coming to that.' Larson hesitates and shoots me an uncertain look.

'Go on, son,' I tell him. 'Whatever you've got, I doubt things could get any bloody worse.'

'I wouldn't put money on it,' he replies. 'The thing is, the lab have managed to get some detail from all but one of them, and they've found images of nine distinct individuals. From the analyses they've done so far on the other items, ten sets of DNA have been identified, and one – presumably Kenny Hughes, appears on all the samples. The others are females. They haven't finished yet, so it's possible they will come up with more. If they do, it may mean we're missing more girls.'

There's a long pause, following which all I can think to say is, 'Shit!'

'Forensics haven't come up with anything else at Oakfield Road so far, either inside or outside,' he continues, 'which means if there are more bodies, they may have been left in another property or perhaps two properties.'

'Oh, that's marvellous!' Grace says. 'That means some poor sods somewhere are living neat, untroubled lives not knowing there are corpses behind their bedroom walls.'

'Wait a minute,' Sillitoe says. 'This doesn't make sense. Kenny Hughes was born into poverty, more or less, and spent his teenage years in a juvenile institution. Yet he flits round the country buying up property for cash – and not just any property. Oakfield Road may not be a leafy suburb, but houses in decent condition in the middle of Bristol come at a cost, and did even back then. Where the hell is he getting his money from? Robbing banks?'

My mind takes a sudden swerve. All the ideas that hadn't quite crystallised in my head come together and become a near certainty. I give silent thanks to little Joseph Drake lying in the family grave in Reigate. I also curse myself for not getting more information on Kenny's mother from Iain Hughes. Sillitoe is right – he's getting money from somewhere. He may not be robbing banks, but was he extracting cash from his grandparents – and possibly from the parents of his victims as well? I push that idea onto the back burner for now and move on to another that has just occurred to me.

'I might be losing it,' I say, 'but here's a theory. Iain Hughes takes a job working for an ultra-religious minister in some decaying backwater mining village. He meets the minister's sassy daughter, who's desperate to get out from under. She falls pregnant and blackmails him into helping her escape. This girl might be young, but she's no fool. Iain Hughes might be intelligent in his own way, but he can't compete. Janet twists him round her little finger, and when Kenny comes along, she makes sure she's got an ally. I mean, we don't even know if Kenny was Iain's child. She'd probably been planning her escape well before he came on the scene. He just happened to be in the right place at the right time.'

'Jesus, Al,' Grace comments. 'That's a bit of a leap.'

'Just hear me out,' I say. 'Iain falls for it, and he and Janet run away together. Kenny is born, and from that moment Iain's chances of making a go of it are zero. She isolates Kenny, raises him to be completely devoted to her, and antagonistic towards his father, and anyone else who gets in the way. Janet is the one in charge, and Kenny is her weapon. She probably encouraged his psychopathic nature – in effect, she made him what he is.'

'If that's true,' Sillitoe objects, 'why kill her? Your theory doesn't add up. He would have done anything to protect her, wouldn't he?'

'That's the part I haven't worked out yet,' I reply, 'but if

Janet's parents are still alive, I may be able to find out.' I pull out my mobile and call Forbes. He answers on the second ring.

'I'll call Cedar Grove right away,' he says, 'and if they make a fuss, I'll threaten them with environmental health. I'll get back to you as soon as I know anything.'

He hangs up, and I realise everyone is staring at me, waiting for me to carry on. 'Look,' I say, 'I'd like to think things through and do a bit more digging into Janet's background before I say any more – I'm still not sure I'm on the right track. But if the first part of the theory is right, and Janet did coerce Iain into taking her on, Kenny might have picked up a few blackmail tips from her and used them later on to keep himself solvent. Perhaps Iain Hughes can shed some light on that as well. Anyway, it's getting late, and I don't know about you, but I could do with some decent food and a good night's sleep.'

Nobody argues, so Grace wraps things up, and we agree to meet up first thing in the morning.

'What's the time, anyway?' I ask Larson as we make our way down to his car.

He consults his watch. 'Just gone nine thirty,' he says.

I let out a groan. 'Shit! It'll take at least twenty minutes to get over to Clifton.' I imagine the accusing look on Chrissie's face, the one that used to say, *Yeah, right. And Rosie was so looking forward to the school nativity play ...*

Jesus, am I still that much of an arsehole?

Larson shoots me a sly grin. 'Don't worry. Rosie took Blue to our place when she got back from their day out. She says she's kept something warm for us – if you want to come and eat, that is. Probably fish fingers – it's Alex's favourite at the moment.'

I feel tears start to prick my eyes. I really don't deserve Rosie or the man sitting next to me. What I do deserve is the fact that Chrissie is out on the town with some flashy bastard or other, making up for the lost years she endured with me. I swallow hard, and my predictable response is, 'Why not? We can have a go at tracing Janet's parents if Forbes comes up empty – if you're up to it, of course.'

'You're welcome,' Larson says, lips curling into the familiar, long-suffering smile.

21

If there's one thing I've learned over the years, it's that unconditional love tends to have conditions attached – except in one instance. Bluebell almost knocks me over in her joyful attempts to lick my face and stick her tongue in my ear. The fact that I abandoned her for almost two days is already, in her head, forgiven and forgotten. I wish I could forgive myself so easily. Once the mayhem has died down, and Blue is happy to alternate between chasing her tail and tangling herself in my legs, I make it to the kitchen, where Rosie is putting out plates of fish fingers and chips – cooked in an air fryer, she tells me as she gives me a hug, presumably to forestall any grumpy comments I might make about what Larson is letting her feed to my grandchildren.

'John told me what you found in Wales,' she says, sitting with us while we eat. 'It must have been awful.'

I throw Larson a glance, and he shrugs. I know how he feels. Being able to offload after the kind of experiences a murder squad detective gets confronted with is pretty much essential if you want to survive. Chrissie did her best, but was never able to take it in her stride. Rosie, on the other hand, is an altogether different proposition.

'Not the best,' I agree, managing to push down the feelings of envy and regret and giving her a smile. 'But we managed.'

Larson finishes his last mouthful. 'I'd better go and check in with Ollie, see how he's getting on,' he says, getting up and squeezing Rosie's shoulder as he makes his way out and up to his office room. Ollie White probably got his head down an hour ago. My son-in-law just wants to give me and Rosie some father-daughter time.

'I'll bring you some coffee,' she says, and once he's gone, she turns to me. 'I'm worried about him, Dad. Is he really doing okay?'

'Better than I thought he would,' I reply, for once unable to give anything but an honest opinion of my son-in-law. 'What we saw in that tank got to more than one experienced officer, and I can't say he didn't turn a hair or two, but he stood his ground. He's got some balls, that husband of yours.'

She laughs. 'You should know that by now.' She gives me an appraising look. 'Why can't you admit you actually like him? It wouldn't kill you, you know.'

'Maybe not,' I say, 'but it might kill him. Right now, I'm not just his father-in-law, I'm also his boss, and I need him on his toes. There's a dangerous man out there. We can't afford distractions.'

She sighs and makes to get up, but I put a hand on her arm, and she sinks back into her chair. 'Listen, Rosie,' I say. 'This is John's first experience of a case like this, and it's going to hit him at some point. My guess is he's not sleeping much, burying himself in all that tech stuff he does – which is good for our investigation, but not necessarily for him. It's not going to be much fun for you either—'

'Dad,' she interrupts quietly, 'I'm your daughter, remember? I saw you go through it all when I was growing up.' She hesitates, then adds, 'And Mum, too. You don't need to worry. I'm keeping an eye on him, okay? It's you we ought to be worrying about – you're on your own, with nobody to talk to.'

'Not true,' I tell her, reaching down to ruffle Blue's ears. 'I've got man's best friend here, and if that fails, I can always offer George Saint a sausage roll at the pub.'

She laughs again, gets up, kisses my cheek and sets the kettle to boil. My phone chooses that moment to come to life. It's Forbes. I slip into the back porch to take the call.

'I'm afraid I have some bad news,' he says. 'Iain Hughes died an hour ago.'

'What?' I feel my heart thud into my shoes. 'How?'

'The home's being cagey about it, trying to blame us for putting him under stress, but it's my guess he managed to get hold of enough medication to take a pretty decisive overdose. He'd made his confession and decided the time was right. Part of me feels sorry for the old sod, but it certainly doesn't make our job easier.'

I close my eyes and, taking a leaf out of the DSI's book, start to massage my temples, thinking of the conversation I've just had with Rosie about her husband's tendency to overwork. I don't hesitate for long. 'Leave it with me,' I tell Forbes. 'I'll get Larson onto it, see what he can dig up.'

I end the call, sigh, and head up the stairs to my son-in-law's study. As I suspected, he's at the computer, totally immersed. He raises his head when I walk in, peering at me through bleary eyes. He looks like a boxer who's just done fifteen rounds with someone way above his weight.

'Maggie's sent through a couple of the photos,' he says, 'and asked me to help with the reconstructions. I should have something good enough to run through the missing persons database by sometime tomorrow. Two more technicians are analysing some of the others.'

I look at my watch. It's way past 11 p.m. 'Leave that for now, son,' I say, then fill him in on what Forbes has just told me. 'I need to find out all I can about the family of Janet Hughes – where her parents were from, whether they are still alive, any siblings – you know the sort of thing. How long do you think it will take you?' I don't need to ask whether it's possible.

He gives me a tired grin. 'An hour if we're lucky,' he says, 'and two or three if we're not.'

'I'll leave you to it,' I say, but he's already turned back to his machine. I take the hint and meet Rosie on the landing, carrying two cups of coffee. I take one and head down to the lounge to wait, Blue padding patiently at my heels.

I OPEN my eyes to a blinding shaft of early morning light stabbing its way into my brain through a gap in the curtains. As I slowly come to life, I realise I'm flat out on Rosie's sofa. At some point, she must have come in and put a cushion under my head and covered me with a blanket. I sit up slowly, stretching out the kinks in my back, and almost tread on Blue laid out on the floor by the sofa, letting out little canine snores. She stirs as I push myself to my feet, and looks up hopefully.

'Come on, girl,' I say, giving her chin a scratch. 'Let's go and get some fresh air.'

We creep out into the kitchen – it's still early, and the house is silent. I put the kettle on and open the back door. I join Blue in the garden, carrying a mug of strong coffee, and settle myself on the bench to think. I've hardly had time to gather my thoughts when the back door opens, and a frazzled Rosie, wrapped in a thick dressing gown, comes over to join me. She's clutching half a dozen sheets of paper and hands them to me as she sits down.

'John only came to bed an hour ago,' she says, 'and he asked me to give you these. He said they were important.'

I glance at the top sheet and freeze, staring. It's a copy of a birth certificate for a Janet Bennet, born 14 September 1951, daughter of Graham Bennet, minister of religion, and Isobel Bennet, housewife. I glance at Rosie, who gives me a satisfied grin.

'He said you'd be pleased,' she says, sitting back and sipping her own coffee. 'He told me you should have everything you need there.'

I move on to the next sheet – the death certificate of Graham Bennet, dated 1979, cause of death, heart failure. The third is for Isobel, who died of old age in 1999. Both are buried in the graveyard at New Vale, somewhere near Pontypool.

'Have you got your phone with you?' I ask Rosie, and she pulls it out of her dressing gown pocket.

'What do you want to know?'

'Can you do an internet search for a place called New Vale, South Wales?'

She fiddles for a minute or two, then grunts in triumph. 'Here it is,' she says, handing me the phone. I'm looking at a small village, maybe two hundred dwellings at most, in the middle of former mining country around half an hour's drive from Pontypool.

'Well done, son!' I mutter, but then realise the information doesn't do much to further our investigation – the two people who could tell us more have very inconveniently died. I let out a sigh.

'That's not all,' Rosie says. 'Keep going.'

I move on to the fourth sheet – another birth certificate. Ruth Bennet, born 28 September 1946 – an older sister. There are two more sheets. I hold my breath and move on to the next. The marriage certificate tells me that Ruth Bennet married Martin Griffiths in her father's chapel in July 1967 – soon after she turned twenty-one, I note – the age of consent for marriage back then. I swallow hard before turning to the final page, expecting to see yet another death certificate. However, I find myself looking at a note from Larson. It tells me that, as far as he's been able to ascertain, Iain Hughes and Janet Bennet never married. More importantly, Ruth Griffiths, née Bennet, is alive and well and living in Cardiff. The note ends with an address and, amazingly, a landline number.

'Jesus bloody Christ!' I can't help saying. 'Your husband's a genius!' I catch myself and add, 'For God's sake, don't tell him I said so.'

Rosie gives me a worried look. 'You're not going to wake him, are you? He looked like death when he came to bed.'

I reach out and give her a hug. 'I think he's done more than enough. Let him sleep. And when he does wake up, tell him everything's in hand, and I don't expect to see him until tomorrow.'

At that moment, I hear faint sounds of stirring inside. I

look at my watch – it's just coming up to 7 a.m. I get up and call softly for Blue. She's at my side in a second.

'Sounds like the kids are on their way,' I say. 'Tell Ben I'll see him later on tonight, assuming he's not in bed by the time I get back.'

'I won't tell him anything,' Rosie replies as we make our way back inside. 'Chances are you won't, and he'll be asleep.'

I nod. 'You're probably right.'

I make my way out, thinking that at least I can give Blue a decent walk back to where my car is parked at West Hill station.

22

Two hours later, after bringing Grace and Sillitoe up to speed and catching up with Maggie at the lab, I pull into a street of imposing Victorian houses in one of Cardiff's more affluent leafy suburbs. Behind me, one of Fitzjohn's technicians is busy checking her pack of forensic equipment, ready to take samples. Jerry Forbes, beside me in the passenger seat, has been unusually quiet, and at first I think he's brooding over whether our visit to Iain Hughes contributed to his apparent suicide. However, when I pull up outside a grand, three-storey example of late nineteenth-century architecture, complete with wrought-iron gates and wide gravel driveway leading up to the front steps, he comes back to life and stares appreciatively up at the house.

'Looks like Ruth Bennet did well for herself,' he comments. 'A place like this in the middle of Cardiff doesn't come cheap.' He sighs. 'Way above my pay grade, and sadly our family firmly believes in primogeniture.'

'You mean when your parents die, the eldest sibling gets the lot?'

'The eldest *male* sibling,' he corrects me. 'The whole pile will go to my brother, Arthur. He's not a bad chap, though, and he won't leave us all to starve – at least, I've told him if he does, I'll do my best to frame him for something.'

'Is he a policeman as well?'

Forbes shakes his head. 'Not anymore. He did a couple of years and said he didn't find it stimulating enough. He's based in London now, doing something for the government – one of those "if I tell you, I'll have to kill you" jobs that takes him all over the world, ostensibly doing trade deals. Read what you like into that.'

I decide to leave my curiosity about Jerry Forbes's background on hold for the moment and focus on the task in hand. 'This is going to be a bit tricky,' I say. 'We've no idea how close Ruth was to her sister, and unless she's very slow on the uptake, she'll know something's wrong the minute we ask her for a DNA sample.'

He nods. 'It's probably better we give her the bad news first. Whether she loved or hated her, it will still be a bit of a blow, and she's, what – getting on for eighty? Not a good age for a shock to the system.'

So, I think, *he does have yesterday's events on his mind.*

'Well,' I say, 'sitting here won't make it any easier. Let's get on with it.' I turn to the tech in the back seat. Bluebell has realised we've stopped, and has poked her head up, looking expectantly through the bars on the hatch. 'How are you with dogs?' I ask her.

'Fine,' she replies. 'I've got two at home. Your Bluebell's a real sweetie.' She reaches through the bars and scratches Blue's ear.

'Good,' I say. 'You stay here with her, and we'll give you a call when we need you.'

Forbes and I crunch our way up the gravel path, take a synchronised deep breath and press the doorbell.

The woman who answers is about as far from my image of a frail seventy-seven-year-old as it's possible to get. Ruth Griffiths is tall, athletic, with long dark hair and barely a wrinkle. She's wearing denim leggings, trainers and an oversized sweatshirt and looks as if she's just come back from a session at the gym. The only visible concessions her body has made to ageing are the mesh of crow's feet round the eyes, and a sprinkle of lines around her mouth.

She gives us a welcoming smile. 'You must be the policemen I was told to expect. Please, come on in. I'll make some coffee – what would you prefer? Americano, cappuccino, macchiato?'

We exchange raised eyebrows and follow her into a substantial kitchen, where she waves us to seats at an enormous oak table and fires up a full-on coffee machine that looks like it should be behind the counter of the local Costa.

Forbes finds his voice first. 'Cappuccino would be lovely, Mrs Griffiths, thank you.'

And for you?' she asks, turning to me. 'And it's Ruth, please.'

'Americano,' I manage to say. 'No milk, three sugars.' I pull myself together and add, 'I'm Chief Inspector Crow, and this is my colleague Detective Inspector Forbes.'

She freezes for a moment, gathers herself and smiles, although there's a touch of uncertainty in her expression now. I realise all the fiddling with the coffee machine is more to hide her nervousness than an act of straightforward hospitality.

'An inspector and a *chief* inspector? It must be something serious to send two such senior officers. Perhaps I'd better get the coffee sorted before you tell me the reason you need to speak to me. Something tells me whatever it is, it's more than a parking ticket.'

We wait patiently while she sorts out the drinks and a plate of biscuits, then joins us at the table, hugging her own mug – black, no sugar.

'It's bad news, isn't it,' she says before either of us gets a chance to speak. 'Has something happened to my husband? Has he been in an accident or something – he isn't ...'

'Nothing's happened to your husband, Mrs ... Ruth,' Forbes puts in quickly. 'He's perfectly all right as far as we know. You don't need to worry.'

She lets out a sigh of relief and visibly relaxes. 'Thank God for that,' she whispers, then blinks at us, confused. 'Then what is this about? He hasn't done anything wrong, has he – been arrested or something?'

It's my turn. 'He hasn't been arrested, and he's not in any trouble, at least not with us,' I say. I pause, glancing at Forbes, who is pointedly studying his mug. 'It's about your sister, Janet. We were hoping you might be able to tell us about her, when you last saw her ...'

I stop. Ruth Griffiths has gone rigid – she's staring at me, the colour rapidly draining from her face. For a moment I think she's about to faint.

'Janet? This is about Janet?' She snatches up her mug in both hands. They are shaking. 'You know where she is? If you've found her, you have to tell me. I mean, is she all right? I need to see her ...' She stops, blinks at us, the implication of our visit dawning. 'Oh, God,' she says, her voice almost inaudible. 'She's dead, isn't she. He found her, and he killed her. All that time we were looking for her, and he knew, and he never said – the evil bastard!'

She dissolves into tears, leaving Forbes and me frowning at each other in puzzlement. She's spilled most of her coffee onto the table, and Forbes gets up, pours a glass of water, grabs a handful of kitchen towel and gently prises the mug out of her hand.

'Here,' he says, 'drink this.'

She takes a sip obediently and puts the glass on the table. We wait until the storm has passed, she's taken a few deep breaths and wiped her eyes with the towel.

'I'm sorry,' I say, aware that this is the second time I've given the same speech in two days, 'but a body has been found, and we have reason to believe it may be Janet.'

'Reason to believe?' She rounds on me, shock turning, as it often does in these situations, to anger. 'What do you mean, "reason to believe"? You come here, tell me my sister might be dead, and you don't know? You might have bloody well bothered to get your facts together before you barge in telling someone they've lost their only sister. You people are unbelievable!'

We wait again until after a full minute she calms down and meets my eye. 'Sorry. I'm sorry.' She picks up her water glass and points to a cupboard. 'If you look in there, you'll find some brandy. I think I could do with a splash in here.' Forbes obliges and pours her a decent slug. She downs it in one and heaves a huge sigh. 'Sorry,' she says again. 'You're saying you're not sure, and you need somebody to identify her, is that it? I haven't actually seen Janet since she was fourteen. She might have changed – I don't know if I'd recognise her now.'

'It isn't that, Ruth,' I say as gently as I can. 'The thing is—'

'Of course,' she interrupts. 'Of course, I wasn't thinking. Nobody can recognise her, can they? They can't because she's been dead all this time. There's nothing left to identify, is there? Do you know when? Can you tell that much?'

'If it is Janet,' I tell her, 'she's been dead a very long time. We think possibly she died in or around 1978, perhaps '79. The remains we've found are purely skeletal. All we know is that the body is a young woman, mid-twenties or so; they were found very close to where Janet lived, and were possibly deposited shortly after she disappeared in 1978. There is only one way to find out whether we have found your sister.'

'Yes – you want my DNA,' she says at once, and nods. 'You can have it. Do what you need to do. If it really is her, I want to know for sure. I think I always knew something like this had happened when her letters stopped coming. God, I should have done something – gone to find her – if I'd been there …'

She's close to tears again, and Forbes takes over. 'I doubt there was anything you could have done, Ruth. You said she wrote to you? When did the letters stop? Can you remember?'

'It was that year,' she says, shaking her head. 'Janet always sent a Christmas card, sometimes just a card, and sometimes with a short letter telling me she was okay, not to worry, that sort of thing. She did the same for my birthday in September, every year without fail. In 1977 I got a Christmas card as usual, but the following September, nothing arrived. I should have known then, but I suppose I convinced myself she'd simply forgotten, and I'd get something in December as usual. But I didn't. Around that time life was pretty hectic – I had two children in primary school and a new baby, and Martin was working all hours. I would have written or phoned, but I had no address, no phone number. She told me right at the start she didn't want me to know where she was, so I never asked. If I had been able to contact her, I would have let her know when our father died, told her it was safe to come home. But you're telling me it was too late by then – she was probably already dead.'

'You said, "He found her, and he killed her",' I say. 'What did you mean, Ruth? Who might have wanted to harm your sister? Who was she frightened of?'

There's a slight hesitation before she answers, her tone full of bitterness, 'My father. The oh-so-holy Reverend Bennet, with all his talk of hellfire and damnation. He was a fanatic, Chief Inspector. And like most fanatics, he was violent and abusive, to me and Janet and to our mother as well. He spent all his time talking about hell, and we spent ours living in it. I would have left way before I did if it hadn't been for Janet. She was five years younger than me, and I didn't want to leave her alone. But then I met Martin, and he stood up to the bastard, told him we were leaving, but for appearances' sake, we would come back and marry in his chapel as soon as it was legal. I wanted to take Janet with us, but it wasn't possible. She was too young, and the law would have just taken her back. I tried to see her, afterwards, but he wouldn't let me in, said he didn't want his only remaining daughter consorting with evil, can you believe? He needn't have worried – he'd already put the devil in her, at least by his standards. You know, as soon as her periods started, he locked her up at night, made sure she never went anywhere alone, not even to school.'

She pauses and pours herself another stiff brandy before going on. 'I managed to see her just once, before Martin and I got married. I went round the back of the manse and threw stones at her window until she woke up and shinned down over the porch roof. She said not to worry, she had a plan and before long she'd be gone. She told me she'd get in touch when she was settled, but wouldn't tell me where she was going – said it was best I didn't know, because our father had threatened to kill her if she ever brought the same shame onto his family that I'd done, living in sin with a heathen. Two weeks later, I tried to see her again, but she was gone. My father saw me in the back garden and came out, waving a poker around and raving, saying he was going to find her and send her to hell. Then he came after me, and I'm sure he would have killed me if Martin hadn't been waiting in his car by the chapel. I jumped in, and we drove off, left my father running down the street after us, ranting – he looked completely insane. In the end he threw the poker, and it cracked the back window.

'We heard nothing more until two years later, just before my twenty-first birthday. Mother got in touch to say that Father regretted his behaviour, was much calmer now, and wanted us to honour our promise to come back and marry in the chapel. Martin said he didn't deserve any consideration, but I told him we'd promised, and I wanted to make sure Mother was all right. So we agreed. It was awful. Father treated us like strangers, and he spent almost the whole day trying to get me to tell him where Janet was. He refused to believe that I didn't know. He got so angry that we left. The last thing he said to me was that he'd find her, sooner or later, and make sure she paid for her crimes against God.

Soon after that, Martin and I moved house, and we didn't tell them our new address. I never saw my parents again.'

A long silence follows, in which we mull over the implications of Ruth's speech. Eventually I ask, 'Ruth, do you truly believe your father found Janet and killed her?'

She thinks about this, then gives a slight nod. 'Yes. I believe he found her and killed her and couldn't live with it. The doctors said he died of heart failure. I think he died of guilt – at least, I hope he did. I tried to get in touch with Mother afterwards, but she shut herself off from everything, became a recluse after his death. In the end, Martin and I gave up and moved on with our lives. She died in 1999, so I suppose we'll never know the truth.'

'I wouldn't say that just yet,' Forbes says. 'If the body we've found *is* your sister, we intend to find out exactly what happened to her, and who was responsible for her death. Is there anything else you can tell us – anything more concrete than a feeling? We need something we can point to as evidence your father may have been involved.'

She shakes her head, brow furrowing in thought. 'No – I can't think of anything … wait a minute!' Her head shoots up. 'Yes, there might be something – not much, but it might help.'

He gives her an encouraging smile. 'Go on – what is it?'

'When Father died,' she replies, 'Martin suggested we get a copy of his will. He owned the manse, you see – not the chapel, that was church property, but the house belonged to him. We wanted to make sure Mother was provided for. He left everything to her, which was a relief, but there was also a clause to say that if she died before him, the property was on no account to be left either to me or to Janet on his death. He cut us out of his will completely. We weren't surprised – he was a vindictive man, so it was only to be expected. But after Mother died, I got a call from a solicitor who told me she had made her own will, leaving the whole property to me. Not to me and Janet – just to me. I was the sole beneficiary. At the time I assumed it was because of the way Janet left, that Mother had deliberately cut her out, but what if it was because she knew Janet was dead? What if she didn't want anyone looking for Janet because it might have exposed her husband as a murderer?'

'Do you have a copy of the will?' I ask, doing my best to keep the eagerness out of my voice.

'I think Martin does, somewhere. I'll ask him tonight, then get him to email you a copy.'

'Thank you, that would be very helpful. And what about the house? Do you still own it?'

She nods. 'I couldn't bear to go back there, and we didn't quite know what to do with it, so Martin suggested we simply board it up, make it secure until I decided. As far as I was concerned, half of it belonged to Janet, whatever the will said, and I always hoped …' She falters, swallows hard and ends, 'I always hoped she would turn up one day, and we could decide together. That's not going to happen now, is it? Oh, God!'

'No,' Forbes says gently, 'and I'm sorry to ask, but do you have a key to the property? It would be really helpful if we could take a look at it. I know it sounds odd, but it could give us more information.'

'Wait here,' she replies, and leaves us to mull over what we've heard in silence. A couple of minutes later, she comes back and hands us a set of keys. 'Keep them as long as you like. Just promise me one thing – you'll let us know as soon as you find out what really happened to my sister.'

'Of course,' I say. 'We'll keep you informed, you have our word. We'll send someone in now to take a swab, if that's okay, and hopefully you'll hear from us very soon.'

'Do you think she's right?' Forbes asks once we've dropped the technician off at Fitzjohn's lab in Newport. 'Kenny Hughes didn't kill his mother – her father did?'

'Who the hell knows?' I reply. 'If you ask me, this is getting far too complicated – and we're no nearer to finding Kenny or Millie. Plus, I have an awful feeling that, despite all the theories about him not killing his victims until they reach a certain age, the longer this goes on, the more danger Millie is in.'

23

For a building that's been unoccupied for over twenty years, the Reverend Bennet's former home looks to be in pretty good condition. Steel shutters over the windows and doors have successfully prevented casual vandalism, and from what I can see, the roof has somehow managed to keep all its tiles – a miracle, given the black-market value of Welsh slate, not to mention lead. Forbes seems to be having the same thought.

'If I were a local villain,' he remarks, 'I'd have been shinning up one of those drainpipes before you could say "baptismal font".'

'If you were a local villain,' a voice says behind us, 'you wouldn't come within a mile of this place. It's got a bit of a reputation round here.'

We turn to see a man, perhaps in his late seventies, who looks like he's walked straight out of the pages of a D. H. Lawrence novel, right down to the pale cream suit, silk cravat and ebony walking cane. Neither of us heard him approach, a fact that makes me distinctly uneasy until I realise he must have come from the rear of the house and across the neatly trimmed front lawn. He smiles and holds out a hand.

'You must be the two policemen my wife told me about,' he says. 'I'm Martin Griffiths. When she said you were on your way here, I thought I'd better come down to see if you needed any help. She forgot to give you the code for the alarm, you see, and we didn't want you to accidentally summon our local PC. Might have been a bit embarrassing.'

We introduce ourselves, and I realise we're staring. He chuckles. 'Oh, yes, sorry about the get-up. I've been putting in an appearance at one of my hotels today, checking on things. We specialise in period experience breaks. This week it's the 1920s – you know, Charleston, gin slings, that sort of thing. I have to look the part.'

One of my hotels? At least, I think, that explains how the Griffithses can afford to maintain a large, empty house for more than two decades.

'You said the house has a reputation,' Forbes says. 'What for? Being haunted by pre-war aristocrats?'

'Now, that would be fun,' he replies, 'but sadly, no. Apparently, my late father-in-law is said to roam the house and chapel, wailing and raving, presumably seeking redemption for his many earthly sins. I've not come across the old bastard personally, but some of the neighbours swear they've heard him banging out the odd sermon in the middle of the night. My theory is water pipes, but you never know. Besides,' he adds, 'it's mostly elderly people in the village now. The teenage vandals are all long gone, and there are enough empty terraces to provide plenty of easier targets.'

'I take it the Reverend Bennet wasn't the most popular preacher in town?' I ask.

Griffiths's smile disappears. 'Unfortunately, he was the only one and universally hated by almost everybody, most especially by his family. People tolerated him because they didn't have a choice. I mean, look at the place. I know the priesthood is supposed to be a vocation, but he wasn't the sort to dedicate himself to caring for the disadvantaged. The only things he cared about were power and control. From what I heard, the church sent him here to get him out of the way, somewhere he couldn't cause too much trouble. A mistake, if you ask me – if anything, it just fed his obsessions, drove him right over the edge. He was the kind of man who would give the Spanish Inquisition a good name.'

'Yet he allowed you to marry his daughter,' I comment.

'Not without a fight. But in the end, avarice won. He needed money, and my family have been hotel owners for generations. At the time we had a string of six high-class hotels, and my father was on the rich list. I'm an only child and was set to inherit the lot. Ruth didn't care about the money, and when I met her, neither did I. We fell in love, and that was that. Graham, though – it was the only thing he did care about. Money would give him more power, and he liked the fact that his daughter gave him power over me. For God's sake, don't tell Ruth this, but I effectively bought her from him. I made a promise to pay for the upkeep of the manse in return for his daughter's hand. I kept that promise, and I'm still keeping it, for different reasons.'

'What reasons?' I ask. 'I'd have thought you and Ruth would have been glad to see the back of it, from what she told us this morning.'

He considers, then answers, 'At the beginning, Ruth couldn't bear to even think about the place. When her mother died, she wouldn't come here or discuss what she wanted done with it. She just wanted it locked up, contents and all, out of sight and out of mind, as they say. I thought maybe after a while, when things had settled down, she might change her mind, so I had it checked out for damp and rot, made secure as you see, and left it. I had an idea in my head that once she was open to the idea, I'd have it restored, turn it into an exclusive guest house. The old pit is still up the road, and there's a market for tours of the disused Welsh mines. Strange what people will pay for these days.'

He stares wistfully in the direction of the former pithead just visible on the hillside behind the village. 'Then we read Isobel's will,' he goes on. 'When Ruth realised Janet had been cut out completely, she was very upset. She and Janet had been very close as children, and although they'd lost touch in the 1970s, she still hoped they would find each other again. She said the only way she'd set foot in this house was with Janet by her side, and in the meantime, we should do nothing, as by rights half of it belonged to her sister. So …' He waves his hands in the direction of the manse. 'Here we are. I've kept it viable, inside and out. Nothing has been changed or moved since the day Isobel died. Now, you're saying Janet might have died more than forty years ago. If that turns out to be the case, I'm not sure what Ruth will want to do.'

One thing I can say about Martin Griffiths – he doesn't shy away from extravagant gestures. Keeping his wife's family home in this condition must have cost him a fortune over the years.

'You say nothing's been moved since 2000?' Forbes asks. 'Nothing at all?'

'Well,' Griffiths replies, 'almost nothing. I got someone in to tidy up after Isobel's death, wash up the dishes, put stuff in cupboards and so on, and of course, we had to take out the body. Apart from that, everything is exactly as it was. A lot of the contents go back to Victorian times, so I suppose I could rethink the guest house idea and open a museum instead, if Ruth ever lets me. But I'm sure you're busy people – come on, let me give you the guided tour.'

We follow him through a reinforced steel door at the entrance porch, protected by an electronic keypad, to a heavy oak front door fitted with two locks and yet another electronic barrier. It's a system my son-in-law would be proud of, I think, as we finally make it into the almost pitch-dark front hall. I instinctively pull a pair of plastic gloves out of my jacket pocket and note that Forbes has done the same. He grabs Griffiths's arm as our host reaches for a light switch, and hands him a spare pair. Griffiths looks confused, but pulls them on, then flicks the switch, flooding the hallway with light.

'Are these really necessary?' he asks. 'Apart from a cleaner and a couple of maintenance people, nobody's been in here for decades.'

For a moment, neither of us answers. We're too busy taking in the pristine state of the place, from the original tiled floor and furniture that wouldn't be out of place on the *Antiques Roadshow*, to the ornate architraves and ceiling roses. Griffiths is right – we've stepped into a ready-made museum, and one that doesn't have a speck of dust or a cobweb anywhere. I blink and pull myself back into the twenty-first century.

'It's just a precaution,' I say. 'In our job, we have to be prepared for anything. You say there are people who come in regularly – do they have keys as well, or do you come and let them in?'

He nods. 'Yes, there are three others who have access. All of them are trusted employees in my hotel in Pontypool, been with us for at least twenty years. I keep the spare keys at the hotel, and they have to sign them out and back in again. I see to it personally. Nobody is allowed to keep a key overnight, even if they are doing a long repair. I pay extra for the inconvenience of course, and I'm absolutely sure none of them would take advantage. I can give you the names and addresses if you need them.'

'Thank you, that would be useful. When did you last come here yourself?'

He thinks, counting up on his fingers. 'It must have been around three months ago. There was a leak in one of the bathrooms, and Eric, our handyman, asked me to come and discuss the options. I have the exact date in my records, so I'll let you know when I'm back in the office. The cleaner comes in once every three months, and her last visit would have been towards the end of June. There are internal maintenance checks at the start of every month, and CCTV cameras covering the outside areas.'

As he talks, he leads us through the ground-floor rooms, which, like the hallway, have been kept spotlessly clean and free of dust and damp. Even the extensive collection of books in what had been Graham Bennet's study has been carefully preserved in several glass-fronted bookcases. I have a feeling Bennet was the sort to set things down on paper, and make a mental note to have a couple of officers go through everything in this room, looking for journals, diaries, letters – anything that might shed light on his movements around the time his younger daughter disappeared. We move on to the kitchen, the only room in the house so far in which concessions to modernity have been made. On a wheeled metal trolley next to the sink, a kettle, microwave and portable electric grill have been provided, presumably for use by the cleaning and maintenance staff.

It isn't until we're halfway up the stairs that I start to feel uneasy. A faint, acrid smell drifts down from somewhere above, in sharp contrast to the thick scents of beeswax and old wood that run through the downstairs rooms. I glance at Forbes – he's noticed it too and raises an eyebrow. Griffiths, though, doesn't seem overly concerned.

'Looks like our plumbing problem's come back,' he comments. 'There was a crack in one of the waste pipes – that's what I was doing here last time. Eric replaced a section of pipe, and I thought we'd fixed it, but it's possible the damage runs further down into the drain. Damn it! That's going to be a bugger to find, and will probably cost a fortune.'

At the top of the stairs, I count five closed doors. The first room, facing the front of the house, is a double, complete with four-poster bed, which must have belonged to the reverend and his wife. Opposite, the door of the first back bedroom is secured on the outside by two hefty bolts, top and bottom.

'That was Janet's room,' Griffiths explains. 'The evil sod used to lock his daughters in at night as soon as they were old enough to, as he put it, be tempted by the Devil and all His works.'

He draws back the bolts and pushes the door open. Inside, the room is bare except for a single bed, a small wardrobe and a chest of drawers. The floor is bare boards; there are no mirrors or pictures on the walls – nothing to suggest this was once a young teenager's bedroom. I stay out on the landing while Forbes steps in, opens the wardrobe door, coughs and takes a step back as an overwhelming stink of mothballs wafts across the room. The meagre contents – a couple of dresses, three skirts and a heavy coat, all encased in clear plastic, are more reminiscent of the 1940s than the swinging sixties. He wrinkles his nose and gently closes the wardrobe door. Meanwhile, something else is niggling vaguely somewhere in the section of my frontal lobe that still works. There are two more closed doors, one on each side of the landing, and at the end, a wide-open doorway leads into the bathroom. From where I'm standing, I can clearly see the toilet and sink and one edge of a Victorian roll-top bath. This, I assume, is the source of the smell coming from the faulty waste pipe. Yet something, my gut tells me, isn't quite adding up.

I start along the landing to distance myself from the equally unpleasant smell of mothballs and to clear my head. To my left, I pass another bolted door – presumably Ruth's former bedroom. The odour of stale urine increases. When I reach the bathroom, it should be even stronger – but it isn't. For a moment, my brain doesn't register what logic is telling me, but then it clicks, and I'm grabbing at the bolts on the second bedroom door, trying to yank them back. The top bolt comes free, but the one at the bottom is stiffer – that, or the tremor that has started up in my left hand is sapping my strength. Forbes and Griffiths are staring at me as if I'm having some sort of fit.

'For fuck's sake!' I snap at them. 'Help me get this bloody thing open!'

A second later, Forbes is next to me, kicking at the bolt. I give him room, and at the third blow it shoots back with such force that the housing comes away, spraying screws, metal and wood splinters in all directions. I hold my breath and open the door.

The room is almost identical to the first – bare except for a bed, wardrobe and small chest in a corner. The difference is that on the bed is a body.

It's that of a young girl, around eight years old, long, mousy-blond hair, wearing an old-fashioned floral dress and dark green knitted sweater. She isn't moving.

For what must be just a fraction of a second that feels like forever, time stops, all three of us paralysed, not wanting to believe what we're looking at. Then the world cranks back into life, training kicks in, and I'm with the tiny, emaciated body, searching desperately for a pulse while Forbes barks orders into his mobile. I vaguely hear the bathroom door slam shut as Griffiths dashes to empty his stomach and probably his bowels as well.

I'm still frantically running my fingers over neck and wrists, trying to find some thread of life, when Forbes crouches beside me. 'An ambulance is on its way,' he says, 'and the whole works. Is this who I think it is?'

I manage to nod. 'Yes. I think I can safely say we've found Millie Drake.'

24

All my instincts are telling me we've come too late. The body is limp and freezing cold. Nevertheless, I carry on trying to find a pulse, and am about to start CPR when Forbes crouches beside me and touches my arm. He's pulled a steel hip flask out of his pocket and is rubbing it on his sleeve. I move aside, and he holds it to the child's lips. For a long, agonising moment we stare at the metal, and then, miraculously, a dot of mist appears on the polished surface.

'Dear God!' I whisper as I lunge for the wardrobe, yank it open and pull out a plastic bag containing a thick overcoat. I tear the package open, and we pack the coat around the girl, then start rubbing her limbs to get some warmth into her. I hear the bathroom door open and at the same time the faint wail of sirens, I guess no more than a minute away. 'Get some water!' I yell at Griffiths without looking up, and hear him clatter back to the bathroom at a run. A few seconds later he's back with a mug. I look up to take it, see the panic in his face, and try to force calm into my voice. 'The ambulance should be downstairs any minute,' I say. 'Go and let the paramedics in, but no one else, understand? When the police arrive, tell them to wait outside until we come down. Have you got that?'

'Yes. Just the paramedics – got it.' He disappears down the stairs.

Forbes dips the edge of a handkerchief in the water and moistens Millie's lips. Her eyes are still closed, but I see her mouth give an almost imperceptible twitch as her instincts start to kick in, drawing some of the moisture into her mouth.

'It's all right, sweetheart,' I say, hoping she can hear me. 'We've got you. You're going to be okay now.'

WE LEAVE the ambulance crew to do its job, and make our way outside. As we reach the front door, Forbes stumbles, has to grab my shoulder to stay upright. I realise he's gone pale, and there's a sizeable patch of blood soaking into his right trouser leg, just above the ankle.

He shrugs. 'Sorry – I'm afraid I might have contaminated our crime scene just a bit.'

I glance back along the hallway and see a trail of blood splashes leading back up the stairs. His breathing is becoming increasingly laboured, and I take his weight as we struggle down the front steps onto the lawn next to the ambulance.

Griffiths joins us, still anxious, although he's managed to calm himself down a bit. 'Is that poor girl all right?' he asks, and then, to Forbes, 'You're hurt – what happened?'

Forbes gives us a weak smile. 'We're not sure about Millie yet. We'll have to wait for the experts. As for me ...' He gestures to his leg. 'I think I've managed to get a part of your bolt stuck in there somewhere. It's a bloody nuisance – this suit cost a fortune!'

At that moment a van pulls up, and a team of SOCOs, already suited and booted, jumps out of the back. I recognise one of them as Meera Kumar, the officer who attended the scene at Wye Cross. She comes across to us, and her expression immediately darkens when she sees Forbes.

'Jesus, Jerry, you look awful – what have you done to yourself?' Without waiting for a response, she digs in her bag, brings out a pair of scissors and slashes her way through his trouser leg to get a better look. A good-sized section of the bolt housing is lodged in his calf, just above the ankle and, from what I can see, dangerously close to the Achilles tendon. More worryingly, blood is pulsing from the wound with alarming regularity. 'Bloody hell!' she remarks, snipping away at the cloth until a length comes free. She ties it round above the wound and pulls it tight. 'The only place you're going is into that ambulance,' she pronounces, then to me, 'Don't let him move. I'm going to let the paramedics know. He needs to get to A&E as soon as possible – I think he might have nicked an artery.'

'Shit!' Forbes comments. 'That's all I need.' Then he passes out.

I watch the ambulance and its two casualties race away, blues and twos at full tilt, heading for Cwmbran, the nearest A&E. A gaggle of uniforms has formed a cordon around the house, while Meera and her team disappear inside to set to work bagging, tagging, photographing and all the rest. I suddenly feel superfluous, and, more worryingly, the familiar nervous tic has started up in my hand, a predictable response to sudden stress, and my right leg isn't listening to my brain. Having no other choice, I stand still, alternating between curses and deep breaths until my body decides to cooperate, then set off towards my car, intending to walk Blue round the chapel graveyard next door while I work out what to do next. I should get to the hospital, but might end up being there for hours, and I'm pretty certain a full-grown Doberman won't be welcome in intensive care. I'm bundling her out of the hatch when Griffiths comes over to join me.

'Magnificent beast,' he says, giving Blue an admiring glance. 'Ruth and I had a Dalmatian until she died last year – fifteen – a good age for the breed. Do you mind?' I gesture for him to go ahead, and he crouches, extending a hand for Blue to sniff, more to provide a distraction than anything else. He still looks pretty shaken. 'What I don't understand,' he says, scratching Blue under the chin, 'is how anyone managed to get in. None of the locks are disturbed, and the alarms are all primed. Aside from me and Ruth, only three other people know the codes, and I can vouch for all of them. It doesn't make sense. I mean, who is that girl, and why here? Why not the chapel or one of the abandoned houses? They would be much easier to get into.'

They are reasonable questions, which deserve reasonable answers. The problem is, the only answers I've got are way beyond reasonable. Even if they weren't, I'm not sure a full explanation of what his nephew might have been up to is a good idea.

'Walk with me,' I say.

We get as far as a bench just inside the graveyard. I've managed to explain nothing much beyond the fact that the girl in his late father-in-law's house is, technically, his great-niece. At that news, the colour drains from his face, and he flops heavily onto the bench, pulls out a handkerchief and wipes his brow.

For a moment his mouth flaps wordlessly until he finally pulls himself together and says, 'Janet had a son?' He shakes his head. 'We didn't know. She never said a word, not in any of her letters to Ruth – nothing. And you're telling me he somehow got into the house and locked his daughter up in there, without food or water? It's – well, it's ...' Unsurprisingly, words fail him. He mops his forehead again, meets my eye and pushes himself to his feet. 'Look, I have to call Ruth, let her know what's happened. And then I need to pick her up and go to the hospital. If what you say is true, we're the only family that poor mite has got, and God knows, she's going to need somebody to look after her.' He sticks out a hand, mouth set in a determined line as if daring me to try to stop him.

I take it and nod. 'I'm sure I'll be seeing you again, Mr Griffiths,' I say, seeing no immediate reason to keep him here, nor to burden him with more gruesome information about Kenny Hughes. The poor sod's got enough to deal with for the time being. 'We'll need to interview Millie, when she's up to it, and we'll have more questions for you and your wife. There will be officers with Millie at the hospital when you get there, and probably someone from social services as well, and they will be able to help.' I give him my card and watch him make his way unsteadily round the chapel to wherever he's parked his car.

I sink down onto the bench and give myself a minute to gather my scrambled thoughts while Blue wanders contentedly among the gravestones. There are too many unanswered questions. Why would Kenny Hughes bring Millie here? And as Griffiths rightly pointed out, the place was well secured, with no sign of a forced entry, so how the hell did he get in? Larson's theory that Kenny only disposes of his victims once they reach their mid-twenties is well and truly screwed.

'Bloody hell,' I mutter as I root out my phone and add, 'Oh, shit!' I put it on silent before visiting Ruth Griffiths, and find myself staring at five missed calls – one from Larson, two from Grace, one from Maggie Ainsworth and one, the most recent, from ACC Forbes. I call him.

'I'm on my way to Cwmbran,' he tells me. 'I've had a quick word with Jerry's surgeon, and he's going to be fine once they've taken the shrapnel out of his leg. I suppose I'll have to deal with his mother when I get there. She blames me for him joining the force – according to her, he was all set to be an accountant before I put my spoke in. I don't fancy his chances with her when he wakes up either, but with a bit of luck I'll be able to keep her at bay for a bit.'

'Believe me, sir,' I say, thinking of Chrissie, 'I know how you feel.'

'Anyway,' he goes on, 'I've filled your chief constable in on things and told Meera Kumar to hand over anything she thinks might be useful to you, particularly documents and that sort of thing. We can deal with the basic forensics, but your technical chap – Larson, is it? Well, he's probably better qualified than any of our people on the computer side. There's no need for you to come down here just yet. They say the young girl won't be fit to interview at least until tomorrow or even the day after. It's a nuisance, but it can't be helped. I'll keep you up to speed, though, and I suggest you send one of your female officers over if you want someone present when we do manage to speak to her.'

'Yes, sir, I'll do that,' I say, but he's hung up, and I'm speaking to empty air.

I'm about to tackle Grace when a PC strides over to me, carrying a cardboard box full of plastic bags.

'Ms Kumar asked me to give you these, sir,' he says, dumping his burden on the bench. 'She said to tell you she thinks you might find them interesting, but our lot have our hands full with all the other stuff. She bagged them straight away, but you'll have to make sure forensics go through them properly before you do anything else with them.'

I wait until he's gone before taking a closer look. There are twenty-two bags, each containing a large, leather-bound book. The front and rear covers are unmarked, but when I turn the top volume to look at the spine, my stomach lurches. Engraved in small characters at the top is a date – 1978. These are journals. I look at the others. They run from 1978 to 2000. Graham Bennet died in 1979. They must, I conclude, have belonged to his wife, Isobel. Perhaps, I think, we might finally start to get some answers.

My phone rings. This time, it's Sillitoe.

'Where the fuck have you been?' she demands. From her tone I get the impression she's been at the receiving end of Grace's frustration, who, in turn, has probably had her ear chewed by CC Gosford.

'Sorry,' I say. 'It's been a bit busy down here.'

'So I've heard,' she retorts, 'from everyone except you.' I hear her sigh; then she goes on, 'Sorry, boss. Everything's a bit mental here. The DSI has been trying to get hold of you, and Mr Larson as well.'

'He's supposed to be at home, resting,' I say. 'What does he want?'

'He says he's got two more likenesses out of the photos

he's been looking at, and he's running through the national misper database now, but it's so vast he could do with some kind of filter to speed things up, and apparently you told him you might have an idea about it.'

'I do,' I reply, 'but I haven't had a chance to find out if it's worth pursuing yet.' I think for a moment, then make a decision. 'Tell him it might be nothing, but try to focus on young girls who went missing aged around thirteen or fourteen, possibly only daughters of fairly well-off parents – the type who would be unlikely to disappear for more than a night or so at a time. Also, for now, concentrate on Wales and the West Country. I have a feeling Kenny Hughes isn't the sort to stray too far from the areas he's used to. Tell Larson I'll be home later this evening. I'll call him then.'

'Okay.' She pauses, and I can tell she's debating whether or not to question my reasoning. Luckily, she decides not to and goes on, 'He also asked if you could get a current photo of Millie – it might be useful to compare with the reconstructions of the mother and grandmother.'

'I'll get one sent through to him,' I say. 'What else?'

'Maggie Ainsworth says she's managed to extract DNA samples from the remains we think are Janet's,' Sillitoe says, 'and she's comparing them with both the ones we're assuming are Kenny's and the swab she's just received from Janet's sister. We should know by tomorrow whether there's a match. As far as Oakfield Road goes, the forensic team say they've taken samples from the cavities where the cat and the third body were found, but there's nothing elsewhere, and they don't think the analyses will come up with anything beyond what we've already got. Plus, the DSI wants to know what the fuck's going on, and when we'll have access to Millie.'

I look at my watch – it's just gone 5 p.m. 'Tell Grace to get the kettle on,' I say. 'I'm just leaving, and I'll see her in an hour or so. Ask Robbie and Daz to wait for me, too – I've got a job for them, and I need a senior female officer from our lot at Cwmbran hospital ready to interview Millie the minute we're allowed in.'

Another sigh, then, 'I'll ring through and tell them I'll be there by seven.' She hangs up.

As I'm settling Blue in the car, a figure comes down from the house, heading for the battered Nissan parked behind me. I recognise DS Peters, Chepstow's answer to my son-in-law.

'Evening, sir,' he says, giving me a cheery smile. 'They say the DI's going to be okay. I've just had his uncle on the phone. They've got the bolt out of his leg, but he won't be very mobile for a week or two. He's not too happy – he's been told that, as he can't do any dashing about, he might as well spend the time going through all the CCTV footage from this place' – he jerks a thumb in the direction of the manse – 'for the last month. Not that I feel too sorry for him. If he hadn't got himself injured, it would have been my job.' His face darkens. 'Terrible about that little girl, though. I mean, it makes you wonder about the kind of people roaming around these days.'

'Yes,' I say to Blue as I heave myself into the driver's seat and set the satnav for West Hill. 'It really does make me wonder.'

Chiefly, though, it makes me wonder where the hell the bastard is, and whether we can catch him before he snatches some other innocent teenager off the street.

25

Grace refills our coffee mugs and sits back, steepling her hands under her chin. She's been unusually silent since I outlined my admittedly shaky theory concerning Hughes's choice of victims. Eventually, she nods and says, 'Polly has a good point. He's getting money from somewhere, enough to fund the purchase of at least one house, if not more. So you're suggesting that he picks his victims with an eye to how much he can get out of the parents? He abducts a girl, with no intention of ever giving her back, then holds the parents to ransom for as long as he can. When the funds dry up, he kills the girl and moves on. So why not look at the records for unsolved cases of kidnapping? Surely at least one set of parents went to the police at some point? Frankly, it's hard to believe he got away with it in every single case.'

'He would,' I say, 'if he had something on one of the parents. Kenny Hughes isn't stupid – in fact, I'd bet he's way above average intelligence. He's meticulous, manipulative and an expert at reading people – in other words, a typical psychopath. He chooses a young, pampered, rebellious teenager, someone exactly like his mother, with domineering parents who have something to hide. He grooms, then snatches the daughter, who I'm sure goes willingly, at least to start with. He's her escape route. By the time she realises her mistake, it's too late. He's convinced her he's her only hope, her only way to get revenge on her evil, misguided parents. So, together they set up the blackmail scam. What she doesn't know is that by complying with his wishes, she's signing her own death warrant.'

'There's one flaw in your argument,' Grace points out. 'From what we've learned so far, Janet Bennet was far from pampered. Her parents treated her like shit, according to the information we've had so far.'

'Okay,' I concede. 'Let's call it "overprotective". Still, it's a case of a daughter wanting to get out from under, whose parents are well off financially, but dirt poor when it comes to real affection for their child. Mum and Dad are more concerned with reputation than anything else, so they cough up without telling the police they've had a ransom demand. He might even get the girl to make the approach – some sob story about needing money for one reason or another.'

Grace shakes her head. 'It's possible, I suppose, although I find it hard to believe anyone is either that clever – or that lucky – more than once. The bottom line is, you're still shooting in the dark, working on a theory with no evidence. Getting Larson to narrow his search parameters to cases that might fit your scenario could turn out to be a monumental waste of time, and if it is, then it won't just be your arse on the line.'

And if I'm right,' I counter, 'we'll get a result much quicker. I've sent Daz and Robbie over to the lab with those journals from the manse. Once Maggie's taken prints and so on, I've asked them both to read through the lot, but especially entries made around the time of Janet's disappearance and Graham Bennet's death. Plus, don't forget, Millie might have something to say once we have access to her. I've asked Polly to let me know as soon as we've got an update on her condition.'

'I don't know about you, but I'm bloody starving.' Grace stretches, yawns and gets to her feet. 'I'm going home. I suggest you do the same. Follow your hunch for now – I don't suppose there's anything else we can do until either Maggie or Fitzjohn come up with their results.'

I'm about to follow her out when my mobile rings. It's Larson.

'You're supposed to be taking a day off,' I say, even though I was about to call him and tell him to get off his arse and get back to work. I can almost see him bristling on the other end of the line.

'Let's just say I've been "working from home",' he replies after a meaningful pause. 'And I'm sure you'll be pleased to know I've come up with something. If you're on your way back to your place, I can meet you there. Ben's got a couple of friends round for a sleepover, and Chrissie's here helping out with Alex, so it's a bit like Custer's Last Stand in my study.'

The mention of Chrissie almost sends me into a spiral, but I take a deep breath and say, 'Sounds good to me, son. You can pick up a takeaway on your way over. I haven't eaten anything since breakfast.'

. . .

HALF AN HOUR LATER, I've just about managed to hang up my jacket, take off my shoes and feed Blue when there's a sharp rap at my front door. Larson walks past me into the kitchen and dumps a bag on the table, from which the marvellous scent of curry sends my stomach into a cartwheel of anticipation.

'Good choice,' I say, grabbing plates, forks and a couple of beers. Then, a little belatedly, 'Thanks.'

'Believe me,' he says, settling himself and unpacking half a dozen cartons, naan bread and a little sack of onion bhajis, 'you're doing me a favour. Rosie won't have curry in the house, and healthy eating is only fun if you can break the rules now and then.'

That, I think, is something I wouldn't have heard my fitness-obsessed son-in-law say a couple of years ago. 'Are you sure working for the police isn't having a bad influence?' I ask.

He jabs his fork into a vindaloo and grins. 'Don't worry, I haven't quite stooped to Sergeant Saint's level yet, although he did offer me one of his Cornish pasties earlier on. I resisted, naturally.'

'Naturally. So which part of "don't come in until tomorrow" did you not understand?'

The fork stops halfway to his mouth. 'I'm fine – thanks for asking. The fact is, I'd already come to the same conclusion as you about where Hughes might have got his money from, so I narrowed the search parameters and set a program running last night. I would have told you, but you were flat out on our sofa. I went to bed, woke up at lunchtime, and the program had come up with a provisional list – still around three thousand or so. Do you realise how many people are reported missing every year in the UK alone?'

'Son,' I say, starting to feel ruffled, 'I'm a policeman. Of course I bloody well realise. I also realise what the clear-up rate is, and the odds of finding an abducted child alive. After all, I tend to be one of the poor sods dealing with the bodies.'

I take hold of myself, aware that as usual, I'm being unreasonable. Larson busies himself pushing chunks of curry round his plate.

'Look,' I say, 'we're both tired and hungry. How about we eat, then you show me what you've got?'

He nods. 'I suppose,' he says, 'I should be used to the average murder squad detective's casual mealtime conversation by now.' He smiles. 'At least nobody's trying to murder *me* this time – unless it's George Saint with his endless supply of sausage rolls.'

'Don't knock it,' I say, raising my glass. 'Take it from me, Sergeant Saint will still be manning the front desk way after you're drawing your pension.'

We eat in silence, although Larson is clearly itching to tell me something. When we've finished, I clear the table while he makes coffee and unpacks his laptop.

'Okay,' he says when I've drawn up a chair. 'I know this is speculative, but you remember those two photographs I showed you from the box – the same girl at different ages?'

'Yes, I remember. What about them?'

'I decided to see if I could get a comparison with the photo of Millie the Oakfield Road neighbour got at the school sports day – it seemed as good a place to start as any. I'm going to do similar comparisons with as many of the other photos as possible once they are cleaned up, but that could take some time or not be possible at all. Anyway, the one we had of Millie wasn't very clear, and she was only around six at the time, so I didn't get very far with it. Then, a few hours ago, I got one from the hospital, so I put the two together and used an algorithm to extrapolate the changes with age. This is what I found.'

I watch the screen as he brings up an image of Millie, aged six, and then the one from the hospital, clearly the same girl, but two years older. He clicks to the next slide, a computer-generated image of the girl as she might look two years in the future, and twice more, until what I see is a young teenager, but still recognisably Millie Drake. The effect is eerie, and I give an involuntary shiver.

'I know,' Larson comments. 'It's weird. But now look at this.'

He brings up another picture and places it alongside the first. It's the younger version of the girl posing in the garden.

'Bloody hell!' I mutter, leaning forward to get a closer look. 'They could be sisters.'

'Not sisters,' he says, 'but if the algorithm is accurate, we're looking at Millie and her grandmother.' He brings up the photo of the older girl and continues to scroll through the computer-generated versions of Millie until we are looking at two women in their late teens or early twenties. The resemblance is still there – if anything, it's even more striking. 'We've already established that these older photos can't be of Millie's mother,' he says. 'Some of the characteristics, like hair colour, are wrong. But I'd be willing to bet this is a picture of her grandmother – the woman who was found under the shed.'

I'm not about to argue with him. 'I don't suppose you've found out who she is?' I ask.

'Now you mention it,' he replies, 'I think I might have. As I said, I've had a program running to try to match this photo' – he brings up the younger, monochrome image again –

'with the missing persons lists. I guessed the most likely dates to focus on would be 1995 to 1998, given the possible age at the point of abduction, and age at death. This is what the search came up with.'

The image of Millie disappears, replaced by an entry from the misper database. A thirteen-year-old girl, Ruby Marx, disappeared from her home near Chipping Sodbury in South Gloucestershire, in April 1996. After a fruitless investigation, it was concluded that the girl was a runaway, probably headed for the bright lights of London. There was no evidence of abduction, and eventually the case was put on the back burner aside from the usual *Have you seen this girl?* posters on lampposts and hoardings. There is a clear head-and-shoulders photograph of Ruby, part of a larger shot, probably taken at a birthday or Christmas party – a laughing, blond-haired teenager playing to the camera. Next to the official file on-screen, the same girl poses in a garden, stiff, unsmiling, dressed in the kind of clothes the girl in the first photo wouldn't have been seen dead in. I wince at the turn of phrase – correction – clothes she *was* found dead in.

Larson points at the image in the police file. 'Look closely – what do you see?'

Aside from the face, my closer examination reveals nothing at first. She's wearing a pink T-shirt, with some kind of logo on it, but the picture is cut off just below the neckline, so there's no way of knowing what it says. She's wearing jewellery – a gold necklace with a heart pendant, a black velvet choker with a pearl brooch in the centre, and … I see it. A pair of earrings that matches the brooch – gold, drop style, with large, expensive-looking pearls. Larson must have caught my expression, because he clicks the mouse again, and in place of the photo from the box, a single earring appears. It's identical.

'I asked Maggie to prioritise the DNA from this,' he says, 'and told her to ring you as soon as she has a result.'

'Shit!' I pull out my phone, scroll to the missed call from the lab, and dial. The phone rings for what seems forever, but finally Maggie picks up.

'Better late than never,' she says. 'Some people do have a life, you know. Have you any idea what time it is?'

I check my watch. It's just gone 10 p.m. 'Since when did you have a life, Maggie?' I retort, cursing myself for my aversion to phone calls. I really do need to get my act together.

'I might not, but Cyril does,' she answers. 'I'm halfway round the block with him, and I can tell you it's not easy to have a serious conversation when you're carrying four full poo bags. However, since, against all the odds, I actually like you, I'll let it pass this time.'

'For God's sake, Maggie!' I take a deep breath. 'You've got something on that earring?'

'I have,' she says, 'and I hope you're giving full credit to that son-in-law of yours. If it hadn't been for him, I wouldn't have looked at it until next week. But I can tell you that, without doubt, it belonged to your first victim. Her DNA is all over it, and so is Joseph Drake's – or whatever you're calling him now. And while I've got you, don't forget that bottle of Jura. If you want this kind of favour in the future, better make it two. I'll get the paperwork over to you first thing, but in the meantime, give John Larson a pat on the back. You know he deserves it.'

She rings off. I glance across just in time to see something closely resembling a smirk on my son-in-law's face.

'Well,' I say, 'as you're so interested in the nuts and bolts of police work, you can come with me in the morning to break the news to her parents if they're still alive. I take it you've got the details for them as well?'

The smirk dissolves. 'Frederick and Georgina Marx,' he says. 'Both still alive, in their late sixties, still living at the same address just outside Chipping Sodbury.'

I suddenly feel exhausted. 'Okay, son. It's probably safe by now for you to go and help Rosie clean up. I'll meet you at West Hill in the morning, eight o'clock.' I see him to the door, and when he's halfway down the path I remember to add, 'That was good work. At least we can give one family some closure.'

'Yeah,' he replies, without looking back. 'I suppose we can.'

26

The mood in the squad room when I arrive is well on the wrong side of cheerful. At my request, Karen Wyatt, our family liaison officer, is waiting quietly next to her desk. Daz and Robbie are buried in the pile of journals from the manse, and Ollie White, Larson tells me, is hunting through birth and death records, hoping to pick out possible aliases that Kenny Hughes might have used. Sillitoe is still in Cwmbran, and I've sent Colin Draper over to New Vale to liaise with Jerry Forbes's lot, who are planning to search the manse and chapel to try to determine how Kenny Hughes got in and out. Grace is in my office, waiting to take possession of Blue – a good excuse for her to stay in the station, catching up on paperwork, and for me to avoid the confrontation with my ex-wife that I've managed to put off up to now. I'm very aware that I'm acting like a child who thinks if they close their eyes, the monster will simply no longer exist. On the other hand, the problem of a new man in Chrissie's life is a distraction I can't afford right now. I give myself a mental shake and join Grace.

'I've given Gloucester a heads-up,' she says, 'and they've offered one of their own FLOs if we're stretched. It's your call.'

I think for a minute, then shake my head. 'Tell them thanks, but I want Karen on this one – it's our first chance to find out exactly what the circumstances were surrounding Ruby's disappearance, and there may well be issues the parents won't want to discuss. I don't want to risk someone who doesn't know the case putting their foot in it.'

'Fair enough. But what about Larson? You really think it's a good idea to take him with you? Isn't having an untrained civilian present at an interview just as much of a risk – to him and to the parents?'

'He can handle it,' I say, with more confidence than I feel. 'And it's worth the risk. He's the only one who can explain some of the more technical details. One thing's for certain – I bloody well can't. Plus, he's the one who made the connection, and I think they would appreciate meeting the man who finally found their daughter, discovered what happened to her. I'm hoping it will make them more inclined to talk to us. My guess is they've been withholding information from the police for a long time, and like you say, Larson isn't a policeman, so his approach might be less, well – intimidating, I suppose.'

Her eyes narrow. 'Okay,' she says eventually. 'But it has to be his choice. I can't order him to go, and neither can you. I won't have you throwing your weight about when it comes to this kind of thing, so no making an offer he can't refuse, understood?'

'Since when did I ever ...?' She gives me a look. I hold up my hands. 'Understood, ma'am.'

'Good.' She tickles Blue's ears and gets up. 'Come on, girl, let's go and find some gravy bones.'

Blue treats me to the canine equivalent of a self-satisfied smile, then trots after my boss, licking her lips, tail thumping against the desk legs.

THE MARX FAMILY home isn't quite what an estate agent would call a country house, but would definitely be described as a picturesque and spacious cottage. By the look of it, it was once two or three terraced dwellings for farm workers, but was knocked into one a good few decades ago, I guess in the late 1940s or early '50s. It stands in roughly an acre of land, the boundary marked by mature trees on three sides, and a low stone wall separates the front garden from the road. I pull up beside the wall and turn to Larson in the passenger seat.

'It's not too late to say no,' I tell him. 'You can wait for us here if you'd rather.'

'You brought me along for a reason,' he says, shaking his head. 'If they have technical questions, I can explain more clearly than you – unless you've changed your mind about that?'

'Fair enough,' I reply. 'It's a tough one. These people have lost a daughter and two grandchildren and have a great-grandchild they know nothing about who almost died the same way as her mother. It's going to be a hell of a shock. There's no way of knowing how they will react.'

He looks me in the eye. 'I'll manage,' he says, through gritted teeth.

I glance at Karen in the back seat. 'You ready?'

She gives me a curt nod. We all pile out and make our

way down the long path to the Marxes' front door like a mini funeral cortege. The only thing missing is a coffin.

Mr and Mrs Marx appear in the doorway before we knock, their expressions telling me they know what we've come to say – part of it, at least. Mr Marx has an arm firmly round his wife's shoulders, almost holding her upright. The years haven't been kind to them. In their late sixties, both look twenty years older. More than twenty-five years of suppressed grief and vain hope have left them visibly diminished, shrunk into themselves in body and mind. He takes in the sight of his visitors – three of us, one a senior officer, one female – and understands what it must mean. Mrs Marx keeps her gaze on her hands clasped tightly in front of her like a protective shield.

I hold up my identification, and he nods. 'Please,' he says, 'come on in. We had a call – they wouldn't tell us anything on the phone. You've got some news for us – about Ruby? You've found her?'

As he speaks, he's waving us through to a large, spotless lounge complete with a cream-coloured shag pile carpet and eye-watering grey and orange geometric wallpaper straight out of the 1970s. There's even a fake tiger-skin rug in front of a tiled fireplace reminiscent of a railway tunnel. I make a silent bet that the bathroom has an avocado suite, and that every room has a wall display of expensive knick-knacks. Given the cottage's chocolate-box exterior, the décor is totally incongruous – and tasteless by today's standards – but then I realise that, for the Marxes, time stopped the day their daughter disappeared, and they have, against all hope, left the entire property exactly as it was, including, without doubt, Ruby's bedroom. One thing is clear – the house and the furnishings would have cost a fortune back in the day. As targets for blackmail, they would have been perfect.

'Please,' Marx says as we sit down, 'call me Fred, and my wife is Gina.' He turns to her and pats her hand. 'Go and make some tea, love. And I'm sure these officers would like some of your fruit cake.'

Gina obediently shuffles off to the kitchen. I give Karen a look; she nods and follows her out.

'Mr Marx,' I start. 'Fred—'

'I know why you've come,' he interrupts. 'She's dead, isn't she? Our Ruby – our lovely girl – you've found her, haven't you …' The dam breaks, and he starts to sob, pulls out a pristine handkerchief, dabs his eyes and collects himself. 'Just tell me one thing, Chief Inspector. When did she die? How long ago? And was it *him*?' He spits the word. 'Did *he* do it?'

'He?' I guide him to the sofa, and he sinks down onto it. 'Who do you mean, Fred? Someone Ruby knew?'

He shakes his head, trying to clear the fog and order his thoughts. I take an armchair and gesture for Larson to do the same. We wait in silence until Karen comes in and sets down a tray, then gently directs Gina Marx to a seat next to her husband. Now, I note, it's her turn to support her spouse, who seems to have crumpled in on himself. She sits straight backed, alert, gripping one of his hands in both of hers. She nods as Karen distributes mugs of tea, then perches on a dining chair brought in from the kitchen.

'He means the man she ran off with,' Gina says, her expression twisting into disgust, as if a dead rodent has suddenly appeared on the carpet. 'Her "boyfriend", she said he was. But he was no boy, and he wasn't anybody's friend. He filled her head with silly ideas, turned her against us, and then he took her away – he must have forced her to go with him, and I told the police so, but they didn't believe us. They said she'd lied about him, made him up, and run off on her own. There was no evidence, you see – that he existed, I mean. They searched, but …' She stops, realising how it must all sound. 'I'm sorry,' she says, taking a deep breath. 'You must think we're both mad. But, like my husband says, you're here because she's …' She can't bring herself to say the word.

Larson has brought a large envelope containing copies of the images we've been working on, and without a word he hands me the old black-and-white photograph, the one of Ruby that must have been taken not long after her disappearance.

'Before I say anything,' I tell them, handing it across, 'I'd like you both to look at this and see if you can identify the person in the photograph.'

They both stare at it for a long time. Even though it's plain from their expressions, I have to ask. 'Is this your daughter, Ruby?'

He doesn't look up, just nods. She meets my eye, her gaze painfully sharp. 'Yes,' she answers, voice brittle as broken glass, 'that's Ruby.' She carefully places the photograph, face down, on the coffee table between us.

I glance at Larson, who is playing his part perfectly, expression sympathetic, but non-committal. He brings out a plastic evidence bag, places it beside the photo.

'I wonder if you could also look at this,' he says. 'Please don't open the bag, but look carefully, and tell us if you recognise it.'

Gina reaches down and picks it up in two fingers, holds it up to the light, turning the bag one way and then the other. Without a word, she sets it down, gets up and leaves the room. Karen makes to follow, but I stop her with a gesture, and we wait in silence. After perhaps two interminable minutes, she returns and without a word places something on the table next to the bag.

It's an earring – the identical twin to the one we've brought from the lab. For a moment I lose my footing. A ripple of shock crosses Larson's face, but he recovers faster than I do, and pulls one of the clean evidence bags I've told him to bring out of his pocket.

'I'm sorry,' he says, 'but we'll need to take this.' He neatly scoops it up and seals the bag. We're all sure, though, that the inevitable analysis won't be necessary. 'You're sure both these earrings belong to Ruby?' he asks. This time, it's Fred Marx who answers.

'Quite sure,' he says.

He's about to say something else when his wife gives him a warning nudge. 'Fred!' she hisses. Then, realising that if there is something she wants to conceal, she's just effectively blown all efforts at secrecy out of the water, she slumps back with a sigh.

I clear my throat. 'I'm really very sorry,' I say. 'I'm afraid there's no doubt now that the body we've found is your daughter, Ruby. From what we've been able to ascertain, she died in or around 2003. She would have been perhaps—'

'Nineteen,' Fred interrupts, 'or twenty. Her birthday was in September, you see. The twenty-first of September. We bought her a present. We've bought something every year since ...' He can't go on.

Gina takes up the tale. 'We make her a cake, too – every year, with candles. Well – just one now. There isn't room for all of them. We thought that maybe one day she'd – well, she'd turn up, that he'd finally let her go, pick on someone else's daughter, get fed up of her. But she's been dead all this time, and we ...'

Grief takes over, and she finally gives in to it, the two of them weeping, clinging onto each other, trying to comprehend a senseless act that took their child from them more than twenty-five years ago. I nod to Karen, who takes over, offering more tea and sympathy, for what that is worth, and I beckon for a pale-faced Larson to follow me out into the hallway.

'How are you feeling?' I remember to ask him.

'Crap – how do you expect me to feel?'

'Sounds about right,' I say. 'But we're not there yet, not by a long way. The next step is an identification of Hughes and a name. Think you can manage that?' The look he gives me could induce apoplexy at fifty paces. 'Okay,' I say. 'Let's get on with it, shall we?'

The Marxes have composed themselves by the time we re-seat ourselves. Fred asks the inevitable questions – how did their daughter die, did she suffer, have we arrested the so-called boyfriend, and if not, why not?

I explain, slowly, what we know – that we believe she died from a single blow to the head, that death was most likely instant. 'We're currently pursuing a number of enquiries,' I end, falling back on the usual formula, 'but as death occurred a considerable time ago, please appreciate it may take a little time for us to complete our investigation. We have two possible suspects, and I'm afraid I can't say more at this stage.'

'When can we see her?' Gina asks – another inevitable question.

I explain that although they are welcome to view the body, it may not be advisable, as the remains are purely skeletal, which leads to the final, last-ditch hope – that we might have made a mistake.

'So how do you know it's her?' Gina demands.

I hand over to Larson, who, to be fair, does an excellent job of taking them through the forensic details and digital wizardry. He ends by handing them a copy of the photo of Kenny Hughes in his persona of the middle-aged Joseph Drake. They both shake their heads.

'Is this him?' Fred asks. 'Is this Carl?'

'Carl?' I say. 'Carl was your daughter's boyfriend?'

Gina takes up the tale. 'Carl Baker – at least, that's what Ruby said his name was. I had to force her to tell me that much. She wouldn't say where he was from, what he did for a living – nothing. I could tell something wasn't right. He was a lot older than her, I know that much. She was only thirteen, much too young to be running around with boys. I mean, only perverts pick on children. She said he wasn't like that, but what did she know at her age?' She stutters to a halt, muttering, 'It was wrong – all wrong.'

'Are you saying,' I ask, 'that you never met this Carl Baker?'

They shake their heads. 'Not once,' Fred says. 'We tried to stop her seeing him, of course. We made sure we took her to school every morning, brought her home in the afternoons, and only allowed her out with friends if they were with us or their parents. It didn't stop her. She must have been sneaking out of school and out of her bedroom at night when we were asleep. A few times I took days off work to keep a watch on the school gates, and Gina sometimes stayed up all night to check on her, but we never saw anything. Then, one morning, her bedroom was empty. She never came back.'

I take a deep breath. 'There's something else I have to tell you,' I say, and see them go still, bracing themselves. I press on. 'Your daughter had two children – twins, a boy and a girl.'

They blink at me, confused – whatever they thought I was going to say, this wasn't it. 'I'm afraid the boy was found with your daughter's body, and we suspect he was a victim of the same person who killed your daughter. He would have been approximately three years old. The girl, however, survived until around two years ago. We're pretty sure that the person you knew as Carl Baker was responsible for your granddaughter's death.'

The silence in the room is deafening. Gina Marx stares, disbelieving, her mouth working, but no sound coming out. Her husband has gone grey, and for an awful moment I think he's having a heart attack, but he takes in a huge gulp of air and thankfully recovers himself.

'Granddaughter?' he whispers, struggling to understand. 'Ruby got pregnant? But …'

'She was only thirteen when she went off with him,' Gina puts in. 'How could she have been pregnant? She was only a child, for God's sake. It's not possible.' She shakes her head. 'He must have – well – you know …'

She lets the word hang and stares at me, willing me to finish her sentence, tell her that her daughter was a victim of rape. *Christ!* I think, trying to think of a gentle way to throw yet more shit in their faces. But there really isn't one.

'The fact is,' I tell them, 'our evidence shows that Carl Baker wasn't the father of the children. We know who was, but he was also murdered, around the same time as your daughter and her little boy. Someone is currently serving a prison sentence for that murder, and we have reason to believe he may also have caused the deaths of your daughter and grandson. Your granddaughter, however, died after this man was convicted, so we are fairly certain Carl Baker was responsible.'

Again, there is a silence, broken by Karen, who asks if they would like more tea. Fred Marx shakes his head. 'Brandy,' he stutters with a vague wave towards a dresser running along the wall of the lounge. Karen glances at me. I nod, and she roots out a bottle and two glasses. The Marxes both take a stiff drink, and Fred makes a valiant attempt to focus, fight his way through the quagmire. Gina simply looks shell-shocked.

'Anything else?' he manages to ask, sticking out his chin, a defeated boxer waiting for the next left hook.

'There is one more thing,' I say. 'Your granddaughter, whose name, we believe, was Pauline, also had a child – a little girl called Millie, eight years old now. Yesterday, we found Millie abandoned in a house in South Wales. She's in hospital, recovering, but hopefully she's going to be fine. We can let you have more information once we've been able to talk to her, and, if social services agree, you may be able to see her. You are, after all, her great-grandparents.'

Larson helpfully steps in and hands the couple two more photographs, the cleaned-up version of the older Ruby, and of Millie. 'You might like to keep these,' he says, 'and look at them a little later, when you've had time to take everything in.'

I get up, and Larson follows. 'If you don't mind,' I tell the Marxes, 'I would like our family liaison officer to stay with you for a while. She'll be able to guide you through all the processes, let you know what happens next, and so on. We'll be in touch very soon.'

They nod dumbly, and when we get to the door, I say, 'Just one more thing. After Ruby left, did you have any contact at all, either with Ruby or with Carl Baker? Letters, phone calls, anything like that?'

Gina pulls in a breath, affronted. 'No – no, of course not. We told the police at the time. She disappeared, and that was that.'

'That's right.' Her husband nods. 'She just left. We never heard anything – not until today.'

'I think,' I say to Larson when we're out of earshot, 'we're going to need to trawl through the Marxes' bank accounts, from 1996 to 2001. Think you can manage that, son?'

27

By the time we're back in the car, Larson is busy fiddling with his phone. While he's occupied, I pull out my own and call Grace to ask her to put in a request for a warrant to access the records of any bank accounts held by Fred and Gina Marx.

'I've texted Ollie,' Larson tells me, 'asking him to do a search for Carl Baker as an infant death, and also for any activity under that name between 1980 and 2000.' When I don't answer, he goes on, 'You really think they're lying – about never having met him, and having no contact with their daughter after the abduction?'

I start the car, having made sure, this time, my phone isn't on silent, and pull away.

'I don't think, son, I'm bloody well sure they are. Plus, I don't think she was abducted. They weren't lying when they said she escaped the house and ran off with him – just like his mother did with Iain Hughes.' I catch his questioning glance out of the corner of my eye. 'Think about it,' I say. 'A young girl, infatuated with an older man, decides to elope with him. She packs a few of her favourite things – a fact, by the way, that the parents decided not to mention – and gets herself dressed up to go and meet him. She puts on her best jeans and T-shirt and her best jewellery, including a very expensive pair of heirloom earrings, probably inherited from a relative. She climbs out of her bedroom window and disappears.'

It takes a minute for the penny to drop. 'She left wearing both earrings,' he says, 'and returned one of them to her parents, or Kenny Hughes did.'

'Exactly,' I reply. 'As proof that whatever request or demand for money in the letter that came with it was genuine. Gina Marx made a mistake showing it to us. I suspect she was so keen to have her daughter's body identified she temporarily lost the plot. By the time she denied ever having heard from either of them, it was too late. To give them credit, they are still trying to brazen it out, even though they must realise we'll get to the bottom of it sooner or later.'

'So why didn't you push it? Why not just search the place for any documents or other evidence?'

'Two reasons. First, we haven't got a warrant – yet. Second, we *have* got Karen Wyatt, and Karen is very good at her job. An FLO isn't all about making cups of tea. Her primary focus is getting information and evidence, just like any other detective. She'll be slipping and sliding around that house faster than a greased pig, you can bet on it. You can also bet she'll find a girl's bedroom left just as it was twenty-odd years ago, complete with a much-diminished wardrobe and a virtually empty knicker drawer, and somewhere in the house a locked office drawer where, more than likely, they've kept any incriminating correspondence.'

'Incriminating?' He gives me a puzzled look, shaking his head. 'Jesus! How the hell do you do this job? We've just told a couple their daughter and grandchildren have been murdered, and their great-granddaughter is barely surviving in hospital, and all you can think of is how to arrest them for something. Are all police officers like this, or is it just you?'

'I know, son,' I say. 'Life sucks.'

I drive in what definitely can't be interpreted as companionable silence until my phone bursts into life. Larson has finally managed to set up the hands-free function, and I press the button. It's DC Colin Draper.

'Sir, we've found something at New Vale. It looks like Kenny Hughes has been in the chapel. I thought you'd want to take a look.'

'You thought right,' I tell him, then turn to Larson. 'Are you up for it?' I ask. 'I was hoping you could go over the security anyway, in case the Chepstow people have missed anything.'

He says nothing, just nods, so I tell Draper we're on our way and head for the Severn crossing.

DC DRAPER IS WAITING for us as we pull up outside the chapel, trying to contain his excitement and not quite succeeding. At least it makes a change from my silent, sulky driving companion.

'It's incredible, sir,' he blurts out as I haul myself out of the car. 'He must have been using this place for years – I've never seen anything like it! It's like some sort of a—'

'I think, Detective Constable,' I interrupt, 'that I'd quite like to form my own opinion of what it's like, if it's all the same to you.'

He coughs, then stands back, giving me room to breathe. 'Yes, sir, of course. Sorry.'

'I take it the scene is secure, and nobody's been tramping all over it – whatever "it" is?'

He nods. 'DC Jones got in touch with Inspector Forbes, sir, and he gave instructions for everybody to wait for you.'

'Good.' I turn to Larson. 'You'd better come along, too, just in case.'

'In case of what?' he asks.

I shrug. 'I'm sure I'll think of something. Lead on, Colin – given the build-up, this had better be worth seeing.'

Draper leads us round to the back of the chapel to where DC Phil 'the Tea' Jones, DS Peters and Meera Kumar are all waiting at the foot of a short, steep flight of steps leading to a large metal hatch – a coal hole is my first thought. The hatch has been opened, and I throw Draper a glance.

'Like I said, sir,' he says, 'nobody's been down there yet. We've just shone a torch inside.'

I nod, and Peters hands me a hefty Maglite. I switch it on and point it down into the darkness. 'Bloody hell!' I can't help muttering as the beam reveals a fully kitted out bedsitting room, complete with table, sofa, fridge and stovetop grill. There's even a microwave oven standing on a set of storage cupboards and drawers, and an electric heater in a corner. It's one hell of a coal hole, I have to admit.

'Is there any other way in?' I ask.

Meera replies. 'Not that we've found,' she says. 'There's a cellar below the main part of the chapel, and this must have been the coal store. At one time there would have been access to it from the cellar, but it looks to have been bricked up a long time ago, probably when the heating system went over to electricity.'

I think for a minute, then make a decision. 'I need to get down there,' I say. 'Just the two of us to start with. The space is too small to have a whole team blundering about. Can you sort out a couple of suits?'

She nods, but doesn't look too pleased. 'If you'll follow me, sir,' she replies curtly, and heads off back to the front of the chapel, where the van containing her team's equipment has been stationed. 'If you'll pardon my saying so,' she says when we're out of earshot, 'we might be provincial as far as you city lot are concerned, but we do have a very experienced team here. We do not "blunder about" – *sir*.'

I stop and turn to face her stony expression. She does have a point. 'My apologies, Meera,' I say. 'I'm afraid it's been a hell of a day so far, and my people will tell you that I do have a reputation for being a bit of an arse, especially when I haven't had a decent breakfast.'

It takes a few beats, but eventually the annoyance melts into a faint smile. 'Apology accepted, sir.' She roots in the back of the van and comes up with two fresh coveralls. We get suited up in silence and make our way back to the hatch.

There's a drop of around eight feet from the hatch entrance to the floor of the concealed room. Getting in isn't that much of a problem, but getting back out again isn't going to be so easy. I send Phil the Tea to hunt for a step ladder or similar, and DS Peters carefully lowers Meera, slightly built and only just over five feet tall, down far enough for her to jump the rest of the way. It's easier for me, being a good foot taller, but I still have to take care letting go of the rim of the hatch. We might be here for a while, so I send Larson off to the manse, where the rest of Meera's team are still going through the rooms, with instructions to inspect the electronic alarm system for possible breaches and flaws.

'There must be a light in here somewhere,' Meera says. 'He's got an electricity supply rigged up somehow.'

After a minute's search by torchlight, I find a table lamp, placed out of sight behind the back of a small sofa and plugged into an extension cable. I flick the switch, but nothing happens, so I follow the lead back until it disappears behind the cupboards. Between the two of us, we manage to move the cupboards out far enough to reach a master switch rigged to a thick cable running through a hole that has been drilled through the brick wall between the room and the rest of the cellar. I turn it on, and we have electricity.

'There must be a master fuse box for the chapel on the other side of the wall,' Meera says. 'He's managed to run a concealed cable off it, and it's my bet that if he uses it sparingly, nobody notices. I doubt they have smart meters monitoring daily usage – they just get a quarterly bill. When he's not here, he can simply turn it off.'

I pull out the lamp, place it on top of the cupboards, and light floods the space. Colin Draper was right to be excited. It really is an impressive hiding place. It's clean, functional and comfortable. There is even a thick rug on the floor. Hughes – or whoever constructed the place, I remind myself – provided himself with every comfort. Someone could hide themselves here for weeks or months at a time. Meera opens the fridge. It's not just empty, it's been scrubbed clean – ready for the next time. It tells us that the occupant is gone, for now. We haven't caught him mid-stay. He did what he needed to do here, and left, but made sure the place was ready for his return. Something tells me he knows we're on to him, and that return won't happen. Kenny Hughes is a step ahead of us. Another thought strikes me. Someone as meticulous as this doesn't abandon his bolthole unless he has somewhere else to go. He already has at least one other place to hide out – maybe more than one. When the fuss has died down, he will simply emerge as someone else – Baker, Drake, whatever – and meanwhile he's holed up in another of his hidden bijou residences. This is one clever bastard. But, I think, he's maybe not as clever as me or Forbes or the combined forces that are rapidly stacking up against him. Wherever he's gone, I have a feeling it won't be far. He's the kind who likes to be in familiar territory.

I pull myself back to the current task and shout up to Peters, who is still waiting up top. 'Get someone in the cellar,' I say, 'and see if you can find a cable running off the fuse box into the wall.'

He goes off, and Meera and I make a start on the search. 'He's got electricity,' I say, 'but where did he get water? If he stayed here for days at a time, what about basic sanitation?'

'That's easy,' she says. 'The chapel has a rest room in the back with a working water supply. The church still uses it for regular services once a fortnight, even though they haven't stationed a permanent minister here since Bennet. It's also used for special occasions – harvest festivals, Christmas, and so on. There's no access from here, though, so he'd have to come out through the hatch and back in through the front door, which is kept locked. He must have had a key cut at some point.'

'CCTV?'

She shakes her head. 'None. They must think there's nothing worth nicking that would justify the cost.'

'Damn it,' I say, 'although from what we've learned of

Kenny Hughes so far, it wouldn't make any difference. We'll have to hope the cameras at the manse have picked him up, but I'm not holding my breath.'

As we talk, we're carefully rifling through the cupboards and drawers. One drawer contains a basic change of clothes – trousers, shirt, socks and underwear. I open another, and all doubt that this is Hughes's hiding place dissolves. It contains a child-sized Liberty-print dress and a dark green ribbed sweater, the 'uniform' worn by every girl to have the misfortune of getting herself entangled with this monster.

'Looks like he's pretty keen on DIY,' Meera comments, rifling through a cupboard.

'What?' I move across to join her.

'There's something here for every occasion, by the look of it,' she says. 'Tools for plumbing, electrics, carpentry – you name it.'

She pulls out a large metal toolbox, opens it and pokes around in the contents – spanners, a wrench, sets of Allen keys and drill bits, and …

'Stop!' I hiss, reaching out to grab her arm.

She lifts her hand away and gives me a questioning look.

Very carefully, I move the tools aside with a gloved finger. Right at the bottom of the box, carefully sealed in several layers of clear plastic and high-strength tape, is a hammer. I swallow and grip the edge of the box with my left hand to hide the involuntary twitch that always, since the shooting, signals a sudden rise in my adrenalin level.

'Right,' I tell her. 'Get your team down here, photograph everything, and send that hammer over to Maggie Ainsworth as quickly as possible. Make it your priority, okay?'

'Right. Important, is it, then – the hammer?'

'More than you could imagine,' I reply, and call up to DS Peters for a ladder to climb up and back out through the hatch.

I'm halfway to the manse when I meet Larson on his way to find me. 'It's a very good security system they've got over there,' he says, 'one of the best on the market. But, unfortunately, a system is only as good as the way it's set up. It's where most security falls down – you know, like people thinking that "password" is a good password for their bank account.'

'You're saying Griffiths used that on his alarm system? For God's sake!'

'Not quite,' he says, his mouth quirking into a grin before he can stop himself, 'but he might as well have done. I suppose he didn't think the place would be broken into by someone who knew his family intimately. He was more concerned about burglars nicking the cutlery.'

'So,' I ask, intrigued, 'what did he use?'

'Two eight-digit codes,' he replies. 'The first, for the outer door, is Janet's date of birth – 04081951, and the second, to disarm the system, is Ruth's – 28081946. It's likely Kenny would have known both dates and been able to work it out.'

Larson's right, but it isn't that which surprises me. 'Are you telling me you remembered the Bennet sisters' dates of birth?'

He shrugs. 'I'm afraid I've got a bit of a photographic memory when it comes to numbers. I can't help it. It drives Rosie mad sometimes, especially when we're out shopping.'

Great, I think. My daughter didn't just marry a computer geek, the man is also a walking calculator. Then I have another thought. 'Janet was born in September, yes? And so was her sister. What about Ruby Marx? Didn't the parents mention her birthday?'

He closes his eyes, recalling the conversation, and nods. 'They said it was the twenty-first September 1983. Why?'

'It may be just coincidence,' I say, 'or my instinct's going way off track, but just suppose one of the criteria he uses to select his victims includes when they were born? They have the same upbringing, more or less, as his mother, he takes them at roughly the same age Janet ran off with Iain Hughes, he dresses them in clothes that are exactly like Janet's, so maybe he also gets as close to her birthday as he can.'

It takes him a minute, but then he gets it. 'It's a very long shot, but if that is what he's been doing, it could save a lot of time. I'll get onto Ollie and tell him to narrow our existing search parameters to missing girls born in September.'

My phone rings. Sillitoe's name pops up on the screen.

'We've been given the go-ahead to talk to Millie,' she says. 'We can get in to see her in an hour or so.'

'Good,' I say. 'I can be there in around half an hour. Come on,' I say to Larson. 'You can bring Ollie up to speed on the way.'

We're intercepted on the way to the car by Phil the Tea, who thrusts paper bags at us and grins. 'Meera said you hadn't had breakfast, sir,' he explains, 'so I nipped off to the café at the end of the village. They do a damned good bacon sandwich, in my humble opinion.'

He leaves us standing, and makes his way back up towards the chapel, clutching enough greasy packages to feed a whole division.

28

Larson hunts around for tissues, finds none, and uses his handkerchief to wipe his fingers. I have to admit that Phil the Tea's humble opinion of the local café's offering is on the nose, and as we reach the main road into Cwmbran, I'm in a much better temper.

'You want to watch it, son,' I say. 'Takeaway curry *and* bacon sandwiches from the local greasy spoon, and all within twenty-four hours. Much more of this and you'll be on the slippery slope to George Saint's sausage rolls.'

He glowers for a minute, then grins. 'I'll never go that far – but it was a very good bacon sandwich.' He pauses, the grin dissolving into a frown. 'I don't understand,' he says. 'Kenny Hughes is smart – he's particularly good at covering his tracks, so if he cleaned out his fridge and made sure there were no clues as to where he'd gone, why leave the hammer? And why wrap it up so carefully? If it actually is the weapon used to kill Ruby Marx and her son and Jimmy Harris, wouldn't he have gotten rid of it years ago?'

'I'm pretty certain it is the murder weapon,' I reply, 'and

he left it because he wanted us to find it. It's his insurance policy.'

My son-in-law gives me a blank look. 'But we already know he's a murderer. He's groomed a number of young girls, kept them completely under his control and then killed them. Why would he want to distance himself from these murders in particular? And how can providing us with the hammer be an insurance policy – it doesn't make any sense.'

'To a normal person, maybe not,' I say. 'But I'm willing to bet the hammer will have DNA from all three victims and from the person he's telling us did those killings – Craig Tyler. He might have got wind of Tyler's appeal, and he'll know that if it's successful, then he will be next in the frame. If I read him right, he'll know we've been to see his father, and guess that we've been told about the hammer attack on Danny Hughes. If we can find Danny and get his corroboration, we can charge Kenny with the more recent murders as well. But in his warped mind, there is a big difference between locking someone away and abandoning them, and the violence involved in smashing a person's skull. It doesn't fit his pattern, and he wants us to know that, which reminds me – Forbes's lot are supposed to be tracking Danny Hughes down. I need an update on that while we're here.'

I realise Larson is staring at me, open mouthed. 'Bloody hell!' he says. 'If this is what Rosie grew up with, no wonder she took up psychology!'

'I know, son.' I shrug. 'It's all my fault, and I've got a lot to answer for. Tell me about it.'

SILLITOE IS WAITING for us in reception when we get to the hospital. 'It's going to be another half hour or so,' she tells us.

'According to the nurses, Millie's recovering well, although she doesn't have much idea what's happened, and she's scared stiff of all the people – never been in a hospital before, so it must be overwhelming, poor mite.'

'What about Inspector Forbes?' I ask.

She grins. 'Still here, and making a monumental fuss. They won't let him out until they're sure he's not going to tear the stitches. At least, his uncle won't let him out – says if he does, he'll be back in by the end of the afternoon because he won't sit still and let it heal. He's in a private room on the top floor, being waited on hand and foot by every unattached nurse who can sneak up there.'

'I can imagine,' I say dryly. 'We'd better go up and rescue him, then. Give me a shout as soon as Millie's ready.'

Sillitoe wasn't exaggerating. We reach Forbes's room just as one nurse is leaving carrying an empty tray, while another is perched on the end of his bed, checking the dressing on his leg. He's somehow acquired a filter coffee machine, next to which is a stack of mugs and a bottle of milk. He sees us and waves us in.

'You're just in time,' he says, grinning. 'Sarah here was about to put a pot of coffee on once she's finished poking me about.'

'Sarah,' Sarah retorts, 'was about to do nothing of the kind. This isn't a hotel. I'm sure your visitors are quite capable of making their own refreshments. You've already wasted the time of one of my students today, sending her off to get biscuits for your colleagues.'

'Only because you gave me strict instructions not to get out of bed,' he says, giving her an innocent look.

She sighs, rolls her eyes and heads for the door, although

she's smiling by the time she reaches us, and gives us a friendly nod on the way out.

'I see you're keeping up your reputation as a spoiled aristocrat,' I comment, pulling up a chair while Larson sees to the coffee.

'Actually,' he says, 'I rather like Sarah. I'm thinking of inviting her for dinner once they let me out. Do you think that's too much of a cliché, falling in love with your nurse?'

'I think,' I reply, 'you've got too much time on your hands. Sergeant Peters said you were going through the CCTV footage from the manse. Find anything?'

At once, he's back in the role of senior police officer. 'I'm not sure. Mr Larson, I'm glad you're here. There's something I'd like you to look at.'

Larson brings three mugs of coffee over and sits. Forbes opens his laptop and brings up the footage from the manse security camera. He forwards the recording to a time stamp of 01:05:00, and freezes it.

'This is from six days ago,' he says. 'Now watch.' He forwards the video, frame by frame. The timestamp jerks forward until it reaches 01:05:30. He clicks the mouse again, and suddenly it's reading 01:07:00. 'Ninety seconds,' he says, with a glance at Larson. 'What do you think?'

'It could be a power outage or a recording glitch,' he says. 'But it could also be a deliberate deletion. Can you play it at normal speed?'

Forbes obliges. The visual record looks seamless – the jump in time would be unnoticeable to an average observer. Larson, who never goes anywhere without his own laptop in its custom-made backpack, pulls it out and fires it up.

'I don't suppose Griffiths has a backup system running?' he asks.

Forbes shakes his head. 'Sadly not – it was the first thing I checked. What I do have, though ...' He rummages in the top drawer of his bedside cabinet, 'is this.' He holds out what I assume is a disk drive in a portable housing. 'I've been using a copy just in case I do something stupid and wipe the whole lot.'

Larson smiles to himself and plugs the drive into his laptop. 'Excellent,' he says. 'Let's hope Kenny Hughes isn't quite the expert in IT that he thinks he is. This might take a while.'

Within seconds, Forbes and my son-in-law are completely absorbed in whatever is happening on the screen, and I've become, as they say, a redundant appendage at a nuptials ceremony. I decide to head back downstairs to Sillitoe, an announcement met by a couple of disinterested grunts.

'I was about to call you,' she says as I join her. 'We can go in to see Millie, but only for a maximum of ten minutes. There's someone from Child Services with her, and Martin and Ruth Griffiths are here, but as yet they've not been allowed to see her. They were in the hospital family room last I heard, arguing the toss with a social worker. ACC Forbes has asked the local force to step back for now, so we've got first dibs.'

I follow her up to another private room, this time on the first floor. A local PC is stationed outside the door, and she stands to attention when she sees us.

'You can go straight in, sir,' she says to me, and smiles at Sillitoe. 'Ma'am.' They are clearly well acquainted.

'Thanks, Jenny,' Sillitoe says, and we enter the room.

Millie Drake is sitting up in bed, clinging tightly onto the hand of a middle-aged woman with a round face and comforting expression. She nods to us, turns to Millie and smiles.

'These are the two police officers I told you about, Millie,' she says gently. 'They're trying to find your dad. Is it okay if they come in and talk to you?'

The child nods uncertainly. She's painfully thin and frightened out of her wits, but she's been bathed, and her long, mousy hair has been brushed out into a ponytail. She looks more like a six than an eight-year-old, swamped by the hospital bed, and so fragile a breath might break her. I suddenly feel a lump in my throat, but swallow it down and put on what I hope is a reassuring smile.

'Hello, Millie. My name's Crow, and this is my assistant, Polly.' This isn't the time to trot out ranks. 'Do you mind if we come in? We've been worried about you and wanted to make sure you're all right.'

Her brow furrows. 'Crow? That's a bird's name,' she says, 'not a person's.'

'That's right,' I say. 'People tease me about it sometimes. There are some who call me "Bird Man" because of my name.'

'Oh,' she says, and after a pause, 'That's not nice. People shouldn't tease other people because of what their name is.'

'No,' I agree. 'I'm used to it now, though, so I don't really mind. Can we come and sit down?'

She thinks, then nods. 'All right.'

We both pull up chairs next to the bed, and I sit with some relief, realising how big I must seem to her, how intimidating.

'Where's my daddy?' she asks, and the question knocks the air out of my chest more effectively than a punch. It's not so much the question, but the look of hope on her face that sends a sliver of ice down my back. She's not afraid in case he turns up – she's desperate to see him.

'We don't know, sweetheart,' I answer after a couple of breaths. 'We're trying to find him. We were hoping you might be able to help us.' What I really want to say is that her father is an evil, murdering bastard who left her locked up to die of starvation and thirst, just as he did her mother and countless other defenceless girls.

She's talking again. 'He said he'd come back to get me, but now I'm here, he won't know where I am, and he won't be able to find me.' The look in her eye is almost pleading. 'I have to go back and wait, like Daddy said,' she says. 'Please will you take me?'

Like hell I will, I think, but before I can answer her, Sillitoe chips in.

'Listen, Millie,' she says. 'Maybe you could ring him, let him know you're okay. You can borrow my phone if you like. Does your dad have a phone number?'

It's a brilliant move, but unfortunately it doesn't work. Millie frowns, puzzled. 'We had a phone at our old house,' she says. 'It was plugged into the wall high up. I couldn't reach it, but Daddy could. We don't live there anymore.'

'Did you ever live anywhere else?' I ask. 'Did your daddy take you anywhere, to stay, like for a holiday, or to visit anyone?'

She frowns again and sticks a finger in her mouth, thinking. Finally, she nods. 'We went somewhere once,' she replies, 'just after Mummy left. Daddy said he thought he knew where she was, and we should go and see. But she wasn't there, so we came home.'

I hardly dare ask the next question. 'Can you remember

what it was like, Millie? Was it a house or a hotel? Was there anyone else there?'

'A house,' she says, after more thought. 'Nobody was in it except us.'

'Was it a big house – bigger than your normal house, or was it smaller?'

'Big. It was a really big house, with lots of rooms with nobody in, just me and Daddy. There weren't any windows. There were places for windows to go, but Daddy said the people who built it forgot to put them in, so it got cold. I had to wear my coat all the time. Maybe Daddy's gone there. Can we go and see? I want Daddy.'

Her lip quivers, and she starts to cry.

The woman from Child Services squeezes her hand. 'I think maybe we'd better leave it there for a while, Chief Inspector,' she suggests. 'Millie's very tired. You can speak to her again later.'

Reluctantly, I agree with her. 'Thank you for helping us, Millie,' I say to the child. 'Don't worry. We'll find your dad, I promise.'

The woman slips out with us into the corridor. 'This place she was talking about,' she says. 'You think her father might be there?'

I nod. 'It's possible. It's going to be difficult to pinpoint a location just from that description, though. It could be any one of a thousand derelict buildings anywhere in the southwest of England or Wales.'

The woman thinks for a minute. 'Millie asked for some paper and pencils a couple of hours ago when I brought her some books. She clearly likes artwork. What if I ask her to do a drawing when she's settled down? Often, children can put things on paper that they don't have the words to describe. Give it an hour or so, and I'll see what I can do. Where can I find you?'

'That could be a really good idea,' I say. 'Thanks. We'll be here for a while yet, so just message me if you manage to get Millie to draw anything.'

I give her my mobile number, and we make our way down the corridor to the lifts.

'I can't bloody believe that!' Sillitoe hisses, her face flushed with pure fury. 'After all that bastard's done to her, all she wants to do is go back to him. It makes me sick!'

'I can't disagree,' I say. 'But right now, there's nothing we can do except wait and hope she literally draws us a picture. Meanwhile, we've got two forensic pathologists, two teams of detectives and a computer wizard all doing their damnedest, so somebody's got to come up with something somewhere. Don't worry, Polly – we'll get him. It's only a matter of time.'

What I don't say, but what we're both thinking, is that the more time goes by, the more chance Kenny Hughes has of slipping neatly through one of the many massive holes in what, so far, has been a very ineffective net.

29

Sillitoe and I head for the ground-floor café to grab a pile of cookies and forestall any further attempts by Forbes to divert star-struck student nurses from their far more vital duties. As we reach the entrance, I catch sight of Ruth and Martin Griffiths seated at one of the tables, absently poking forks into pastries that have probably been sitting in front of them, uneaten, for the last hour. Exhausted, I feel unwilling to risk being drawn into yet another awkward conversation.

Sillitoe taps my arm. She's clearly had the same thought. 'There's a bakery just across the road,' she says. 'Fancy trying that, boss?' I nod, and we make our way out onto the street. 'What's going to happen, do you think?' she asks. 'About Millie, I mean. When all this is over, where is she going to end up?'

'Eventually, who knows?' I reply. 'In care, initially, but after that, things are going to get very complicated. The Griffithses would probably be her best shot, but what they don't know yet is that she isn't their great-niece at all – neither

Kenny Hughes nor Janet are genetically related to Millie, and that will have an effect on the official decision-making. Also, they are in their late seventies, and that will go against them. On the other hand, she is the Marxes' great-granddaughter, but they are more than likely going to end up with a criminal record, at the very least, for obstructing the police, and they are almost as old and less suitable – after all, Ruby Marx couldn't wait to get away from them. Whichever way it goes, Millie is already severely damaged, and it's going to get worse before it gets better for her.'

'The poor little beggar,' she says. 'You know, boss, sometimes I bloody hate this job.'

'Me too, Polly,' I agree. 'But we're not social workers. At least, if we're good enough and get a few lucky breaks, we can get our hands on the man who started it all.'

'Yeah,' she says. 'But I'm starting to wonder who, exactly, that was.'

The cake shop is as busy as the hospital café, and it's another half hour before we finally get into the lift to the top floor, laden down with a selection of pastries and muffins that would give even George Saint's fridge palpitations. Jerry Forbes gives us a wide grin as I dump our offerings on his bedside table.

'If you treat all your team like this, I'm putting in for a transfer,' he says cheerfully, rooting through the bags and pulling out a chocolate muffin.

'Believe me,' Larson mutters, 'this is definitely a one-off.' Nevertheless, he helps himself to a Danish pastry. 'We were about to call you,' he says, through a mouthful of pure cholesterol. 'We've managed to recover one or two of the missing sections. Come and look.'

We gather round the laptop screen. They've been

working on the section containing the missing ninety seconds. This time, the gap is filled by the appearance of a shadowy figure coming across the front garden from the direction of the chapel. For what can only be a second, the camera catches a full-frontal view as he approaches the front door and turns his face away. To my annoyance, it's too dark to see any detail beyond the height – around six feet – and a lean, fit-looking build. Larson freezes the image and taps at his keyboard. Suddenly, the figure is much clearer, enhanced by the digital filters in the software he's using. For the first time, we're staring at a crystal-clear, current image of Kenny Hughes.

'Good-looking sod, isn't he?' Forbes comments. 'And if I'm not mistaken, that's a very expensive cashmere overcoat he's wearing, probably bespoke. I'm not an expert, but I'd say he's the sort who wouldn't have any difficulty getting young, impressionable girls swooning over him and jumping at the chance to become a runaway bride, wouldn't you?'

I have to agree. To an experienced eye, or to be more accurate, one more jaded by the realities of life, the warning signs are there in the man's bearing – just that little bit too upright, too confident in his ability to control everything and everyone around him. The real giveaways, though, are the mouth, its resting expression a slight, supercilious smile, and the eyes – bright, piercing, even in the near-pitch dark, and utterly devoid of warmth or empathy of any kind – the eyes of an out-and-out killer. We're looking at an image of a monster, but one that a young, inexperienced, lovestruck teenager would never recognise as such. I realise that the hairs on the back of my neck are prickling again.

Just in case there is any doubt, Larson brings up a copy of the only other photo of Hughes we have, taken several years previously. He's made a few small changes to his appearance – a short, neatly clipped salt-and-pepper beard, and the greying hair is a little longer, fixed in a trendy ponytail. He's in his late fifties, but to a casual observer wouldn't look much over forty.

'Have you sent this over to Grace?' I ask Larson.

He nods. 'To her, and to ACC Forbes as well. There should be an all-forces alert out by the end of the day.'

He starts the sequence running again, and we watch as Hughes deftly keys in the code, slips inside and closes the door behind him. It's taken him less than a minute.

'It's not the first time he's done that,' I say. 'He must have been coming and going to that house for some time.'

'I would say so,' Forbes agrees. 'We can be certain of one thing, though. He won't be coming back.'

'So where the fuck is he?' Sillitoe puts in, with real venom, and we all stare at her until she shrugs. 'Sorry. This bastard is doing my head in. I mean, he's got to be somewhere close by, probably laughing at us.'

'It's my guess he's hardly thought about us at all,' I say. 'As far as he's concerned, until very recently we probably haven't registered as a threat – at least not a serious one. Yes, he knows we're looking, but he's underestimating just how much information we've got. We've found his dumping ground in Wales and the Oakfield Road bodies, which is annoying for him, but he may not be aware that we have the resources to recover the deleted CCTV footage, or that we've identified Ruby Marx. The only thing I don't understand is why he abandoned the house he'd been perfectly safe in for more than two decades, and left before disposing of the bodies and picking up his little box of souvenirs.'

'Because he was threatened,' Forbes says. 'Not by us, by

somebody else. Someone spooked him so much he ran, left everything behind. Maybe he thought he could come back later and sort it all out, but he never got the opportunity. Possibly he didn't think the house would sell so quickly, or he figured he could wait until the new owners went on holiday. Whatever, things didn't work the way he wanted them to.'

'In that case, why sell it at all?' Larson asks. 'Why not wait until it was safe to clear it out, then put it on the market?'

We fall silent, trying to work that one out. The lull is interrupted by a call from Grace. I put it on speaker.

'Al, I think you should get back here,' she tells me. 'There's an update on the forensics, and Daz and Robbie have something they think you ought to see. Have you spoken to the Drake girl yet?'

'Yes, ma'am,' Sillitoe replies for me. 'She remembers going somewhere with Kenny, and we're trying to get her to draw a picture of it.'

'Okay, You stay with her, Polly,' Grace says. 'And let us know the minute you get anything. What about Larson?'

'Here,' I say, 'with me, helping Inspector Forbes with the CCTV analysis.'

'Good. Bring him with you – Maggie's asked if he can go over to the lab. I'll see you in, say, an hour?'

She hangs up.

I DROP Larson off at the forensic lab, with a promise to call in on Maggie later, and carry on to West Hill. I walk into the squad room to find Grace, Daz and Robbie huddled at a desk piled high with the manse journals. They are all so engrossed they don't even notice as I come up behind them. Blue, however, curled under the desk, shoots up like an erupting volcano, almost upending the desk and splashing the contents of a half-drunk mug of coffee dangerously close to the sheaves of documents.

'Christ, Al!' Grace hisses, grabbing piles of paper and lifting them up while Robbie dabs at the spill with a pile of tissues. 'It's too late in the day for heart failure. Pull up a chair and look at this.'

I oblige, struggling to stop Blue jumping up and licking my ear, and Daz props a heavy journal against his laptop screen so that we can all see. 'This is 1978,' he says, 'the year before Graham Bennet died. The entries are written by his wife, Isobel. The relevant passages start on the twentieth of August. You want me to read it out, boss?'

I nod. He clears his throat and begins.

'*G got a call from Bishop Frost this morning. Richard's mother died last night* – we think Richard is, or was, Richard Brownlow, a Methodist minister in Chepstow. *He's been asked to fill in until after the funeral, so he'll be away for at least a fortnight, just back for the Sunday services. I'm worried about him. As always, he works too hard, and his health isn't what it was.*'

He pauses and flicks forward a couple of pages.

'This is where it starts to get interesting. 22nd *August. G made his first visit to the school today. It is a most terrible place, full of sinners of the very worst kind. The staff do their best, of course, but he is determined to bring the word of God even to Satan's doorstep. If just one of the heathens is brought to Christ, he says, all his efforts will have been worthwhile.*'

'Jesus bloody Christ!' I mutter, and everyone glares at me. 'Sorry – it's no wonder Ruth and Janet Bennet got out of there as soon as they got the chance. So Graham Bennet was at Wye Cross the year Janet disappeared.'

'That's not the half of it,' Grace says. 'Daz, get on with it!'

'Yes, ma'am.' He skips a few more pages and resumes.

'*15th September. G did not call last night, nor tonight. I am worried. If he had fallen ill, or, heaven forbid, been in an accident, I would have been informed. Perhaps, as so often happens, his zeal has run away with him, and he has lost track of the days. God knows, from what he says of that dreadful place, he has been given a hard mission, and my husband has never been well disposed to failure.*

'Now we get to the interesting bit,' Daz comments.

'*20th September. G arrived home five hours ago in a dreadful state. He went straight to his study and locked the door. He refused to open it even when I took his evening meal. It is past midnight, and still he will not let me in, nor speak, even through the locked door.*

'*22nd September. This morning, G finally came out. He had stayed in his study all night, and I don't think he slept. He told me he saw her walking in the grounds of the school, in the woods near to the cottage used by the caretaker there. He was at the top of the hill, some distance away, but was not, he said, mistaken. At once he ran down to the cottage, and is sure she must have seen him, because when he got there, she was gone, hiding, perhaps, in the woods. That night, he left his lodgings in town and went back. She seemed to be alone – her, and her child, a boy, he said, around twelve or so years old. The next night he did the same, and the next, until he was sure there was no one else with her. On the final night – the night before he came home, he intended to knock on the door, although he admitted he had no idea what he would do. But she came out to get wood. He went to speak to her, and there was a terrible argument. She struck him – he has a dreadful* *bruise all down one side of his face – and ran off towards the school. He went after her, of course, but she disappeared inside, even though all the doors were locked and the windows barred. It was, he said, the Devil's work. The next morning, he went to the school and demanded to see our daughter. They knew nothing about it, they said, and there was no way any person could get in or out of the building after dark. Nevertheless, they went down with him to the cottage and spoke to the boy, who was on his way to school in the town. His mother, he told them, had gone out early to catch a train to Cardiff, where she was due to meet his father, who had been away visiting family. My husband, he said, was a madman who had most likely stumbled in the dark and hit his head. The school board agreed and so told G to go home and rest.'*

'Ruth Griffiths was right,' I murmur. 'Graham Bennet did find Janet and could have murdered her. Jesus – as if this investigation wasn't complicated enough!'

'The next significant entry is in 1979,' Daz goes on. 'It's dated the fourteenth of September.'

September again, I think, but say nothing. He reads it out.

'Today, my dear husband took his place among the worthy and walks in the light of Jesus our saviour. It is a year, almost to the day, since the terrible events that caused the illness from which he never recovered. The doctors say it was his heart. It was indeed, but not as they described it. He returned, many times, searching for our daughter, but the place was all shut up, and the school board told him that our Janet had gone away with that dreadful man, leaving their child behind. They asked him if he would take the boy, who was an inmate of the school by then and had caused no end of trouble. He refused, which is just as well. I have no desire to witness the product of her sin, who might well have been spawned by Satan himself in the guise of a man. Once I

have laid my beloved Graham to rest, I will never think of them again.'

Daz puts the volume aside, and Robbie hands him another, labelled 1981. He turns to October and continues.

'8th October. Yesterday I received the most dreadful letter. The boy has been released from the school and has written to me. He tells me that G died, not of a broken heart, but of guilt. He says he has proof that my husband attacked our daughter, that he left her, mortally injured on that night, to die. He says G is no doubt condemned to the torments of hell, and that so shall I be when my time comes. He asks for money. He says if I do not give it to him, he will visit the same fate on other women who, like his mother, are unloved and unwanted, the issue of pure evil. He says that if any die, the fault will be mine. He is trying to frighten me. I do not believe his threats. Today, I burned his awful letter. He will get nothing from me but contempt and, God forgive me, my eternal hatred.'

There's a long silence broken only by a gentle whine from Bluebell, hinting that it's about time someone gave her a bathroom break, not to say dinner. I scratch her ears, and she responds by resting her chin heavily on my knee.

'Fucking hell!' I say finally.

'I'd say that was an understatement,' Grace comments. 'If we can trust what Kenny Hughes said in his letter – and if we believe Isobel Bennet's diary – Graham Bennet caused Janet's death. Kenny tried to blackmail Isobel, and when that didn't work, the killings started.'

But why not blackmail Graham?' Robbie asks. 'He was the one responsible. Isobel had nothing to do with it.'

'Because he was locked up in Wye Cross until 1981,' I reply. 'Graham Bennet died a year after Kenny was put in there, and it was another two years until he was released at age sixteen. He wanted revenge and couldn't get to Graham, so Isobel was the next best thing. I would imagine Janet tarred them both with the same brush, and from some of the things Isobel wrote in her journal, it sounds like she was as bad as he was, in Kenny's eyes at any rate. They both made their daughters' lives a misery – Janet and Ruth. Note that he's never targeted Ruth, even though her husband is a very wealthy man.'

Blue whines again, and I get reluctantly to my feet. 'Is there anything else there?' I ask, pointing to the pile of journals.

'We don't know – yet,' Robbie answers. 'We were aiming to carry on for another couple of hours, then start again in the morning.'

I look at my watch. It's way past any reasonable hour, and I still need to catch Maggie before I go home. 'If you do any more tonight,' I tell them, 'you'll be bugger all use in the morning. You've done a great job so far, but it's time to get your heads down. I'll see you in the morning.'

They nod gratefully and push back their chairs. Grace follows me out to the lift. 'Do you know if the Cardiff squad have searched the old school building yet?' she asks.

'Forbes said they had three or four uniforms go through it, but didn't find anything.'

'I think,' she says, 'it's time I had a word with ACC Forbes and get them to do another search – a thorough one this time.'

30

Maggie and Larson are waiting for me in the laboratory building's basement kitchen, a dingy, windowless room used by the cleaning and warehouse staff and furnished with a kettle, fridge, plastic table and chairs. Dogs are strictly forbidden near the labs, but down here the rules can be bent occasionally, thanks to Maggie's obsession with Cyril's health and well-being. Thankfully, Maggie's malodorous pet is absent, although his scent lingers, and Blue spends a good two minutes sniffing vigorously and raising her eyebrows at me before finally settling under my feet.

'You've got something for me?' I ask Maggie.

She nods. 'I do, and so has John. That hammer of yours was very interesting – four clear sets of DNA, all identifiable. I suppose you want to know whom they belong to?'

'You suppose right,' I say, settling in for one of Maggie's long hauls. Surprisingly, she gets right to the point.

'You'll be relieved to know that one clear set of prints

belongs to your good friend Craig Tyler. That should help put a spoke in his appeal attempt, if nothing else. There are three more sets of DNA – Jimmy Harris, the woman you've identified as Ruby Marx, and the child.'

I realise I've unconsciously let out a huge sigh of relief. 'So Tyler murdered all three of them. Maggie, you've made my day!'

She grins. 'Maybe, maybe not. The thing is, Al, Tyler's fingerprints were on the haft, where he had gripped it. The samples for Ruby, Jimmy and the child were on the head, as you would expect if they had been struck with it. However, Harris's prints were also on the haft. At some point, he took hold of it. For what reason, of course, it's impossible to tell.'

'That,' I say, 'could be accounted for if there was a struggle between him and Tyler, and he grabbed hold of it at some point.'

'I don't think so,' Maggie replies. 'If there had been some kind of struggle, with both men grabbing hold of the weapon during the fight, you would expect Harris's prints at some point to overlay Tyler's, and vice versa. However, all the examples show that while Harris's prints were frequently partially obscured by Tyler's, none of Tyler's prints were overlaid by Harris's. My conclusion from this is that Tyler most likely killed Harris, but before that, Harris handled the hammer and might have used it to kill Ruby and her son. On the other hand, it might simply have been his hammer, and he used it for DIY around the house.'

'Oh, for fuck's sake,' I mutter. 'This is getting out of hand. What about Kenny Hughes?'

'Nothing,' she says. 'There is no evidence that he touched it directly, so how and why it was found among his possessions is a mystery. Clearly, though, he must have known what it was, and what it signified, as he wrapped it very carefully and kept it hidden.'

'Well,' I say, 'at least there's one piece of good news. I wasn't wrong about Craig Tyler. That will make the chief constable's day.' I turn to Larson. 'You have something?'

He hands me two sheets of paper. Each contains a printout of a teenaged girl who, like Ruby and her daughter, Pauline, is posing outdoors, wearing the dress and sweater we've become accustomed to seeing on Kenny Hughes's victims.

'The lab reconstructed these from two of the photographs in the box,' he tells me. 'It looks like they were taken in a back garden, but at a different location from Ruby and Pauline, so it lends weight to the theory that Hughes owned more than one house, or rented one previously. I suppose the next step is to try to marry up the photos with the bodies found in the tank.'

'Which won't be easy, if it's possible at all,' Maggie puts in. 'In any case, it won't be a quick job, so don't hold your breath. If they are among those victims, we've got six to go through, and even with Fitzjohn's team working on them as well, it could take weeks if we're lucky, months if not.'

'In the meantime,' Larson goes on, 'the images have been fed into the misper database. We just have to wait to see if anything turns up.' He hands me another sheet, this time copies of birth and death certificates for an infant by the name of Carl Baker, who succumbed to measles at six weeks old. 'I guess that confirms another theory,' he says. 'Ollie is delving through all the usual records – property transactions, driving licences and so on. We'll let you know the minute we find anything.'

I suddenly feel a heartfelt desire to shut myself away in

my own living room, preferably with a decent beer and a Chinese from the takeaway round the corner. I really need some time out to think things over. I push my chair back, causing another minor eruption from Blue, who is clearly thinking it's way past dinner time.

'I need to get my head down,' I say, and to Larson, 'You want a lift back?'

He shakes his head. 'I'm going to give it another hour. Maggie will run me home when she leaves.'

'Don't work too late,' I warn him. 'Take it from one who knows – it's a slippery slope. Too many late nights and the kids will forget what you look like.'

He gives me his 'keep your nose out of my business' look.

I make my way to my car, Blue trotting contentedly behind me.

I'VE JUST FLOPPED down on my sofa and am about to unwrap my long-awaited portions of chicken chow mien and special fried rice when Blue shoots up, shattering my moment of peaceful anticipation with a series of ear-splitting barks punctuated by threatening growls. As an intruder alarm, I have to admit she does a very good job. A moment later there's a quiet tap on my patio door. There's only one person it could be. It takes a minute to settle Blue down, and she follows me, still growling under her breath, to the back door. Clive Gingell's gangly silhouette is slumped awkwardly in one of my garden chairs, instantly recognisable despite the oversized hoodie and the black scarf wrapped round his face, leaving nothing visible but the eyes glittering at me in the darkness. I can't help thinking that the largely redundant disguise is more to cover his acne than his identity. As he catches sight of Blue growling and baring her teeth behind me, he shoots upright and takes a step back.

'Fucking hell,' he mutters under his breath. 'Ain't you had enough of those fuckers? You're bloody mad, you are.'

I give him an innocent look. 'What? You mean Blue? She's a sweetheart. Come and say hello – I'm pretty sure she won't bite your hand off, although I'm not a hundred percent.'

'Fuck off,' he mumbles, trying for bravado and not quite succeeding. 'I come yesterday,' he goes on, 'but you wasn't here. Shark wants to talk to you – says it's important.'

He pulls out a burner phone and waves it at me. 'He said I was to ring him when you're here.'

Well, I'm here,' I say, 'so you'd better ring him. By the way, aren't you supposed to be doing your GCSEs? I thought your grammar would have improved by now. Doesn't Shark want you to do a law degree? You need language skills for that, you know.'

His upper lip curls. 'Mind your own fucking business.' He lets out a huge sigh and deflates into the chair like a punctured balloon, giving a rare glimpse of the child lurking behind the macho gangland exterior. 'It's dead boring,' he says. 'We have to do Shakespeare and stuff, and his English is really crap – the actors talk funny, and his spelling's rubbish.' He pauses, considering. 'Some of the stories are good, though,' he admits. 'Macbeth was a total tosser, just doing everything his missus said – it was his own fault he got wasted. We had a school trip to the Odeon to see *Henry V* as well. It was all in black and white, but the battle at the end was good. I joined the archery club after, and that's really cool.'

He catches himself, realising that he's actually talking to

me as if I were a human being, jabs at the phone and sticks it to his ear.

'I got him here,' he says into it, then holds the mobile out to me.

'Is there something you want me to know?' I ask.

I hear Shark take a drag on what is probably a joint, hissing the smoke in through his teeth. 'First,' he says, 'you tell me – what's happening with Tyler? Is he going to get out?'

'Not a chance. You know I can't give you any details, but take my word for it – his appeal isn't going anywhere.'

He grunts with satisfaction. 'Your word had better be good, Bird Man.'

'It always is,' I reply. 'What have you got, Shark?'

'Been asking around,' he says. 'Seems there are things about Jimmy I didn't know.'

'Like what?'

'Like that the guy over in Oakfield Road paid him to put a shed up, back in summer 1999. While he was there, he got friendly with a girl living in the house, and word is he got her pregnant. Word also is the guy paid him for that as well.'

For a minute I can't speak. If what Shark's source says is true, it might explain one hell of a lot. 'Are you sure about this?' I ask. 'How reliable is your source?'

'I believe what he says,' Shark replies, and I have to acknowledge that when Shark believes a story, the likelihood is it's true. 'Truth be told, Jimmy would do anything if he was paid enough.'

'Anything else?' I ask.

'Plenty, according to what I was told,' he replies. 'The girl had the kids – twins, a boy and a girl, but the guy she was with didn't treat her right, and she got worried about the babies. Jimmy was going around, doing stuff in the garden, and she told him she wanted out, and could he help. He said no way. I mean, she wanted to move in with him, her and the kids, and Jimmy wasn't the type to get tied down, know what I mean? So he stopped going to the house. Then, a couple or so years later, she turned up on the street, asking for him, with one of the kids in tow. She'd run off from the house, and asked him for money to get somewhere where the old man wouldn't find her. He was doing some good business by then, said she could kip down on his floor for a couple of nights while he sorted something. According to my source, two days later Craig Tyler wasted Jimmy, and the girl and the kid disappeared.'

I pull in a breath. 'So how come you knew nothing about all this? I thought you and Jimmy were joined at the hip back then.'

'We were in business,' Shark agrees, 'but Jimmy wasn't the type to throw his personal crap in the street. He had his own secrets – everybody keeps things close round here, you know that.'

'Okay – so who is this source of yours, and how come they know so much?'

I hear Shark chuckle and the snap of his Ronson as he lights another rollup. 'You know better than to piss in the wind, Bird. Put it this way. The guy I spoke to was a brother once, back in the day. He and Jimmy were close; they had a thing going – not the kind of thing I would have wanted to know about, if you get me. Anyway, he helped Jimmy with the shed.' He pauses, presumably considering whether it's wise to say more, and decides I'm worth his effort. 'He knew

Jimmy got paid to knock the girl up, and figured it was worth him hanging around to see if there were any more odd jobs needed doing. He told me the guy who owned the house was mental and paid huge amounts for next to nothing. The other thing ...' Again, Shark pauses, making a decision. 'He was still around after Jimmy died, but he'd moved over to New Park by then.'

'New Park? That was Tyler's territory, wasn't it?'

'Let's just say,' Shark replies, 'there was a change of allegiances. He got well in with Tyler, but for a while he still risked coming onto our patch now and then. I've got no proof, but I reckon it was him who introduced Tyler to the old guy, and Tyler got paid to waste Jimmy, the girl and the kid. But the thing you should know is, the other kid, the girl twin – it must have been around eight or nine years ago – he says the old guy paid him five grand to get her pregnant.'

'And he did?'

'So he says. But after, he remembered what had happened to Jimmy, and figured a contract might be put out on him, too, so he disappeared, left the country, hasn't come back. Don't bother looking for him – he was spooked enough that I rooted him out, and there's no way he'll come back here – he'll be a dead man if he does. That's it, Bird Man. Now you do your job, yeah? Get the bastard who paid Tyler to kill Jimmy. You'd better be quick, though, because if we find him first, you'll have a truckload of shit to clean up.'

'Don't worry,' I say. 'I'll get him.'

I hang up and am about to hand the phone back to Clive when I have an uncomfortable thought, nip inside, give the handset a thorough wipe down and wrap it in a sheet of cling film before handing it over.

'That's just paranoid,' Clive comments, with an incredulous grin as he gets up, preparing to shin over my back fence.

'Better safe than sorry,' I reply. 'Are you sure you'd rather not leave by the front door like a normal person?'

It takes him a minute to catch the irony. 'Fuck you,' he says cheerfully, and starts climbing.

31

By the time I get to the station, there's a message on my desk from Grace – hand scribbled, to avoid any excuses from me about not having time to check my email. I head up to her office and find her sitting behind her desk, entertaining Carol Dodds, who greets me with her usual ball-freezing expression, plus a suspicious glance at Blue, who immediately makes herself comfortable under Grace's desk.

'Morning, Carol,' I say, aiming for a cheery smile.

'Chief Inspector Crow.' She gives me a less than perfunctory nod as I draw up a chair and make myself comfortable.

'I've been explaining the latest results from forensics,' Grace says, just about managing to keep a straight face. 'Unfortunately for your client, Ms Dodds, it does look pretty conclusive – wouldn't you say, Al?'

'Indeed,' I agree. 'I'm sure, when you read the report, you'll find there's no doubt the hammer was the murder weapon, and that Craig Tyler's prints are all over it, as well as DNA from three victims. You have to agree that continuing to pursue an appeal in the light of this new evidence would be fruitless. In fact, we fully intend to charge him with the other two murders, so even in the very unlikely event the appeal went to court, he would have further charges to face.'

Surprisingly, Dodds doesn't look too concerned by our revelation. In fact, a ripple of satisfaction flashes across her usually frosty expression.

'You don't seem too upset,' I can't help commenting.

She smiles, or rather, the corner of her mouth twitches as if she's thinking about it. 'I'm a barrister,' she says. 'To be accurate, I'm a defence barrister – a very expensive one. You know very well that it is not my job to form relationships with my clients. They pay me to present a case that includes reasonable doubt as to their guilt. Sometimes, that isn't possible. I agree that it would now be unwise to continue with an appeal against conviction for Harris's murder. However, my client will need a defence in relation to any other charges.' She stands and picks up the copy of the forensic report that Grace has helpfully placed on the desk for her. 'You don't mind if I take this?'

'Be my guest,' she says, 'and we look forward to seeing you in court in due course.'

After Dodds has left, Grace comments, 'She's going to make a fortune out of Tyler. It's one way of making sure he doesn't benefit from his stash of drug money, I suppose.' She pauses, then adds, 'Odd that she never charged your Rosie a penny when she defended her. Working pro bono isn't normally her style.'

I shrug. 'Maybe, for once, she knew she was defending someone who was actually innocent,' I suggest, although Dodds's rare display of generosity has always been a mystery to me. 'At one time, I thought she might try to capitalise on it, but so far, she never has. I get treated with the same contempt she's always shown towards hardworking arresting officers.'

'Ah, well, it will have to remain one of policing's obscure mysteries,' Grace replies. 'But at least she's got the good sense to know when she's beaten, and we can get back to the real job. You think Shark Johnson's actually telling us the truth, for once?'

'In so far as he understands it, yes,' I say. 'He's got no reason to lie, and he seems as anxious as we are to see Kenny Hughes off the streets. Everything he said more or less fits with what we know, and it explains how Jimmy Harris got to be the father of Ruby's children. That piece of info will save us a lot of time trawling through sperm bank records. It also solves the mystery of Millie's parentage – it's a shame we didn't get a name from Shark, but not a surprise. I would imagine Millie's biological father is holed up as far away as possible from Shark and from us – South America probably. He'll be on the West Hill gang's hit list for sure, and if he shows his nose here, I'd lay a bet they get him before we do. They don't particularly like turncoats.'

'Whoever he is,' Grace comments, 'he's not on our radar – at least not for anything serious. We'd have his DNA on record otherwise.'

There's a tap at the door, and Karen Wyatt sticks her head through.

'Sorry to interrupt, ma'am,' she says, 'but I thought you should know, Mr and Mrs Marx are downstairs.'

Grace and I exchange a look. 'What do they want?' I ask.

'To confess,' Karen replies, with a smile. 'I think they realised they were going to get found out sooner or later, so they showed me a bunch of letters they'd received back around the millennium, asking for money. They say all of them are in Ruby's handwriting, but it's likely Hughes dictated them. They ended up giving him more than sixty thousand pounds over a period of three years.'

'Bloody hell!' Grace says. 'That's a tidy amount, especially back then.'

'You're telling me.' Karen nods. 'They say they ran out of their own savings after the first year and had to take out loans, saying they were for a car, holidays, home improvements and so on. In the end they remortgaged the house to pay them all off. The letters stopped in 2003.'

'The year Ruby died,' I point out. 'That makes sense – and gives us a definite answer to the question of where he got his money. He must have blackmailed, or tried to blackmail, the parents of the other girls he lured away as well. Is Daz in yet?'

'Yes, sir. I saw him park up a minute ago.'

'Okay. Fill him in on what you've got, both of you interview them, get a statement and then bail them pending further investigation. I doubt they're going to flee the country. Make it clear, though, that there are likely to be charges, of obstruction at the very least.'

'Yes, sir. It'll be a pleasure.'

She disappears down the corridor, and I let out a grunt of frustration. 'Jesus! How stupid can you be? I hope they realise that if they'd come to us the minute they got the first demand, their daughter might still be alive – not to mention some of the other victims.'

Grace gives me a sidelong look. 'That may be true, Al, but don't forget, Ruby Marx and her daughter were the last two in a long line of girls whose parents almost certainly withheld information from the police. If you want to blame anyone, aside from Hughes himself, I'd be more inclined to go for Graham and Isobel Bennet. They mistreated their daughters, didn't report Janet's disappearance even though she was only fourteen, and after Graham's death, Isobel didn't report Hughes's threats. If either of them had come to us, perhaps nobody would have died.' She sighs and shakes her head. 'Sometimes I wonder who the real villains are in cases like this. So far, it seems like the only innocents in this mess are lying in the morgue. Al – are you all right?'

For a minute I can't reply. The thought has struck me with the force of a 200-watt light bulb, and now that I see it, I realise it's bloody obvious. Grace's first sentence has triggered a sudden certainty that I'm right.

'He's stopped,' I say, half to myself.

'What?' Grace frowns, clearly wondering whether I might have finally lost it. 'What do you mean, "He's stopped"?'

I hold up a hand. 'Just give me a minute.'

She nods, goes over to her coffee machine and pours us both a mug, adding three sugars to mine, plus one for luck.

'You said Ruby and Pauline were the last two,' I say as she pushes my coffee across to me. 'That means he killed his last victim around two years ago, and Pauline wasn't the result of an abduction – he raised her from childhood. The same goes for Millie. It's my guess Ruby was the last girl he lured away.'

'Why?' Grace asks. 'I mean, why suddenly stop or change his MO? This kind of killer normally sticks to the plot – they can't help themselves.'

'He didn't stop altogether. For some reason he walled Pauline up in Oakfield Road, and only he can tell us why. But think about it – according to Isobel Bennet's journal, he blamed Graham Bennet for his mother's death. In his mind,

Isobel was as guilty as Graham, so when Graham, his principal target, died, he transferred his attention to Isobel and tried to blackmail her. She didn't play ball, so he carried out the threat, making her indirectly responsible for the subsequent murders. I think ultimately what he wanted was a confession from the Bennets, to see the things they valued most taken away from them – their faith and their reputation. You have to admit, from what we know of them, they were a pretty nasty pair.'

'So you don't think Kenny Hughes killed his mother?'

'No, I don't. My problem is, I'm not sure Graham Bennet did either, but let's leave that aside for the moment. The point is, in 1999, Isobel died. And in 1999, Kenny paid Jimmy Harris to get Ruby pregnant.'

'Doesn't that mean your theory that he was taking girls to try to father his own offspring is blown out of the water?'

'If I'm right, I'm afraid so. The thing is, we always assume that crimes against young girls are sexual, and nine times out of ten, we're right. But now, I don't think Kenny Hughes had any intention of having sex with his victims. The thought probably horrified him. But when Isobel died, and he no longer needed to kill Ruby, he had another idea. Perhaps he actually fell for her, loved her in his own way, and wanted to give her children, but couldn't do it himself, so he hired Jimmy as a stand-in.'

I see understanding dawn on Grace's face. 'Jesus, Al. You're saying Ruby and Jimmy had sex ...' She thinks for a minute and almost laughs. 'But it backfired – Ruby fell in love with Jimmy and ran off with one of the children, hoping he'd take her in. Hughes found out, flew into a rage, and realised if Ruby talked, his game might be up.'

'So he sent Craig Tyler to shut Jimmy up permanently

and, my guess is, to bring Ruby and the child back. But something went wrong, and Tyler ended up killing all three,' I finish for her.

'That still leaves Pauline,' Grace points out, 'and what about Millie? Why leave her in the manse? There must be far less risky places to put her if he didn't want her to be found.'

'That's just it,' I say. 'He *did* want her to be found. He knew the place well, had visited many times and even had his own bolthole under the chapel. That means he also knew precisely when the maintenance crews did their rounds, and counted on one of their routine visits to find Millie. He didn't want to kill her. Hang on.'

I pull out my phone and call Martin Griffiths. He answers after one ring. Yes, he says, a routine maintenance check was due two weeks ago, but the man caught Covid, so the date was put back. He would have been due to make his visit in three days' time. He's still at the hospital with Ruth, so I promise to catch up with him later in the day, then hang up.

'If the maintenance man had come when he was supposed to,' I say to Grace, 'Millie wouldn't have been harmed at all. And if we hadn't turned up when we did, he would have found a dead body.'

Grace sits back and considers, massaging her temples with finger and thumb. 'It still doesn't explain how Ruby and the child ended up under Hughes's shed,' she says at length, 'and we're assuming Tyler killed them. Even with the evidence from the hammer, we can't say without any doubt that he did it. I want you to go and see him again, Al. He'll know by the end of the day that his appeal attempt has failed, so maybe he'll be a bit more forthcoming.'

'Bloody hell, Grace!' I groan inwardly at the thought. 'Do you really think it's worth it? He'll also know we're about to charge him with the other two, and that won't put him in the best of tempers.'

'And if he wasn't responsible,' she counters, 'he won't want to extend his sentence beyond the five years he's got left, and more importantly, he won't want a reputation as a child killer – you know what kind of ride they get inside. He'll end up doing most of his time in the hospital wing, if he makes it that far.'

I haven't got an answer to that.

'Good,' she says. 'I'll let them know you're on your way.'

Down in the squad room, I find Robbie Robbins, Larson and Ollie White waiting for me. 'I think I've found something, sir,' Ollie says, thrusting a printout into my hand. It's a copy of an old set of estate agent's particulars, offering a house for sale on the other side of town, near the Staple Hill district. It's dated 1991.

'What am I looking at?' I ask.

'With luck, Kenny Hughes's other house,' Ollie replies, puffing out his chest. It was purchased by Carl Baker back in 1991, and, sir ...' He draws in a breath and announces, with an air of triumph, 'He sold it in 1996, to someone called Edward Page.'

'And how does that help us find him, exactly?' I snap, rather unreasonably I realise, given the amount of work he must have done to root out these details. The thought of my upcoming second interview with Craig Tyler has put me on edge, but that's no excuse.

'Edward Page,' Larson puts in quietly, 'died of diphtheria in 1965, aged four months.'

For a moment, the power of speech deserts me, and all I

can do is stare at the faded photograph of a large, shabby and, if truth be told, ugly detached house, only partly visible behind an overgrown hedge of privet and brambles. These were the days before gentrification and TV shows extolling the virtues of home renovation and easy-care gardening. It's just the kind of place Hughes would choose – an anonymous, private, down-at-heel house in a big-city suburb where neighbours keep to themselves and don't pry into each other's business.

DC White is fidgeting beside me, waiting for a verdict. I tear my eyes away from the paper and give him a pat on the back. 'Well done, son – bloody well done. If he's still using this place, we've got him.'

32

Daz and Karen join us as we're poring over the estate agent's particulars.

'We've bailed the Marxes,' Karen says, 'but I think I ought to stay with them for another day or two. I'm concerned they might try to get over to see Millie, which wouldn't be appropriate at this stage, and besides, they're both still pretty shaken up.'

'Serves them right,' I say uncharitably, but then, on second thoughts, 'You're probably right, though. They've been stupid, but they've also been through a lot, and there might be more evidence in the house they haven't told us about. You'd best keep an eye on them for the time being.'

I take a minute to think. The squad is stretched tighter than George Saint's waistband, with Sillitoe at the hospital, Colin Draper liaising with Forbes's team in New Vale, and Karen shepherding Fred and Gina Marx. We don't even know whether Kenny Hughes is still using the property in Staple Hill, so any kind of major surveillance operation might turn out to be a waste of time and, more importantly as far as the chief constable is concerned, budget. Without evidence of activity, anything electronic is out of the question, and unfortunately, the insistent tingling at the back of my neck doesn't count as evidence. Nevertheless, the place has to be watched, and that means a minimum of two officers and a car, an unexpected boost to the income of the local takeaways, and a corresponding dent in the force's bank account.

'Right,' I say, making my mind up. 'Daz and Robbie, I want you to get over to Staple Hill. If a cat pees in the garden, I want to know about it. And go easy on the coffee – I don't want Hughes turning up while you're both in the lavatory.' I give Daz a meaningful look.

They both roll their eyes at me. 'Where will you be, boss?' Daz asks.

'In Wales,' I reply. 'I want to check in with Colin at New Vale, and then I'll be at the hospital.' I turn to Larson. 'Can you stay here with Ollie and keep digging in the records? Keep in touch with Maggie, and let me know if there's any movement on identifying the other victims – and maybe keep an eye on Blue till I get back? Ollie, you can mind the shop.'

Larson nods. 'No problem,' then adds, man and dog raising eyebrows in tandem. 'If you're not back by teatime, I'll take her home to see Ben, and you can pick her up from there.'

We both know I'll probably not get back at all tonight.

COLIN DRAPER IS WAITING when I arrive at New Vale manse. These days I can't look at him without being reminded of Blue at around six months old. He bounds over to my car with such enthusiasm I have to push down the urge to dig in my pocket for a treat and ask him to sit before he bowls me over. I decide he's going to need watching – he's the type to rush into a situation without a second thought for his own safety, or for the safety of any officers he might be with, and that worries me.

'I'm glad you're here, sir,' he says, almost wheezing with excitement. 'We've found something I think you'd like to see.'

I try for a look that's halfway between withering and exasperated. 'Detective Constable Draper,' I say, through gritted teeth, 'are you having some kind of panic attack? Because if you are, I suggest you find a paper bag, bury your head in it and take some very deep breaths.'

He turns a shade of boiled beetroot and thankfully manages to get hold of himself. 'Yes, sir. Sorry, sir.'

'I should bloody well think so. Cut the dramatics and act your age. This is the police force, not the local Gilbert and Sullivan society. Now, what have you found, and why might I be interested?'

'It's a box, sir,' he replies, aiming for calm and collected, but just missing the target. 'Like the one we found at Oakfield Road. There are photographs, trinkets and suchlike, but all in much better condition.'

The prickling under my collar intensifies. 'You found it in the coal hole at the chapel?'

'That's just it, sir. It wasn't there – it was in a tin box in the manse kitchen, mixed in with old tins of coffee and tea bags and stuff. Sort of hidden in plain sight, you might say.'

We're walking up the path towards the manse, where the forensic team is still working, but with less urgency than yesterday. 'Now, that is interesting,' I say. 'So, son, what do you make of it?'

He screws up his eyes, thinking, and finally says, 'I don't think Hughes hid it there, sir. I think one of the Bennets did – probably Mrs Bennet, as she would be the most likely to hide something in the kitchen. I think Hughes knew she had it, and one of the reasons he came back here was to look for it, but he couldn't find it.'

'Very good,' I say. 'We might make a detective of you yet. But why did Isobel Bennet have it in the first place?'

He thinks again, coming to a sudden halt, as if walking and concentrating at the same time is a task just beyond him. I see the lightbulb come on.

'Because Hughes wanted to get his own back. He wanted her to know he'd carried out his threat, so he sent her evidence to show he'd killed each victim.' He pauses, frowning. 'But why didn't she take the photographs to the police? We could have identified the girls and maybe stopped him much quicker.'

'Yes,' I agree, 'Maybe we could have, and maybe we could have stopped him earlier if the Marxes had called us as soon as he started blackmailing them. But nobody did. Nobody called us because they were all too wrapped up in their own reputations – well-to-do couples obsessed with their standing and power in the community, terrified of any scandal, no matter how small, and putting more importance on what people thought of them than on their own children's welfare.'

'You mean they were all stuck-up shitheads, sir?' he asks.

'You took the words right out of my mouth, Detective Constable,' I reply, and we carry on walking.

DC Draper has not, for once, overestimated the importance of the find. There are seven photographs, well enough preserved to see the faces clearly, including the now familiar snap of Ruby Marx. For the first time, I'm staring at the dazed, unsmiling faces of the six girls Kenny Hughes murdered and disposed of in the septic tank behind his parents' cottage at Wye Cross. I realise my hand is twitching as I reach for my phone and fumble to bring up Larson's number.

There's a long silence when I tell him what I'm looking at, except for a few deep intakes of breath. 'Bloody hell!' he says finally.

'Careful, son,' I reply. 'Any more of that and you really will turn into a policeman.'

He ignores me. 'Can you send them straight over? We can put them through the system right away if they're clear enough.'

Meera Kumar is still here, supervising the search of the upper rooms. She breaks off to pull out her laptop and send copies of the photos through to West Hill, together with shots her team have taken of the other items found with them.

'If you look carefully,' she says, 'you can see that all the girls are wearing jewellery –bracelets, necklaces or earrings mostly. It's my guess he gave them as presents and persuaded them to wear the items for the photos, together with any they had been wearing when they left home.'

'And then,' I add, 'he sent a photo and one of the trinkets to the parents, another to Isobel Bennet.'

'Precisely. There's no picture of Pauline, the girl you found behind the wall, because by that time Isobel was dead.'

'That's what's confusing me,' I say. 'Pauline was Ruby's

daughter, so there were no parents to blackmail, and his revenge campaign against the Bennets ended with Isobel's death, so why take a photograph of her, and why kill her?'

'That, Chief Inspector, is for you and Inspector Forbes to find out.'

I ARRIVE at Cwmbran hospital just in time to bump into Jerry Forbes, who is hobbling through the foyer on crutches, deep in conversation with Uncle Freddie. Forbes Jnr gives me a cheery wave and a grin that turns into a wince as he forgets the crutch and puts weight on his injured leg. I go across, shake his hand and nod to the ACC.

'Are you sure you should be out of bed?' I ask.

'He is – but I'm bloody well not,' Freddie replies. 'He's discharged himself against medical advice. I told him he can do what he likes, but if he ends up killing himself, he damned well won't get a payout from the compensation board.'

'If I kill myself, I won't need compensation,' Jerry puts in. 'Stop fussing. You're worse than Mother.'

'She's not your superior officer,' Freddie retorts. 'I am, and I'm telling you, you'd better not start racing around making yourself worse, because I won't approve any extended sick leave.'

'With respect,' I say with emphasis, and they stop and stare at me indignantly, 'perhaps we could set the family quarrels aside for the moment? I'm going to need both your minds on the job if we're going to catch Hughes before he does any more damage.' I pause, look at ACC Forbes and add, 'Sir.'

He colours a little, but nods. 'My apologies, Chief Inspector. You're quite right. Now is not the time—'

We're interrupted by Sillitoe, who bursts out of the lift as if the place has caught fire, phone jammed to her ear. A second later my mobile rings, but then she sees us, and it stops. She runs over to us, reminding me of my earlier experience with Colin Draper. She's got something, and it's important.

'Boss, I think we've got it,' she says, breathing hard, then remembers her manners and nods to the ACC. 'Sir.' She turns to Jerry. 'Have you got your laptop with you?' she asks. 'My phone screen is too small.'

Freddie holds up a bag. 'It's here. We can go to the office at reception.'

He waves his ID at the startled receptionist, and we all pile into the back office. A minute later, Jerry is bringing up the source of her excitement on his screen. It's a drawing – a very good drawing, done with coloured pencils, of a building that's instantly recognisable. Millie is a pretty good artist.

'That's Wye Cross!' Jerry remarks. 'But we searched it – twice. There's absolutely nothing there, I'd stake my job on it. There's no sign anyone has lived or even been inside the place since it was shut down, apart from the usual graffiti and a few piles of needles and so on. There's nothing to suggest Hughes made himself a hideout in there at any time.'

I know enough about Jerry Forbes to take him at his word. Yet Hughes did go there – and relatively recently, with Millie.

'I managed to get a few minutes with her,' Sillitoe says, 'when she gave me the drawing. She doesn't remember much, only that it was a long time ago – that could be anything from weeks to years, the way children her age measure time – and that it was cold, she had to wear her coat all the time, and she says all the food was cold too, and they didn't stay there long. Daddy had something to do, she said, and she only went with him because Mummy had gone away.'

It suddenly makes sense. Hughes paid a visit to the tank every year, on the anniversary of his mother's birthday, or her death, to re-dress the skeleton and leave flowers. Millie would have stayed at the Bristol house with Pauline. But Pauline died, and Hughes had to take Millie with him. My adrenalin level shoots up as a faint possibility gives a ray of hope.

'Polly,' I say, 'can you go back up and ask Millie if she knows what time of year they went to Wye Cross? Was it summer, autumn – what was the weather like? You know the sort of thing.'

Sillitoe frowns, but doesn't question the request. 'Sure, boss.'

She heads back to the lift, and the rest of us file out of the office and into the coffee shop next door, where I fill Jerry and his uncle in on the latest development in Bristol.

'I suppose it's good news of a sort,' Jerry comments. 'There's a possibility he'll go back there if he still owns the place. Clever bugger, though, isn't he? God knows how many more boltholes he's got.'

'It's hard to say,' I reply, 'but given that he milked Ruby Marx's parents for around sixty grand, and if we assume he got a similar amount from the families of the other six victims, it's possible he has one or two more.'

'I'm not so sure,' Uncle Freddie puts in. 'Don't forget, he's never had a job as far as we know, aside from a short stint as a labourer on a building site in his twenties, so he would have had to put away a fair amount for living expenses. From what he was wearing in that CCTV footage, he has pretty upmarket tastes, even if his houses are falling apart.'

'True,' I agree, 'but looking at where the houses are, he'd be pretty conspicuous if he had a Mercedes parked in the drive and a pool in the garden. He might dress well when he wants to, but he's good at keeping a low profile, too.'

'Great!' Jerry mutters. 'A bloody chameleon!'

Sillitoe rejoins us, looking excited.

'What?' I ask, and realise I'm gripping my thigh under the table to hide the tremor that's started up in my left hand.

'I asked Millie if she could remember when Hughes took her to the place in her drawing, and guess what she said?'

We all stare at her until Uncle Freddie finally says, his voice clipped with irritation, 'We're not on *Family Fortunes*, Inspector. Just get on with it.'

Unbowed, Sillitoe grins. 'She said of course she could remember, because Daddy went away at the same time every year, and once she asked him where he was going, and he said it was to remember the day his mummy died, and to put flowers on her grave. She couldn't give a date, though.'

'No,' I say, 'but I think I can.' I pull out my phone, call Larson and ask him to go back through Isobel Bennet's diaries, the entries for September 1978. It takes a few tense minutes for him to ring back, and he starts to read them through. 'Jesus Christ!' I breathe when he gets to the fifteenth of September. 'What date is it today?'

'Thirteenth of September,' Larson replies, confused. 'Why?'

'Because,' I tell him, 'we've bloody well got the bastard. Stay where you are – I'll ring back when we're sure.' I hang up and turn to my bemused audience. 'According to Isobel Bennet's diary, Graham Bennet rang her every night when he was away. The first time he missed was the fourteenth of September, and he didn't contact her again until he returned home on the twentieth, in what she described as a "dreadful state". He didn't ring his wife because Janet died on the fourteenth of September 1978. And every year, without fail, Kenny Hughes has gone to Wye Cross on the fourteenth of September, the anniversary of her death.'

'And today,' Jerry says, 'is the thirteenth. He's going to be there tomorrow. But when? Bloody hell, what time is it now?'

I glance at the clock above the coffee shop counter. 'Just coming up to a quarter to two,' I say. 'He might already be there. We need to move – now.'

'God Almighty!' the ACC groans, wiping a hand across his brow. 'Do you have any idea how big that place is? We'll need a bloody army – and it's going to cost a fortune! And do you really think he's stupid enough to keep to a routine? He must know we're onto him by now.'

'He knows,' I reply. 'He just doesn't care. He thinks he can outsmart us.' I get up. 'If we're going to need an army, we'd better start rounding up the troops.'

33

There's a flurry of activity as ACC Forbes gets CC Gosford on the phone, barking out a string of urgent requests for officers, armed backup and whatever else he can think of to combine with the Welsh division's resources. While he's wrangling over budgets, overall control, deployment and all the other bureaucratic and practical necessities involved in a full-scale police operation, I call Grace. I'm in the middle of explaining what's going on when Sillitoe's mobile rings.

'Boss,' she hisses, the urgency clear in her face.

'I'll call you back, Grace,' I say, and to Sillitoe, 'What is it?'

'Daz,' she replies. 'He needs to speak to you right now.'

I snatch the phone out of her hand. 'What have you got, Daz?'

'He's here, boss,' he tells me. 'Arrived a couple of minutes ago – strolled up the front drive like he didn't have a care in the world. He's inside now. Robbie's gone round the back to make sure he doesn't go out that way. She knows to stay out of sight.'

'You're sure it's Hughes?'

'Positive. There's no one else it could be. I ...' There's a pause, then, 'Shit!'

'What's happening?'

'He's just come out – with a girl, boss. He's got a girl with him, young, blonde, around fourteen or fifteen, jeans and a low-cut top, hanging onto him like a cat that's got the cream. What do you want us to do? I'm sure we can take him—'

'No!' I snap. 'If you lift him now, all we've got is a love-struck teenager who's likely to back up any story he's decided to spin. I'm pretty sure he's headed for Wye Cross.'

'Wye Cross? But why—'

'I can't explain now. Just get Robbie and follow him and make sure you're not spotted. If he crosses the bridge and heads for Chepstow, you can peel off and meet us at the police station there.' I glance at Jerry Forbes. He gives me a nod of understanding. 'I'm going to give Inspector Forbes your number. Stay in constant touch with him, and he'll have officers to take over when you cross into Wales. Can you get a photo of the girl?'

'Already done,' he replies, 'and I've sent it to Ollie. Sorry, boss – gotta go.' He hangs up.

I give Jerry the number. His uncle finishes his call, and we bring him up to speed.

He nods gravely. 'You'd better be right about where he's going. We've got an AFO squad – that's eight armed officers – plus another six uniforms. Apart from present company, it's best we stick to our own force – they know the area better than your people. Also, I've withdrawn everyone from around the tank and taken down the cordon. With luck he hasn't been down to it since we dug it out, and he won't know we've been inside until he actually gets there. Your DSI is coming down, and if your sergeant does his job properly, we can take over after the bridge and give the heads-up when Hughes gets to where he's going. We'll have the place surrounded in minutes. Let's just hope minutes isn't too long.' He frowns. 'I'm not happy about the girl. It's one hell of a risk letting him run with her. Do we know who she is?'

I shake my head. 'Not yet, but given what my sergeant has said, she's new, probably taken within the last few days, and almost certainly local. I'll get Larson to go through the missing person reports for the last month to see if anyone fits the bill. I think it's more of a risk trying to arrest him while he's got her so close. I don't want him using her as a hostage. If he's true to form, he'll leave her somewhere to make his visit to the tank, and we can get her out before he realises his error. Looks like old habits die hard.'

'I'd prefer a different turn of phrase, Chief Inspector,' he replies dryly, 'but it certainly looks like it.' He turns to Jerry. 'Okay, Inspector Forbes, let's get hobbling.'

'Right you are, sir,' Jerry replies, struggling to his feet and giving me a wink as he follows his uncle out. Injured or not, there's no way Forbes Jnr is going to sit this one out. Likewise, Polly and I make a dash for the car park.

'We'll take my car,' I tell her. 'It might not be as nippy as yours, but it's a damned sight more comfortable, and I can hear myself think.'

Once in the driver's seat, I call Grace back. She echoes Forbes Snr's concerns.

'Jackson had better not bloody lose him, Al,' she says. 'A young girl's life is at stake here.'

'Only if he gets wind of us,' I reply, hoping I'm not

making a big mistake. 'There's a better chance of getting her out in one piece this way. We'll be at Chepstow in around half an hour if the roads are clear. I'll see you there.'

IN THE END, thanks to four interminable waits at temporary traffic lights thanks to builders, a burst water main and two sets of roadworks with no identifiable purpose, it takes forty-five minutes to get to Chepstow police station. Grace is already there, having had the advantage of a car with blues and twos, and we find her with Jerry and Freddie Forbes in Jerry's small office, which, with the addition of the two of us, makes it standing room only.

'We've got all the entrances covered, and all vehicles out of sight,' Freddie says. 'According to Sergeant Jackson, Hughes is driving a Volvo estate and stopped in Chepstow for around twenty minutes. He and the girl went into a supermarket together – it's my guess he didn't want to leave her in the car on her own in case she changed her mind and legged it. DC Robbins followed them in – risky if you ask me, but she got away with it. They bought sandwiches, a cake, a bottle of white wine and four bunches of flowers. They also got some teen magazines and a couple of cheap bracelets. The girl couldn't decide, which explains the length of time they were in there. Then they went to a coffee shop and got takeaway and left a few minutes ago. I've got a couple of our officers following them now, and your two are on their way here. I've asked ex-sergeant Evans to accompany them, as he knows the lie of the land better than any of us.'

'And when he gets to Wye Cross?' Grace asks.

'There's no way he can get through our cordon without being spotted,' Jerry says, 'whether by car or on foot. He won't see us, though. Once he's in, we close the circle, wait until he leaves the girl, then pick him up at the tank.'

My phone rings. It's Larson. I put him on speaker. 'We've identified the girl,' he tells me. 'Kayleigh McBride, aged fourteen, reported missing from home in Portishead by her parents an hour ago. She's been missing since four o'clock yesterday afternoon. The parents assumed she'd gone off with friends.'

I curse silently. So much for my theory that there would be no more victims. This time, however, I get the feeling this has nothing to do with revenge. What he wants now is insurance – and if true, that means he knows we're close. 'Yesterday?' I snap at Larson. 'They waited nearly twenty-four hours before reporting a missing fourteen-year-old? Who the hell are these people?'

'Whoever they are, they're coming down to the station,' he says. 'Any instructions?'

I think for a minute. Aside from Ollie White, whose people skills are only slightly better than mine, there's no one from the squad left in the building. I decide.

'Okay, go down to George in reception and tell him to make them comfortable, but on no account to allow them to leave. He can tell them we're dealing with it, but no details. Just keep them calm, and keep them there, understood? If they start making a fuss, tell him to ring through to CC Gosford. It's about time he got out of his office and did some real police work for a change.' Grace grins at this, but says nothing. 'Have you got that?' I ask Larson.

'I'm on my way,' he replies, and hangs up.

'At least we've got a name,' Sillitoe comments, as a knock at the door announces the arrival of Daz and Robbie, who squeeze into the already overcrowded office with some difficulty. A second later, the police radio on Jerry Forbes's desk crackles into life. It's the senior firearms officer.

'Hughes has arrived, sir. He left his car a mile or so back in a stand of trees, and he and the girl are making their way across country, heading for the main Wye Cross building. They don't look to be in any sort of a hurry – I'd say at this pace it's going to take them anything between half an hour and an hour before we can start moving in. It's bloody unbelievable, sir. It's as if he doesn't have a care in the world – he must be out of his mind!'

'I think,' Jerry replies, 'that's exactly what he is. I'll bet he's not missed a single year since his mother died, and he's damned well not going to miss this one, and bugger the risk. But why not leave the girl back in Bristol? If I were him, I wouldn't want an idiot teenager slowing him down and getting in his way.'

'Two reasons,' Grace says. 'First, she's too new. He's had her less than twenty-four hours, so he won't have had time to groom her completely. He can't take the chance that she'll have second thoughts and go back to her parents or run to us. Second, she's his insurance – it may even be why he took her in the first place. He knows we can't move while she's close to him, and as long as she's within arm's reach, he's safe.'

'But he won't take her with him to the tank,' I say, 'so he's got to leave her at some point.'

'We won't find that out, Chief Inspector Crow, until we get there,' ACC Forbes growls, unconvinced, 'so we'd better get moving. DSI Helston, you can ride with me. DCI Crow, you take the rest of your people.'

'And what about me?' Jerry asks. 'If you think I'm going

to sit here playing poker with the desk sergeant just because I've got a sore leg, you've got another think coming – sir.'

'Oh, for goodness' sake!' Uncle and nephew glare at each other until Forbes Snr holds up his hands in defeat. 'All right, but you can sit in the back seat and stay there. I'm not having you wandering around the countryside, tripping over your crutch and giving the game away.'

'Certainly not, sir,' Jerry replies, with a wide grin. He hauls himself to his feet and brandishes his crutch towards the door, making Daz and Robbie duck. 'Well,' he says, 'what are we waiting for? Let's go and nick the bastard!'

34

Of all the tasks that fall under a police officer's remit, there are two I particularly try to avoid. One, understandably, is having a gun pointed at me. The other is sitting for hours on end in the pitch dark and freezing cold, waiting for the appearance of a dangerous and very likely armed killer of defenceless young girls. We've been holed up in the woodland behind the septic tank for almost three hours – me, Polly, Daz and Robbie, and from the Welsh side, ACC Forbes, clearly relishing the rare opportunity to see some action, DS Peters and three firearms officers. Jerry Forbes and Grace, together with DC Phil 'the Tea' Jones and a small contingent of uniforms from Chepstow are keeping watch on the main house, covering all possible ways in and out, and the rest of the AFOs are spread along the route between the house and the caretaker's cottage that Hughes used to call home. Hughes himself is somewhere inside the massive former school building, and the girl, Kayleigh, is with him.

I risk a quick glance at my watch. It's almost midnight.

Nobody has spoken for over an hour, and aside from the odd rustling and snapping of twigs as the local wildlife goes about its nightly business, it's deathly quiet. Sillitoe is around two metres to my left, although I can't see her, and she's probably as bloody uncomfortable as I am. My knees ache, an itch has started up underneath my bulletproof vest, and as always in situations like this, I'm wondering what the hell I'm going to do if I need to pee. All these concerns vanish, however, as a crackle from Forbes's radio rips the silence with the force of a gunshot, setting off a violent tremor in my hand and spiking my heart rate to critical. We all hear Jerry's message.

'He's on the move, sir – just left the building, alone, carrying a large sports bag, heading your way. We'll go in and get the girl out as soon as he's over the rise. One thing – he's not using a torch, so you might not see him coming.'

'Received,' Forbes replies, and I hear a click as he turns his radio off.

At the same time there are three more soft clicks – safety catches on firearms being released. The sound makes me feel slightly sick. There's no need for further instruction. The silence descends again, made even heavier by expectation. We wait.

After perhaps another twenty minutes, I hear a distinct rustling coming from the direction of the old cottage, getting closer, and too heavy for an animal. A stiff, chilly breeze has whipped up, adding numb fingers and freezing ears to my growing list of discomforts. I find myself understanding why the hoodie has become the gang member's uniform of choice. Footfalls are clearly audible now, a regular snapping of twigs and crunching of dead leaves. Then they stop. Hughes has reached the tank. The top sections, removed to allow extraction of the bodies, have been hastily replaced so that the initial impression is that the chambers are still intact. In daylight, the disturbance would be obvious from a hundred metres away, but now, at one in the morning, the illusion holds. Even now, a clever solicitor could argue that their client was guilty of nothing more than trespass – not even a criminal offence – was simply paying a nostalgic visit to his old home, or out in the woods hunting rabbits. His female companion (not girlfriend, as that *would* be illegal) would, of course, back up the story. Hughes is simply a friend who took her for a nice day out in the country. Yes, we can most likely get him for Pauline's murder and for blackmailing Ruby's parents, but for the rest, until he tries to open the tank, and so prove he knew the other bodies were there, all evidence is open to other interpretations. The parents of the dead girls, whatever their faults, deserve to have their daughters' names read out in court.

I hear a soft thump – the sports bag being placed on the ground, I guess, and a second later an area no larger than a dinner plate is illuminated by a dim yellow glow that nevertheless seems painfully bright after several hours of sitting in suffocating darkness. My eyes acclimatise, and I can just make out the shadow of a man crouching over the lid that has been replaced on the smaller chamber of the tank. He reaches out, hesitates – there is something wrong, but it doesn't quite dawn on him what it is. He looks around, completely still, listening. Nothing moves. Satisfied, he grabs the lid, starts to open it – then he realises, frantically hauls it up, and lets out a shattering, inhuman howl, a combination of horror, fury and despair. The sound knocks the breath out of me, bringing me out in a cold sweat. The small light he was carrying falls into the tank and goes out.

Then all hell breaks loose.

A bright light, trained on Hughes, momentarily blinds everyone. There's rapid movement everywhere, and a good deal of yelling from the firearms team as they surge into the clearing, closely followed by Sillitoe and ACC Forbes. It all happens in no more than a second – but, as my vision clears, I know it's a second too long. Even before the spotlight was turned on, Hughes had a shotgun in his hand, and what must have been years of practice hunting in these woods with his father has made him an expert. He takes out the spotlight with a single shot, and once again we're plunged into darkness. With officers already in the clearing, the AFOs can't risk firing and hitting one of us or each other. Almost at once there's a second shot and a scream – a woman's scream. Either Sillitoe or Robbie Robbins has been hit. There's a second, blood-curdling cry, but no shot this time, a loud thud as a body hits the ground, and an urgent shout.

'Quick! Here – I've got him!'

It's Robbie's voice. At once, torch beams are everywhere, and the AFOs are surrounding a struggling Hughes while Robbie, who has thrown herself on top of him, disentangles herself and dashes across to Sillitoe, who is on the ground some five metres away. Daz Jackson, handcuffs out and ready, throws me a glance, and I nod.

'Go ahead and do the honours, Daz.'

'Sir,' he replies as he rushes past.

When I reach Sillitoe, Forbes is on his radio, calling for an ambulance and prisoner transport. Robbie is, miraculously, helping her to sit up, between sobs and curses of relief.

'Fucking hell, boss,' Sillitoe spits. 'The bastard shot my

bloody foot off! It cost a sodding fortune – do you have any idea how much a bionic leg sets you back these days?'

She glowers at me; then I see her mouth twitch. Within seconds, the three of us are giggling like schoolkids, the pent-up tension leaking out of us.

'Polly,' I say when I've brought myself under control, 'once the chief constable has given you your medal, I don't think he'll have much choice but to foot the bill – if you'll excuse the pun.'

'I see the paramedics aren't necessary,' Forbes comments, joining us. 'I don't think they can do much with artificial limbs.' He pauses, then observes, 'Well, I think I can safely say that was a bloody pig's ear. It's lucky he just had a double-barrelled shotgun – only two shots before having to reload. Still, we got him. Transport should be here any minute. We'll get him booked and into a cell and interrogate him in the morning. I thought I'd leave that experience to you and my nephew, if that suits you, Chief Inspector?'

'It would be a pleasure, sir,' I reply. 'What about the girl?'

He frowns. 'They're still looking. She must be hiding in there somewhere. Poor kid's probably terrified.'

A couple of minutes later, two Land Rover Defenders come over the rise and trundle down to us. Daz, being the arresting officer, has the honour of escorting Hughes across to one of them, accompanied by a hopping Sillitoe and two of the AFOs. The rest of us take the other vehicle and head back to the former school to help with the search for Kayleigh McBride.

We arrive at the main Wye Cross entrance to the welcome sight of Phil the Tea doling out cups of steaming coffee from catering-sized vacuum flasks.

'Any sign of her?' I ask, wrapping my freezing fingers

gratefully around a cup and breathing in the scent of Nescafé.

'Not yet, sir,' he replies. 'We're going through every room, but the place is huge, and there are plenty of nooks and crannies, cellars and outbuildings as well. If she thinks all this is purely to drag her back home, she's likely hiding somewhere, hoping we'll give up. At least we've got Hughes, and we know she hasn't left the building, so she has to come out sooner or later.'

Jerry Forbes appears at the main door and hobbles across to join us, looking concerned. 'There's no bloody sign of her,' he says, shaking his head. 'We've got two teams on it, starting from either end of the building. Your DSI is heading up one, and I've been with the other. We met in the middle a few minutes ago. I'm damned if I know where she's gone. We're taking a quick break, then doing another sweep.' He grabs a cup from Phil's hand, takes a sip and flinches. 'Shit, that's hot!'

A minute or so later, Grace comes across, looking equally worried. 'How's Polly?' she asks. 'ACC Forbes told me that for a minute he thought Hughes had killed her.'

'She's fine,' I reply as we both move away from the crowd for a more private word. 'Just minus a prosthetic and spitting nails. Thank God he didn't hit her other leg. I'll have to have a serious talk with DC Robbins. She behaved like an idiot, breaking ranks and jumping on him like that – if he hadn't been out of bullets, it could have been the last thing she ever did. Plus, she was largely responsible for the AFOs not being able to get a clear shot in.'

'Not now, though, Al,' Grace warns. 'It's two in the morning, and we still haven't seen a trace of this wretched girl. All we know is that she definitely hasn't come out, so she's still inside somewhere.'

'Well, you've got some extra bodies to help now,' I tell her. 'What about cupboards, wardrobes and so on. Could she be hiding inside something?'

Grace shakes her head. 'The whole place was cleared out years ago. There might be a few bits and pieces here and there, but nothing big enough to conceal a teenager. We found the remains of their picnic in one of the second-floor rooms – an empty wine bottle and a couple of magazines. Getting around is a bit dodgy, though. Some of the wooden stairways have rotted, and DI Forbes put his foot through one of them – nearly ripped his stitches out.' She grins. 'He made me swear not to tell his uncle.'

'What about outbuildings?'

'A barn and a couple of collapsed greenhouses,' she replies. 'Two of the AFOs went over them, but didn't see anything, and besides, we'd surrounded the house within ten minutes of their arrival, and neither of them could have left from any of the exits without being spotted.' She gulps down her coffee. 'We'd better get started on a second sweep. Are you coming?'

'No. I think I'll take Jerry and have another look outside. It sounds like he needs to be kept away from staircases for the time being. I'm sure his uncle will be more than pleased to head up a team – he seems to be enjoying himself.'

She laughs. 'To be honest, Al, so am I, in a way. It's not often us pen pushers get out from behind our desks. Are you going to give Daz the arrest? It's a good way to bump up his respect level with the team.'

'Actually,' I say, 'I was thinking of making it a joint effort with Robbie, once I've read her the riot act. After all, Daz put the cuffs on, but Robbie brought him down.'

She gives my shoulder a squeeze. 'DCI Crow, I always knew you were an old softie at heart.'

Before I can reply, the search parties are reconvened, and she's gone.

Jerry limps over to join me. 'No chance of me getting back inside now that Uncle Freddie's here,' he says gloomily. 'He's obviously had Mother chewing his ear off again.'

'Don't worry,' I tell him. 'You're with me, making sure she hasn't sneaked out into one of the outbuildings.'

He shrugs. 'I don't see how, but worth a shot, I suppose.'

'The thing is,' I say as we make our way round to the rear of the building, 'Grace told me there was a window of about ten minutes between Hughes and Kayleigh entering the house and our people getting close enough to monitor the exits. Ten minutes can be a pretty long time.'

'And in that ten minutes,' Jerry retorts, 'they went up to the second floor and settled in for a romantic picnic. We found the remains of it in an upstairs room. Hughes clearly didn't suspect we were here, or he wouldn't have gone in the house in the first place.'

'Unless,' I say, 'he had another agenda, and the stuff you found upstairs was arranged to give the impression they were there.' As soon as I say it, the hairs on the back of my neck tell me it's true. 'Think about it,' I go on. 'They bought packets of sandwiches – where are the wrappers? All you saw were two magazines and an empty wine bottle. If you've searched properly – and I'm sure you have – you know the place is empty. Didn't you ever read Conan Doyle as a kid?'

He laughs. 'Of course – required reading for all budding detectives.' He stops in his tracks and stares at me, understanding. 'It was in *The Sign of Four*, wasn't it? Sherlock Holmes said to Watson, "When you have eliminated the impossible, whatever remains, however improbable, must be the truth." They arrived, the officer watching the house saw them go in at the front, reported that they were inside, and then, while we were getting into position, they went out the back, he hid the girl and went straight back into the main house alone.' He groans. 'Oh, shit – she's out here somewhere.'

We get to the back of the house, which looks out onto the old kitchen gardens. In the light of our torches, we can see two completely collapsed greenhouses – a jumble of rotted wood and broken glass. There's nowhere there for anyone to hide or, I think grimly, to hide a body. On the other side of the garden, a huge outbuilding, probably once used for farm machinery and maybe housing for chickens, rabbits or some such, looms in the darkness. We make our way across to it, trying to avoid the trip hazards of low walls and rubble, the remains of raised vegetable beds that would have been a hive of enforced activity back in the day.

There are two doors. One is hanging open. We cautiously peer inside. It's empty. We turn to the other, which is closed and padlocked. Jerry examines the lock by the light of his torch.

'This is quite new,' he pronounces. 'There's no sign of rust, and it's been oiled, too.'

We exchange a look. 'Christ!' I whisper. 'She's in there – she's got to be.' Then, as an afterthought, 'For God's sake, don't try kicking it off this time. We need a lever of some sort or a screwdriver. I don't suppose you've got a Swiss army knife in your back pocket?'

He shakes his head. 'There must be something lying around.'

'No,' I say, and get onto the radio. 'There's a quicker way.'

A minute later, a firearms officer appears round the corner of the building at a run.

'Can you shoot that padlock off?' I ask.

He gives it a quick examination and nods. 'If you wouldn't mind standing well back, sirs,' he advises.

Once at what he considers a 'safe distance' a hundred yards or so away, we hear two rapid, horribly loud shots and a clang as the mangled padlock hits the ground. We come up behind him, and with the pistol still at the ready, he nudges the door open with his foot and shines his torch inside. The place is full of abandoned farm machinery and tools, everything from garden rakes to tractors, all long since left to rust. He takes a step inside and almost falls headlong onto the blade of a rusty hoe.

'Damn!' he hisses, and then, shining his torch at the entrance, 'Be careful. There's a concrete lip there.'

We step over it and gingerly make our way forward, our torches playing over the jumble of equipment – tractors, diggers, hand tools and an assortment of stuff that looks like it was once housed in the school's kitchens – pots, pans, a huge old catering oven, fridges and a couple of chest freezers. The whole place is a minefield disguised as a scrap merchant's Aladdin's cave.

Kayleigh McBride is here somewhere – I feel it in my bones – alive or dead.

Jerry and the AFO start hunting through the mass of scrap metal, calling her name, reassuring anyone who might be here that we're the police, and she isn't going to come to any harm. I stand still, thinking. Something is niggling at me, and it takes me a while to realise what it is. When it does come to me, it seems obvious. Kenny's mother, blindly running from Graham Bennet, headed for the barn, where she tripped on the same lip that almost sent the AFO flying headlong into a pile of rusty metal. She, however, wasn't so lucky.

'Janet died here,' I whisper to myself as, suddenly, everything makes sense. 'Stop!' I shout, and at once the two officers come to a dead halt, turning to me, startled. 'Stop,' I say, more quietly. 'Listen.'

Jerry opens his mouth to say something, but I hold up a hand. All three of us stand stock-still. The wait seems interminable, but after what must only be a couple of minutes, there's a sound, an almost inaudible scuffle coming from one of the barn's dark corners.

Jerry shrugs. 'Rats?' he mouths silently.

I shake my head, finger to my lips. There's another scuffle, then silence. It's coming from the far corner, where the old kitchen appliances have been dumped. We all move in the direction of the sound, slowly, straining to hear the slightest sound. There's nothing. We reach the freezers, and hardly daring to breathe, I lift the lid of one of them while Jerry takes the other. Although there's no real need, the AFO stands back to cover us, giving us extra light from his more powerful torch to allow us to use both hands while listening for further sounds. Both freezers are empty. We move on, examining two tall fridges and the cavernous oven, without a result.

Suddenly, Jerry grabs my arm and points. Behind the oven, almost invisible under a thick layer of grime, is a third chest freezer. We scramble over a pile of old metal crates, and as the torchlight plays over it, my stomach lurches.

There's a smudge by the handle where the dust has been disturbed, and beneath it, the freezer lid has been sealed shut with thick, industrial wire – the kind that's way too tough to be tackled by anything but wire cutters or heavy-duty pliers. If the girl is in there, she's had nothing but stale air for several hours, and the scuffle we heard might have been her last feeble effort at escape. Using a gun is far too risky – at close range it could easily punch through the freezer wall and hit anyone who might be inside.

Jerry shouts to the AFO, 'Can you find something to get this wire off? Quick – we might only have minutes!'

For what seems forever, the three of us scrabble around for something that might be of use, but most of the tools scattered around are completely rusted and useless.

Finally, Jerry shouts, 'Here!' and brandishes a hefty metal mallet, almost too heavy for him to lift. 'If the screws on the handle are weakened,' he says, 'we might be able to bash it off.'

'Give it to me, sir,' the AFO says, 'and stand back. I've done a fair bit of weight training, so with respect, I've got more chance than either of you.'

We don't argue. On the sixth heavy blow, the handle shatters into three pieces, two of which fly off and land with a clatter some distance away. One more strike, and the remaining fragment comes away – and, with it, the wire. I take a deep breath and open the lid.

Inside, curled on her side in the cramped space, is the silent, unmoving body of Kayleigh McBride.

The firearms officer is already on his radio, letting the teams know we've found her, and giving the location for the ambulance crew as Jerry and I struggle to lift her out, clear a space in the clutter and place her gently down. For a horrible moment – the second in two days – I think we've arrived too late. But then an arm twitches; she blinks and takes in a huge, rasping breath.

'Thank God,' Jerry mutters. Something, though, isn't quite right. Her head is lolling, her eyes unfocused – she's as limp as a rag doll. 'Drugged,' he says. 'Probably Rohypnol or similar – in the wine.'

I nod my agreement. 'It's probably what saved her life. She was relaxed, semi-conscious, so she didn't struggle and use up the air.'

I leave him to tend to the girl, and pull out my phone. It's gone 3 a.m., but somehow I doubt anyone at West Hill will be sleeping. Larson answers in less than two rings.

'Are the McBrides still at the station?' I ask.

'Yes,' he answers. 'We all are. You've got Hughes? What about Kayleigh?'

'Hughes is in a cell, and the girl is with us – alive and well, we hope. I'll tell you more in the morning.' Two paramedics appear in the doorway. 'Watch your step,' I warn them, and direct them to where their patient is lying, semi-conscious, wrapped now in Jerry's Barbour jacket. 'Where will you be taking her?' I ask.

'Cwmbran,' one of them replies. 'It's the nearest A&E.'

'You can tell the parents their daughter is on her way to Cwmbran hospital,' I tell Larson. 'Ask George to find a uniform to go with them – I assume he's still in the station as well?'

'He's up here with us,' Larson replies. 'He went off shift hours ago, but he's been supplying us with sandwiches and coffee. And don't worry about Blue – Rosie picked her up when she got Ben from school.'

'Okay. Get the McBrides off; then all of you go home and get some sleep. Tomorrow's going to be a busy day.'

I hang up, watching as Kayleigh McBride is stretchered off to the waiting ambulance.

'You know something,' Jerry says, coming across to join me. 'You want to tell me your theory?'

I clap him on the shoulder. 'Not yet. It is still a theory, although I'm pretty sure I'm right, particularly about what happened to Kenny Hughes's mother. I want to hear it from his own lips, though, in case I'm jumping to conclusions.'

'Fair enough,' he replies. 'I don't know about you, but I'm bloody knackered, and we need to have our wits about us when we interview Hughes in the morning. It's a long way back to Bristol – do you want to stay over at my place for what's left of tonight? I've got a very well-equipped guest room, and I do a decent breakfast, although I say so myself. What do you reckon?'

I'm far too tired to argue, and for once, the sensible part of me takes over. 'Lead on,' I say.

35

Jerry Forbes is true to his word. As I suspected, his apartment is a large, trendy bachelor pad in the old part of town, looking out over Chepstow castle and the River Wye. I can't remember falling asleep, and wake to mid autumn sunlight seeping through the curtains of an airy, well-equipped guest room with its own bathroom. I take advantage of the facilities, make myself presentable, and join him at the breakfast table, realising that for the first time in God knows how long, I've slept for five straight hours without waking in a cold sweat after some nightmare or other.

He greets me with a grin, a plate of scrambled eggs on toast and a mug of coffee. 'All I could do at short notice,' he says. 'I haven't had the chance to shop lately. Hope it's okay.'

'Perfect,' I reply. 'What's happening with Hughes?'

He checks his watch. 'The duty solicitor should be arriving about now,' he tells me. 'I expect they'll have quite a bit to go through, so we're scheduled to interview him at eleven. It's just past nine thirty now, so there's no rush. The station is only a ten-minute walk from here.'

'He's asked for a duty solicitor? I'd have thought he'd have his own brief tucked away somewhere.'

'Apparently not. Maybe that's the disadvantage of having multiple aliases and trying to stay under the official radar. I just hope he doesn't take the "no comment" route – he must realise it won't do him any good.'

'It's the standard advice,' I say, 'and most are happy to toe their brief's line. Somehow, though, I get the feeling Kenny Hughes is going to be different.'

AT ELEVEN PRECISELY, we open the door to the interview room and get our first real look at the man who has murdered at least seven women, possibly more, over the last four decades. He's tall, slim – someone, I think, who likes to keep fit – impeccably dressed in a dark suit and pressed white shirt, open at the neck. His tie, of course, was removed when he entered the cells. His hair, greying but still with a good smattering of black, reaches just below his shirt collar and has been neatly combed back, the short beard carefully trimmed. The only evidence of last night's events are two large mud stains, one on the front of his shirt, the other on his jacket. He's fifty-eight years old, but could easily pass for early forties. As we enter, he looks up, meets my eye and gives me a slight smile and a nod before moving on to greet Forbes in the same way. He's completely relaxed, untroubled. Something about that fleeting look sends a shiver down my spine. By contrast, the duty solicitor, a young man in his early thirties who I guess hasn't been long qualified, seems totally overwhelmed, glancing nervously first at his client, then at us. He looks like a rabbit that's been forced to sit next to a panther.

We take our seats. Forbes goes through the necessary identification procedures, and I'm about to ask Hughes if he understands why he's here when he jumps in before I can take a breath.

'I would be grateful, Chief Inspector, if you could tell my mother where she is. She's a little confused, you see.'

It's the first time I've heard him speak, and it takes me by surprise, although given his appearance, it shouldn't. It's the voice of an educated man, the tone deep, soft, but firm – what Joyce, my ex-mother-in-law, might have described as 'a honey tongue', usually followed by the comment, 'I wouldn't trust him as far as I could throw him.'

At once, the solicitor pipes up, 'I thought we agreed, Mr Hughes—'

Hughes doesn't look at him, but keeps his eyes on me. 'Does this person really have to be here?' he asks. 'We would like him to leave.'

We? And *Tell my mother*? That's all we bloody well need – the diminished responsibility gambit. On the other hand, it means he knows he's run out of road.

'I wouldn't advise that, Kenny,' I say, finally getting a word in. His eyes narrow at the sound of his first name, so I go on, 'Or would you prefer Kevin – or Carl or Edward or perhaps Joseph? Just let us know your preference.'

A brief flash of tension runs through him; he takes a deep breath and regains control.

His brief tries again. 'Really, Mr Hughes, I—'

He turns his head and gives the kid a look that could freeze burning oil. 'If you are to remain,' he hisses, 'you will be silent. Do you understand?'

He gets a nervous nod in response as the solicitor gives up and sits back, arms folded.

Hughes turns, this time eyeing both of us. 'Please, call me Kenneth. Would one of you care to answer the question?'

Forbes takes it up. 'I assume you are referring to the remains found in the smaller section of the tank behind your parents' former cottage? They are currently being examined, and once the examination is complete, a decision will be made on what happens to them. In the meantime, perhaps you could tell us how they came to be there?'

Hughes spreads his hands in a shrug. 'It was where she asked to be,' he says simply. 'She wanted to be close to our home, where I could always see her. I carried out her wishes. It's what a son does for his mother, yes?'

'I suppose it is,' I say. 'So tell us, Kenneth, when exactly did your mother make this request?'

'When I brought her back from the big house,' he answers without hesitation. 'She was on her own, you see. I couldn't leave her where she was – it was most unsuitable. She said she wanted to go back home, so I took her.' He sighs. 'My father had gone, and it was just the two of us. I took her home and looked after her.' He frowns. 'But then you people turned up and forced me to leave. You shouldn't have done that. Mother was very upset. She didn't want to be on her own. She said if you found her, you'd make her go elsewhere, just like *he* did before, you understand? So I made sure she had a place to hide, close to home, and went back to see her often, to make sure she was all right. It was difficult at first. I'd been away in the big house, you see, so there was no one to tend the woodland, with both me and my father gone, and mother kept telling me she didn't like to be outside, alone. But then, men came and cleaned out a perfect home for her, with room for her friends, too. I moved her there, and then she was happy.'

The solicitor sits up and takes a breath. I know what he wants to say, and I shake my head. Hughes gives him a look, and he slumps back down.

'I think I do understand, Kenneth,' I say. Forbes glances at me, eyebrows raised. 'When you say *he*, you mean your grandfather, Graham Bennet.' He gives me a single nod, and I go on, 'Bennet caught sight of your mother when he was working at Wye Cross. He tried to persuade her to go back to New Vale with him, but she ran away. She couldn't get into the main house – it was all locked up, so she headed for the barn. There's a nasty lip at the entrance. She tripped, fell and hit her head, was knocked unconscious. Bennet thought he'd killed her, panicked and hid the body in an old freezer. But she wasn't dead. She came round and couldn't get out. The air ran out, and she suffocated. It must have taken you a long time to find her, Kenneth. You must have been very worried.'

He nods again. 'It took me three days. I searched the woods first. I could hear her calling to me, but she wasn't there, or in any of the places in the big house – the secret places. But then I realised, she wouldn't have led *him* to any of those places. So I went to the barns and found the trail she left me.'

'Trail?' Forbes asks. 'What kind of trail?'

Hughes doesn't look at him, but keeps his focus on me. Nevertheless, he answers. 'From the door to where she was hidden. Once I saw it, everything was clear.'

A trail of blood, I think. She must have cut her head when she fell, and bled onto the floor as Bennet moved her to the freezer.

The young solicitor is fidgeting in his seat, and I know we haven't got long before we'll be forced to terminate the interview, for now at least. Before that happens, however, there are a few more questions it's vital we have the answers to. I step carefully.

'Can you tell me about the others – the ones we found with your mother?'

He smiles – a genuine, wistful smile that could, under other circumstances, be interpreted as affectionate. 'You mean her friends. She always had very good friends. She wanted me to make sure she had people with her. She would have been lonely otherwise. We all need that, don't we? Mother knew what it was like to be lonely, unloved. But when you have people around you who understand, who can share their experiences – well, it's a great comfort, don't you think?' A flash of bitterness crosses his face. 'I wasn't allowed to go back to live with her. That was wrong. A mother and child should always be together. She understood, though. It was a very difficult time. I did everything I could to make sure she wasn't alone, had other women with her who had been through the same thing, knew what it was like. She chose them to be her friends. They were very lucky.'

'And the parents of the girls your mother chose – what about them?'

He lets out a dismissive grunt. 'Mother said they deserved no consideration. Their children were neglected, unhappy, just as she was. She asked me to help, care for them until they were old enough. Their parents were happy to pay for their keep, of course. After all, I relieved them of that burden. I'm sure you will agree, they were also very fortunate. Mother asked me to let *them* know they were wrong, that their children were happy. I did as she asked. They were not good parents to their children. They know that now.'

Forbes looks as if he's going to respond to this, but wisely keeps silent. We both realise that, as far as Hughes is concerned, he might as well not be in the room.

I decide to move on. 'Can you tell us about Ruby?'

For the first time, I see genuine emotion in his expression, an upsurge of anger and, beneath that, grief. He reins himself in, and his answer is calm, measured. 'We loved her,' he says. 'We both loved her. But she left – her and little Jason. Mother chose their names, you know – Pauline and Jason. I took Pauline out to the park – Jason was unwell, so Ruby stayed to care for him. When I got home, they were both gone. I knew where. Mother was very angry. She told me to find them, bring them home. It was dangerous for them to be out there, alone – the world is so full of evil people, and terrible things happen to young women and children out on their own at night.'

He pauses, shaking his head, completely, it seems, unaware of the irony of the statement.

'She went to Jimmy Harris,' I say.

Again, the anger, and this time he can hardly control it. 'There was a man – a local man who helped out sometimes. Never in the house, you understand, but outside, keeping everything tidy for the children. Mother is very particular about her garden. She loves flowers. I always make sure the garden has all kinds, especially roses. They are her favourite.' He smiles, his gaze far away; then he snaps back to the present. 'The man said he knew where to find Harris, and he could bring Ruby and Jason back.'

'Do you know his name?' I ask.

'Craig. Craig Tyler. I told him if he could bring them back safely, he would be well rewarded. He left, but returned later that night without them. He told me that Harris had been taking drugs, that he'd ...'

His composure finally cracks, he clenches his fists, lips taut with rage, and out of the corner of my eye, I see Forbes's hand drift towards the panic button under the desk, although we are both aware that his uncle and DS Peters are watching from behind the one-way mirror running the length of the room. To my astonishment, I see a tear roll down Hughes's cheek. When he speaks, his voice is unsteady.

'Craig told me they were dead. He said Harris had set on them and beaten them to death. Of course, Mother was distraught. She so loved Ruby, had so looked forward to having her close by, and of course, she loved her grandchildren, too. She said we had to protect Pauline. She wouldn't be safe as long as Harris lived. So I told Craig to see to it, to make sure Ruby and Jason were put somewhere quiet, where they would never be disturbed.'

'And Craig Tyler did as you asked?'

'Mother said it was poetic justice.' He nods. 'Craig used the same weapon Harris had used on Ruby and Jason.'

'But we found the hammer among your possessions, in the chapel at New Vale. How did you come by it?'

His mood changes again, back to the calm, unruffled individual we encountered at the start of the interview. 'I wasn't certain Craig would do as we asked,' he says. 'I had to make sure, so I followed him. I saw him kill Harris, then throw the hammer into a refuse cart. I retrieved it. Mother said it was a good idea, since if Craig became difficult later on, it would be evidence that I was innocent. I paid him very well, of course, but these days, you never know whether you can really trust people.'

'It seems,' I point out, 'that Tyler had the same idea. When did you realise that Ruby and Jason were buried in your garden?'

His eyes widen, partly in surprise, partly acknowledgement.

Yes, you bastard, I think. *You really did underestimate us.*

He takes a heavy breath, and there's another quiver of anger, quickly suppressed. 'I received a phone call,' he says. 'It would have been at the beginning of June. Tyler told me he was lodging an appeal and would be released soon. He wanted compensation, he said, and if I didn't agree, he would tell the police what he knew, and that I was responsible for Ruby's death. The evidence, he said, was "close to home". I dismissed his threat as groundless, but Mother knew. She told me we had to leave. I had to look after little Millie – she needed me. I told Mother I had to bring Pauline home first – she was ready, you see – but Mother said no, there was no time, and Millie was more important, so we did as she asked, and left straight away.'

He lowers his eyes, frowning, and I wait. Finally, he says, 'Thank you – for looking after Millie. I miss her terribly. When you see her, please tell her I love her very much.'

'You left her,' I point out. 'You left her locked in a room, and she almost died, Kenneth. Why do that if you love her so much?'

It takes him a long time to answer. 'Mother wanted her,' he says at last, almost in a whisper. 'Mother wanted her, but I wanted her more. Millie is my daughter, my blood – not like Pauline or any of the others. Millie is mine – just mine. Mother has lots of friends now, but she always wants more. I told her she couldn't have my daughter. Everyone is entitled to a child of their own, wouldn't you agree? Mother had me, and I had Millie.' He shakes his head. 'Even the best parents can sometimes be very unreasonable.'

Outside, Hughes's young brief collars us on our way to the observation room as Hughes is escorted back to his cell. 'I know, son,' I tell him. 'We'll have a mental health assessment arranged within the next couple of hours.' I smile. 'Don't worry, you'll be back to a simple "no comment" housebreaker tomorrow.'

'There was nothing I could do,' the kid stutters, clearly shaken. 'He just wouldn't take any advice. I've never seen anything like it.'

'Believe me,' Forbes puts in, 'neither have we.'

We watch as the solicitor makes his way reluctantly down to the cells for a debriefing with his client, and then we join DS Peters and Uncle Freddie.

'What do you think?' Jerry asks his uncle. 'Mad or bad?'

Forbes Snr shrugs. 'I don't think it matters. It's a life sentence either way. The only difference is how comfortable that sentence is going to be. If he's clever enough to fool the medics, he'll understand that, and I'll give you fifty to one he ends up with the comfortable option.'

'You want me to bet on a no-brainer?' Jerry says. 'Sorry, I can't afford it.'

'I think he'll find,' I comment, 'that Broadmoor isn't the Shangri-La he's hoping for. Mind you, given the nature of the crimes, the chances are he won't live long enough to get there.'

36

We've been waiting in silence for around an hour for the attending psychiatrist to report back when my mobile rings. It's Maggie, even more excited than usual. I listen, hang up, then stare at the phone, trying to absorb what she's just told me.

'What?' Jerry asks.

It takes me a minute. 'Jesus fucking Christ!' is all I can say. Everybody waits. I pull myself together. 'That was Maggie at our lab,' I explain. 'She's just had DNA results through from samples your people took from Iain Hughes's body and from Graham Bennet – apparently they were able to extract DNA from the notebook he used to prepare his sermons – amazing what technology can do.'

I pause, making sure I've got the information straight in my head, until Forbes Snr snorts in frustration. 'Well?' he demands. 'What did she say?'

'Quite a lot,' I reply. 'Firstly, she and Fitzjohn are in agreement that Iain Hughes was not Kenny's father.'

There's a short silence while this information is absorbed.

'Do they know who was?' Jerry asks.

I nod. 'His natural father,' I say, taking a deep breath, 'was Graham Bennet.'

'Dear God!' Jerry comments, and his uncle simply shakes his head.

'Do you think Kenny knows?' the ACC asks.

'I don't think so. Remember, he said Millie was his daughter – his blood – and this brings me to point three. We know there is no genetic relationship between Kenny and Millie. What we haven't known until now is that there *is* a relationship between Millie and Iain Hughes. She's his granddaughter.'

'There's more, isn't there?' Jerry says when I don't go on.

I nod, my brain struggling to catch up. 'There's a gang boss, over in West Hill,' I say finally. 'Now and then he passes me information. Jimmy Harris ran with him back in the late '90s, and Craig Tyler was with a rival gang. He told me that Tyler definitely did for Harris, but there was a third party, a former gang member who defected to Tyler's lot. This third man was paid by Hughes to get Pauline pregnant. He wouldn't give me a name, and it probably wouldn't do us much good anyway, as he fled the country some nine years ago.'

'Just after Pauline got pregnant,' Jerry murmurs.

'Exactly,' I say. 'But here's the thing. Maggie's team have been doing extensive analysis on the hammer that was used to murder Ruby and her son and later Jimmy Harris. Originally, they found four sets of DNA – mother, child, Harris and Tyler. They've finished a second run-through, just to be certain, and they've come up with very faint traces of a fifth individual. This fifth profile has characteristics in common with both Iain Hughes and Millie, but neither is a perfect match.'

There's a short silence; then Jerry catches up. 'My God!' he breathes. 'Danny – Danny Hughes, Kenny's half-brother – at least, Kenny thinks he is. Danny is Millie's father? And Kenny must be aware of that.'

'Oh, yes,' I reply. 'Remember what he said in the interview? *Millie is my daughter, my blood – not like Pauline or any of the others*. Yes, he knew all right. What he doesn't know is that Jimmy Harris most likely didn't kill Ruby and Jason, and neither did Tyler – Danny did.'

'That's a bit of a leap,' Forbes Snr remarks, raising an eyebrow. 'You can't know that for certain.'

'No,' I agree. 'But it's a pretty good bet. Think about it. His DNA is on the hammer used as the murder weapon. When they were children, Kenny attacked Danny with a hammer and damn near killed him. That sort of thing isn't easily forgotten, especially in gangland circles, and Danny ended up running with one of Bristol's most vicious gangs at the time, according to my source. He saw his chance for revenge, and he took it, with the added bonus that Harris, one of his main rivals, would take the fall. Don't forget, Danny and Craig Tyler were in the same outfit, so it's likely he knew where to find Kenny. My guess is that after Tyler was sent down for the Harris murder, he reacquainted himself with his long-lost half-brother, olive branch in hand, and took over as Kenny's odd-job man. I wouldn't be surprised if it wasn't Danny who buried the bodies under the shed and told Tyler about it later on. As you say, though, it's mere speculation. Even if we had enough evidence for an international murder hunt, it probably wouldn't get us anywhere.'

'No,' the ACC agrees, 'but we can still put out a call for him as a witness. You never know, something might turn up. For what it's worth, I think you've summed it up pretty accurately.'

There's a tap at the door, and the attending psychiatrist joins us, a lithe, middle-aged man, bald save for a few remaining wisps of greying hair, sharp, pointed nose supporting a pair of round, John Lennon-style spectacles. ACC Forbes greets him warmly – they clearly know each other well.

'Come on in, Charles,' the ACC says. 'You know my nephew, of course. This is Chief Inspector Crow, from Bristol. Chief Inspector, this is Charles O'Connor, our mental health expert.' We all shake hands, and the ACC goes on, 'What's the verdict? Are we dealing with a nutcase or a straightforward murderer?'

O'Connor gives him a disapproving look. 'You know as well as I do, Freddie, that we no longer refer to those with mental disabilities as "nutcases".' He grins. 'However, in this case, I'm afraid it's difficult to say with total confidence. What you are really asking is whether or not Mr Hughes is capable of understanding the charges against him and of answering questions put to him during interview coherently. In both cases, my answer is yes. I would urge caution, though. He is quite volatile and likely to behave irrationally if he gets upset.'

'Thanks, Charles – that's all we need to know for now. We'll go carefully, and hopefully I can call on you again if necessary?'

'Of course. I'll be in Chepstow for the rest of the day –

you have my number. Maybe see you in the pub later, when you've finished here?'

The psychiatrist makes his exit, and ACC Forbes gets up and straightens his jacket. 'Right, gentlemen,' he says. 'Time for round two, I think.'

IT MIGHT BE MY IMAGINATION, but when we enter the interview room for the second time, I detect a slight difference in Hughes's attitude – a little less confident, a little more wary. His solicitor, now thoroughly resigned to being a redundant part of the proceedings, is sitting back in his chair, arms folded, gaze fixed on a patch of desk immediately in front of him. DI Forbes and I settle into our seats, and by prior arrangement, given our prisoner's clear reluctance to engage with Jerry, I kick things off.

'I'd like to ask you a few questions about your garden shed,' I say. 'Is that okay with you, Kenneth?'

An eyebrow twitches – he wasn't expecting the question. Nevertheless, the gaze fixed on me is steady.

'By all means,' he says smoothly. 'What would you like to know?'

'You asked Jimmy Harris to build it for you sometime in 1999, is that correct?'

He nods, but says nothing.

'Why?' I ask. 'I mean, why choose a local gangster to put up a shed? He clearly wasn't an expert – he didn't even put down a proper foundation. Unless, of course, you asked him not to. But why would you do that unless the shed was simply there to cover something up – like a couple of dead bodies, for example?' I see the muscles in his jaw tighten, and go on, 'If that was the case, you were taking a risk, weren't you, letting Harris in on your little secret? You can see how it looks.'

At last, I get a reaction. 'You know nothing,' he hisses through clenched teeth, leaning forward and jabbing the table with a finger. Then, realising he might be revealing a weakness, he takes a deep breath and forces himself to sit back, mouth curling into a dismissive smile. 'You know nothing,' he repeats, once again calm, controlled, 'about the things in life that matter. Friendship, loyalty, honour – these things transcend all boundaries. Is that not true?'

'In most circumstances, yes, I would agree,' I reply. 'You are saying there was a degree of loyalty between you and Harris? You'll excuse us if we find that a little hard to believe. Harris was a drug addict and a thug, and according to you, he ran off with Ruby and Jason. I don't see much loyalty or honour in that.'

Hughes responds with a snort of contempt. 'It appears, Chief Inspector Crow, that you are not quite as clever as you pretend to be. Or perhaps' – he glances at Forbes – 'your assistant here hasn't been as diligent as he should. As you know, I was separated from Mother, sent to live in the big house with the other boys. I was young then. It was very difficult at first. I missed Mother very much, and some of the other boys were very cruel – but not all. There was one boy, much older – he must have been seventeen at the time – who protected me, taught me how to survive there. His name was Gavin – Gavin Harris. He was released a few months later, but gave me an address in Bristol to look him up when I got out, and so I did. Little Jimmy was a toddler by then. I knew him nearly all his life and was happy to help out whenever I could, to repay the debt I owed his father.'

I feel Forbes tense at the suggestion that he is my

'assistant' and, what's more, that he hasn't done a thorough job. Hughes notices it too and flashes a brief, satisfied grin.

At least he's explained the presence of Jimmy Harris on the scene. I get back to the matter in hand.

'You were going to explain why you asked Jimmy to build you a shed,' I prompt.

Hughes shrugs. 'He said he needed somewhere to store some of his belongings, away from his flat. I didn't want him to have free access to the house – I had great affection for him in those days, but I have always been a realist – he was young, headstrong, and not totally reliable. I wanted somewhere to store my tools, so I suggested he build a shed in the garden, which he could then also use for his own purposes. The arrangement benefitted us both. I'm afraid I can't comment on the quality of his work.'

'Fair enough. You say you had affection for him – so much so that you allowed him to pursue a sexual relationship with Ruby Marx, or, rather, persuaded him to do so. This resulted in the births of Pauline and Jason. However, when Ruby fell in love with Jimmy and tried to leave with Jason, you hired Craig Tyler to murder him – not a very affectionate response.'

His eyes harden, the anger rising back to the surface. 'You are repeating yourself, Chief Inspector. I have already explained – at length – Jimmy killed Ruby and Jason. Mother insisted on justice for them. There was nothing I could do.'

'You could have got your facts straight,' I reply. 'We now have fairly strong evidence to suggest that Jimmy Harris did not murder Ruby and her son.'

For the first time, I see a glimpse of real confusion in his expression. He recovers, though, and shakes his head. 'No –

you're lying. Craig found them in Jimmy's flat. They had been beaten to death. Mother knew what Jimmy had done – she always knows. The weapon was still there, on the floor, Craig said, by the bodies.' He pauses, struggling to keep his emotions under control, but can't keep the anger out of his voice as he says, 'They both betrayed us – Mother was furious. We took them in – Jimmy, then Craig. We helped them out, made sure they were well rewarded for everything they did, but they turned against us. First Jimmy, then Craig told me where Ruby and Jason were. They'd been there twenty years. Twenty years!' His voice rises to a shout. 'All that time, and they could have been safe, with Mother. It was unforgiveable!'

He slams a fist on the table, and for a moment I think he might actually burst into tears, but with a supreme effort, he regains some composure. Still, I think, with a glance at Forbes, he's finally starting to crack. Forbes raises an eyebrow in agreement.

'Craig told me he was going to appeal his conviction, and was giving me fair warning. If things went against him, he would tell the police where Ruby and Jason were, make out that I'd killed them. That's when mother said we had to leave. I wanted to at least take Pauline with us, make sure she was safe, but Mother said no, there wasn't time. So I left with Millie. But it all went wrong. Mother decided she wanted Millie to stay with her. I told her it wasn't possible. Millie would have missed me, you see – she was my child. I would have done anything for her, even if it meant disappointing Mother. We had a huge argument, and Mother stopped speaking to me. That's when I decided to leave Millie where she would be found by Mother's sister. Ruth would know what to do. She is a good woman; she would care for her.' He sighs. 'It was unbearable – to be without Millie, and with Mother so silent. Then I had an idea. It was nearly time for me to visit Mother, and if Craig Tyler hadn't interfered, I could have taken Pauline to her. That would have made her happy. I thought that if I could find another friend for her, she would forgive me for not giving her Millie. Then things would be as they were between us.'

'So you took her Kayleigh McBride,' I say.

He nods. 'She would have liked Kayleigh. She was just Mother's sort of girl. But now ...' He glares at me, a look of pure venom. 'Now, she has no one new to be her friend, and she will never forgive me. She hasn't spoken to me, not since I left Millie for Ruth to care for, but I won't change my mind. Millie is my daughter, and it's for me to decide what's best for my child.'

He shouts this last sentence, eyes raised to the ceiling in defiance, as if challenging his phantom mother to do something about it.

I decide the time has come to take the chance. 'Kenneth,' I say, trying for a sympathetic tone, 'we know you had contact with Danny Hughes – that Danny is Millie's biological father.'

His eyes widen. I see his mind working, wondering if it's worth denying it. After a long pause, he nods. 'Danny came to see me – it would have been in the winter of 2000 – Ruby was expecting the twins. He said he'd had some business with Jimmy and had been directed here. He stayed a short while, and we became reacquainted. He visited regularly after that, around Christmastime each year, and in fact, he introduced me to Craig, who was a friend of his looking, he said, for occasional work. That was in 2003, after Jimmy had let me down a few times, and ... well, you know what happened later that year. It was in 2014 that I had the idea. Mother didn't like the idea of me – well, having *that* kind of relationship with the friends I chose for her. But I wanted a child of my own. I had Pauline, but she wasn't really mine. Danny and Pauline got on well – I could tell he liked her. I put the idea to him, and he agreed straight away. The child would be mine, and it would have my blood – mine, but separate from Mother, do you see? When Millie was born, I knew I'd done the right thing.'

He's smiling now, eyes half closed, distracted, reliving the memory. I give Forbes a slight nod, then glance at the solicitor, who has been perfectly still and silent throughout, not daring to say a word. The ACC and Sergeant Peters are on the other side of the one-way mirror, and there are two PCs outside the interview room door. If Hughes is going to crack, it will be now. I take a deep breath.

'Kenneth, I'm afraid I have some bad news for you.' He opens his eyes, suddenly alert, back in the present. 'We ran some tests. Danny is Millie's father, but I have to tell you that you are not related to him in any way. Therefore, Millie is not related to you either. There is no genetic relationship between you, not even a distant one. It means that Iain Hughes was not your natural father.'

Hughes is suddenly upright, rigid in his chair, staring at me in disbelief. Before he can speak, I go on.

'We also found traces of what we believe to be Danny Hughes's DNA on the hammer used to murder Ruby Marx and her son, Jason. We think it highly likely that it was Danny, not Craig Tyler, who killed them, then buried the bodies under your garden shed. It's very possible Tyler was following Danny's instructions, not yours.'

Hughes has started to tremble with fury, too shocked to

speak. The atmosphere is barely breathable, the eye in the middle of a coming storm. I play my final card. 'We have been able to establish, however, who your natural father was. It was Graham Bennet, your grandfather.'

Even though we were expecting it, the speed at which Hughes moves takes us all by surprise. I've hardly finished speaking before he's on his feet, and in a single motion hoists the chair he was sitting on above his head and brings it down with all his strength, at the same time letting out an ear-splitting howl of pure rage. I duck, a fraction too late, and the back of the chair crashes into the side of my head with the force of a truck, followed by Hughes's body as he slithers across the table and falls on top of me. Reeling from the blow to the head, I vaguely see a blurred fist aimed at my face, but thankfully the punch doesn't land, as Jerry Forbes leaps onto both of us, grabbing Hughes's arm and wrenching it back, using his weight to pull Hughes off me before any more damage can be done. A second later, the two PCs have cuffed our prisoner's hands behind his back and are dragging him out and down to the cells.

'Are you okay?' Jerry asks, sitting up and leaning back against the wall, breathing hard.

For a minute I can't answer, blinking hard to try to focus. I get to my knees and risk feeling the side of my head. There's a reasonably large lump rising behind my left ear, and my hand comes away wet. Any minute now, I'm going to have one hell of a headache.

'Damn it!' I reply. My vision returns to normal, and I see a movement out of the corner of my eye. The solicitor has curled himself under the desk, head between his knees, muttering to himself.

Forbes Snr appears in the doorway, looking from one to

the other of us. He holds out a hand and hauls me to my feet. 'Looks like you've been lucky, Chief Inspector,' he says, handing me a clean handkerchief to dab the wound. 'It's only superficial, by the look of it. Do you want an ambulance?'

I shake my head, a mistake as it's starting to pound. 'I shouldn't think so, if you've got a police surgeon here. It probably just needs a plaster.'

'There's one on the way – should be here any minute.'

'I'm fine,' Jerry pipes up, getting to his feet. 'Thanks for asking.'

The ACC grins. 'Well, you've both done a great job – I think we've got plenty to be going on with. The only question now is, who do we charge – Kenneth or his mother? I'd better get off and make sure everyone is doing what they are supposed to. Sergeant Peters will show you down to the medical room. If you need anything, let him know.' He holds out a hand. 'Thank you, Chief Inspector. I'm sure we'll meet up again in the next few days.

'Meanwhile, my nephew will deal with all the tedious details and keep you informed. I suggest you head home if the surgeon gives you the green light to drive – if not, we can arrange a car. I'll call your DSI Helston and bring her up to date – save you the bother.'

I shake his hand and clap Jerry on the back. 'It's been a pleasure,' I say, and follow Peters down to the surgeon's office, hoping he won't decide I need stitches and an interminable wait in A&E.

37

The entire team is waiting for me when I get back to the station – head fully repaired and in working order – including Larson, who looks like he's lost a stone over the last week or so, and Sillitoe, who has acquired a temporary replacement leg from somewhere. I walk into the squad room to a chorus of cheers and whistles and an overexcited Doberman, who nearly knocks me over in her eagerness to get reacquainted. Everyone, including me, is totally exhausted, but sloping off to a quiet corner isn't going to be an option.

Daz hands me a beer and grins. 'You've got no bloody chance, boss,' he says. 'Nobody's letting you out of here until we've got the whole story – word for word, and no shortcuts, okay?'

'Oh, fucking hell!' I protest feebly, and spend the next twenty minutes giving a full account of the interview and the list of charges, ending with, 'Now, for God's sake, bugger off home, the lot of you, unless you want to spend the rest of the day on paperwork. Full briefing, nine o'clock tomorrow.'

They all slowly file out until only Larson and Blue are left. He's still at Ollie White's desk, head bent over the screen.

'Didn't you hear what I said, son?' I ask, going across to join him.

'We've identified four of the six girls,' he tells me, not looking up. 'I just need to find the other two before … Shit! What the hell …?'

He shoots to his feet, far too quickly, staggers, and has to grab the desk to stay upright. Once he's recovered, he glares at me or, rather, at the plug dangling from my hand, which a second ago was powering his monitor.

'They've waited all these years,' I say, aiming for a reasonable tone. 'Another twenty-four hours isn't going to make a lot of difference. Now, do as you're bloody well told and go home before I call a couple of uniforms to escort you off the premises.'

For a moment he thinks about squaring up to me, but then his body sags; he wipes a hand across his brow and hitches his jacket from the back of his chair.

'Right – you're right. God, I'm tired.'

'We all are, son.' As he moves past, I break the habit of a lifetime and grab his shoulder. 'You did a good job, John,' I say. 'A bloody good job.'

He looks me in the eye and gives me a bleary grin. 'Can I have that in writing?' he asks, and heads off down the corridor.

Finally, I'm alone and slump into my office chair, Blue leaning into me, her head on my lap. I'm just dozing off when a tap at my door jerks me back to consciousness.

Grace takes the chair opposite and kicks off her shoes. 'How's the head?' she asks.

'Fine. It was just a scratch. The police medic gave me a week's supply of paracetamol and told me to stay off the Scotch, that's all.'

'Good. I've got some news for you,' she says, tickling Blue's ears and pulling out a bag of gravy bones.

I look at her suspiciously. 'Are you sure I can take it?' I ask.

She smiles. 'Oh, yes. I've just had a call from Carol Dodds.'

'Jesus Christ! That's all I need.'

'Believe me' – Grace laughs – 'you'll want to hear this. Craig Tyler has dropped his appeal. He has also – finally – admitted to the murder of Jimmy Harris.'

'Bloody hell! Has he overdosed on something?'

She shakes her head. 'I simply informed Dodds of Hughes's arrest, the fact that his statement confirmed he was an eyewitness, and reminded her that this goes nicely alongside the murder weapon with Tyler's prints all over it. Apparently, Craig has been persuaded to come clean on condition he isn't charged with the murders of Ruby Marx and her child.'

'But we know he didn't kill Ruby and Jason, so we can't charge him anyway.'

'Really?' Grace's grin takes on a mischievous tinge. 'I knew there was something I forgot to mention. Too late for Dodds to do anything about it now, I suppose.' She gets up. 'Are you going to go home sometime this week? If not, do you fancy some dinner? I could murder steak and chips.'

It's a decent offer, and I'm about to take her up on it when my mobile rings. I dig it out, look at the screen, and my world starts to spin. Grace sees my expression and nods.

'Another time, Al,' she says. 'Take care,' she mouths as she leaves.

My hand is shaking as I take the call. 'Chrissie?'

'Sorry to call you at work, Al. Can you meet me? It's important.'

Suddenly, my mouth is sandpaper. I swallow and make an effort to sound as if my world isn't about to fall apart. 'When?' I manage.

'In half an hour – maybe a bite to eat somewhere?'

In other words, I think, she wants to meet me in a public place, while it's still daylight, somewhere safe where I'm not going to make a scene when she tells me she's in a relationship with someone, and would I mind finally buggering off out of her life.

'I've got Blue with me,' I say. 'It will have to be somewhere that allows dogs.'

The excuse doesn't work. 'No problem,' she says. 'How about the Old Mill on the harbour? There's a beer garden there, and it's just about warm enough to sit outside.'

'I'll be there,' I say and hang up. It's only then I realise my other hand has strayed into my pocket and is clutching the screwed-up paper napkin on which George Saint scribbled Chrissie's new companion's number plate.

BLUE SPOTS HER FIRST, sitting at a table in the far corner of the beer garden, sheltered from the breeze by an old oak tree, its leaves just beginning to turn. She's fiddling anxiously with her gin and tonic – no ice, no slice – eyes fixed on the glass except for the occasional glance at the pub's rear door, which won't help her, as I've come in the back way, through the car park. I'm reminded of our first date, thirty-odd years ago – two nervous kids in our late teens, trying to act grown up and making a total mess of it. I was the first to arrive that time, and in a flash of misguided inspiration ordered a beer for myself and, because it seemed sophisticated, a port and lemon for my would-be girlfriend.

She crept up on me as I was busy rehearsing my equally terrible chat-up lines, and remarked, pointing at the drink, 'I thought you were supposed to be dating me, not my grandma.'

Today, she's got the drinks in, and there's a half of real ale sitting on the table opposite her. I swallow the lump in my throat, let Blue off the lead, and watch as Chrissie greets her with an enthusiastic pat, looks up and meets my eye. I do my best to put on a smile, and join her.

'Rosie told me you got your case wrapped up,' she begins, aiming for small talk. 'She says John's completely wiped out. You look tired, too. Are you okay?'

No, I'm bloody not, I think. *I've not been this not okay since the day our divorce papers came through and you ended up going off with a con artist who almost got you killed.* 'I'm fine, Chrissie,' I say. 'I need a good night's sleep, that's all. You said you wanted to see me – that it was important?'

She nods, digs in her bag and produces a brown envelope. 'I want you to promise me, Al,' she says. 'Promise you won't be angry.'

Angry? Christ, I'm bloody furious. 'I promise,' I say, by some miracle keeping my tone level. She pushes the envelope across the table. 'What's this?' I ask.

She doesn't answer, just gestures for me to open it. I try, unsuccessfully, to hide the tremor in my hand as I pull out a single sheet of paper and unfold it. Whatever I might have been expecting, nothing has prepared me for what I'm looking at. For a minute, I desperately try to understand what it means, but all I come up with is confusion, my brain taking on the characteristics of the scrambled eggs Jerry Forbes served up for breakfast.

'What the bloody hell is this, Chrissie?' I ask. She flinches, and I realise I'm shouting.

'Please, Al,' she says, her voice trembling, 'you said you wouldn't get angry.'

I swallow hard and take a deep breath. 'I'm sorry. Just tell me. You know I can't accept this – I just want to know why you think you need to give it to me.' I pause, then add, 'I don't want a payoff, Chris. If you've – well, if you've met somebody …'

Her head jerks up, and she pins me with an incredulous stare. 'Met somebody?' It's her turn to shout. 'You think I've got somebody else?' She starts to laugh. 'For God's sake, Al. Sometimes you can be so stupid. You really think if I was having a relationship with someone, I wouldn't tell you? Especially after last time – in fact, this is because of last time.' Her eyes narrow. 'What are you telling me? Have you been following me, making sure I didn't get into another mess? You have, haven't you? Christ, Al, you're impossible! I mean, why the hell do I bother?'

'Of course I haven't,' I retort, which is, I know, only a half truth. 'And you're the one who's shouting now. You've just given me a statement that says £75,000 has been paid into my bank account. What am I supposed to think?'

It's her turn to take a breath. 'Okay,' she says. 'I want you to listen – I mean really listen. Will you do that?'

With an effort, I pull myself together. 'I'm listening.'

'I've gone back to work,' she says matter-of-factly. 'It's taken a while – you know, after what happened with Terry.

It's been – difficult, and I didn't think I'd be able to get back into it. I mean, graphic design is a young person's game these days. I didn't tell you because I wasn't sure I could compete anymore. I didn't think anyone would take a chance on a fifty-something-year-old with nothing in their portfolio for near on ten years.'

'That's crazy!' I interrupt. 'You were always brilliant – any firm would be lucky to have you.'

She glares at me. 'For the love of God, Al, just shut up and listen!'

I snap my mouth shut, sit back and fold my arms. 'Sorry.'

She softens a little and smiles. 'As it happens, someone did take me on as a freelance – a big media outfit in town. I did a couple of commissions for them.' She pauses and gives me a rueful laugh. 'Believe it or not, they were for a campaign to sit alongside a TV series on how to avoid getting scammed out of your savings – ironic, don't you think?'

For once, I'm speechless, thinking of Terry Markham, the man who not only made sure our marriage was dead and buried, and almost destroyed my relationship with Rosie, but also stole damn near all the equity in our jointly owned house. Still, she hasn't explained where all this money has come from. 'So, what—' I start, but she silences me with another look.

'The company liked what I did, and put it up for an award. It won. The prize money was a hundred and fifty grand. It was a bit embarrassing, really. There was a big awards ceremony over at the TV studio. I had to get dressed up, and they sent a chauffeur-driven car to get me – one of those new electric things – I felt a total bloody idiot. I haven't worn that dress for years! Anyway, I had to totter up and give a thank-you speech and receive the cheque, plus this awful metal thing that looks like a cross between a dinner gong and an ashtray. Mum's put it on the bloody mantelpiece, would you believe?'

She offers me a tentative smile. 'Anyway, when Terry Markham conned me out of the house, it wasn't just me who was left with nothing. Half of it was your savings, Al. And now, I've given it back.'

For a moment I can't say anything. I have to screw my eyes shut with the effort of controlling the tremor that seems to have taken over my whole body as pure relief washes through me, and the full import of what she's saying sinks in. She went to probably the most important event of her life in a chauffeur-driven Tesla, wearing the dress I gave her all those years ago. When I open my eyes again, she's smiling at me.

'For Christ's sake, Chrissie,' I say when I finally manage to speak, 'why the bloody hell didn't you tell me?'

She reaches across the table and takes my hand. 'I wanted to,' she admits, 'but I knew that if I did, you wouldn't have accepted the money. I asked Mum and Rosie to keep quiet, and Rosie gave me your bank details. Nobody else knew, not even John. Actually, it was Rosie's idea to simply transfer it and not say anything until it was a done deal. Now it is. There's nothing you can do about it, and you can't give it back – not unless you want to spend the rest of your life playing financial ping-pong. So – are you going to accept defeat gracefully or not?'

I go through her argument and, as usual, can't find a single flaw. I sit back and hold up my hands. 'Okay, you win. I'll tell you one thing, though – I'm starving. The very least you can do is let me buy you dinner.'

. . .

The next few weeks are spent wrapping up the various loose ends left by the Hughes case. Hughes himself, having spent a week on remand, was transferred to Broadmoor, where he is, according to the latest report from Jerry Forbes, being treated for a severe but as yet undiagnosed delusional disorder while awaiting trial. Thanks, I have to reluctantly admit, largely to Larson's efforts, most of our time has been spent on the unpleasant task of locating, informing and interviewing the parents of the victims found in the tank at Wye Cross. All were blackmailed at some point by Hughes, and so were technically guilty of at best obstructing the police, at worst, aiding an offender. The consensus, however, is that no purpose would be served by prosecuting any of them. A search for Danny Hughes has, as I suspected, so far been a futile exercise.

Finally, at the beginning of December, Grace called me upstairs to inform me in no uncertain terms that I had a month's leave owing, exactly thirty-one days in which to take it, and therefore I should 'bugger off home and not show my face until the second of January'. Sillitoe, she told me, was more than capable of dealing with anything that might crop up, particularly as, thanks to the police insurance fund, her new bionic leg worked even better than the old one. As with all the women in my life, Grace is not the type to lose an argument, so I gave in without a fight, and am now, as the political euphemism goes, 'spending more time with my family'.

. . .

'Hey, Grandad!' Ben throws open the front door and, after a brief pause while Blue sticks her tongue in his ear, grabs my hand and drags me inside. 'You're just in time,' he says. 'We're opening door number two.'

I allow myself to be hauled into the kitchen, where Rosie is leaning against the worktop, waiting for the kettle to boil, and little Alex is standing to attention, gazing up at the wall, on which two advent calendars have been pinned just out of her reach. She holds her arms up, jiggling with excitement.

'Up, Gandi,' she demands, and Rosie gives me a nod.

'Okay,' I say, hoisting her the extra couple of feet. 'You ready, Ben?'

He nods. 'Let's go!'

Alex leans forward, and I guide her finger round the numbers until we arrive at the right door. She gives it a hefty jab and comes up with a tiny chocolate reindeer. Ben, a few seconds ahead of us with his own calendar, whoops in triumph.

'I won! I found it first.'

'Okay,' Rosie says, laughing. 'That's it for today. Ben, take your sister and go and play with Blue. I want to talk to your grandfather.'

They disappear into the garden, and Rosie hands me a mug of coffee. 'Have you told him yet?' I ask.

She shakes her head. 'I thought I'd leave it to you. You're the one he seems to talk to about anything remotely sensitive. I guess it's a parent thing.'

'That, or he's a terrible judge of character,' I reply. 'When will they be here?'

'John left around an hour ago. I reckon any time now if the traffic's okay.'

'Right – better get on with it, then.'

I give her a hug, and we make our way out to where Ben, Alex and Blue are playing what looks like a multi-species game of Piggy-in-the-Middle, with Alex sitting on the grass, giggling while Blue chases Ben in circles around her. Rosie retrieves a rather muddy Alex, and I beckon Ben to come and join me on the bench by the shrubbery.

'Do you remember Millie Drake?' I ask when we're settled.

'Sure,' he says. 'She's the girl from our class who went missing. You said you'd found her, and she was okay.'

'That's the one. Well, she's got new people now to look after her, some foster parents, and she'll be coming back into your class after the Christmas holiday. What do you think about that?'

He frowns, considering. 'She wasn't very nice to me when she was in our class before,' he says at last. 'I don't think she likes me very much.'

'I think that used to be true,' I agree. 'But she's changed quite a lot. She's been through a really bad time, and I think she's going to need a friend – someone to look after her, make sure she settles in all right. I also think you're the right man for the job. You wouldn't just be helping Millie, you'd be helping me as well – you could be her unofficial "police protection". What do you reckon? Are you up for it?'

He thinks for another minute, then grins. 'Sure, Grandad.' He puffs out his chest. 'I'm your man!'

There's a commotion at the front door, and Blue shoots up, dashes inside to see what all the fuss is about. 'Your mum's invited her over for lunch,' I tell Ben. 'Sounds like she's arrived. You want to get started?'

We go inside, and as soon as we reach the hallway, Ben stops dead, mouth open, eyes on stalks, watching Millie as she drops to her knees, giggling as Blue makes a valiant attempt to give our visitor a thorough face wash. The girl is almost unrecognisable now – rosy cheeked, long blond hair combed back into a ponytail, dressed in the current fashion of jeans, hoodie and trainers.

She looks up and catches sight of my grandson still gaping dumbly. 'Hi, Ben,' she says. 'Is this your dog? What's its name? Is it a boy or a girl?'

Ben swallows and finds his voice. 'Hi, Millie. This is Blue – she belongs to my grandad. You want to come and play ball with her?'

'Sure,' she replies, and scrambles to her feet. On the way to the garden, she sees me and gives me a sunny smile. 'Hi, Mr Crow,' she says. 'I love your dog – she's dope!'

'Dope?' I ask Rosie as we watch them from the kitchen window.

'It's what the kids say these days,' she explains, laughing. 'I think it means "very good".'

I make for the cupboard to root out some plates. 'Jesus bloody Christ!' I say, but can't help smiling at the sight of two laughing children taking turns to throw a ball for one delighted dog.

ABOUT THE AUTHOR

H J Reed lives and writes in Bristol, where she graduated with a PhD in psychology and began a long career lecturing in psychology and criminology, both in mainstream universities and in the prison education system. Her evenings were spent writing novels and short stories in various genres and styles, and pondering on the strange workings of the criminal mind. After a number of publication successes, she gained an MA in creative writing and went on to teach literature and the arts. Now, she is able to follow her lifelong passion and write crime fiction full time. When she is not writing, she can be found being taken for long muddy walks by a middle-aged, temperamental toy poodle, or in far-flung foreign cities thinking up new plots.

Did you enjoy *A Fatal Pact*? Please consider leaving a review on Amazon to help other readers discover the book.

www.hjreed.com

ALSO BY HJ REED

DI Crow Series

Her Last Chance

The Killing Ground

A Fatal Pact

Printed in Great Britain
by Amazon

2e7a361d-bc4b-4a16-bca3-e1efe1b8bfabR01